The Chronicles of Borea

Book I

The Making of a Bard

Preludio

D1518401

By Joseph E. Koob II

Illustrations and Cover by Robert Haselier

Seven-Book Fantasy Series

Book I	The Making of a Bard	Preludio
Book II	The Making of a Bard	Gigue
Book III	The Making of a Bard	Siciliana
Book IV	The Making of a Bard	Ciaccona
Book V	IXUS	Corrente
Book VI	Civil War Threatens	Tempo Di Borea
Book VII	The Great War	Grande Finale**

**The book sub-titles reflect the musical emphasis in the series. Taken from the Baroque period, all except the Finale are found in J.S. Bach's *Three Sonatas and Three Partitas for Solo Violin*. *(See Next Page for descriptions)*

ISBN: 978-1-097-48540-6

Sub-Titles

Preludio (Prelude) – short introductory piece of music, improvisatory in style, usually begins a work of several movements

Gigue (Giga, Jig) – a lively dance often serving as the final movement of a suite of dances in the Baroque period

Siciliana (Siciliano) – Baroque Dance/movement in an instrumental work in a slow $^6_8$ or $^{12}_8$ time with lilting rhythms, that resembles a slow jig or tarantella, characterized by dotted rhythms and usually in a minor key. It can elicit a pastoral mood.

Ciaccona (Chaconne) – series of variations over a ground bass (short, repetitive bass line) that sets the harmony

Corrente (Courante) – triple meter dance, often found in the Baroque suite

Tempo Di Borea (Bourree') – lively dance in duple meter with an upbeat quarter note

Grande Finale (Finale) – ending section or movement of a larger work – sonata, suite, etc.; often with thematic material from other movements and related in Key to the whole

Acknowledgements

Much thanks to everyone who has influenced me over the years.

Thanks to: my wife, Lisa; my children, Nathan and Elise, and **Pat, son-in-law,** who have been readers throughout the development of this series and helped me in innumerable supportive ways with this project; Anne Duston, one of my regular readers; Carolyn K.; as well as other readers and friends. Special thanks to my good friend and expert editor, Steve Bridge, who set me on the path to righteousness early on in this process, and who has been instrumental in making the final editions so much better. Thanks also to Stephanie H. of SLL Editorial Services for her early editing; Phil Lang for his work on the cover; and my cousin, Robert Haselier, for his wonderful illustrations and cover art.

Website: **chroniclesofborea.com**

Blog: chroniclesofboreabooks.wordpress.com

Contents

Map of Borea

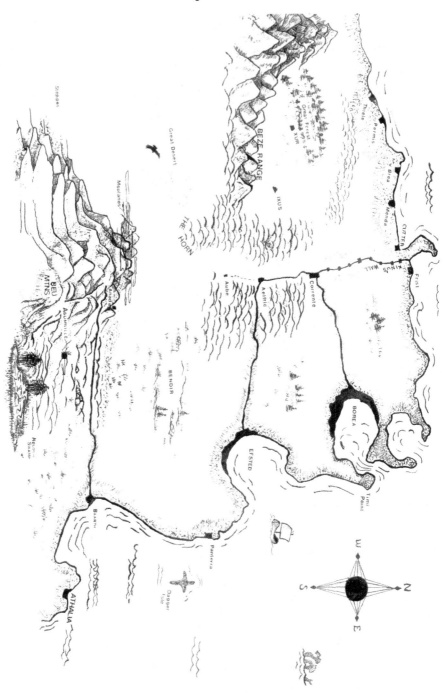

Death in the West

"Kla-a-ng, Kla-a-ng!" The deep pitch resound of the village bell echoed across the scattered boulders of the high hills. The heads of the two hunters came up at the first peal. The older lad slung his bounty of coneys over his shoulder and shouted, "Come on, Jared, the boats must have come early." Broad of shoulder, he grinned at his younger brother and then took off with an easy trot down the slope toward the stockade. However, by the time they neared the narrow path that led through the rock outcropping between them and the village, the younger lad, almost as tall as his brother and more lightly built, passed him.

The bell continued ringing, and as they hurried through the twisting route to the pasture above the town, Jared glanced behind him and gasped out, "Something must be wrong, Ge-or. Hurry!"

They came around the last bend in the path and slid to a halt on an overhang that led down to the lower fields of barley and oats. In an instant, they took in the implausible scene below. Jared yelled again, "Qa-ryks!" Dropping his rabbits, he plunged down toward the stockade. His brother followed several steps behind, both unslinging their short hunting bows as they ran.

From their vantage point above, they could see that the western stockade wall had been breached in several places. Gaping holes, blasted in the sturdy logs by some immense force, were filled with the struggling of men and large beasts as the villagers strove to stem the attack of the marauders. Inside the town's perimeter, old men, women, and even children were trying to erect a secondary line of defense around the buildings that fronted the town square. The whole scene was a frenzy. Many villagers fought fiercely with whatever they had been able to bring to the battle: short swords, axes, heavy hammers, as well as pitchforks, hoes, and other farming implements. They were keeping the onslaught at bay, while others piled carts, rugged hand-hewn furniture, and miscellaneous crates up into a makeshift barrier at the center of the hamlet.

As they broke into a sprint, the brothers were more than three-hundred paces from the closest attack point. Jared ran at full speed, using the downward slope to gain even more momentum and distance with each long stride. He was soon far ahead of his brother. As he neared the log wall of the outer fortifications, he could see that the battle had moved inward toward the heart of the village. Running toward the nearest breach, he could now see the charred logs and hot coals from the blast that had leveled a good part of the wall. Moving quickly north to gain access, he was about to step through the opening toward the noise of the fighting when his brother gasped out from behind, "Wait, we'll get better shots from the roofs." Jared spun around and waved, waiting for Ge-or to come up. Keeping watch for any beasts that might head their way, he held his bow at the ready with one of his hunting arrows nocked.

From where he stood, Jared could see the devastation of the initial attack. Bodies of both men and Qa-ryks lay in contorted positions along the fiery path. The

---

**Considering the unique linguistic characteristics of Old Borean, and Ge-or's heritage, historians have agreed that his name would have been pronounced "Gay-or" in contrast to the current popular vernacular "Gee-or" or the more vulgar "George."

eight-foot-high stockade had been struck by some mysterious power, which had burnt a twenty-foot-wide section of the heavy logs. Several houses inside the wall had also caught fire from the intensity of the blast. These were also burning fiercely, and other nearby buildings were smoking from the heat. The close proximity of the houses in the mountain hamlet, built to help withstand the ravages of fierce winter snows and cold winds from the sea, made fire a threat to the whole village. Though the townspeople were always prepared to fight a fire, this was no ordinary blaze.

As soon as Ge-or reached Jared, the two young men ran to the east along the inside of the stockade wall until they came to a dwelling that was untouched by flames. Replacing his bow over his neck and shoulder in order to give his brother a boost, Jared helped hoist Ge-or up onto the roof.

Once Ge-or was perched precariously on the steep slant of the rough wooden shingles, he reached down to give his brother a hand. As Jared began to climb, a Qa-ryk appeared from around the building to the north. Ge-or drew back and yelled, "Look out!"

Jared instinctively pushed off from the logs, rolling to the side as he hit the ground. Not having time to retrieve his bow from his back, he drew his hunting knife from the sheath on his belt as he came to rest on his knees.

The Qa-ryk, wielding a wicked double-bladed axe in one claw, rushed at him, roaring. Ge-or, above, had nocked an arrow and was drawing back as the broad blade began to descend toward Jared's head. The younger lad, warrior-trained, crouched ready to jump clear of the blow.

The arrow from above struck the hairy beast in the back of its thick neck, causing the stroke of the axe to go wide. The Qa-ryk reared back; and Jared, using the opening, lunged forward, driving his knife deep into the creature's gut. Ripping it sideways, he withdrew the sharp blade in a gruesome swath through its stomach and intestines. Mortally wounded, the powerful beast was still able to reach out and claw at Jared as it fell away from the knife in its gut. The four-inch-long nails of its left claw ripped across the top back of the boy's light leather jerkin and right shoulder. A second arrow from Ge-or struck the Qa-ryk in the center of its chest, and the enemy warrior swayed for a moment before falling back, full-length in the dirt.

Jared, having spun to the side, began to straighten when his brother yelled from his perch on the edge of the roof, "Are you all right?"

"I guess I'll manage," Jared answered. He could feel blood leaking from the wound, but it did not hurt any more than if he had been hit with a heavy punch. "He caught me in the shoulder. It's not bad. Give me a second to stop the bleeding."

"Get the arrows; we'll need them," Ge-or shouted.

Trying to focus in spite of the flash of pain that hit him as he moved, Jared ripped a length of cloth from his woolen cloak. Working quickly, he managed to staunch the flow of blood with a hastily tied bandage.

Bending over the dead creature, Jared began to cut out the two arrows. He was seeing one of these massive humanoids close-up for the first time in his life, yet he had butchered many a big game animal; and since the anatomy of all mammalian creatures is similar, he made quick work of the grisly task. Cutting quickly through red flesh and sinew, he reached the carefully crafted steel arrow heads and drew them out.

The beast was heavily muscled and a foot taller than Jared. It had sparse, short, coarse, brownish-red hair on its body and limbs. On the nails of one of its clawed hands, Jared could see the red crimson of his own blood and several clots of

9

pink flesh. He swallowed hard, pushing down the threat of nausea at the sight.

Though its features were twisted in death, Jared noted the heavy jaw, sloping forehead, deep, close-set eyes, and long upper fangs that curved slightly in toward its chin, all of which gave the beast its fearsome visage. Until this attack, Qa-ryks had never been this far north to threaten the Borean seacoast hamlets. Jared and Ge-or's only exposure to them had been on long treks to the south and west during trapping parties with their father into the Dark Forest. They had always given the beasts wide berth when they had seen them.

A hissed, "Hurry!" from above brought Jared back to the immediacy of the task at hand. Dismissing the heavy battle-axe as too cumbersome for either of them to wield, Jared turned back toward the building and began to climb.

A minute later, with Ge-or's help, Jared was on the roof. He handed an arrow to his brother. "The one in his neck broke when he fell. I cut out the arrowhead."

"The axe?"

"Too big even for you to handle, Ge-or. Come on, let's go." Both boys turned and scrambled quickly up the slope of the roof.

When they reached its high peak, they could see that the battle was now focused in the center of the village. Running down the far slope of the roof, each, in turn, leapt across the four-foot distance to the next roof. Ge-or led the way. They had to leap across several more roofs before the beasts were in range of their shortbows, ending up perched on the edge of a small house at the far southwest of the square.

The smoke from burning houses drifted all around them. It was difficult, even from their vantage point, to get a good perspective of the state of the battle. The fighting was fiercest in the northwest corner of the newly fortified square, where the major Qa-ryk thrust was aimed. Many of the beasts were crowding together, trying to smash their way through the hastily formed barricade to get at the villagers. Even the older women and young lads were fighting now. The din of the battle was a deafening, continuous roar -- the beasts' guttural battle cries mixing with the clanging of weapons and the frantic shouts and screams of the defenders.

The two lads stood on the north slope of the roof and nocked arrows to their bows trying to pick out targets within range. They shot carefully, aiming to wound each beast they hit badly enough so it would be out of the fighting. Their hunting arrows and light shortbows, while meticulously designed and formed under the watchful eye of their father, were intended for small animals, rabbits and squirrels, and the occasional deer. They were not powerful enough to bring down a Qa-ryk warrior unless the shot was extremely accurate. Though both boys were excellent marksmen, capable of skewering a running rabbit at thirty paces, the swirling smoke and decreasing light made it difficult for them to find targets.

Jared, the better marksman, caught one big Qa-ryk neatly in the eye with his first shot. The creature straightened, stiffened, and pitched backward, dead before it hit the ground. Ge-or's first shot stuck deep in the neck of one beast who was trying to claw up a sturdy oaken chest to get at two women fending it off with pitchforks. The beast grabbed at its throat, collapsing backward as the two pitchforks stabbed into its chest.

The two boys continued shooting – picking off the closest beasts with carefully placed shots. Unfortunately, it took only a few minutes for them to use up most of their small supply of arrows. Finally, Ge-or stood, handing his last three shafts to his brother. "Here!" he shouted above the din, "we've got to get more arrows and our swords. Stay as long as you can, then head back over the roofs to our house. I'll meet you on my way back. Watch out! If they see you, they might still have buoas. Good luck." Ge-or clapped his brother on his unbandaged shoulder; then he ran to the side of the roof and leapt across to the next dwelling to the east.

Jared, swinging back around, loosed his arrow as it came to bear on the first vital point he focused on – the ear of a beast trying to push through a breach in the defenses. The shaft hit dead-center and penetrated about half-way into the beast's brain; the Qa-ryk thrashed wildly as he fell. Jared caught a loose nail with his boot, causing his next shot to go a bit wide, hitting the Qa-ryk he had seen sneaking around the house below him in its shoulder, just above the heart. The beast roared in pain and ducked back around the building.

Swearing at the less-than-perfect shot, Jared nocked another arrow and searched through the smoke for a target. Suddenly, a gust of wind blew the dark gray haze from the square, and he caught a glimpse of the whole battle. He immediately realized how hopeless the situation truly was. A large company of the monstrous beasts had attacked their village; the entire square was now surrounded. Though the villagers were putting up a stalwart defense, they were over-matched; and there was no place to which they could retreat. The beasts had surrounded the makeshift barricade; and already several had clawed their way through the obstacles before them, engaging the defenders within the village center. Jared's and Ge-or's fine shooting had slowed the breakthrough in this quarter; unfortunately, most of their fellow villagers were not trained fighters.

Jared knew that there was something terribly wrong about this whole scene. Qa-ryks roved in small bands, seldom more than ten or twelve in a group. Even a clan was rarely more than twenty-five or thirty of the beasts. That was why the mountain villages, though settled near the eastern part of the Qa-ryk range, were considered safe from attack. Their only concern with the beasts was when hunting or trapping teams were out far from their protective stockade. These groups could be vulnerable to being ambushed. From what he could see, their village had been assaulted by over a hundred of the fierce warriors; the two hundred inhabitants, only a third men and women of fighting age, didn't stand a chance.

Even so, the resistance was determined. A bright flash of light, rising above one part of the beleaguered square, caught his eye. Jared immediately recognized the flaming blue arc of an elven sword rising again and again above the fray. He knew that his father – one of the best weapons-men of the early Qa-ryk Wars – was leading the defense at that point. There, the men and women were holding back the worst of the attack.

Jared took heart and resolved to move in closer to the melee to make sure his five remaining arrows counted. He leapt across several roofs before bracing for another shot.

Suddenly, the sky darkened, as if night had descended instantaneously instead of waiting for the twilight to progress further. A rush of wind accompanied the blackness as a massive form swept down from above toward the northwest corner of the square. For an instant, the fighting stopped throughout the whole village. The Qa-ryks broke off their attack and backed hastily from the crude fortifications.

A second later, a huge belch of flame came from the huge beast's open maw as it swept down close above the square. The blast of flame roiled out, engulfing the center of the defense. The bravely wielded blue sword, caught in the center of the liquid fire, faltered in its highest arc and fell.

11

That was all the boy saw, because the smoke from the new blazes and the tears streaming from his eyes obscured the rest. Now he knew what magic the Qa-ryks had used to breach the village walls. However inconceivable it was, the normally reclusive beasts had somehow enlisted the aid of a red dragon. The horrific winged creature had destroyed the last serious defense in one fiery blast; with a bellowing roar, it turned neatly on its tail and flew off into the west.

The burst of intense fire from the red dragon changed the whole scene from one of willful resistance to a complete rout and massacre. Qa-ryks renewed their assault and streamed into the square from all sides, cutting down men, women, and children as they charged inward. Those villagers that could get away, ran toward the eastern gate. Their last hope was to out-distance the lumbering beasts. Most, however, were met and brutally torn apart by long claws and sharp fangs.

Jared, fighting back tears, kept shooting. He was nocking his next-to-last arrow when one of the beasts espied him on the roof. Just in time, he saw the flick of the beast's wrist, and he dove backwards and to the side. An instant later, a wicked spiral blade buried itself in the wood shingles only inches to the right and above his forehead. Getting up quickly, Jared ran further up the slope trying to reset his arrow. As he was setting up for a shot, he looked down and saw the beast bringing his arm up to throw again. Knowing his shortbow and hunting arrow were no match for the deadly buoa thrown by an experienced warrior, he judiciously scampered over the peak of the roof. Running as fast as he could on the shingles, he headed toward the southeast corner and leapt for the next roof. He had to find his brother.

Roof followed roof as he ran to the east. The steep slopes were hazardous and made of rough-hewn slats; nonetheless, Jared's half-elf agility gave him a distinct advantage. He was as sure-footed as any. He and his brother had often played games scampering up and down the steep roofs while practicing their swordplay. He would be able to outdistance the slower Qa-ryk, but not by much.

At one point he caught a glimpse of the big beast still following him, though he lost sight of it as he ran over another peak. Jared was now more concerned with the fate of his brother than for himself. Ge-or would need to know what had happened in the square. As he neared their house, he shouted his brother's name. He got no reply.

The last house before his own was burning brightly, so when Jared reached the edge of the roof he knelt down, grasped the eave, and spun over the edge, dropping lightly to the ground. Running past the burning dwelling, he finally caught sight of Ge-or. His brother was standing in front of their log house fighting, keeping two of the dread beasts at bay with his sword. One dead Qa-ryk lay at his feet. He could see that Ge-or was bleeding from several superficial claw wounds, yet he seemed to be holding his own.

Ge-or was a remarkable swordsman; nevertheless, in the close confines between houses, and pressed by two of the heavy beasts, he was giving ground slowly. Jared knew his brother was waiting for the right opening to gut the foremost beast, but he also knew they had little time before other Qa-ryks would be upon them. Their house, which Ge-or was backing toward, was also beginning to smoke.

As he moved forward, Jared brought up his bow, drawing back as he raised it. When his aim came to bear, he let it fly into the back of the nearest Qa-ryk's neck. The arrow struck the beast, penetrating deeply, just as Ge-or parried a swipe from the foremost beast. Flipping the blade under the creature's arm, Ge-or plunged it deep into its upper belly. At that moment, another Qa-ryk appeared from the left and swung at Ge-or with a massive cudgel. Dodging under an attack by the beast that Jared had shot, Ge-or saw the swipe coming an instant too late. The heavy club struck Ge-or's temple with a loud sickening thwack. Jared saw his brother sink slowly to his knees, falling face-forward onto the packed earth.

Readying his last arrow for a shot, Jared caught sight of the Qa-ryk that had been chasing him as it came between the houses to his right. Seeing the buoa in its claw, he changed his mind and tried to get past the one with the club. He ducked forward, running as fast as he could toward Ge-or's crumbled form. Reacting on pure instinct, he grabbed the quiver of arrows from his brother's back as he passed, ripping upward until the leather strap broke; then he swung into the open doorway of their smoking home. Dashing through the large main room to the back, he flung himself at the window, closing his eyes tightly as he smashed through one of the few luxuries they had owned – a glass window his father had purchased for his elven wife. Landing on his side, he rolled to his feet and raced to the left past another flaming house.

The whole village was afire now; Jared had no choice but to flee. He had watched his father die in an instant from the dragon's fiery breath, and now saw his brother felled by a Qa-ryk club. With a massive beast following, the burning anguish in his chest would have to wait. Tears blurring his vision, he ran alongside the stockade wall, hoping that some of the villagers had managed to get to the eastern gate and safely onto the road to Permis. Once on the road, they might be able to outdistance the heavy-legged Qa-ryks. With luck, they could make it to the next town to warn their neighbors. Having only a quiver of arrows and a hunting knife, Jared knew he was of little consequence to what remained of the battle.

Crying bitterly, he made his way as fast as he could to a small door in the southern wall of the stockade. Ahead, he could see other beasts rushing toward the eastern gate, but no other villagers were in sight. Opening the door, he stepped through, glancing back once again to see if there were any others who might make it out that way. When he looked left, he saw the large Qa-ryk with the buoa come around the corner of the nearest house. Jared immediately slammed the heavy panel shut behind him. Searching the area around the door, he found a small log, which he wedged up against the heavy panel. Finally, he turned and ran for the hills to the south and east.

Jared was tired. A three-hour weapons training session early that morning with their father, as well as the day's work helping with the harvest in the fields, had taken a toll; and the early evening hunting trip up in the hills with his brother had taxed him further. He was, however, young and able. The swirl of emotions tightening his chest helped him make good time up the rocky slope. At first, he didn't think about where he was going; he went up and away, trying to put some distance between him and the beast that was trailing. As his jumbled thoughts began to settle and his grief subsided into a slow-burning rage, he oriented himself along a well-worn path due south, that went up into the hills.

Jared had no doubt the Qa-ryk was tracking him. From what his father had taught him, he knew they did not give up on fugitives readily. As a half-elf, he would be a special prize this far to the north. If he were taken alive, he would be tortured mercilessly for days. He was not going to let that happen.

He was too far from the eastern road to cut over easily; still, he figured that if he got high enough into the hills and either outpaced or killed the Qa-ryk, he could wend his way back to help any who might have gotten free from the fighting. He knew this terrain well. He had spent his youth moving in and out of the many nooks and crannies of the rocky slopes on adventures with his brother. He and Ge-or often began their hunting expeditions heading up this very path.

He began to think more clearly and to formulate a tentative plan as he loped easily along the pebbly dirt path through the rocky terrain. After ten minutes, when the rocks began to get larger and more difficult to maneuver around and the path narrowed considerably, Jared struck off to the west. This was as good a place as he would find to set an ambush. The large brute would have trouble maneuvering on the narrow path, and the boulders would give Jared enough cover to get off one clean shot before the beast could spot him. If he was accurate, he might survive.

Two minutes later found Jared crouching on a small ledge in a natural hollow formed by two large boulders. This spot had been his secret hideaway for many years. It was a place where he had been able to think, read, and make up tunes while accompanying himself on his small portative harp. He always carried it on his back, even when hunting, for he never knew when a new tune might come to him.

As he waited in the increasing dark for the Qa-ryk, Jared reached back underneath his cloak to touch the strings and rosewood frame through the well-used cougar-pelt carry case his mother had made for it. Though he always felt the weight of the instrument on his back, it was reassuring to feel the light tension of the strings. With a deep sigh, he wondered if he would ever feel like singing again.

Turning his attention to his bow, he eased an arrow from the quiver. Nocking it, he pulled back slightly on the string, feeling the tension of the wood in his left hand. He prayed that his aim would be true for this one chance, because that would be all he would get. If he missed his aiming point, the beast would be on him in a second. He wished he had picked up Ge-or's sword; but in his frenzy to get away from the Qa-ryk, he barely had time to get the quiver.

Jared sensed the Qa-ryk's approach a moment before he heard scraping noises amongst the rocks. He drew back the bow string, relishing the feeling of resistance of the tightly-wound, carefully waxed gut. He waited. The large warrior became aware of Jared a split second after he came around the boulder; that instant cost him his life. Jared smoothly released the arrow at the yellowish gleam of the beast's left eye. Dropping the bow before he knew whether the arrow had hit where he had aimed, he vaulted up and back over the boulder behind him, drawing his hunting knife as he prepared for what might happen next.

A roar greeted the night air, convincing Jared that he had been true to his mark. Teetering on its heavy legs, it fell forward, the arrow protruding from its left eye socket. The beast was likely dead before it hit the ground; Jared wanted to be certain. He slid sideways around two boulders to come up behind it, lifted its heavy head, and slit its throat. The creature did not move; the arrow had penetrated into its brain.

As Jared stood over the fallen Qa-ryk, he saw that the creature was one of the ranking clan members. It was dressed in a chain mail shirt never found on their regular soldiers, and it had an ornate two-handed sword in its left claw. He stooped over the eight-foot body of the humanoid and began to search the corpse.

First, he drew out the beast's long hunting knife from its leather sheath. Small for a creature of this size, the blade would serve as a sword for Jared. Cutting out his arrow next, he returned it to his quiver. Thankfully, the wood had held and not snapped when the beast fell. Finally, he cut off the Qa-ryk's food pouch, which he re-tied over his shoulder. Slipping the long knife into his own belt, he bent over and picked up the remaining buoa from the dead creature's claw. He handled the wicked spiral throwing blade gingerly, deciding at the last to place it in the large food pouch in between the dried meat and bread he found there.

Stepping back from the body, Jared closed his eyes and whispered a thank you to the gods. He was on his own now and would need to survive in the hills for at least a few days. Making a decision, he stepped toward the dead beast again and bent to search the body for a purse, eventually finding a small one tied around its belt. Jared cut it loose with his hunting knife and tied it to his own belt. He knew he would need everything he could find that might prove of any use. Thiele was destroyed, his family members and friends killed. He did not know if he would be able to go back to salvage anything within the next few days... or if he would ever wish to.

As he was about to leave, he noticed a large, irregularly shaped stone, bound by some light-colored metal, hanging from a leather thong around the beast's neck. Bending over, he cut the cord. Without looking at it, he tied it around his own neck to examine later. If it had any value, he might be able to trade it for supplies. He left the beast for the crows or its comrades to find and headed back to the southerly path, thence, further up into the high hills.

The Black Priest

He stood on the hillside above the village looking down at the dying embers of the fires. The sight had a nightmarish quality to it, which pleased him. Swaths of orange-red gleamed in the darkness, lighting in various places the sooty gray pall of smoke that had settled over the destroyed hamlet. It was pleasing to his eyes and to his dark soul. It had been a good day. Well, mostly a good day. One task completed; one other he hoped to take care of quickly enough. With the dragon as an aid to the battle, the Qa-ryks had an easy victory. Overkill – more of the beasts were left for the next attack he planned. That would come soon enough, too, if all else went well.

The inspiration to use the red dragon, Fis, had come into his plans a few years ago, when he saw the beast flying far up, outlined against the western mountains. There weren't many of them left in Borea, and most were unreachable in their lofty lairs far in the west. This one's nest, though it had been difficult to reach, had been on the eastern slope of the range. He had thought he might be able to use the old beast someday. The great elven sword had been the perfect lure to bring the thing out of its stuporous existence. Now, thanks to his foresight, that horrific blade was also beyond the kingdom's reach. Thankfully, there were few enough of those dread weapons about these days. Many had been lost in the dragon wars. Still, one fewer would make his ultimate task that much easier.

He wondered if they had any notion of what they had lost. The Boreans! He sneered at the kingdom's elite which had ruled for far too many centuries. The lushes and dandies that strutted about the court in their silk doublets with rapiers to hip probably had no idea the great weapon even existed. The best elven mages and dwarven smiths had crafted the blade during that age of the world when the two races were close, sharing secrets and working their arts together. Not only had they used the best metals, the sword had also been imbued with the most powerful of magic. No, he didn't think that even the young elf, who had passed the blade to the human warrior,

16

had known how valuable a weapon it was for the good. Its history was only pain to his brethren; they were well rid of it.

It was an unusually sized weapon. Shorter than the typical long sword, yet still long enough that only an elf warrior or a tall human could wield it effectively one-handed. Double-edged, with two long blood-grooves that ran the length of the blade, it could be honed to a razor tone that would retain its sharpness through even a long battle; such was its making. There was weight in it as well; but it was light enough to wield for a long time, making it ideal for either thrusting or swinging in broad strokes in the close quarters of a pitched fight. The human who had owned it had been a renowned fighter. Now, he was dead as well, which was all for the betterment of the Black Druids' cause.

Yes, he knew the sword well enough. It had been many years since the blade had briefly fallen into his hands. He still bore the faint scars from where it had burned him when he had tried to pick it up. Its searing blue light was death to those of their ilk. Now it was safe. Fis would covet it for centuries to come. He was still deadly; that he had just proven. Yet, Aberon doubted he had even seen a smattering of what the old beast could really do. Though he had no current plans to use him again, he would keep the dragon in mind as a potential source of insuperable force in the future.

Of his other tasks – well, he was a bit irritated that the stone had escaped him for the moment. He had tried to acquire it numerous times. Unfortunately, the stupid Qa-ryk chieftain would not part with it. It was his "bauble." He had tried to coerce the beast out of it, resorting to bribes in the end; Raugghh would have none of it. Of course, he could easily have taken it from the brute, but then it would have been next to impossible to get the dull creature to agree to the assault he had planned. The burning village below, one of several places that were thorns in the sides of his brethren, would still be standing elsewise. Eventually, the Black Druids would eliminate all these northern sea-coast towns and rule the entire west. That, however, would have to wait until he finished his current tasks.

It had taken most of his skill to negotiate the planned attacks as it was. Qa-ryks were slow mentally and their natural clannish tendencies were hard to break. It had taken three separate trips to their diverse strongholds, using his wiliest conjurations, to bring these clans together under Raugghh. He had not wanted to jeopardize that delicate balance by absconding with the beast's treasure.

The big Qa-ryk wouldn't even tell him where he had found it. All he could get out of him was, "Mine, Won. Mine, Won," whenever he had asked. Aberon's own desire to acquire the pendant had caused the dumb beast to be even more covetous; the brute had gone to tying it about his neck.

So, he, dark priest of the void, had used another approach. Nothing like killing two birds with one arrow, so to speak. Qa-ryks enjoyed a pitched battle, close quarters, kill or be killed. They loved ripping a few throats and lapping up the blood of the fallen. It was how they proved themselves and gained status in their clans. Raugghh was a big mean brute who liked nothing more than to show the others his strength and prowess. The biggest and bravest of the beasts were always at the fore of any attack. They never held back or let the young ones take all the glory. They lived to throw down their opponents, and in their blood lust to bite their victims' throats.

He had used that knowledge and cast a curse on the Qa-ryk leader. He reasoned that with providence working against him, the great brute would catch a stray arrow in a vital area or be gutted in the first charge. It had not worked out quite that neatly, at least not right away. Raugghh had entered the fray at the fore of the massed clans as Aberon predicted he would. The beast had been quite impressive. Yet despite the powerful spell, he had come through the battle with only minor wounds.

He hadn't counted on the young half-elf, either. It turned out that he was both a blessing and a curse. The lad had managed, with a well-placed arrow, to kill Raugghh – not a feat that any one human would likely have accomplished without the curse weighing the beast down. His plan to take the stone had been foiled again when the boy had cut it off the chieftain and taken it for himself. Well, it was a small enough matter after all. He would trail the lad in a day or so. He had no qualms about using whatever deadly effort was needed to destroy him and take the pendant. The lad was nothing to him; the stone – everything. After that, he would have all that he required to complete the other tasks of his current quest. If he succeeded, the Black Druids would raise him up to become part of their inner cabal, which was the next step toward his ultimate goal.

Enough with all this pleasant reminiscing; the Qa-ryks were approaching up the hill carrying their loot and their dead. His most immediate task would be to speak with them about a new leader. He had the perfect brute in mind, too. Raugghh's son, Ka-ragh, had been eyeing his father's position. He had already eclipsed his father in height and weight; thus, there would not likely be any others who would fight for chieftain once his clan put him forward. He would make sure that happened this night.

The only drawback to all of this was that it took the beasts a full day to put their prospective clan head through the brutal initiation required to prove his worth. He would have to stay for the festivities; it was expected. Well, there was nothing for it. Thankfully, the half-elven lad was wounded, and thus not likely to go far without rest. He would be able to scry him easily enough. Once he knew where he was, he would make plans to dispose of him and take the stone. The thing threw off an aura that was hard to miss if you could read such. Repugnant as its coolness and wholeness were to Aberon, at least he would know where to find it.

Tonight, he, Aberon, Priest of the Void, would celebrate his victory with these beasts, a victory that had cost him little enough. Certainly, they had lost a couple dozen Qa-ryks; but that was of no real consequence to him. The monsters bred quickly. Kan had seen to that. There were always young pups eager to join the fray. It was a good thing that he had expended so little effort on this attack; he would need his powers soon enough. The next fray he planned would not be as easy.

Thistle

Leaving the dead Qa-ryk behind, Jared broke into an easy lope up the winding path to the hills. He was more than tired now, but he knew he could run this way for a long time. His father had always emphasized fitness first, weaponry second. At the moment, he didn't have any clear plan – just to get as far away from the Qa-ryks as possible.

He had to assume that they would make every effort to find their fallen leader. Their patrols were composed of close-knit relational groups from the same clan. If he was correct in his assumption, this attack had been by an extended clan. Why they had felt the need to gather a large force to destroy the remote coastal village of Thiele, Jared didn't know. Every way he thought about it, it didn't seem to make much sense. The beasts, according to the long-range trapping and hunting groups that had gone out all year, had been holed up deep in the Dark Forest. They had not proven to be any threat to the men while they worked their lines, and they had appeared content to ignore the humans encroaching on the edge of their range.

When one figured in the red dragon, the attack made even less sense. He had never heard of anything like a dragon joining forces with Qa-ryks. He and Ge-or had listened to their dad tell many stories about the early Qa-ryk wars, when the beasts had been driven by evil dark priests to attack the dwarves' and gnomes' homeland. Nothing had ever been said of dragons or their ilk being involved.

Dragons were memories of times long gone. Even Jared's father had only seen one a couple of times at a great distance. The few remaining in Borea lived far to the west, past the Qa-ryk lands. As far as anyone knew, these few kept to themselves. These fell beasts of a by-gone age were a diminishing race, as were the elves. It was only the eldest of the elves, dwarves, and gnomes who recalled the days when these great races had all lived together as friends. That is, if one could believe the old, old tales.

It was nearly full dark when Jared rounded a large boulder and saw the barest silhouette of a darkness that was not part of the rocks ahead. As he watched, it eased back into the shadows. It was not a Qa-ryk. He knew that they could remain still and quiet, surprising even a good hunter in broad daylight; nor was it likely a gzk, as the grey-green forest dwellers were rarely found this far to the north. There were other creatures of the night, though; and Jared was not going to take any chances. Not today.

He eased the Qa-ryk's long knife from his belt as he jogged a few more paces further up the hill. Just before he reached another large rock, he suddenly slipped off the side of the path. Sliding quickly and quietly around one boulder, he leapt up over another. He was upon the creature before it knew he had changed directions. He tackled it from behind, grasping at the head and drawing its neck back by the long hair he felt in his fist. As they fell to the path, he raised his knife for a thrust at the throat. Before he could plunge the blade down, they both hit the dirt and rock. Jared could feel the soft, smooth skin of his victim's limbs. An "Ouch!" followed by an indignant, "What are you doing?" greeted him as he rolled away from a young girl.

From the little light provided by the crescent moon and the stars, she appeared to be young and slight of build. Before he could sheath his blade, she was attacking him with her fists and cursing him with words he only half-knew himself. After a brief scuffle, he was able to subdue her sufficiently to get her unwilling

19

attention. Pushing her hands forcefully down to her sides, he half whispered, "Quiet, you little waif. We're not out of danger here. You'll have the whole Qa-ryk clan on our backs. What in hell are you doing here anyway?" He bent to pick up the knife that he had dropped when he had defended himself against her fury.

"What the hell am I doing..." She started to shout again. Jared raised the hand with the knife in it, palm outward to shush her. She quieted to a forceful whisper, "...here? What are YOU doing here? Too scared to fight and die like the rest of the MEN? Going to kill me instead?" She spat out the last word at him, standing her ground defiantly.

Jared backed away from her, flushing deeply, though she couldn't tell that in the dark. She had hit a nerve.

She paused, sensing his discomfort; but she continued a second later, alternately sobbing and gasping for air. "My hus... fiancé... sent me out... when the fighting started. We were near the east gate. He went back to the fighting. I... they... I didn't think it would be so bad. The dragon... Did you see my parents? They left before the alarm. I... It wasn't fair." She began to cry, tears streaming down her face, her shoulders heaving.

Jared, angry in general and shamed by her words, did not try to comfort her. She had struck at the one thing that had bothered him since he had gone through the door in the stockade to head into the hills – Should he have stayed? He also knew they were far from being out of danger, and that is what he needed to address in spite of his chagrin and her anger.

He spoke rapidly in a harsh whisper. "We don't have time for whimpering either. I suppose you'll have to come with me; I doubt that you will be anything except a major hindrance. The village is destroyed. I don't know who may have escaped. I don't know about your parents. If they left early, they might have survived. I saw my father and brother die before I got away. We can decide tomorrow where we'll go, but we have to move, now!" He grabbed her arm and pulled her roughly toward the path. "Can you use a knife? Are you strong enough to run for a while?"

The girl stopped crying and looked up at Jared with anger burning in her eyes. After a moment, though, she nodded "Yes." He handed her his hunting knife and pushed her behind him on the worn rock. "I know the paths for a few more leagues. Follow closely and don't stop for anything. I'd as soon leave you here as a Qa-ryk meal if you give me any trouble. Come on!"

Jared started up the path again at an easy trot. The girl hesitated; then she followed, catching up to him easily. After that, she stayed close behind as they ran up the trail.

They covered a league or more at a good pace, always further up into the hills. The girl had been able to stay with him so far and had not complained, so she was at least fit. Jared could tell, however, that she was suffering. She wasn't dressed for the high hill country in the early fall. She had on a light linen dress and house sandals, hardly appropriate wear for the rocky terrain they were crossing, and certainly not adequate for the prospect of chilly, windy nights. Luckily, Jared had on his tough hunting boots and a leather jerkin above his work clothes in addition to his short woolen cape.

They stopped briefly at a small stream to drink, but didn't speak to each other. The girl remained sullen and withdrawn, and Jared was in no mood for conversation anyway. The truth was, he didn't feel well. His head had begun to throb with the effort of trying not to think about what had happened to his family and the choices he had made. He felt weaker than he reasoned he should. After barely a minute's pause, he motioned to the girl to follow, and they were off again.

About half an hour later, Jared began to feel quite dizzy. He kept going, though he couldn't seem to shake off the feeling. Shortly after they crossed a flat grassy expanse before the next rocky climb, he felt something warm and wet trickle down his side. Suddenly, he remembered the clawing he had gotten from the Qa-ryk. He felt under his arm. His whole right side was sticky with blood. The binding he had managed to tie on the wound had fallen off, and his shooting and running had opened the gashes. He had lost a good deal of blood. Though the arm did not hurt, he was light-headed by the time he finally stopped. He turned to the girl coming up behind and started to say, "I have to get this..." Then he fainted, slowly slipping to the earth as she looked on in disbelief.

He woke only seconds later, lying crumbled on the path. The girl was leaning over him crying softly, "Please, please wake up. I don't know where we are. Please..."

"I'm all right... I..." he managed to say, trying to sit up by pushing with his elbows. The dizziness returned, so he eased back down onto the path. "You've got to help me. My shoulder is bleeding and needs to be bound. I've lost a lot of blood. I think... I'm afraid I'll faint again if I try to get up. Take my cape and tear off a piece to bind it."

Jared paused, trying to think past the dizziness. "We can't stay here for long; it is too open. I'm worried the beasts may be tracking us. I killed one of their officers. They will want revenge if they find him. I'm sorry... I'm not in much shape to fight anymore." Jared slumped down, his head spinning with the small effort he had made.

Still angry, she wanted to snap at him; but after feeling his shoulder and side with her hand, she realized that the boy – he really wasn't much older than a boy – was in bad shape. The blood was thick and viscous coming down from the wound and caked where it had dried. Wilderness-raised, she knew what to do. Setting her resolve, she eased his cape over his head. That is when she saw the harp case tied beneath. "Oh," she exclaimed, "you must be Ja...." She stopped; he had fainted again.

Within a couple of minutes, the girl had bound the wound tightly with strips from the cape and managed to pull Jared slightly off the path. She eased his back up against a small hillock to give his head some support. She also raised his legs up with the rest of the rolled cape. Jared woke up half-way through her ministrations, too dizzy and weak to help in any way. She spoke to him when she saw his eyes were following her movements. "Listen, Jared, I'll try to find some water. There must be a stream somewhere up ahead with all this deep grass here. I'll look for a place to rest as well. I... ah... my name is Thistle. I'm sorry I said those things before. I didn't realize you were wounded. I... well, I'm sorry." She turned to go, turned back and added, "I heard you play in the village. It was beautiful."

Jared closed his eyes and lay there for what he figured must have been at least a half hour. He kept the long Qa-ryk knife in his lap ready if he needed it, yet he doubted he could have wielded it in any case. He kept drifting off, but would waken almost immediately to his shame.

What the girl had said had hurt him deeply. He could not help feeling guilty about being alive – about leaving the battle and the village, even though it had seemed hopeless, even suicidal, to stay with the massive Qa-ryk on his trail. At the time, he had taken what he considered to be the best course of action – find a place where he had the advantage over the beast and try to kill it. After? He didn't know. Had he panicked? Should he have gone back down, instead of further into the hills? Could he have made a difference? What would his brother have done in his place? His father? His thoughts were spinning off in every direction. He didn't know what he should have done.

He kept asking himself if he could somehow have done more. He had no answers. He had done what he had, and now he couldn't change it. Finally, too weak to move, he drifted off for a time in spite of his throbbing headache.

When she returned, Thistle found him asleep with the Qa-ryk knife in his hand by his side. She bathed his head with the wet cloth she had brought back. When he woke up under her ministrations, she squeezed some water in his mouth. His forehead was hot to her touch. She knew he would have to rest completely as soon as possible. "There is a stream up ahead that winds next to the path for a bit, and a small cave a little further past that. Do you think you can make it?"

"I have to," he muttered, not meaning to sound harsh; yet the effort he made trying to stand up made it sound so.

Thistle stared at him for an instant with an angry glint in her eyes. "I said I was sorry!" she cried. She looked like she was going to stomp her foot, but she didn't. Instead, she looked away for an instant and whispered forcefully, "Here, put your arm around my shoulders. Now let's go." She reached out and grabbed his good arm to help him get up, pulling firmly, though not roughly, despite her feelings.

Within a couple of minutes, they discovered that they could not navigate amongst the rocks with him leaning on her. They stopped in the middle of a wider section of the path. Jared, breathing heavily, pushed her ahead. "Go before me, Thistle. Here take this." He handed her his lyre, pondered for a second and also handed her his bow, quiver, and the Qa-ryk knife. "Carry these. I'll follow you. Go slowly. I think I can make it. I'm not angry, not at you, Thistle. I'm angry at myself. I..." His voice trailed off. He added weakly, "Go ahead, while I still can move."

It took them a long time to cover the distance to the water where they took another long rest. Jared was weak and exhausted, yet he couldn't fall asleep. His forehead burned with fever. After a couple minutes, he whispered to Thistle. "I'm sorry I treated you like a child. I... I saw my father burnt by the dragon, and I saw so many others die as well. I felt so helpless. I still find it difficult to believe that this isn't just a horrid nightmare. There was no warning. No hint of danger. The Qa-ryks have been far to the west and south this year. Before this..." He paused; the pain of remembering even this much brought tears to his eyes.

As he was barely whispering, Thistle moved up next to him to listen. She reached out to bathe his forehead again with the wet wool.

He stared at her, not remembering what she had related earlier. He said, "You're not of our village. I would recognize your face or voice. Why were you in Thiele?"

"My parents were arranging my betrothal with Baldo, son of Guido."

Jared searched his memory for a second; finally, he nodded. He had heard of the betrothal. Baldo was not a good friend of his or Ge-or's, but he was a sturdy fellow and true. He was older and well-settled, a farmer who would have made a good match.

"I am from Permis. My father received a gift of furs for my hand. Times have been hard this year in our village with the fur trade being what it is. We, my family and his, were at the east wall before the attack started. My father and mother had left for home only minutes before the alarm rang. Baldo and his parents were with me. I wanted to stay and do what I could, but they insisted I go into the hills. They all went back to fight. I never saw them after that, or anyone, until you came up the path. It all happened so quickly."

They fell silent for several minutes, each trying to deal with their grief in their own way. After a deep sigh, Jared broke the quiet. "How old are you? You seem young to be wed?"

"Almost seventeen," Thistle sniffed. "Well, not almost. My father deemed me old enough to give away. One can hardly blame him. He has five daughters, and I am the eldest." She smiled at Jared, and that was when he first noticed her simple, pure beauty. She had long brown hair that looked soft and fine in the moonlight, a thin face with strong, graceful features, and startling green eyes. Her delicate fingers toyed with his hunting knife. She asked shyly, "How old are you, Jared?" She looked down while she waited for him to answer.

"I am half-elven." He paused to let that information sink in. She did not act surprised; but he knew that while people oft recognized his elven features, few understood what that meant developmentally. "Though I have seen a few more years than you, I am still not considered a man. Today I think I have had such responsibilities forced upon me sooner than I would ever wish."

Thistle looked up into his eyes. "Yes, I guess there is something elven about you. It is quite rare to find the elves this far north?" She ended the sentence with a slight rise in pitch – as a question. This time Jared did smile. There was something about her…

He shook his head, interrupting his own thought. "My mother was elven. My father met her in the latter days of the Qa-ryk fighting in the southern mountains. It was a fortuitous meeting. He was a brave and renowned fighter before he lost his arm. She was taken by his charm and prowess. She died years ago of a rare illness. I guess I take after her the most. She taught me to play and sing. My brother is… was… more like my father, sturdy and dark-haired. I am lighter in hair and in form, though we are both tall and quick."

He continued, a bit more excitedly, something stirring in the depths of his mind. "My father," he began, as the memory of the bright sword rising high over the field of battle flashed into his consciousness, "went to his death with his sword, a warrior to the end." Jared stopped, suddenly seeing the vivid picture of the dragon's breath searing and engulfing the blade as it rose for the last time. He exclaimed, a little too loudly, "The sword! My father's sword! The Qa-ryks must have taken it!

"That's what I must do!" Jared began to struggle to his feet. "It is a power weapon. I have to win the sword back. It is an elven blade and magical. I cannot let it remain in their hands. I must have it back!" Jared's voice continued to get louder and higher. "I..."

"Jared." Thistle's raised her voice in warning. "Sh-h-h. Don't be a fool. You are weak and ill. We must first think to our safety. The weapon is lost. You and I would be no match for a patrol of Qa-ryk warriors fresh from the kill, much less a large company. Come, we had better get to the cave. You can rest there."

Jared persisted about the weapon. "I must get it. I will have it back for my family. I..."

Realizing it was the fever that spoke, Thistle slapped him across the face, hard enough to get his attention. "Jared, you're feverish. Come on. It's only a bit more to the cave." She pulled him up. In hopes of placating his fierce focus, she said, "We'll get the blade tomorrow. I'll help you. Come on!"

23

The blow stopped Jared's jabbering, but he was quite dizzy. He was finding it difficult to focus. He followed the girl only with great effort. Somehow, amidst the haze of the fever, he felt he could redeem himself if he got the sword back. Stumbling after Thistle's form in the dim light, he held the burning blue blade before him in his mind.

It was within a couple hours of dawn when they reached the small cave. Off the path by a dozen paces, it was set in the face of a small cliff and overhang. About twenty feet deep, it was only four feet in diameter at the mouth. When they both crawled in, they found they could rest comfortably behind a jutting angle of rock that would keep passing eyes from seeing them. Thistle half-pulled Jared around the corner. He collapsed into a deep sleep immediately.

Thistle tried to make herself comfortable at the corner, leaning up against the curved rock wall with her feet extended toward Jared's. She wasn't frightened now, yet she was worried. She was wilderness bred; she would deal with whatever happened. However, she was really concerned about Jared. He had a fever and by all signs it was getting worse. His head felt hot and he was moaning in his sleep. If she dared make a fire at dawn, she would clean his wounds better, sew up the two longest gashes, and bind his shoulder more tightly.

She carried in her leather purse, as all the women did and most of the men, a small kit of "necessities." You never wanted to be without needles, from the finest for linen to heaviest for leather, a bit of thread and heavy twine, flint, and a small knife. You didn't want to have to run back to your cabin every time the need for any of these arose. The only difference in her accoutrements pack from average was the quality of the small knife she carried. Her father had insisted on his daughters learning how to defend themselves. Thistle's blade was well-balanced, and she did know how to use it.

She had never sewed up a wound, but she had watched her mother do so on more than a couple of occasions. If she focused, she would be able to do it. For now, she would have to wait until it got light. If they both lived that long, she would face that for Jared.

Thistle adjusted her position once more, turning slightly onto her side so she could see the opening to the cave. It was quite dark, yet her eyes had adjusted well enough to the bit of starry light that she could make out Jared's form as well as the edge of the grotto's wall leading outside. She placed the Qa-ryk's long knife in front of where her right hand lay.

It was ludicrous to plan on attacking a Qa-ryk – a wisp of a girl and a wounded, half-elven musician – but she wasn't going to give up. Now that she had oriented to the current situation, she was of stern enough upbringing to steel herself for the morrow. She closed her eyes; after a long while she did fall asleep.

About three hours later, Jared awoke sweating heavily. Still hot and dazed, he could see light streaming in from outside. Suddenly, he felt threatened, though he wasn't sure why. He listened carefully. He heard a sound unlike anything he had ever heard in the wild before. It was coming into the cave. It sounded a bit like someone slurping soup from a bowl. The sound approached the angle in the cave steadily. Whatever it was paused just out of sight, close to Jared's feet, which were stretched along the wall to the point of the angle.

Easing his knife out of its sheath where it lay next to him, Jared tried to move

24

slightly so he could see the corner of the cave. He got ready to lunge. A moment later a cold, rubbery thing touched his ankle. He reared up from his position to strike. Thistle screamed.

Sart

The cleric stood in the middle of the town square, the heart of the devastation. Tears were streaming down his cheeks. He had been too late. Eight months of tracking, watching, and waiting and when he was most needed, he had failed. He sank to his knees, bowed his head, and prayed, asking Gaia to bless those who had fallen here, to show him his hubris and the mistakes he had made, and to lead him further along the path set before him.

He did not stay kneeling there for long. He had work to do, not the least of which was to look for wounded, if there were any in this awful destruction, and elsewise, to bless the dead.

Over four weeks earlier, he had been hot on the evil priest's trail. It led westward and south into mountains a long way from Aelfric, the border town where Sart had discovered this evil maggot lurking. He had long ago passed any place he recognized. Then, a day after climbing ever upward on a roundabout path on the side of a massive range of seemingly impenetrable mountains, he had seen a sight that he had never thought to witness.

A great beast of rusty red had burst from a cave high above, launching itself into the air and swooping down the side of the mountain toward the east. Upon its back, the fell priest clung.

Caught off guard, Sart saw the object of his quest speeding away with nothing for it but to watch. A red dragon, a dragon with a rider – it was a sight from lore so long ago that no one even spoke about them anymore. The elves had written records of days of yore when dragons and elves spoke to each other and shared magical things; when the fair ones rode about the skies and fought great battles with dark creatures and races; a time when unicorns, griffins, winged horses, and other fantastical and magical creatures roamed the earth. Such times were long, long past; they had already been waning at the end of the first age of this world.

It was Mangor's great evil that had been the final stroke leading to the demise of those fell winged beasts. The war between dragons, elves, and the other Borea races had been long and devastating to all. After it was done and all the races diminished except for men, the few dragons left had flown west, far west, never to be seen again. The land, too, was diminished; the elves had retreated to their enclave in Moulanes. For a time, the world was ruled and molded by sturdy races of dwarves, gnomes, and, as time went on -- men.

As he watched his adversary flee upon the dragon's back, Sart had looked on with both awe and dismay. Dragons and men had never gotten on well together, not since the elves' diminishment and self-exile. As man pushed ever westward searching for more lands to settle, the remaining dragons preyed on their livestock, resisting incursions into their ranges.

The great beasts loved all things bright and magical, things also coveted by men. Thus, the battle had been joined between the two races. Men prevailed because they were much more prolific, determined, and perhaps more than anything, always out to prove themselves better than the next. Dragons became the target of men's own form of pride and avarice. Over the years there were ever fewer of the beasts. They had reportedly gone even further into the west and settled in the impassable mountains. Few had been seen since. Yet, here was one flying off to the east with a rider upon its back!

He was now witnessing the unthinkable – a great beast enlisted by the enemies of Borea for what task he could not imagine. He well knew that only something of great value could entice an ancient dragon to leave its lair. It was most likely something magical that the beast coveted.

Sart had finally shaken off his surprise at seeing this unlikely duo flying eastward and had cast a scrying charm as the dragon sped away. Just in time, he was able to enhance his sight to see the beast drop from the sky into the heart of a Qa-ryk stronghold far to the east and north. Moments later, free of its burden, the beast had launched itself back into the air. It was returning west, directly back toward the mountain upon which he stood gaping.

Sart decided, fortuitously, because the dragon was coming much faster than he would have expected, that he did not want to be caught exposed on the side of the mountain with his trusted and very edible mule when the beast returned. Pulling the four-legged beast after him, the two had scrambled, rolled, and scrabbled straight down the steep slope until they were able to get amongst the trees. From there, for many long days and nights of hiking through the deep forest, Sart had headed in the general direction of where the evil priest had been dropped off.

Almost two weeks passed before he picked up the trail. Exhausted and with virtually no hope that he could catch them, Sart had trudged on following what appeared to be a massed Qa-ryk company now led by the dark priest.

He continued on through the days and nights with little sleep, moving as quickly as the terrain would allow. Unfortunately, the beasts had too much of a lead. The dread priest drove the heavy-legged Qa-ryks doggedly through the forests and hills north toward the coast. Sart didn't know their final destination; however, he had a good idea where they might be headed. There were villages and farmsteads carved out all along the northern seashore. First built for the prolific fur trade, several were now full-fledged, self-supporting communities centered around agriculture and the cattle, sheep, and goats they raised for wool and food. He also knew that they wouldn't stand a chance against a force this large. They had defenses, but they were designed for keeping out wolves, or for repelling small raiding parties of young Qa-ryk patrols out for blooding.

It was early evening on his twenty-second day from the dragon mount that Sart rounded a bend in the high trail and saw the sea afar to the north. He was over a league away and well above sea level on what had been a bright, sunny day. Unfortunately, the sun was already westering. He had a clear line of sight to a village that nestled in the hilly terrain south of a natural harbor. It had been many years since he had been this way, so it took him a couple of seconds to recall the names of the larger walled towns along the coast – Cutter-by-the Sea, Menda, Brea, Permis, and finally, Thiele. A pleasant place was Thiele, he recalled – the western-most village. They were a sturdy folk who were generous and kind to wandering clerics. It was to this small village that the death cleric led his minions. He could see the beasts below; he was too late.

As he leaned against a rock outcropping, Sart tried to summon what strength he could. From his vantage, he could see the Qa-ryk horde crawling and edging inexorably through the rocky area to the west of the town, sliding from one hiding place to another as they moved into place for an attack. He thought that perhaps there was some hope if he could get a bit lower, perhaps close enough to send some signal or warning. Though he was exhausted, he had alchemical tricks that might work. Where he now stood, he was too far off to be heard or seen, not unless someone was

27

specifically looking for a sign from him.

All of that changed in the next instant when he heard the whoosh of wind come from the west. There, set against the yellow of the sun, was the great red beast hurtling through the sky toward the town. Panicking, Sart released the mule's halter and began loping down the slope, skirting the twisting path as best he could. He was in no shape to run, tired as he was from weeks on the trail. Still, the steepness of the path allowed him to build up speed, as much from slipping and sliding as from his own efforts.

The dragon hit the side of the stockade with a massive blast of fire as Sart fell to his knees, skidding to a stop when he rounded a sharp bend a bit too fast. As he watched, the winged beast circled. Turning adroitly on its tail to attack again, it blew in another section of the logs with its liquid fire. The effect was awesome and terrifying to behold. The heat from the blast was so intense that anything flammable within its direct path was incinerated instantly. Even the heavy logs of the stockade simply vanished into ash and smoke.

Satisfied with its work, the dragon rose high into the sky, spiraling upward until it was a speck against the sun. There it hovered as the Qa-ryks roared from their positions toward the breaches in the stockade walls.

Sart was done for. He had pushed himself past endurance for days. He dropped into a half-sitting, half kneeling position on the dusty, rock-strewn path, helplessly gasping for air. Some half a league below, he saw two lads run into the village's upper pasture from the foothills above and race pell-mell toward the town. He wanted to call out to them, to save at least these two; but the roar of the beasts attacking below was now almost drowning out the frantic clamor of the village's alarm bell.

Minutes later, he managed to pull himself up, grabbing a hold of the mule's saddle when it ambled next to him. Even with the aid of the beast, he only made it a few hundred more paces down the hill. When Sart stopped again, it was only in time to see the dragon swoop once more to blast the willful resistance of the townspeople in the center of their square. After that, he could watch no more. He swooned against the rocks in defeat and grief, finally giving into his exhaustion.

He came back to his senses far into the night, a couple hours before dawn. He was still tired beyond belief, yet had managed to pull himself into the mule's saddle and ride slowly down into the upper pasture where he paused to rest again. A small rivulet coming out of the hills gave the two of them sustenance. While his mule grazed, Sart stood on the lonely hillside with his bare feet rooted in the earth, his arms spread wide in full view of the devastation below. He meditated as he gathered his strength for the morn. He prayed that there would be something he could do when he reached the town. He knew how brutal and completely merciless the Qa-ryks were. He could at least bless the fallen and pray for their peace in the afterlife. It seemed such a small thing at that moment.

By all signs, the Qa-ryks had been thorough. Sart moved throughout the village checking each body for any sign of life. When he saw they were past his help, he would touch the person with his rood, offering a quick blessing to the gods. The beasts had removed their own dead as was their wont, but had left the torn and bitten bodies of the villagers where they had fallen.

Some said they were cannibals. Sart knew the truth of it –they bit their enemies in the throat as a sign of their fierceness and valor; and they tore at the bodies sometimes when in battle rage, especially if the victim continued to struggle. Though they appeared to relish the taste of fresh blood, he had never known them to eat the flesh of the humans they killed. Their own dead they respected and honored. Their brethren's bodies would be burnt nearby or borne back to their enclave.

He had seen worse devastation than this in his many years of adventuring and doing battle against the forces of evil; however, this was one of the hardest things he had ever had to face. It wasn't the burnt and mutilated bodies or parts of bodies, nor the hellish way the beasts had rent many of the victims apart, nor the ample evidence that they had bitten many throats in their bloodlust… it was the regret. Knowing that IF he had been sooner, IF he had caught the evil priest before he met with the dragon, IF… There were too many IFs. He didn't know these people personally, yet he knew their quality. He knew that all they desired and worked for was a solid life amongst family and friends. He had spent time here years ago when he was a young priest They had accepted him as one of their own. He had been the recipient of their kindness and generosity when he had been in need. They hadn't deserved this horror.

Sart had moved into the southeast corner of the village, near a section of homes that were only partially burnt, when he heard a low moan. He rushed around the corner and saw part of a body. The man's boots were sticking out of a doorway into the pathway at an odd angle. He saw no movement, nor did he hear another sound as he approached. It looked like the man had wrapped his arms around the entryway, attempting to pull himself inside. There he had either died or fainted. Most of his upper torso was out of sight, which Sart later determined may have saved him from having his throat bitten.

Kneeling next to the man, Sart gently probed the body, starting at his exposed side and working upward. There certainly was enough blood, from several clawings and from a blow to the head. When he reached the neck during his examination, the man twisted slightly at the cleric's touch and moaned again.

Working quickly, Sart rolled the man... Half-elven! He's a half-elf! onto his back. Sart could now see the slightly elongated ears, high cheek bones, and other features marking the man as having at least some elfish heritage while he tried to assess his injuries. There was a good bit of blood on the right side of his face, running down his neck and darkening his tunic; it was not enough that he would have fainted from the loss. There was also a large knot on his temple. Sart probed the wound gently. The lad, for he was still young for a half-elf, groaned again. Luckily, his head did not appear to be fractured; he had taken a severe blow and likely had a concussion. Sart adjusted his position so that he could address the lad's injuries. Not having to heal a broken skull would make his work considerably easier.

Sart decided to use what inner strength he had left, rather than relying on his purely medicinal skills. He placed his hands on the head wound and let healing energy bind the cut and ease the swelling. During his ministrations, the large fellow relaxed. Sart was then able to check him thoroughly. Remarkably, the lad was in generally good shape – a few cuts and abrasions, but no deep wounds that needed stitching or healing energy. The Qa-ryks must have seen the blood loss and considered him dead and already bitten.

Following the examination, Sart managed to get the young half-elf further inside and into a sitting position with his back to the wall of the house. After, he left to check the rest of the area in hopes of finding others. Unfortunately, his search was in vain. This quarter of the village was devoid of bodies aside from the young half-elf. He found a few others further on, scattered along the path leading to the eastern gate, brought down while fleeing. He prayed that a few had made it free to the east.

When he returned to the house, he examined the immediate area more closely. The half-elf must have fallen while fighting. His bloodied sword and hunting knife were lying near where his feet had been. He had also dropped a bow before being felled by whatever beast had hit him. The curved, strung wood lay in the dust near the doorway. There were other pools of blood and many scrapes upon the ground, which lent evidence to a fight with one or more Qa-ryks having been slain in the immediate vicinity.

The fellow was starting to waken, so Sart washed the boy's face and hands with water from his pouch.

"Father?" Ge-or immediately noticed the man's cowl and robe as his eyes adjusted to the light. The priest was large, massing more than Ge-or's bulk. He had a full head of medium brown hair and a broad friendly face.

"A priest of the Earth, my son. You are safe. The beasts are gone."

"My brother? The village." Ge-or was starting to reorient. A rush of memories flooded in as he glanced about frantically at what little of the devastation he could see.

"I'm sorry, my son. No one else lives. I came too late. I am terribly sorry. I have seen naught of another half-elf amongst the slain. Perhaps he escaped to the east."

"No, he would have fought and died with the others." Ge-or choked back tears. "I will find him and honor him." He tried to rise, but dizziness hit. He had to settle back against the wall.

30

"He is not here, my son. I have searched the entire village, checking all in hopes there were others still alive. I found no other half-elven." What he didn't add, and feared, was that this man's brother may have been taken alive. That would mean days of insidious torture, followed by merciful death. "Rest a moment my son; you need to regain your strength. You received a tremendous blow to your head, and you are lucky to be alive. I have ministered to your wound. Nevertheless, it will take more time to overcome the effects of your injuries."

"The sword!"

"What?"

"My father's sword." The half-elf had shifted directions so suddenly that Sart backed away wondering if there had been more damage than he had suspected. The lad's eyes, however, were focused and bright. He did not seem disoriented.

"The beast took it, the dragon. I saw it in his talons when he spun around in the air to leave, just before I was attacked. It is why he came. He must have coveted it. The dragon came to take the magical blade of my father. I must have it back!" Ge-or tried to rise once again, and again he had to sit back. "What is wrong with me?"

"You are in shock, and you probably have a concussion. I eased the pain and swelling with my power, yet it will take some time and rest for you to regain your strength. You are still wounded, and you have seen your village destroyed. You must rest and gather yourself. You can do nothing until…"

"I must after the sword. I have to. It is too valuable to lose. I will have my revenge on that beast as well. I will have it. I…"

Sart could see that the young half-elf was still in shock, and now giving in to his anger and hurt. He knew that the worst he could do right now was to head vaingloriously out into the wilds after a red dragon seeking revenge – perhaps another day, not right now. Sart also knew that any warriors capable of such a feat were only memories to most in this world.

"My son, what is your name?" Sart took a hold of his shoulder in his strong grip and held on. "Listen to me. I will help you, but we must make sure you are whole first. Your name?"

"Ge-or, Ge-or of Thiele, son of Manfred. I will avenge his death. I will…" He struggled against Sart's efforts to hold him in place.

"Ge-or, good. Now listen, my son. I will help you. First you must calm yourself. Look at me. Look into my eyes."

Ge-or stopped struggling and looked up into Sart's dark brown eyes.

"Good, good. Now, tell me about the sword, and we will decide what must be done."

"It… it is elven, magical, a great blade from the first age. My father was gifted it during the early Qa-ryk wars when he saved an elven prince during a battle. It was forged by the masters of the first age. It was a kingly gift."

"Manfred, formerly of Panterra? Manfred of Borea?"

"Yes, did you know him?"

"Only in tales; he was a great warrior and swordsman by all accounts."

If this one is of his ilk, Sart thought, maybe there IS someone who could best a dragon. He is young; too young to… Well, he did know that the lad's father had been world-renowned before he had lost his arm.

"One of the best fighters of this age from the tales," Ge-or said, "though he never spoke of his own feats. Don't you see? It was what the dragon was after; it was how they got him to join this fight. They say the dragons ever lusted after powerful

31

magical weapons."

"Yes, I believe you are right, my young friend. You have helped answer a question I have had puzzling me for many long days. It makes perfect sense."

"Why did the Qa-ryks come? What did they want here? We are... were... a small village. Nothing to them."

"It is not the Qa-ryks, my son; it is the evil force that drives them. There are fell priests that are said to be organizing the beasts' diverse clans into fighting units, large fighting units. They are the same group that led the first of the Qa-ryk invasions to the south that your father fought so bravely against. They failed that time, but they have reorganized. They are expanding and proliferating once more. My guess is that Thiele was simply in their way, for it was a fell priest that led this attack."

"I will have my revenge on this priest as well." Ge-or's eyes flashed.

"Nay, you had best leave that one to me. He is deadly, and his force will need to be met by a like force. I will be back on his trail on the morrow. He is my quest; my life's work, it appears," Sart said tiredly.

"Go, if you must, after the dragon. I urge you to think on it before you make that leap. You are trained in arms; and if you have learned from your father, you will have skills. Know this – dragons are formidable foes. Many a fine warrior has fallen to their ruin by these great beasts. From what I saw, this is one of the eldest – old beyond your ken, yet still powerful. He likely wields magic as well as his fiery breath. Do not take him lightly."

"The beast will be mine. I will swear upon my father's grave."

"Ge-or, trust what I now tell you. There is work to be done here -- to honor the dead, your father included. After, if you must, go for the beast. Still, I urge you to gain much more knowledge, power, and skill before you do so. You are young; yon beast will be far to the west in its lair a year from now, or ten. Seek experience, quality weapons and armor; learn what you can of the beasts before you start a quest against any dragon. Their lore is ancient, and there are still a few who know about these things if you seek them out."

"I understand your concern, Father. But my anger thirsts. I will for this beast now."

"Then let me place my hands on your wound once more, for you must leave whole." Sart placed his fingers gently on Ge-or's head as he lowered it for the ministration.

Ge-or felt a tingling energy start in his head and trickle throughout his body. The throbbing he had barely noticed before suddenly flared painfully; an instant later it disappeared. He opened his eyes; he wasn't sure how long it had taken. He saw Sart looking at him, seated across the room on a rickety stool.

"Better?"

"Much; that was amazing. Was I... ah... out for long?"

"A few minutes. Come, here is a potion that will also help with your recovery. Drink it all." He handed Ge-or a small vial filled with a murky liquid. The lad took it and drained it in one gulp. He grimaced at the muddy taste as he handed the vial back to Sart.

"Good, now sleep, my son. I will be gone when you wake. I apologize for the subterfuge; however, you need to rest. Good hunting to us both." Ge-or was already nodding off from the powerful sleeping potion the cleric had given him to drink.

Sart made a small bed for Ge-or, and another for himself from the shreds of linen and wool left inside the house. He was beyond tired himself. The day had drained him, the healing more. He would rest until morn, before setting off on his continuing quest against the dark priest. The roof was whole, and the partially burnt walls provided enough protection from the breeze off the coast that they should be comfortable for the rest of the day and the night.

Sart woke a few hours before dawn and gathered his belongings. He knelt and blessed the young lad before he left. Ge-or, he knew, would sleep another full day before awakening fully rested and hopefully a bit more sensible about his plans. For now, Sart had Aberon to catch up to. His greater mission called. He hoped that the evil priest had not gotten too far ahead.

Yolk

"Jared, don't!" Thistle reached out to grab his arm. Jared, however, had not calculated for his wound; and as he lunged forward, a searing pain flashed through his arm and shoulder. The knife fell from his hand to the ground.

The creature that had touched Jared's bare ankle quickly disappeared around the corner of the cave. Jared moaned deeply as Thistle scrambled past him. "Yolk! Yolk!" she cried. "Please, don't leave me again. Please..."

Jared held his shoulder, trying to blink back the tears of pain. His whole right arm and upper back felt as if they were on fire; his mind was hazy with fever. While trying to make some sense from Thistle's words and actions, he crawled forward until he was peering around the curve in the cave wall. Thistle was kneeling, just back from the mouth of the cave, coaxing a small leathery-looking creature toward her. "Come. Please come, Yolk. He's not going to hurt you. Please! He thought you were attacking us. Please don't leave me again. I need you."

Tears formed in her eyes as she reached out toward the creature. It hesitated only a second longer, then it undulated toward her outstretched hands. Jared felt he must be totally consumed with fever, his mind playing tricks on him. The animal looked like a brown fried egg, but it was a good foot or more in diameter. It was basically flat, the color of the dusty earth, with a bump in the middle of its leathery body. The bump stared at Jared with two large unblinking yellow eyes. It scuttled toward Thistle. The thing moved by folding its flat body over the earth. As it got closer, Jared once again heard the strange slurping sound that had awoken him.

The creature finally reached Thistle's hands and flowed up onto her arms. As soon as she had it, she drew it quickly to her breast, hugging it close. Thistle began to sob as she held the animal. "Oh, Yolk, I honestly believed you had left me. I'm so glad you came back. I need you so badly." Jared sat back against the cave wall, closed his eyes, and tried to clear the haze of pain and fever from his head.

A moment later, Thistle's light touch on his cheek made him look up. "Jared, Jared? You are so hot. We have to get your fever down. I'm sorry Yolk woke you. He's... well, sort of a pet, a friend. I'll explain later. Let me look at the wound." Jared turned so she could untie the bandage. He was still dizzy and very hot. His shoulder pulsed with the pain of the cuts. Even Thistle's gentle touch sent flashes of fire down his arm. He grimaced at the fierceness of it.

As Thistle eased off the last wide strip of bloody cloth she gasped when she saw the flaring, puffy wound. Jared's shoulder and upper back were swollen and a fiery red. "By-the-gods, Jared!"

Jared looked over, raising his arm to try to see the angry gashes. The back of his whole upper arm and the part of the shoulder he could see were bright red and inflamed. Strangely, the wounds already appeared to have healed partly over with scar tissue, and no additional blood or pus was oozing from the few areas that were still open.

"Water," he whispered hoarsely. "I need water."

"Jared, it looks infected or poisoned, and we have no herbs. You can't die. You can't!" Thistle began to sob again. Jared fell back against the wall of the cave, heat burning up his awareness.

"Water, please get me some water," he moaned. He lost consciousness.

Sometime later, Jared struggled back to awareness; the haze of heat had passed. He felt cool, with little or no pain in his shoulder. He tried to push himself up. The effort woke him completely. After fighting unsuccessfully to rise, he gave up, settling back onto the warm cushion he had been lying on. Opening his eyes, he saw Thistle was looking down at him, smiling slightly.

"So, you finally decided to wake up, elf-kin. Here, let me help you." She reached behind him, pulled out the bundle of leaves wrapped in his wool cloak, and pushed it up against the wall of the cave, so Jared could ease himself into a sitting position with the bundle supporting his lower back.

"Drink this. The fever is gone. You'll need to get as much liquid as possible into you." Thistle held out the animal he had seen earlier toward him, holding it at eye level. It was upside down with its "head" cupped in her hands. He could see that the folds of the brown body were filled with a clear liquid.

"What is it?" He asked.

"This is Yolk... Ah, sorry, you mean the liquid. It's water, silly. Don't worry, it's fresh. Just drink it or I'll hit you." She leaned forward. As she did, the floppy creature slowly lowered one side of its body toward Jared's mouth. Soon, a thin trickle of water was flowing down onto Jared's chin. He opened his mouth somewhat reluctantly and tasted. It was fresh spring water. Getting over his squeamishness and realizing that he was desperately thirsty, he drank deeply. He kept drinking for what seemed like a long time, yet the water in the creature's middle did not appear to diminish. Jared finally put his hand up. The animal lifted its flap, stopping the flow. The water disappeared; and the creature righted itself, going back to clinging to Thistle's front.

Jared looked at it and again at Thistle. "What? How does it do that?" he asked.

"I really don't know how he does it; but if you leave him immersed in water for a short time, he kind of fills up. He can carry a lot of water, much more than his size would indicate. He regurgitates it, I guess. It always tastes as fresh as if just scooped from a stream. He's like an instant water bag. He...."

Jared interrupted her. "I mean, what is it? Your friend? I've never seen or heard of anything like it. What else does it do? How did you get it? I..."

This time Thistle interrupted him by clamping her hand over Jared's mouth. "Shhhh, we don't have time for all that right now. You've been asleep for a day and night. I haven't seen any sign of Qa-ryks, though we shouldn't take any chances either. You need to drink more and eat. I have some rabbit roasting outside. After that, we should decide where we will go, if you think you can walk?"

Realizing that they were still in an untenable situation, Jared began to get up. "Wait!" Thistle pushed him back gently. She reached toward his wounded shoulder. "I need to look at that. Does it hurt?" She began to untie the bandage.

Jared raised his arm and flexed the muscle. He felt no pain, only some soreness and stiffness in the upper arm and shoulder. "No, it feels much better."

Thistle gasped and pulled back in surprise when she took the last bandage off. She could see the broad lines where the Qa-ryk claws had raked Jared's shoulder deeply, as well as the shallower cuts on the back of his upper arm. Somehow, in the past day and a half, the wound had healed completely over, leaving only the bright pink and white lines of fresh scars. She looked at him quizzically. "Do half-elves always heal this quickly?"

He peered over his shoulder at the wounds. "No, well, at least I never have

35

before. I can't imagine what…? Could it be the stream? Or Yolk?"

"No, I don't think so. I drank and washed in it also, and I have a small cut on my hand. It hasn't healed, not like that. I've always used Yolk for water when I've needed to, so I doubt if it's him. Unless he changed in some way since he left me."

"Left?"

"When we got to Thiele, he left me while I was sleeping, the first night after we met Baldo and his family. He, I mean, Yolk, doesn't like some people, and for some reason he was ill at ease in their home. I really thought I had lost him, or that I would have to choose between him and getting married. He came back last night."

"Yolk? What?" Jared looked like he wanted to ask much more. He didn't quite know where to start.

"All right, I'll tell you what I know; then we must eat and make some choices. He came to me when I was thirteen; he just showed up. Well, that's the way I think it happened. One night I went to bed; the next morning I woke up to find this brown, fried-egg-like creature on my stomach staring at me."

Jared chuckled. "Is it a he?"

"Actually, I don't know if he's a 'he'. No way to tell, as far as I can see. I wanted to call him Eggy, but my sisters kept saying Yolk. Not to mention all the stupid puns and jokes that four little girls can come up with. So, the name stuck."

Thistle reached over and touched Jared's scars, effectively changing the subject. As a final test, she pushed in on them. He assured her the pain was gone. His fever was gone, too. Except for some soreness and stiffness, he felt good, much too good for having been gravely wounded, lost a great amount of blood, and struggled through hours of fever. However, they didn't have any more time to waste pondering the fast healing of Jared's wounds. Thistle helped him up. Crawling to the mouth of the cave, they went out to where she had two nice-sized rabbits roasting over a smokeless fire.

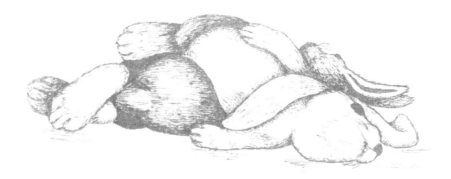

Jared flogged himself mentally for thinking that this wisp of a girl would be a worthless burden. She had killed the coneys – not a small feat in the rocky hills of this part of Borea – gutted and prepared them, and had cooked them over a fire made from a dry, nearly smokeless and odorless wood. He wanted to praise her resourcefulness; but as he sat down in front of the fire, he suddenly felt awkward and shy. He accepted the hind quarter of the rabbit she handed him with a meek, "Thanks, Thistle."

He ate hungrily, accepting more rabbit as she divided them, also taking a piece of toast she proffered. "It's from the Qa-ryk's pouch," she said. "It's quite stale;

36

toasted it is edible. There were some pieces of meat in the sack, too. They didn't look very appetizing, so I threw them to the crows. I hope you don't mind my going through your things, Jared. I was hungry." She stopped, looking steadily at him while she nibbled at a piece of the hard bread.

Jared tried to smile at her; he only managed a slight lifting of his lips at the corners. "Thanks, Thistle. I... I really am sorry about... Well, about how I have been acting. I'm really not mean-spirited. It's been a bad time for me, for us, I guess." He paused when he saw her brighten as he spoke. He continued, feeling a bit more at ease. "You are right, we have to decide what we're going to do." He stopped again, then went on slowly.

"Where do we go from here? You have a family, a village to return to. I feel lost. I've always had my family, and now..." His voice trailed off.

Thistle stared at him silently. Without answering, she stood up and began to cover the fire with dirt. Jared, looking at her fully in the daylight for the first time, realized that although she was slim and of a moderate height, hardly reaching his shoulder, she was hardened, as most of the women were who lived a difficult life in the west. She was also quite young and comely, even beautiful. Her light brown hair flowed about her shoulders, and she moved with a litheness that reminded him of his own elven heritage. Her face was thin, delicate in build, with a finely crafted nose and high cheekbones. There was a strength to her visage, too. Perhaps it was simply in her gaze and how she looked at the world… And those green eyes, they penetrated to one's soul.

Thistle broke his train of thought when she straightened from her work and looked at him squarely, almost as if challenging him. She immediately started asking a stream of questions, as if she had been waiting for this opportunity to quiz him. "You mentioned something about a sword when you had the fever. Is it important? I mean, is it important for you to find it? We could try, couldn't we? Are you positive the Qa-ryks took it? Why is it so critical to get it back? Can we try? I would like to help. Do…" She stopped just as suddenly when she saw his deepening frown.

Jared looked up toward the sky, as if suddenly noticing it was daytime and the sun was shining. He remembered now that his father's sword must have been taken by the Qa-ryks. He had last seen it when the dragon's breath had consumed all the resistance in that quadrant of the square. Based on what little he knew of the great old blades, even that intense flame would not have damaged it.

He sat frowning for a minute with his hands clasped tightly together. Finally, he said, "It is an elven sword – an old, magical blade that was given to my father when he saved an elven prince who was captured by the Qa-ryks. It was how he eventually met my mother. She was the prince's sister. In the right hands, it is a powerful weapon for the good. I do not really think I could use it. It is too big for my light frame. I could certainly never wield it as well as my father did. He meant it to go to my brother, Ge-or, but now…"

He paused, looking into her intensely fascinating eyes. "I don't know, Thistle. It would be worth a great effort to win it back for Borea. It is a blade that can only be used effectively by the good. In evil hands, it would be useless. It might even be damaging for them to try to wield it.

"I would think, from what my father told us, that they would try to destroy it or hide it. I don't think they could use it against us." He paused, speculating. "Do they have it? Yes, I would think so. Qa-ryks plunder anything of value after victory. My father said they use valuable items to trade with the Black Priests for the buoas they use – their throwing weapons. They are made from megas-metal, and that is rare and expensive."

"The spiral blade in the food pouch?" Thistle asked.

"Yes, they are deadly. Luckily, because of the dearth of megas-metal and how expensive it is, they usually only have a few of the weapons in each clan. Those are carried by their best warriors. They would have coveted the sword because they would have known its worth from seeing it used in battle.

"Can we get it back? I don't think we could... I mean, we wouldn't stand much of a chance against a company of Qa-ryks, even if we can follow them."

Thistle took Yolk from off her chest and took a long drink from its well of water. She passed the creature to Jared who stood holding it, unsure of what to do next. The animal felt like a supple leather in his hands, like fine suede. "Hold him close and he will let you drink. He isn't afraid of you now. He wouldn't have touched you the first time if he had considered you dangerous. I don't think he would have come back to me if he didn't like you."

Jared did as she instructed. Yolk lowered his flap closest to Jared when he drew him near. The water appeared in his middle. Jared began to drink as Thistle continued. "We could try to track them, don't you think? I mean find out where they take it, and what they do with it."

Thistle paused looking at Jared as he lowered the creature from his mouth. She clenched her fists, and he saw an angry glint in her green eyes. "I want to DO something, Jared. Anything! Something worthwhile, constructive. I can't..." She hesitated. "I don't want to go back to my village until I have done something to get even, to make a difference. I didn't want to leave the battle. I could have fought, but they wouldn't let me stay. And... and though I didn't really know him, they killed my husband to be. Jared, can't we at least try?"

He handed the floppy animal back to Thistle, studying the anger in her eyes and the determination written on her face. Finally, he nodded. "Finding their trail should be easy enough, they are heavy-legged, lumbering beasts. Catching up to them and staying with them in this country? I don't know. We can try. You are right, we wouldn't stand a chance against them in a fight. Maybe we can trick them or steal the sword at night. Or if, or when, they try to trade it, we take it. I want to do something, too." He stopped again. A minute later he said more quietly, yet more determinedly. "I want, I NEED to do something. I feel like I am burning up inside."

Finally, he shook his head sadly. "We have both lost so much. It seems like my former life is over. I can't go back to what was. It wouldn't be the same even if I tried. Who could have foreseen such a change in one's life? My brother and I, we often had dreams, romantic adventure fantasies, boyish plans perhaps; but now he is gone." A tear slid down Jared's cheek. He caught himself and shook his head angrily, looking up at Thistle.

"We will try." He stood up, looking into the west. "We are over a day and a half behind them. The company is probably long gone, back to the forests, heading for their main camp. My guess is that if there were any following us, we have either given them the slip or they figured we weren't worth the effort to chase down. Our best bet would be to try to intercept their trail by heading south and west from here."

Thistle nodded. "Let's try, Jared. Please don't take me home, don't make me go home. I don't want to go back to that life. It... it has no meaning for me anymore. Let's at least make some effort for those that died."

"I don't know, Thistle. It will be extremely risky. We could easily die; do you

38

understand that?"

She nodded again, her face set and determined.

A minute later, Jared said, "I left, Thistle, when I could have stayed. I don't know why I didn't. I keep asking myself over and over why I left at that moment, when I could have stayed and fought. I don't know. Maybe I panicked. I can't remember. A Qa-ryk was chasing me, and the defense in the square had been destroyed by the dragon's fire – the whole town overrun by the beasts. I had seen my brother felled by a huge beast with a wooden club. I ran. I just ran." His voice trailed off, his cheeks flushing a deep red as he bowed his head, shamed at his actions and the words that bespoke them.

Thistle stepped close to him, putting her hand on his left arm. "Jared, don't torture yourself thinking like that. You had no choice. You're alive! And as long as you, we, stay alive, we CAN do something. Had you stayed, you would be dead now." She stopped, remembering how frightened she had been.

"I probably would have eventually gone down to the village and been killed. You saved my life." She looked at him with that unwavering gaze. He could well understand the force of the inner pain that was driving her. She tightened her grip on his arm. "Let's find the sword. We have to try."

Jared took a small step back. He looked into her eyes, trying to read all that was there. He knew she was right; they had to do something. They had lost too much to just forget all that had happened. They couldn't start a new life built around what little was left of the old. For now, he really didn't feel like he had a choice. That old life held no meaning for him anymore. From what she had said, Thistle felt similarly.

They would make a go of it. He was, after all, the best tracker in their village. His elven-enhanced skills might give them the edge they needed out in the wilds. They would have to be careful; he lacked experience and he knew it.

He reached out and touched Thistle's cheek lightly, as if to comfort and yet agree with her. Then, his shyness returning, he blushed and turned suddenly away. He walked from her toward the cave, saying, "I'll get the rest of the gear. Maybe you had better get whatever it is... ah, Yolk, filled with water. We will need him unless we can find a water bag."

Thistle smiled and said, "Yes, Yolk. I don't know what he is, though he is cute." Her voice sounded relieved, with a bit of a lilt to it.

Jared mused as he crawled into the cave; at least relevant to this, he felt he had made the right decision.

Several minutes later, they had gathered their few weapons and belongings together in a small pile in front of the cave. Jared handed Thistle the hunting bow and quiver of arrows. "Here, you might as well take these. My arm is still sore, and you seem to be a good shot. I'll use the knife."

Thistle handed the bow back to him. "I've never shot a bow before. I got the coneys with this." She held up her small knife. "I learned to throw knives when I was a little girl. My father believed we should be able to protect ourselves with something."

Jared looked at her while slinging the bow onto his shoulder. That she could have thrown such a small blade accurately and brought down two conies was remarkable. Grinning broadly, he said, "I guess I have a great deal to learn about you, Thistle. Maybe you can teach me a few things."

"Only if you promise to teach me how to play and sing a little," she smiled back at him.

When she mentioned his music, Jared's face darkened; he brusquely turned away. He had already securely tied his instrument to his back, but he had purposely avoided touching the strings. The pain of the past few days had cut him deeply. He wasn't sure he would ever want to play again. Yet, he could not bear parting with the small lyre. It was the only thing he had that was from his mother.

After a deep breath, he turned back and awkwardly picked up the wool cloak, brushed off the remaining leaves, and held it out to her. "Here, you had better wear this. It will be cold while we stay in the hills. I'm afraid we're poorly provisioned for a trek. Those sandals won't last long either. Maybe we should go to your village first. I..."

"No!" Thistle's reaction was angry and immediate. She stomped her foot, looking as if she would be willing to take on a clan of Qa-ryks. "If we don't start now, we will never find the trail; and I am not going back first. You'll leave me there, or someone will force me to stay. We go after the sword!" Her eyes flashed, and she planted her feet apart on the trail, glaring at Jared.

Jared grinned at her again, wondering how this small, slim, brown-haired girl would stand up to a seven-foot Qa-ryk warrior, or whether or not the Qa-ryk would stand up to her.

"All right, Thistle. I wanted you to be more comfortable. We'll have to be careful, even a small injury could delay us for days in these hills."

She answered determinedly. "I can make some revelins from rabbit skins if I cure them in ashes and work them when we stop to rest. Maybe I can use the sole of my sandals to reinforce them. We'll manage. I'm a western girl, bred and raised. I could walk a long way in my bare feet, though I would prefer not to in these rocks. I do admit that I know little about tracking. Where do we go from here?"

Jared knew the short, light-weight laced boots Thistle was working on would work well enough if she reinforced the sole, as she had suggested. Still, they would find they were without many things soon enough if they continued trekking through the woods. "Well," he answered, " if we are going to intercept their trail, our best bet is to head west to begin with. We should retrace our steps until we find a path leading up into the hills to the south and west. We can work our way further west from there. We will have to be constantly alert. I'm hoping that we have not been followed. I'm almost convinced they would have attacked by now if we had been.

"Intercepting the trail initially should not be too difficult. The Qa-ryks won't try to hide their passage. Plus, I do have some skill tracking all manner of beasts. It is one of the things my father taught Ge-or and me at a young age. They are unlikely to be afraid of pursuit. Unless they use magic, they will leave a wide trail."

"There is a path heading southwest past the stream. We could try that, and Yolk could get filled up."

"Good, Thistle, that might work. I'll scout it while you wait for Yolk. Let's go."

The two adventurers headed back north, Thistle leading; her "pet" clung to her chest under the wool cloak. They were an unusual trio set on an impossible task, and they did not know they were being watched.

Resolve

By nightfall Thistle and Jared had covered almost three leagues in an erratic course through the rocky hills. En route, they killed two more coneys and ate late in the afternoon, saving the remaining meat for a cold supper. By the time they set up camp, they were both exhausted. Jared's wound looked like it had healed completely; still, he was still weak from the fever, and the difficult terrain had sorely tested his strength. Thistle's sandal straps had broken several times; so, when they finally settled into a small cavity off the trail they were following, she began to work on the rabbit skins, carefully pounding and working the hides toward a pair of revelins.

While she worked, Jared retraced their steps, diligently hiding their trail with all the skill of his mountain training and elven heritage. As full dark settled over the hills, he returned to their hollow and began dividing the food for their meal.

When they had finished the last of the rough Qa-ryk bread and cooked rabbit, Thistle, still working in the dark on the sandals, asked Jared, "Shouldn't we set a watch? I'll need to work on these for a while, so you can sleep first. The moon will be up shortly, and I might be able to get them done."

"We should be safe. I covered the trail completely, back past several turns we made. We are still several leagues from where we should intercept the Qa-ryk trail. It's more important to rest while we can."

"Well… I'll finish these if I can. I have to get them done before we leave tomorrow. My sandals are falling to pieces."

"Wake me if you hear or see anything. Goodnight, Thistle." Jared settled back against the smooth wall of the hollow, watching his newfound companion work for a few minutes before closing his eyes. Thistle whispered, "Goodnight, Jared." She smiled at him, blushed slightly at something odd she felt; then she shook her head as if to say to herself, It's nothing. She returned to her work.

Looking up a second later and seeing he was still looking at her, she added, "What we're doing is crazy, isn't it?"

Jared nodded. "More than a bit, I'm afraid. Qa-ryk warriors are fierce and powerful. Our only real hope to retrieve the sword will be through guile, and I'm no thief, Thistle. I can move quietly – as you saw when I changed directions and came up behind you on the path."

Thistle frowned and cleared her throat at that comment, yet she smiled again when Jared stopped and stared at her.

"I don't know what else to do, Thistle. I'm at a loss. My family is dead; I know of no other relations, except perhaps in Moulanes – and no one who is not a true elf has been allowed in the elven stronghold in decades. I have nowhere else to go, no one I can really rely on. I…" His voice trailed off. He continued a second later, "You could…"

"Stop right there, half-elf." Thistle's benign, concerned countenance changed in an instant to a grim resilience when she realized where he was headed. "You may be older, but you don't rule my life. I did not make a hasty choice back there at the cave. I have four sisters and times are hard in my village. The harvest is poor this year, the sea has been fitful and difficult to fish all summer and fall, and the fur gathering in and around Permis has been tapped dry. If I go back, I would be seen as one more mouth to feed, one more girl to take care of."

Jared was taken aback a bit by her vehemence. She certainly had a mind of her own, this wisp of a girl, counted as a woman by wilderness standards. There was a toughness about her. She hadn't complained at all during their hard trek through the rocks. And she was stubborn, no doubt about that.

Thistle eased off her forceful tone slightly when she saw he was intently focused on what she was saying. "I'm sorry, Jared. My heart aches as yours does, and yes, I could go back and see to my sisters. You know as well as I that my fate would be to be married off as quickly as possible. My father cannot put up with five daughters much longer. He is even working on a match for my next youngest sister, and she is only fourteen. I was not happy about being thrust into a marriage with Baldo; yet he seemed a decent and stalwart man. For my parents, I would have done so. Now, I feel I have a choice. Maybe that means another kind of hardship, perhaps even death; but you can't imagine how much better it feels to be free from all of that. And now that I do have a choice, it feels like I have been a slave to an untenable situation and to convention. No matter how desperately it was conceived by my parents, I know that being married off and living such a life is not what I wanted."

Thistle paused and wondered what Jared was thinking. In the deepening dark, she could not make out his features very well, so she could not judge his mood.

Actually, he was thinking: She is feisty and well-educated, judging by her choices. I like her; I think I like her a lot.

"Let's take our own path from here, Jared – whatever comes of it. We may be fools, yet we have a purpose. We have something worth pursuing. Perhaps it will lead to something else we cannot ken right now."

"You are determined, Thistle, and I am resolved as to our fate." Jared laughed lightly. "We make a fine pair out here in the wilderness. Yes, let's make what we may of our fortunes. Though my heart is heavy with sorrow, you have helped give me hope for something better. I must rest now. My wound drags at me still. Good night, Thistle. Please get some rest, too." With that, he settled back once again, a slight smile on his lips as he held the soft lines of the girl's silhouette close to his broken heart.

Thistle, roused by her own words, moved toward the entrance of the hollow and sat down to work on the skins in the moonlight. Yolk folded his way next to her.

Jared opened his eyes briefly at the movement. The last thing he remembered before he fell asleep was the creature staring up at Thistle with his large, unblinking yellow eyes.

Thistle worked for a long while. She felt drained by the events of the past few days, yet there was something within her that seemed to be energizing her spirit. Her thoughts drifted from her immediate work, and she soon found herself blinking back tears. For some reason, an image of the first time she had seen her husband-to-be flashed into her mind. She had not loved him, or even known him well; still, the idea that a person could be taken away so abruptly, someone who was a decent, hardworking sort, made her incredibly sad.

Baldo was ten years older than Thistle. He had lost his first wife to the fever the previous winter. He was good-looking in a wilderness sort of way – medium short in height, sturdy, well-muscled, bearded, and with a dark sun-tanned complexion. Initially, Thistle had been incredibly nervous at the idea of being wed, of leaving her family and starting a new life with someone she barely knew. In spite of what would likely prove to be at least a year-long engagement, she had felt uncomfortable with the whole idea. Interestingly, when she had met Baldo, he had seemed as shy of her as she was of him.

42

After the formalities of their families meeting one another, and a light noon repast, he had shown her about the village. She had liked his kindness and deference toward her. The small two-room house he had built on the south-east side of Thiele had been about as perfect a place as she could have imagined to start their life together. He had shown her the garden patch he had carved out in the communal area, the goats that were the beginning of his stock, and the small skiff he used for fishing. Thistle knew the value of all of these; with five girls and no boys crowded into their three-room home in Permis, her family was considered poor by coastal village standards. Baldo had the makings of becoming successful, even moderately prosperous, compared to others in the region.

He had proudly told her of an expensive breed of goat he hoped to introduce into his herd within a year or two, and how he believed they would do well in the hill environs surrounding Thiele. Possessing fine, long hair, the relatively new strain of goats had been bred in the southern mountains. They had only just begun to be introduced to the north and west.

That evening there had been a village gathering to celebrate their betrothal. She had warmed to the man a bit more, though she could not shake the ill-ease within. When the festivities had turned to music and dancing, she had danced several reels with him and the men of both their families. It was there she had noticed the beautifully skilled playing of a young man with a lyre, supported by the drums and recorders of several other villagers.

Coming back to reality, she glanced over toward where Jared lay curled up against a boulder, his bow and quiver near to hand. She knew his portative harp was hidden beneath his cloak near his back. Just then, a different emotion welled up deep within. She stopped her work, wondering where the powerful feeling had come from. Suddenly, she couldn't see what she was doing, because of the tears flowing freely from her eyes.

She gasped in some air, tried to stay in control, but a slight sob escaped her. She saw Jared stir. Thistle quickly turned aside and put her hand up to her mouth. It took her a while to regain her composure. When she did, the weight of all that had happened hit her and she couldn't keep her eyes open anymore. Confused by the strong feelings that had welled up so quickly, she clutched the partially finished skins to her chest. As she did, she felt Yolk move up, as if to offer her support. At that, she relaxed a little. Giving in to her exhaustion, she lay back and fell asleep almost instantly.

Searching in the Dark

He had found the half-elf easily enough – he appeared to have picked up a young girl along the course of his retreat. Aberon had discouraged the beasts following the pair with a slight tweaking spell sent from afar. He didn't want the louts to catch the half-elf and potentially discover the gem. Then he would have had to find another way to extract "the bauble" from whichever beast had it. He didn't have any qualms about killing these two humans once he had the stone in hand.

What he didn't understand was why they were heading west, when the nearest village was over a day's long hike to the east and north. That was a puzzle to be sure. It might be worth a more benign approach to find out. When he caught up with them, he would strike up a conversation and play the kindly monk until… well, until it served no more purpose. When he felt the time was right, he would strike and take the stone. Neither would be much trouble to deal with. Flies already stuck in his trap. He simply needed to swat them after he had the artifact.

There was one troubling element, something he had yet to figure out. One of the two had some hidden force about them. He hadn't sensed it in the half-elf when he had witnessed the killing of Raugghh. He had stayed well back watching that little fracas from up above in the rocks. Perhaps it was only the stone. It was probably sensing that its place in the world had shifted once again. It would begin to open up and assert its influence, which was something he definitely wanted to prevent. He would be careful, spending a brief time with them to ascertain what he was up against before he struck. He wondered if the boy had given the stone to the girl, for thus were the ways of men. Well, he would find it, whichever one had it.

For now, he would camp nearby and approach them in the morning. A shapeshift might be in order, so he would not frighten them unduly. His natural form, tall and skinny almost to emaciation, seemed to put people off. He couldn't understand why.

Hah! He laughed at himself. The rituals necessary to follow the black arts wore on the body, but asceticism suited his personality anyway. He disliked most foods, though he found an occasional piece of raw meat a tasty treat. He rarely drank anything except a strong anise-based tea, which he steeped with other bitter herbs that helped him rejuvenate his energy and to focus. Still, though he always kept a decent larder on his travels, he rarely indulged. It was more useful for him to have such provisions along when he had to cajole or spell some other wayward soul to his purpose. Food and drink helped people ease up. Tonight, he would have neither meat nor tea; he would simply enjoy the memory of a nice piece of fresh liver he had chewed on two evenings ago.

Priest

The first grey threads of dawn were streaking the sky when Jared awoke abruptly with Thistle's hand clamped over his mouth. "Shhh, something or someone is coming down the path," she whispered in his ear.

Picking his bow up and sliding an arrow from his quiver, Jared crawled slowly and silently toward the opening to their hollow. Thistle had his hunting knife drawn. She slid quietly to the other side of the opening, the blade to the fore. Yolk had flowed over to the farthest corner of the rock enclosure. The little fellow suddenly reversed direction and went rapidly back to Thistle, creeping up her leg and under the wool cape. As the sound approached, Jared tensed, drawing the bow string back. Thistle gripped the knife, ready to draw back for a throw.

They could easily distinguish the sound of shuffling footsteps and the half-muttering, half-humming of a man as he approached. Jared signaled Thistle to wait with a wag of the tip of his bow. Just before they caught sight of the man, he spoke loudly. "Hello, there. Please don't worry. I'm quite harmless, just an old priest on a penance. I saw you yesterday and was hoping to catch up to you. I must admit you led me a merry chase. Yes, quite a merry chase. It is lonely in these hills, quite lonely."

Appearing a second later from around the rock was a short, rotund, odd-looking fellow, dressed in a long, ankle-length black robe and cowl. Jared would have said there was some edginess to the man's features, particularly his long thin nose; but the puffy pinkish cheeks appeared to belie that. He carried only a staff and a large black satchel at his side. He looked like the last person one would see wandering the high hills on the edge of the Qa-ryk range. Smiling jovially, he turned toward Thistle and bowed low. Turning back to Jared, still smiling, he said, "Well, well, my pleasure, I'm sure. Put your bow down, young man. As you can see, I don't even carry a weapon, unless you consider this old stick dangerous." He brandished his staff, flourishing it about to his fore with some dexterity, though it was a least a foot longer than he was.

"My name is Aberon," he continued. "I'm a priest on penance. You know, silence and meditation and all that. Once in a while I do have a great need to see another face. Positively delightful to find two young people here in the wilds. You must tell me what you are about. I haven't talked to anyone in...? Why it must be several months now. Very lonely out here with no one to talk with except my mule."

Jared relaxed the bowstring as the man continued to chatter amiably, letting the arrow slip into his left hand. Thistle was smiling at the stranger, yet Jared still felt ill at ease. The man appeared to be as harmless as a ground squirrel. Yet, something was not right. Jared's neck was prickling. He wondered if his elven sense for danger was warning him or whether he was being overly cautious because of their circumstances.

Finally, because he had no reason to doubt the priest, he extended his hand. Yet, he resolved to stay alert. He was well aware that things were not always as they appeared, especially in the wilds. "I'm Jared of Thiele, or I should say lately of Thiele."

The rotund priest's grip was oily and weak. "The Qa-ryks destroyed my... ah, our village a few days ago." He gestured toward Thistle, deciding to include her, though she had not yet truly been a part of Thiele. "We got out at the last minute; there was nothing left, no-one was alive. It was horrible. I shot as many arrows as I had and then saw my father fall. There was a dragon. My brother was killed." His voice trailed off and for some reason he took a step back, distancing himself from Aberon.

"A dragon?" Aberon stroked his chin. "Ah, that must have been the pall of smoke I saw to the north and east. I was headed there when I caught a glimpse of you two moving west yesterday afternoon. Nothing left? No one to be cared for? I'm so sorry. Is there anything I can do? No, I guess not. I am terribly sorry. How do you come to be traveling west? I know of no settlements or camps in that direction"

"We are resolved to go after the Qa-ryks that did this to our families," Jared said angrily. He stepped down into the center of the hollow and planted his feet firmly apart. With a grim expression, he dared Aberon to gainsay their right to revenge.

"That is..."

"Foolhardy. Yes, we know," Thistle broke in. "We have to do something. They..." Her expression was determined, but her voice faltered as a swirl of emotions came from the depths of her being.

Jared took up where she left off. "We have nothing else left. The Qa-ryks stole our lives. Thistle's betrothed and so many others are dead. I saw my father and brother killed. I was wounded and chased by this Qa-ryk captain. I... ah, we want to do something, anything. There is a sw..." Jared caught himself, wondering why he felt so compelled to go on. He was not usually so loquacious. Why was he finding it so easy to keep talking? Why had he said so much to this stranger? He backed up another step and gestured toward Thistle.

"Sorry, I am rambling and forget my manners. This is Thistle of Permis. She was betrothed to a man of our village. You are welcome to sit with us a while, though we cannot offer you anything except idle words. Our provisions are few, and we will have to hunt for our victuals. We plan to head further west today; there is game aplenty in the hills."

"I, on the other hand, am well stocked with provisions," Aberon said cheerfully. "And it is nigh time I broke my fast. I hope you will join me in a morning meal. Believe me, to be with you young folks and to share idle chatter is just what this poor lonely fellow needs. My mule is up the path a few dozen paces. Jared, if you would be so kind as to fetch the old critter, we can have some tea, bread, and whatever other delicacies I can dig up in the saddle bags. Luckily, my penance does not include starving myself." He patted his ample stomach. "As you can tell, I enjoy a good meal now and again. Well, perhaps a bit more often than now and again. Go, young man. Thistle and I will see to reviving your fire."

The three of them were sitting back enjoying tin mugs of a minty herbal tea after a surprisingly bounteous repast. Aberon had been serious about the delicacies. He had tins of fish and sweetmeats, rich aged cheeses, and flour, honey, and spices that were quickly mixed into fresh campfire bread Thistle cooked on the stones. Both Jared and Thistle dug in with a relish, realizing how meager their provisions had been the past few days.

"So, you're bent on revenge?" Aberon broke the silence while they were eating. He hadn't eaten much except to nibble on this or that delicacy, and finally a piece of the newly baked bread Thistle had offered him. "Well, I guess I can't blame you. The Qa-ryks show no mercy. I must try to dissuade you if I can. Both because I am a priest, and because it is a bit foolhardy for two youngsters to be chasing a company of Qa-ryks. No?"

Thistle flared up at that, "No is right! We're not going to attack them, just follow them. We have to see where they take the sword."

Jared glared at her. He had almost spoken of the blade himself. Already he was finding the man before them something of a problem. He hadn't liked what he felt when he had shaken his hand; now he was convinced there was something manipulative about the priest.

Aberon, however, did not appear all that interested in talk of the weapon. "Ah, a family heirloom? Well, do what you must. I won't interfere. I'd like to have some company for a day or two. It is lonely in these hills. Very lonely indeed, and I have six more months on my penance. You see, that's what I get for not being able to control my impulses. I'll never drink again. By all the saints in the heavens and the gods above them, I'll never even taste beer again... or... at any rate I won't drink to excess." He grinned broadly at his little joke.

Thistle laughed at him, a bubbly laugh that burst out. Even Jared couldn't help smiling. The fellow was somewhat comical, both in looks and in his affectations. For one thing, he kept stroking his chin like he had a beard, yet, he was clean-shaven. Another odd thing that Jared noticed was that despite supposedly being in the mountains for some months, he had managed to avoid getting much sun. His complexion – what they could see of his hands, feet, and face – was deathly white.

Aberon began to gather the tin plates. Thistle, though, would have nothing to do with him cleaning up. "I will do them, Aberon. We are grateful to you for having provided us with such a wonderful meal. I'm afraid we took off with no thought to provisions. Thankfully, the land can provide much this time of year. I'll get in a quick morning bath at the stream while I wash these. I'll be back in a few minutes." She picked up the small stack of tins and headed out of the hollow.

Jared, suddenly feeling ill-at-ease again, stood up and began checking over his bow and arrows and other things in preparation for the day's journey.

"Stay a moment, my son. No rush to leave, I trust. The Qa-ryks are heading south and west as you guessed. They are in no hurry to get home. I crossed their path yesterday and can lead you directly to it. That should save you some time.

"Come over here and at least let me examine your wounds. You said you had been hurt. Is there naught I can do to hasten the healing, to ease your pain?"

Jared looked up from the small pile of arrows he had been carefully going over to insure they were in top condition. "I was clawed, but it is already well healed. I guess it wasn't that bad."

"Healed? Did you not say the battle was only a few days past? That would be extraordinary, especially considering the nature of a Qa-ryk claw wound. They have irritants under their nails. Quite painful, I am told, and a certainty for infection. Could I see where you were struck?"

"I... I guess." Jared knew that many priests and clerics were healers. It still felt uncanny that his wound had closed over so quickly. He kept thinking it would burst open and show that only the outer layer had healed. He was still anxious whenever he put any stress to that shoulder and arm. He drew down his jerkin to the side, revealing his upper shoulder and back.

"I would not call that a minor wound, young man. That is a near death wound from a Qa-ryk. The claws raked deep. From the angle he caught you, I would warrant it barely missed penetrating to your lung. I am surprised you did not have any muscle damage. You can move it all right?"

Jared nodded, moving the shoulder forward, up, and back.

"Qa-ryks are not known for their cleanliness, to say the least. Unfortunately, they also often coat their claws with a slow-acting poison. You are certain you feel all right? No fever? Pain?"

"No. Really, I feel fine. I'm still a little stiff, not really sore anymore."

Aberon drew in closer to Jared and began pressing the long scars with his thin, delicate fingers. Jared, feeling quite uncomfortable, let the priest continue to examine the wound.

"What can you tell me about this? How did it happen?"

"I don't remember very much; everything happened so quickly. I received the wound early in the fighting, when my brother and I came down from the hills. The beast came on me while I was trying to climb to the roof. After we killed it, I bandaged my shoulder hurriedly; then my brother and I went on to fight from the rooftops. Later, Ge-or went to fetch more arrows and our swords. I caught up with him near our house, where he was beset by several of the beasts. I shot one, but a blow from a club felled him. When I saw him go down, I fled with another hot on my trail. I grabbed this quiver of arrows from my brother's back as I ran past." Jared gestured toward the pile he had been sorting through. "There was no time for me to get anything else. I ran.

"Later, after I had killed the beast following me, I came upon Thistle. She was in the hills where her betrothed had sent her. She helped me through the first two days. I became delirious and feverish the first night and do not remember much else. I do remember a good bit of burning. It felt like my shoulder and back were on fire. When Thistle changed the bandage, my whole shoulder was a fiery red and I had a fever. When I awoke a day or so later, the fever was gone and it… it was like you see it now."

"Odd, very odd, indeed. There must be something else at work here. Are you or Thistle healers?"

Jared pulled his jerkin back up, chagrined again at having so easily spilled so much to this oily man. Aberon stepped back to his pile of belongings and began to rifle through his satchel.

"No. I know I'm not unusually quick to heal, and Thistle didn't understand this either. I have had many cuts before. The small ones took a week or more to heal. I can't think of anything that… Wait, there is one thing out of the ordinary, at least from my perspective."

"Yes?" Aberon drew up from his search, holding a small jar in his hand. He took a step closer to Jared, his eyes intense again.

"Ah, Thistle does have this creature. It is, or seems, a wee bit magical? She says it has never helped her heal or had any healing affect that she has been aware of. It's mostly a friend, I guess. It's an odd-looking animal."

"A pet? What does it look like?"

"No, it is a friend, as Jared said, not a pet." Thistle came around the rock into the hollow. Setting down the tins on the blanket, she drew Yolk out from under her tunic where he had been since Aberon had entered their campsite. When Thistle held him up. the little fellow was rolled tightly into a cylinder with his eyes on top. "He is shy of strangers," she said.

"Well, well. What do we have here?" Aberon moved one step closer to Thistle; however, for some reason he kept back several paces, content to examine her companion from there. He stared intently at Yolk for several seconds. When Thistle's little friend opened his eyes for an instant to look at the newcomer, the priest jumped back a half step. Perhaps thinking better of his own valor, the little creature shut them tightly again.

"Oh, ho, now I know. Those eyes are unmistakable. You have an ovietti. My, that is quite unusual. They are rare, you know. Quite rare. What does he feel like? Might I touch him?" Aberon reached out with his hand hesitatingly, but Yolk unrolled and quickly slipped back under Thistle's cape.

Thistle looked puzzled. She said hurriedly, "He really doesn't like strangers. What did you say he is?"

"An ovietti. They are a magical species, or so I'm told. I've never seen one before this, only artists' renditions –paintings and sketches, you know. No one knows much about them; they are extremely rare. They are supposed to have various powers, magical effects of a sort; but these have probably been exaggerated. From what I can remember, accelerated healing isn't one of them. " Aberon shrugged. "I really couldn't tell you more. Where did you get him, my dear?"

"Well, I really didn't get him. He got me. He was just there one day. He came to me one night; and except for one short time before and during the attack on Thiele, he has been with me since."

Aberon raised one eyebrow. "Hmmm, yes, well, I guess I had heard that also. They choose an owner, as it were. Cute little fellow. Does he have any magical powers that you are aware of?"

"Not really," Thistle said, hugging her chest. "He can hold a lot of water, and he can change colors. You know, like a chameleon, only to grays and browns. That's all I've ever noticed. He did wake me up when he heard you approaching. Mostly, he's been a good companion."

"Sorry," Jared butted in, a bit uncomfortable with Yolk's reaction to Aberon, and suddenly anxious to get moving. "I would like to head out as soon as possible if we could. We are most grateful for the breakfast, but we have a lot of territory to cover today. Perhaps we can talk further while we walk?"

"Yes, I understand. I'm an inquisitive sort. It is how one learns. Yes, let us be off. We will get to know each other better on the road."

Aberon was troubled. The stone was already influencing. That was obvious, else the half-elf would not have healed so quickly from such a deep wound. He would take the thing soon enough. It was time to move ahead with his plans.

The Chase

Aberon led the way, immediately taking a jog off the trail they had been following onto a path leading due south. Jared would have continued more to the west; still, he felt he should give the priest a chance to prove himself.

They had to go single file for a couple of tough leagues; and though the rotund priest looked out of shape, he set a demanding pace. Jared walked slightly behind and to the left of Aberon, while Thistle led the mule at the rear of the small procession. The animal didn't appear to have any name except "Mule." She had made an effort to befriend the sturdy beast. Looking well-cared for physically, "Pesky," as Thistle now thought of the animal because he wanted all the attention she gave him and more, would still shy away anytime Aberon approached.

As they neared the higher hills, the short, scrubby trees of the rocky slopes began to give way to the first hardwoods. Once they entered the woods, Aberon said they would meet a wider track that would lead them directly to the Qa-ryk trail.

Autumn was in the air. Jared and Thistle enjoyed the hint of coolness on the breeze and the smells of the forest as it was preparing for winter. Leaves were beginning to turn to radiant colors, the first frost in these hills a week or more past. They saw late wildflowers, thistles, and flowering shrubs growing in scattered clumps along the more open parts of the trail. Thistle and Jared both managed to pick pocketfuls of walnuts, some late berries, and a variety of hearty herbs as they walked.

Jared, however, was still uncomfortable; and though he wished he could relax, he had a nagging angst that he could not shake. Yolk's defensive reaction to the strange cleric had put him more on guard. He managed to alert Thistle to his feelings at one of their brief rests, when Aberon left for a few minutes to tend to necessities. She had nodded in agreement; she also felt uncomfortable with Aberon. They resolved to keep alert.

Jared was well aware that clerics could wield a great deal of power – both for good and for evil, depending on their orientation and the religious beliefs they followed. He also knew that the rotund priest's staff, which he had so deftly brandished, could have magical properties or even be a conduit for some type of power. He would keep his eyes open and his knife handy. They lived in a world where the forces of good and evil vied for dominance, and at the edge of the Qa-ryk range, evil held sway. They would have to be very careful.

At their second stop in the ever-thickening hardwood forest, Jared volunteered to scout ahead to look for a small deer for their dinner. He returned to them an hour before dusk carrying a haunch of venison on his shoulder. It would be a change of pace. Aberon seemed thrilled at the prospect of fresh meat as well.

"The rest of the deer is ahead," Jared said. "I left it near a small stream where we might make camp. I tied it up off the ground, but figured I better ensure we had some meat for the night." He slapped the haunch as he finished tying it to Mule's back. "I don't know this country well; it is possible a bear or wolf might get at it."

"Still a bit east for bear country these days," Aberon said. "The Qa-ryks chased them out long ago. It should be safe off the ground. Otherwise raccoons, fox, and skunk would have at it soon enough. I am hungry, too. Did you save the liver? I am partial to organ meats. Or perhaps I could have a bit of the heart?"

Jared nodded to both questions. Many a mountain-bred or wilderness-raised relished these organ meats. They were considered delicacies. Jared had never developed a taste for them; he had eaten them in stews and meat pies often enough. His father had also insisted that he and Ge-or eat the hearts of their first kills. "I skewered them with a scraped stick and stuck them in the ribcage. They are not my favorite parts. I prefer the back-strap roasted or cut to chops. You are welcome to anything you like."

"You are sure? Well, I appreciate your generosity, young half-elf. Let us get to your chosen campsite and there we can feast on fresh venison.

"Perhaps we can set a good portion on wood racks to smoke and dry through the night. I have some salt and spices we can use for a rub to make a tasty jerky. I noticed both of you gathering herbs along the way; they will add to the flavor. Those juniper berries you picked, Thistle, will be quite tasty as an addition. Liver jerky is quite nice you know."

Thistle's and Jared's mouths began to water at the prospect of fresh-killed, roasted meat. By now, their morning meal was much too long ago. They needed no other coaxing; soon the three of them were striding side-by-side on the main trail west.

"It is an old logging and trapping trail," Aberon explained. "The wagoners would drive out to the west in the spring to meet the trappers with their sleds on their way eastward. It was a system that worked for many years, that is until the Qa-ryks overran the west. Some would say, the good ol' days; though the truth is, there were more gzks, goblins, and ogres back then. Life in the hills and forests has never been an easy one; you both know that history, I suppose, being from trapping communities.

"So, Jared, tell me more of this Qa-ryk captain you slew. You are positive he was an officer? What was he wearing? Bearing? Did he have anything of value with him? The officers often carry special prizes with them that they have taken from their victims."

Jared, feeling ever more uncomfortable with the cleric, answered the priest's questions politely, purposely avoiding any specific details. He was relieved when they finally reached the stream where he had tied up the rest of the deer carcass. Busy with making dinner and eating their fill, he avoided further inquiries until they finally settled down for the night.

51

Awakening

Ge-or rolled over onto his side and slipped off the bedding Sart had hastily gathered for him to rest on. Bumping his head on the log wall jolted him awake. Memories flooded back. He drew himself up on his knees and felt his head, searching for the wound. He realized that the cleric – Sart was his name, he remembered – had spoken truly. He was whole again, with no residual pain or evidence of having been clubbed. Actually, he felt amazingly good, well-rested and only slightly groggy.

Sitting back on his heels, he considered his situation. The priest had tricked him – given him something that made him sleep. Ge-or was smart enough to realize that the good fellow had actually been right about many things. He had needed the rest, and he needed to think things through carefully. He definitely felt that though he was better able to make more intelligent choices, the delay had not lessened his resolve to recover his father's sword. First, however, he knew he had things to do here. It was his duty to care for the dead. It would speak to his honor to make the effort. He dreaded the task, but it would not do to wait further for possible help arriving from Permis. It might be days or weeks before any dared venture west to take care of the fallen.

As the sun began to rise in the east, Ge-or started his labors by gathering bodies from about the entire compound. Each of the villagers – all had been friends, acquaintances, and comrades – he wrapped in whatever sheets, blankets, capes, and robes he could find. He reverently picked each body up in his arms and wheeled them in a barrow to the dock, arranging them as carefully as he could from one end to the other of the long wooden structure. It was no small feat, as there were over sixty bodies. When all had been gathered, he began collecting, as respectfully as he could, all the body parts he could find, no matter how small, placing them in a row at the end of the dock.

Finally, he took a large flat-bladed shovel and scooped up wheelbarrow after wheelbarrow of ashes from the places where the dragon's breath had obliterated everything in its path. How many of his fellows had been incinerated, he didn't know –he wanted to honor all the dead, so he labored on. These remains he shoveled into large wine tuns placed in the forecastle of the large fishing boat that was tied to the eastern side of the dock. When he was done, the sun was beginning to wester. On impulse, with his emotions finally overcoming him, he dove off the end of the pier into the icy northern waters. He swam as hard as he could out toward the open sea.

It took him a long time to calm enough to slow his pace. Then he realized he was a long way from shore. Treading water for a few minutes, tears streaming down his face, Ge-or turned back south, trying to grasp the meaning of what had happened to his family, his village, his friends, his life. Eventually, resigned to what he had left to do, he swam slowly back to the dock.

He worked for several more hours gathering enough kindling and logs from the burnt houses to load the bottom of the boat. During the remaining time until dusk, he deferentially transferred body after body and all the other remains into the boat until they were piled on top of the wood. Finally, he poured what pitch and pine tar he could find over the top of the pile. When he finished, he knelt on the dock and begged the gods, though he did not truly follow any religion, to guide his friends in the afterlife. It seemed the right thing to do. Many of the people in Thiele had given at least a nodding credence to the old gods. He did not know what lay after, but the old religion offered as good an explanation as any he had heard.

He raised a single sail, hoping the westerly wind would catch in it and help the boat into deeper waters when he shoved it off. The light breeze might be enough if he could get the boat in motion with a push from the dock.

Lighting several torches with his flint and knife, Ge-or hurled them one after another into the boat. When it was well ablaze, he cut the thick ropes holding the boat to the dock and gave a mighty heave, his right leg braced against one of the dock posts. Slowly, the craft eased out into the small bay. The wind fluttered the canvas for several seconds, finally catching. The craft began to pick up some speed sliding to the northeast. After a few minutes, the boat was fiercely ablaze and the sail caught, too. It slowed and began to settle. Ge-or knew it would nestle deep enough beneath the waves to rest undisturbed. Turning his back to the funeral pyre, he went through the ruins of the village to his bed. There he collapsed, incapable of watching his life disappear below the waves.

Betrayal

When Jared awoke, Thistle was already sitting up working on her new footwear, making adjustments to the fit. Yolk was still out of sight, clinging tightly to her lower chest underneath her dress. Aberon was humming and muttering to himself by the campfire as he mixed up portions of several herbs in a small pan for tea.

While their morning meal cooked, Jared made an effort to get more out of the priest, in effect reversing the probing Aberon had done the night before. The priest adroitly evaded Jared's questions. Though he offered a great deal of information about himself and his wanderings, none of it really gave Jared any insight into the man's true identity or background. Jared tried to be polite, but his tension and anger rose as he was continuously put off. As they were packing, following their repast, he asked, "What religion do you follow, Master?"

"None you would have heard of, my son. It is strict. My, my, it is so very strict. Why all I did was go on a small – really small, mind you – binge; and I get stuck out here in the wilderness for a whole year, with Qa-ryks and what-not-all ready to split my skull. I have been through some close ones, too. Just days ago, I barely missed being jumped by that band of Qa-ryks that must have attacked your village. It was only through faith, yes, through the deepest faith, that they didn't see me. I tell you, my son, never think that faith doesn't count. Whatever gods you follow, it is important to have faith. Saved me innumerable times. As weak and helpless as I am, I have the power of faith behind me. I sit here before you today, sipping tea, because I have my faith."

It was difficult not to be drawn in by the man's deeply resonant, charming voice. Jared shook his head as if he were mesmerized by the priest's last discourse. He stood up abruptly, throwing the last venison rib bone to the side of the fire. "Well, I'm afraid our brief meeting is at an end, good Master Aberon. Thistle and I have a quest and duty of our own. I hope you excuse any impoliteness of our hasty departure, but we must be on our way. We hope that you will not have to spend the rest of your penance time alone."

He paused to see if Aberon would react in any way to his partially prepared speech. He and Thistle had decided the eve before that they were too uncomfortable to continue with the strange priest. They wanted to move ahead free of any encumbrances. The rotund cleric stood himself and nodded as Jared continued.

"We have left you a portion of the venison jerky; we both sincerely thank you for what you have shared with us." He looked toward Thistle, who had also risen and was gathering their belongings. She nodded in agreement.

"Yes, well, I am pleased to have met you," said Aberon. "Truly sorry you must go. I do see you are anxious to rush ahead, and I would probably slow you down. I wish you Gods-speed on your quest. I must warn you again that Qa-ryks are fierce and crafty. Yes, indeed, they are crafty, and evil. Do be careful. Bless you, my children." He waved them on. Within a minute, Thistle and Jared were down the path and out of sight of the small hollow. Jared felt the tension in his shoulders ease as they loped along at a steady pace.

They all but ran a half a league before Thistle eased back. "What is wrong, Jared? Yolk was petrified of him, and I must admit I didn't feel comfortable either. He seemed genuine in some ways, though..." Her voice trailed off.

"I don't know, Thistle. There's something hidden beneath that benign countenance. He has strength of some kind, and somehow, I don't think it is for the good. Unless he has powers beyond my imagination, I don't see how a fat priest on foot can outdistance two of the western-bred. If my calculations are correct, we should cross the track of the main party of Qa-ryks within the hour. After that, we can make better time."

They alternated loping and walking for most of the day, with only brief stops to refresh themselves and to examine the Qa-ryk trail that led toward the south and west. Jared felt as if he had never been wounded. He couldn't explain why he had healed so quickly, yet he was glad he had. Even skipping lunch did not affect their energy. They made good time over the hills through the hardwoods, finally making their way into the thicker forest where the trees were beginning to change over to more evergreens. By early evening, they were exhausted and had slowed to a walk as they continued through the sweet-smelling autumnal forest. At last, famished and with cramps in their legs, Jared called an early halt.

"Let's stop here, Thistle. I don't think we can go any further today," he said, gesturing toward a small grove of trees and shrubs to the left of the path they had been following through the forest. "We should be able to keep out of sight of the path in that thicket, and still be able to see anything coming from either direction." He was mildly concerned about gzks, as on rare occasions the forest dwellers did venture this far north. On the other hand, with the fall weather and with Qa-ryk activity nearby, they were likely already moving south.

Leaning heavily on the walking sticks they had picked up earlier from the forest floor, they both walked over to the grove. Thistle plopped down as soon as she had gotten through to the center of the thicket. The tiny clearing looked like a deer bedding area, the leaves matted down in large ovals. Thistle moaned to Jared, "You go get some dinner. I'm starving, so get plenty. I'll start a fire as soon as I can move. I didn't think you would ever stop." She was smiling, so he knew she was only tired, as he was.

Jared smiled back at her, briefly wondering what she was thinking and feeling. Other emotions soon threatened to push the good feelings he was beginning to have away, so, dropping his walking stick and the Qa-ryk pouch, he took the bow from his shoulder and nocked an arrow. "This may take a while; I'll be back as soon as possible. Rest a little." He turned and followed a deer track out of the grove.

Two hours later, as the last shreds of light disappeared from the evening sky, Jared sat back against a small tree in the grove. Though he had not found the deer, he was stuffed with roasted rabbit, squirrel, and with nuts they had found in abundance in the forest. They decided to keep the dried venison for days when they didn't have the time to hunt or when game might be scarce. They had filled their pouches with sweet nut meats for the next day. After their repast, they were ready for sleep.

While Jared had been hunting, Thistle had prepared two cozy nests of leaves and pine needles in the hollow center of the small grove. Jared felt comfortable, almost pleasant, but he couldn't quite relax. Something within him was keeping a tight control over his emotions, not allowing him to feel the agony of his pain and loss. He hadn't even thought about his music, at least, not without painful memories threatening to engulf him. Luckily, the barrier to that pain kept snapping back in place. He couldn't remember a day when he hadn't sung before. Now, he couldn't even think of the joy it had always brought him. A dark, black, indistinct mass lurked in his mind, where once the wonder of a thousand tunes of youth had murmured.

He sat against the tree for a long time trying to immerse himself in the calm and comfort of the night. He couldn't completely put to rest the concerns he was trying to avoid, so finally, he set aside the arrow shaft he had been working on and wormed himself down into his snug bed.

Thistle, who had been working the skins of animals they had gotten that day, looked up from her task and smiled at him. The light of dying coals played across her face in a strange way accenting her simple beauty. "You know, Jared," she said, "things have happened so fast. This morning already seems so many years ago – the priest, tea, and bread..." She paused, wondering, "Do you think he followed us?"

"Aberon?"

She nodded.

"No... well, at least, I hope not. Did Yolk really warn you he was coming?" Jared could see the cute little fellow wrapped about Thistle's legs, his two large, unblinking yellow eyes taking in everything she was doing.

"Well, he woke me, and he was definitely frightened."

"He will probably be enough of a guard for the night, but keep your knife handy." Jared looked at her, for a time enjoying the comfort of her warm smile. Unfortunately, within only a few minutes, the blackness returned to block his happiness. He looked away. "Goodnight, Thistle."

"Goodnight, Jared." Then, a moment later, "Jared?" He turned slightly back toward her. "This all seems kind of silly, doesn't it?"

"Yes, it does. As you said, it is our choice now. We have to do what we feel is right, what we feel we need to do for ourselves. It is odd how it all happened."

"Yes, truly. Somehow, it's like we have known each other all along, and that this was supposed to happen to us one day. Do you know what I mean?"

Jared turned away again as she spoke, clenching his fists as the memories of fire and pain flooded back. He answered with difficulty, the words coming out haltingly. "Yes... I... I'm sorry; it's still too close. I..." His voice caught and he didn't finish.

Thistle could hear the tightness in his throat. She could almost feel the effort he was making to keep the memories of the battle away. "I know. I'm sorry, I didn't mean to..."

"It's all right, Thistle. I will have to face it soon enough, but no more tonight. Sleep well. Maybe we'll catch a Qa-ryk tomorrow."

"You catch one. I'll watch."

"Thanks."

Jared was exhausted and had hoped to drop right off to sleep, yet he couldn't shake the feeling that they had done something wrong. He realized, especially since they had spent a short time with the well-provisioned priest, that they had been more than foolish in taking off with nothing to hand to help them in their quest.

He was more than a competent woodsman, and Thistle had already proven her worth in practical matters relevant to surviving outdoors. Even her little friend was proving useful. However, winter was coming; and though he knew they could survive with their knives and his bow, hard work, and a bit of luck, they should have reasoned the whole situation through more.

As he turned from one side to the other, Jared listed in his mind all the useful things they might have gleaned from a quick search of Thiele. It now seemed completely insane that neither of them had chosen to circle back, check for survivors, and pick up what they could use, though he knew that it was unlikely the savage beasts would have left anyone alive. After his two days down with a fever, he figured it even more unlikely that any of the wounded would have lived through the cold nights. Still, they could have at least gathered what they might from the refuse of the battle for the quest they had set for themselves.

A horse or mule would have been invaluable, as well; yet, it was unlikely they would have found either. The Qa-ryks would have taken them for food. They probably could have scavenged backpacks, maybe recovering some foodstuffs, a pot or two to cook in and other utensils, some good rope, warmer clothes and heavy wool winter cloaks, and some tools. If they were lucky, they might have found a sword, or at least something he felt more comfortable with, rather than the poorly made and unwieldy Qa-ryk knife. His head was aswim with the things they could have used. At least Aberon had insisted they take a second woolen cloak and a small pot that he proffered. He was also more than grateful for the extra victuals the priest had insisted they take. Perhaps the man was what he appeared to be – a strange priest on a penance.

He hoped they might happen upon an old trapping cabin or deserted hut as they proceeded further west into the forest. In such a place, it was possible they might find odds and ends that had been left for the next year or an old cache of useful items. Finally, too tired to continue his train of thought, Jared began to doze off.

Jared tossed and turned for a long time before he fell into a fitful sleep filled with images of fire-breathing dragons, dark demons, and evil priests. The dreams were an indistinct and continuous merging of frightening scenes in which he tried desperately to defend himself with a magical sword he was unable to wield or control.

At last, one scene began to solidify: he was sitting upright in a brightly lit tree grove on the side of a large hill trying to reach his bow, which lay only inches from his grasp. Somehow, a power he could not overcome was preventing him from picking up the weapon. At first, he could not focus on the source of what was immobilizing him. He could only see a large, towering black mass off to his side that was threatening another figure with a tremendous force.

Finally, the picture began to clear. He saw Thistle lying inert on the ground with the Qa-ryk knife clasped tightly in her small fist. A dark figure was bending over her, pawing at her clothes, searching for something it could not find. Frustrated in its search, the darkness turned toward Jared. Then he knew – he knew they had been right about the fat priest.

Aberon, Priest of Darkness, strode purposely toward the young half-elf, and still Jared could not move to his own defense. The priest had changed from a short rotund figure into a tall, thin, blond-haired man dressed in the blackness of the void. While Jared struggled against the spell that bound him, knowing that the dream he had been dreaming was real and that he and Thistle were in terrible danger, the evil priest approached within a foot of his outstretched hand. Waving his black staff, which was engulfed in a bright red flame, Aberon dealt Jared a forceful blow to the chest. He fell backwards to the earth, helpless as his opponent bent to search him.

With the foul breath of the priest in his face, Jared continued to struggle. He knew, when he saw the gleam of triumph in those wicked eyes, that Aberon had succeeded in his hunt. The dark priest ripped the cord from Jared's neck. Stepping back from his victim and holding the pendant high, Aberon drew upon his inner power and encased the gem in a spell of evil. With a horrible laugh, he placed it in his purse and strode to the edge of the grove. Waving the staff a last time in the air, Aberon shouted. A column of flame descended on the clearing, engulfing the two bodies on the ground. He laughed again and vanished, leaving the smoldering thicket behind. Jared knew no more for a while.

Succor

He struggled to consciousness with great difficulty. Something warm and heavy, but not really uncomfortable, was resting on his forehead. He recognized, as if from a great distance away, the intonation of words, a chant. He could hear the subtle rising and falling of tones reminiscent of the modal scales of the old religions. It was soothing and peaceful. For a time, he simply let himself float with the ethereal melody as it swirled about him. Instinctively, he seemed to understand that such music could not come from evil, so he accepted it as it was.

It was some time before he was able to distinguish the individual sounds of each syllable as they formed into a flowing, coherent whole. With a start, he realized that the intonation was in the ancient elven tongue, "...the peace of the earth shall rise in your heart, and you shall become as one with the world. Take my hand and the strength of the firmament will be yours. Peace be unto you, elf-kin. I bid you well."

He finally answered. Opening his parched lips, he sang a simple response to the tune and words. "Hail to you, ancient father. May the peace of the world rest upon your brow and give you strength."

Suddenly, he was fully awake. He managed to open his eyes, blinking as acrid smoke stung them. Above him, he could see the brown cowl of the man whose hand was resting on his forehead.

Reacting quickly, Jared lunged to his right, away from the man, diving for his bow and quiver. Putting arrow to string, he stood and drew in one fluid motion. By the time he had set the arrow and drawn back, aiming at the priest's chest, he had conquered his fear. The man was not Aberon. What he had been saying in the ancient tongue was a blessing that no evil priest could feign to speak.

This cleric was tall, broadly built, and dressed in a long brown robe; his cowl was the color of freshly tilled earth. He carried a long oak staff in his left hand, and around his neck was a brass chain on which hung a curiously worked cross. Jared could tell from the way he held himself that the large man was wearing chainmail as well. He could also see the bulge of a weapon hanging underneath his long robe on the right side. Jared released his draw, then bowed low, saying in the old speech, "Forgive me, Father, I mistook you for another."

The priest was not ancient or even that old. Jared guessed he was a man in his late thirties or early forties. He had short, tousled dark brown hair – a mop that wanted better tending and that looked to be kept short without the benefit of a mirror. The cleric inclined his head toward Jared and answered in the common tongue, "I am sorry I arrived so late. He moved faster than I believed he would. I was...."

"Thistle!" Jared suddenly became aware of their surroundings – the utter destruction of the clearing by the sheet of flame from Aberon's staff. He spun around looking about. He saw her lying on the burnt ground to his left, right where she had been. Something was dreadfully wrong. In a panic, he turned back toward the priest with a desperate question in his eyes. The cleric reached out to grasp Jared's shoulder.

"Hold, young half-elf. She is alive and resting. She had a rougher time than you did. The spell that protected her was not nearly as powerful as the one protecting you. Try not to wake her; the healing will progress better if she can rest."

Jared managed to relax slightly, though he was confused by what the cleric was saying. He slipped out from under the priest's hand and went carefully and quietly through the ashes across the space to where the Thistle lay. There he knelt, bowing his head in an attempt to pray.

The priest moved up behind Jared as he knelt next to Thistle. He laid his hand gently on Jared's shoulder and said, "I am sorry I cannot do more for her right now; my power is limited by my ignorance and by the trials I have faced recently."

Jared picked up Thistle's small hand in his and began to stroke it lightly. Her skin was amazingly soft and smooth. He had never actually touched a girl in such a way. He had only begun to think girls were of any interest, beyond being nuisances, this past year. As he knelt, he found himself holding his breath. Another emotion began to well up inside, one he had never felt before. He forced it back down and turned his attention fully to her condition.

She was breathing easily, as if in a deep sleep. Jared could see that she had suffered from the fire. Her hair had been burnt around the edges by the flames and the exposed skin of her face and neck was swollen an angry red, though there appeared to be no charring of flesh or blisters from the heat. Even the woolen cape she had been wrapped in and all of her clothing down to her waist had been blackened and burnt in places by the fire. Below the waist, curiously, the blast had not touched her. Jared could see the bump of Yolk's head beneath her cloak, yet the odd-looking creature had not moved. Luckily, the cloak had sustained only minor burns at the point where Yolk lay clinging to Thistle. Jared figured the animal had not been severely injured by the flames either.

Jared laid her hand back down. He looked up as the priest gave his shoulder a slight squeeze. "Come, young elf-kin," he whispered. "We have much to relate to each other, and your Thistle needs the rest. It will be dark in a few hours. And though you may not like the idea, we should have a fire. Gather some wood, and I will lay out food and drink. Go." He smiled at Jared, before turning away.

The priest whistled softly to the east. About a minute later, a large scruffy-looking mule appeared. At the sight of Jared and the priest, the beast made a noise that sounded somewhat between the neigh of a horse and the mournful low of a cow. It ambled up and put his nose forcefully into the priest's stomach. "Oomph. Ah, Crunch. I wish you would stop doing that," he said, scratching roughly behind the mule's ears. "Here meet..." and the cleric bowed low, waving toward Jared.

"Jared... Jared, lately of Thiele," Jared said, bowing slightly toward the cleric.

An instant later, the mule had flattened Jared to the earth with the same unusual form of greeting it had given its master. Only Jared seemed to have received an even firmer blow to his gut than had the priest. The young half-elf found himself looking up into the animal's grinning, he would have sworn, face.

"You'll have to forgive Crunch. He always says hello that way. I've tried to break him of it, but he has a mind of his own. I am Sart, cleric and follower of the Earth; oft, unfortunately, referred to as one of the 'Earthbirds.' I am at your service, if I can be of some further assistance to you."

While he was speaking, the big man went over to the mule and pulled him, none too gently, from his position over Jared. As the half-elf rose and dusted himself off, Sart began to unpack one of the saddlebags that hung on the animal's ample back. "I have new apples, vegetables, dried meat, and spices," he said. We shall have a good stew brewing by the time the young lady awakes... but only if we have a nice fire." He looked up from his task with one eye cocked at Jared, who nodded, smiling at the mule as it stood eyeing him mischievously. He took one more glance at Thistle to make sure he was not dreaming of all that had just transpired; then he scampered for the edge of the clearing.

An hour later, Sart and Jared were sitting in the sole unburnt spot of the clearing – the place where Jared had been laying that eve. About fifteen feet away, outside the damaged area, a pot of stew was simmering over a small fire. Sart purposefully drew Jared closer to the center of the burnt area so they could keep an eye on Thistle, while he questioned him about what had happened.

When Jared sat down, he began examining the circle of grass and leaves of the untouched spot where he had lain. It contrasted drastically with the charred remains of the rest of the clearing. He pulled a blade of thick grass out of the moist earth, twirled it in his fingers, and wondered aloud, "Why was this area untouched? Why was I saved from the flames and not Thistle?"

"I was going to ask you that very question," Sart answered. "Only a powerful spell or talisman could give you this kind of protection. Are you a spell caster, Jared? Do you have some other form of protection? A rood or a ring? A stone of some power?"

"No, none that... I don't understand." Jared stopped. Suddenly, he remembered his dream and Aberon's search. He said excitedly, "The pendant! I had forgotten I had taken it. He was after the necklace."

Jared grasped at his neck to feel for the stone and thong. He looked up at the cleric. "He took it. Aberon took it!" He stared at Sart, as if the cleric might know something of what he spoke, but the cleric frowned and shook his head.

"It was a large stone, or gem," Jared went on, "about the size of my thumb. It had a silver-wire mounting that was strung to a piece of leather. I took it from a Qa-ryk leader I killed. I don't know why I removed it from the beast's neck... in my village we are taught to respect the dead of our enemies. I think I felt it would fetch a price, so I could purchase supplies later. Aberon took it from me last night before he cast the spell of fire. I remember he was searching Thistle for something. He couldn't seem to find what he was looking for – that's when he came over to me. He pawed through my clothes and discovered it. He had to be looking for it specifically; he was elated when he found it. It had to be the pendant, because it is gone."

Jared rose and began to pace back and forth. Sart watched him for a moment, then asked, "This necklace, the stone, can you describe it? Did you notice anything about it that was unusual? Any effects it might have had on you when you had it on? Anything you noticed could be important."

Jared returned to a spot directly in front of the cleric. "I don't know. I don't even know what it really looked like. I cut the cord off of the Qa-ryk captain's neck and tied it around mine. I never took it out again. I never even thought of it until just now. To tell you the truth, I'd forgotten about it. Too many other things happened afterward. It stayed around my neck until that dire priest took it.

"I do remember it felt fairly large, the stone I mean. I vaguely remember it had what looked and felt like a wire mesh mounting; and as I said, it was tied to a simple leather thong. The light was dim when I took it, so I could not see it clearly. Beyond that, I really don't know. Nothing unusual has happened, except that I was untouched by the flames. I...

"Wait! My wound!" Jared began to take his shirt off, as he continued. "I was wounded. Here," he pointed to his upper back, "on my upper shoulder and arm by a Qa-ryk during the battle. He clawed me badly. That was only a few days ago. By yesterday it had already healed over. The first night it was red and raw and really swollen, and I had a bad fever. Now, except for some stiffness, it is fine."

Sart stood up. He stepped toward Jared to examine the long pink scars on his upper back. As a healer who had studied the medicinal lore of the land, he knew immediately that some power had been at work to help this lad's wound close so quickly. When he was rested and in his own power, he could do deep healing work. But it was always draining. It had taken him years of study, prayer, and communion with the earth to develop that much power. By the look of the clawing Jared had received, it was a miracle the boy had survived. The wounds had been deep.

He resumed his seat on the soft earth before speaking. "Only a potent healing spell could close a wound that fast. If you have no other talisman, we must assume that the pendant protected you from the effects of this wound and also helped it to heal. It likely helped protect you from the flame spell, too, even after it had been taken from you. Its effect must have stayed with you for at least a short time after the pendant was removed. That would suggest a powerful talisman. Based on my understanding of such things, it is unlikely it is still providing any protection now. Yet, its power must be very great to leave so powerful a residual effect. Most stones of power have to be worn if they are to affect the owner in any way; once removed, the effect is no more.

"You say your shoulder was swollen? It was red and you had a fever?"

Jared nodded.

"It is likely the Qa-ryk's nails were poisoned. They often treat them so to distract and discomfort their enemies. The pendant cured you of that as well," Sart mused.

"The Qa-ryk chieftain wasn't protected from my arrow."

"There can be many reasons for that, my son. Magical devices often provide only certain forms of protection. In addition, I would guess that this stone is a magical item aligned to the good. It may have had the opposite effect on the Qa-ryk, causing him to be more vulnerable, rather than less vulnerable." Sart scratched his chin as he reasoned. "It is possible it might shield the owner from magical attacks, though not from conventional weaponry. Magically imbued items have limitations. It is wise to always remember that, Jared. I can't know what this stone is and what type of power it may have, unless I have a chance to examine it. It seems that it is an item of considerable power."

"What about Thistle? Why was she only partially protected?"

"As to Thistle, that I truly don't understand," Sart replied. "She could not have been protected by the stone unless she held it for some time?" He looked questioningly at Jared.

Jared shook his head. "I don't think she even knew I had it, unless she took it from me when I was feverish. She said she searched for things to help me when I was unconscious. We could ask her when she wakes."

"Since the earth has been burnt between you and her, the sphere of protection you were in could not have protected her. It is also curious to see that she was only in some measure protected, as if from a partially completed incantation by the looks of it. Or perhaps she has some other magical device of power about her... on her ankle, perhaps? Is she a spell caster, or an apprentice witch?"

"No, not unless she has been concealing it from me," Jared said.

Sart nodded. "I doubt she would have the knowledge at her age to wield that much power anyway. From all the signs, it appears that whatever protected her was an intense shielding sphere or bubble. The odd thing is that it was not fully in place. Therefore, she was partially wounded by the blast. Half the shell was in place, but the top part of the sphere had only incompletely formed. What was there, luckily, provided some protection; else she would be dead. Aberon's power is immense. The fire he called down would have felled a dozen Qa-ryks."

Sart shook his head. "It doesn't make much sense. It would take an even greater mage to counter his evil force. Perhaps Thistle will remember more. When she wakes, we must ask her. There are too many unanswered questions here. And now, Aberon has the biggest mystery of all in his grasp. What is this necklace you found? Why did he covet it? Where did it come from? And why did a mere Qa-ryk chieftain possess so powerful a device for the good?" Sart shook his head. Looking at Jared, he shrugged.

"Unfortunately, now that Aberon has it in his possession, it could be dangerous for us. If it is that which truly healed and protected you, then he will likely try to destroy it. He and his kind want to rid the world of such artifacts. If only I had not delayed so long at the village, perhaps I could have gotten here in time. Still I needed to re-provision. Nor could I leave without helping where I could, though for the most part there was little to do except pray for the fallen."

Jared sat down opposite Sart, looking into the cleric's eyes intently. He asked, "You mentioned Aberon before, as if you know him. Who is he and what is he? Why have you been following him?"

Sart lowered his voice, as if to speak his words loudly would draw evil to them. "Aberon is a priest of darkness. He is the one of the vile black priests, apprentice to the Black Druids, the leaders of the Qa-ryk hordes. He...."

Jared interrupted. His thoughts ran quickly ahead. "The Black Druids? There has been talk of them in our village for years. We often heard rumors of them, but few believed they really existed. If I had known he was one, I would have done something. When he joined us, I sensed something was wrong; something didn't feel right. I should have listened to my gut. I should have shot him when I had the chance."

Sart shrugged and gestured with his hand. "It would have done no good." His lips turned up in the slightest of smiles. "You never had the chance, Jared. He would have deflected your arrow as easily as you brush off a leaf, and destroyed you with a wave of his hand. He almost did anyway, were it not for the pendant you wore. He would have taken it from you when he first caught up with you, but he is more powerful at night. He didn't want to risk failure, against the stone's power to do good."

Sart's voice took on a harsher tone. "He is powerful, Jared, more powerful than I, or so I am beginning to realize. Perhaps I could have done more if I had arrived at the village in time. I did all I..." the cleric's voice trailed off.

"You have mentioned a village twice. Were you at Thiele?" Jared asked.

"Yes, I was at Thiele. Too late to do much good, I am afraid. If I had not lost track of Aberon in the mountains, I might have arrived in time to help – more than I did, anyway. I am not positive even my powers could have stemmed a powerful coordinated attack of so many Qa-ryks. And, there was the dragon. It added another dimension altogether. Aberon has been about much more than I understood. Your village just happened to be useful to his plans.

"I have been following this evil 'thing,'" Sart spat out the last word, "for many months, trying to catch him off guard. He is quite clever. I followed him far to the west. That is where he enlisted the aid of the fell beast that destroyed your village. I lost him when he rode it to the Qa-ryk encampment. It took me too long to catch him up. By then, there wasn't much I could do. I do not have the powers to fend off a dragon in any case. I have to imagine that this stone, the pendant you found, was part of his plan. Perhaps it is the central part to his ultimate goal, whatever that may be."

Jared looked puzzled. He asked, "Why didn't he take it from the Qa-ryk himself? He must have known the beast had it. I never heard of anyone in the village owning any artifact like this, so the beast couldn't have picked it up there."

"There could be many reasons for that, my son. The Black Druids have tried several times to corral and organize these fell beasts for their conquests. Aberon could not afford to affect the careful balance of spells and favors that keep them under their sway. It is why we priests of Borea are keen to learn as much as we can about them.

"I originally ran across Aberon's path purely by accident. When I did, I decided that this was an opportunity to learn something more about these evil druids who drive the Qa-ryks to their barbarous acts of destruction and violence. I am powerful enough that he did not want to risk a fight with me. I have to admit that he has toyed with me and led me in circles. I have not learned much for my efforts either. I am dearly sorry that I arrived too late to help your village. Perhaps I could have warned them in advance, with time enough for them to flee."

Jared shook his head sadly. "They would not have left their homes. They would have fought, no matter the odds."

Sart nodded. "I thought so... still, one wishes one could have done more."

"It was Aberon, who led the attack? Not the dragon?"

"Nay, Aberon did not lead the attack. I doubt that he was even there until it was over. He likely watched it from afar. He did enlist the aid of the dragon, and he drove the Qa-ryks into a frenzy for the assault. The Black Druids and their evil priests do not often fight, not unless through dire necessity, or when a goal requires their magical abilities to succeed. When they do fight, they use their evil powers to destroy. The Qa-ryks would only be a minor inconvenience to Borea if these dark priests were destroyed."

Jared hesitated before asking his next question. "I have hoped against hope... were there any survivors at Thiele? I left... I ran after I saw my brother fall. There was a large Qa-ryk after me, the one I eventually slew. I was wounded and... I guess I panicked. I found Thistle as I was running up into the hills from the battle." He hung his head; the pent-up tension and guilt of the past days overflowed at last. Tears began to stream down his face. His shoulders heaved as he sobbed.

Sart let him cry. Placing his hand on the boy's shoulder, he drew him into his arms. After several minutes, Jared's sobs subsided. Sart consoled him. "Do not blame yourself, Jared. The fight was done by the time you fled, and by the looks of those scars, you were gravely wounded. Your only chance was to flee. From what you have related, you slew a great beast, and saved Thistle. The gods move in strange ways. Perhaps this was all meant to happen, to bring us together. One can only deal with what is, not with what was, my son.

"Now, as to your question," Sart continued. "There were signs that some made it out the eastern gate and fled toward Permis, but I did not go so far. I have been remiss in not telling you this sooner... well, it was necessary to deal with what I found here. I only found one alive, badly wounded, yet still breathing – a stout fellow named Ge-or. He mentioned a brother."

"Ge-or is alive?" Jared abruptly pushed back from Sart. He knelt down in front of the cleric and grabbed his hands, looking intently into his eyes. "My brother lives? He survived the blow?"

"Aye, he has a hard head, though he did have a bad concussion. It took my remaining strength to heal the damage. He..."

"Where is he? Did you leave him? Was he...?"

"Shhhh, quietly, lest we wake Thistle from her rest. As to your first question – he was still in Thiele when I left. I gave him a potion to help him sleep, so he could regain his strength. He was determined to charge out after the red dragon to retrieve an elven sword of some value. Something taken from your family, your sire? He said the beast had it. My guess is that he would have woken yesterday. I don't…"

"The dragon took the sword?" Jared asked, thinking quickly. He was surprised at how wrong he had been about several things. "I… I guess that makes sense. I… We…" Jared gestured toward Thistle, "we believed the Qa-ryks had it. We were determined to trail them and seek a way to get it back."

"Well, you are certainly both cut from the same mold, I'll warrant that. Ge-or wanted to rush right out after the dragon. This sword must indeed be a great weapon."

"One of the finest of an age gone by, or so our father spoke of it. He only allowed us to see it unsheathed once. He always meant it for Ge-or. It is too big for me to wield easily. Do you think he, I mean Ge-or, has gone after the dragon?"

"I cannot say. I tried to dissuade him, but he was headstrong. Unfortunately, he also thought you were dead; so, it is doubtful he would be looking for you. I had to leave quickly; I was worried about what mischief Aberon would do next. It appears I did not leave soon enough. From what you have told me, the pendant is a great loss to our cause. Now, it is of even more importance to track this dread priest.

"Listen carefully to me, my son." Sart drew Jared a bit further away from where Thistle lay. He laid his hand on his shoulder again. "It is important that you understand how hopeless things were. You cannot blame yourself for leaving the battle. Had you stayed, the Qa-ryks chasing you would have killed you, quite easily considering your condition. Out in the country you had a chance, and you probably saved Thistle's life. Be thankful for that. In addition, you have told me much I did not know that speaks to Aberon's intentions. I will need to ponder all of this, yet I feel this priest has more mischief in the works. You may have helped delay his plans a few days, which may help me thwart what else he intends."

Jared sat back on his heels, wiping the tears from his eyes. Eventually, he stood up and began pacing again, troubled by many things and still bothered by his feelings of guilt. "I saw my father and many others killed and... and so many others. I can't help feeling that I should have done something, something more to help."

"I feel the same way, my son," Sart said sadly. "Had I not lost Aberon's trail I might have been able to warn your village, or helped repel the assault, had there not been a red dragon; and if my strength hadn't failed me at the end... There are many ifs in life. For whatever reasons, the gods did not will it to be otherwise. I must trust in that. I must believe that there are reasons for the difficulties we face. If nothing else, they can make us stronger and wiser, though only if we choose to learn from them.

"Unfortunately, the choices are not always ours to make. Many times, it seems…" Sart reached up with his left hand and began to caress the old rood that hung from his neck… "the power that permeates all things moves in strange ways, and only rarely can we affect its direction. However, sometimes we do have to try. Else, what is life for?"

Jared turned to the priest. "Yes, that is why Thistle and I are here and not at Permis. We wanted to make a difference, to avenge our losses. We both wanted to do something. Our old lives are past…"

Sart suddenly motioned with his hand; Jared stopped in mid-sentence. The cleric pointed toward Thistle.

The White Wizardess

They strode toward Thistle's prostrate form. Sart had seen her stir.

"Jared? Jared?" Thistle called out weakly. She tried to push herself up from the charred bed.

Jared jogged over the last few steps and knelt down. Putting his arm behind her back, he helped ease her up to a sitting position. "I'm here, Thistle." He choked back angry tears. "Don't try to get up yet; you've been badly hurt."

"What happened? I'm so hot... Where is Yolk? Why can't I see you?" She began to struggle in his grasp, panic edging her voice. "Jared! I can't see. Everything's so blurry! Jared, help!" Thistle grabbed at him frantically. He pulled her close to his side, grasping one of her hands.

"It's all right, Thistle. I'm right here. Aberon attacked us last night, and you were burned. Yolk is right here on your stomach. I don't think he is hurt. I..." Jared stopped, unsure of what else to say. While he paused, the little creature on Thistle's stomach began to glide up higher on her chest.

"I can't see, Jared! It's all cloudy. I can't see!" She cried out the last words.

Sart knelt down next to her. He pressed a small clear crystal vial to her lips. "Here, my dear girl, drink this. Do not fear; you are in good hands. The blindness is only temporary. If I were not so weak, I could heal you faster. This potion will ease the pain and hasten the healing. Your sight should return to normal by morning next."

Thistle drew back at the strange voice, grasping Jared's hand tightly. "It's all right, Thistle. This is Sart, a priest of the Earth, who has been tracking Aberon. Go ahead and drink; the potion is safe."

At Jared's assurances Thistle relaxed more, pressing her face into his chest. After a moment, she pulled away and opened her mouth to drink the proffered potion. Soon she was able to sit up by herself. Bolstered by blankets from the mule's backpack, she hungrily ate the stew they brought to her. As she ate, they filled her in on what they had discussed.

When she had finished eating, Sart said, "You should rest as much as possible, several days would be ideal. I'm afraid that we will have to move before nightfall to find a safer place to camp. This place reeks of evil. I would away from it now that you are awake, child. How do you feel? "

"I still feel hot," Thistle said. "The pain is gone. Thank you. I guess we have been careless."

Sart put his hand on her forehead as he spoke, "You couldn't have known. I'm the one who has been careless. I understood the cunning and power of my enemy, yet I underestimated his speed." Done with his examination, he sat on the ground next to her. "I need to ask you about one further thing before we move on, Thistle. Can you tell me how you protected yourself? You are too young to be a potent witch."

"I don't know of what you speak, Father. No, I am no witch. I know no spells. I really don't know what could have aided me. Aberon said ovietti have magical powers, but I don't know if Yolk has any. He's a friend."

"Yes, ovietti are indeed magical, and I am amazed to see one has chosen such a young person. Their power is to enhance magic, not to protect one from it. I have only seen one a couple of times before this. One of those was in the company of a powerful elven princess near Moulanes; the other was with a Wizardess. My understanding is that they only choose those who are already powerful in the ways of magic. It is their wont to enhance what is already present. That it has chosen you is curious. You are positive you have no powers? Perhaps as a seer or prognosticator?"

Thistle replied, "No, none I am aware of. I'm a simple country girl from a large family. No one I know of is magical in any way. We do have a hag in our village who makes mild potions for this and that. She specializes in herbs and other general treatments."

"And you did not study with her? Or help in any way with her devices?" Sart continued to probe.

"No," insisted Thistle. "We rarely went to her; my father is wary of such healers. We only went if the need was great. Elsewise, I only saw her at village gatherings, and that was from afar."

"Ah, well, we have a puzzle, don't we? Do you mind if I call your friend to me?"

"No, not at all, if he will deign to come. He is particular about people. He didn't like Aberon, which is one of the things that concerned both of us."

"Ah... so, let us see if he will abide me. Come here, Yolk, and greet a bungling priest."

Yolk opened his eyes. After blinking once at Sart, he folded out of Thistle's arms and over into the cleric's hands. Sart picked him up, stroking the top of Yolk's head softly. Yolk rolled his eyes closed contentedly.

"I guess he likes you," Thistle said. "He would not come to you else. Now I can truly relax."

Sart laughed heartily, his deep voice booming. "He does seem content enough, doesn't he; and he is certainly cute. Here now, Yolk, go back to your mistress. She needs you more than I do." Sart waited while Yolk folded his way back to Thistle's arms. He asked, "Is there anything else you can remember about last night that might explain the protection spell?"

"What little I remember is more like a dream. I woke to find myself being pawed over by that horrible priest. I couldn't move, no matter how hard I struggled. I felt trapped, as if I were tied tightly, though nothing was holding me down."

"A binding spell of some type, I'll warrant," said Sart. "Please go on."

"He was looking for something. When he didn't find it, he left and went over to Jared. I began to struggle even harder, but I still couldn't move.

"At that point, the dream began to shift... I saw a tall woman in the distance, bathed in white light. She was blond and exceptionally beautiful, with shoulder length hair -- dressed in a long white and blue robe, radiant with energy. She was trying to talk with me or tell me something. At first, I couldn't understand the words at all; suddenly, I understood that she wanted me to repeat what she said. I began to say them aloud, even though I did not understand them. As I did, she faded away, and I saw the clearing again; yet I could still hear within my mind what she wanted me to say. Soon a shimmering began to form around me, and Yolk was... well, he was gleaming, too.

"That's all I remember. I guess I blacked out after that... Wait! I do remember a bright flash. That was all."

"Meligance," Sart mused.

"Meligance?" Jared and Thistle said together.

Sart explained, "She is the White Wizardess of Borea, the only one I know who is powerful enough for a sending of this type. You have described what she looks like when she is within her power. I don't really understand this at all, unless you have latent magical powers, Thistle. Thus, I would guess, she was able to connect with you. She obviously knew of you, even if you knew nothing of her.

"However it happened, you received a dream-sending – a conjuration cast from mind to mind. Your limitations and the great distance, or both, made the spell only partially successful. What is more intriguing is why she felt compelled to send protection to you? How could she have known you were in trouble? Have you had no dreams before of this woman?"

"No, none I remember. She was a stranger to me," Thistle replied with certainty.

"We must thank the gods for your good fortune," Sart said. "Remember this, child, you have been touched and blessed by a power far beyond any other in this world that I ken. She is one of a kind, and for some reason the two of you are linked." Sart looked intently at Thistle, trying to discern whether there was anything about her that would indicate latent magical powers. Being drained of his own strength, he was unable to learn anything further.

Sart stood, satisfied that he had at least part of the truth for now. He gestured toward his mule. "We must move from this area. It would not be safe to stay the night. We will find a better resting place. In the morn, I think you two should go back to Permis where Thistle can recover properly. I must..."

Thistle's reaction was sharp. "No! If Jared's brother is going after the sword, then we have to help you recover the pendant." She crossed her arms in front of her chest and thrust her chin out. "I won't go back. I don't care what either of you say. If I have to wander around in the forest half-blind for two days, I'm going on!"

The outburst startled Sart. He looked from Thistle to Jared and back again. Jared was grinning broadly. He shrugged his shoulders when Sart looked at him again. "If she wants to go, she'll go. I found that out soon enough. She's worse than my brother for stubbornness. I agree with her, though. We have too much of ourselves wrapped into this quest, if one can call this strange series of occurrences an adventure. The sword is now out of our reach, but we can still go after the stone. If it is as valuable as you say, it should be regained. Aberon would never have come after us if it had not been important."

"Important? Yes," Sart said. "I would warrant it so. It may be more important than any of us realize. I don't think Meligance would have entered this, elsewise. Perhaps this is what she sensed. I do not try to second guess the White Wizardess." He paused and did not say what he honestly thought, which was that the White Wizardess's interest might have more to do with Thistle than anything else. "You both need to understand that it will be dangerous – dangerous beyond your imagination. I fully intend to go after Aberon myself. Especially now that he has the stone you found, whatever it may be. Nonetheless, this is no quest for a half-elven lad and an even younger girl. We may all be killed. Do you both ken how fell this dread priest is?"

Jared frowned. Until a few days ago, he had not understood the true power of evil. Now he was caught up in a whirlwind, something that was indeed beyond anything he had ever imagined. The fantasy adventures he had shared with his brother paled in comparison to the bizarre tale of which he was now a part. On the other hand, he was also an expertly trained fighter. He had learned weaponry from one of the true masters of the age. His father had drilled both him and Ge-or relentlessly for the art of war. He would not shirk from danger, whatever its form.

He answered the cleric, "Nay, Sart. I do not truly understand what we will face, but I am for it. If Thistle wants to come as well, it is her choice. I cannot tell her what she should do. If she is old enough to be given in marriage, she is old enough to make her own choices. I, myself, have naught else to go back to, unless I wish to find my brother. It seems that separate paths are being laid before us by providence. I, for one, will accept this challenge for good or ill."

Thistle spoke, tears welling up in her eyes. "Jared is right. We have been set upon an adventure we did not seek. I am also determined to see it through. As long as we are not a hindrance, I hope you will take us with you. We may prove of more mettle and use than even you can know."

"Who am I to gainsay the gods?" Sart declared. "You both obviously have many talents, and I can use all the help I can get. Know this – Aberon will probably lead us into the heart of Qa-ryk territory. We will face many more dangers than his wrath when he sees I have not given up the chase." He looked back and forth between the two several times. Their resolve did not waver.

At that, Sart clapped his hands together. "Well, enough! We can decide more tomorrow. Tonight, we must at least move from here and find a place secure for resting. I need to sleep myself. More than anything, I need to meditate to rejuvenate my powers. And Thistle, in spite of your bold pronouncement, you are weak. You must recover your strength." He gestured ahead. "Come, let us pack quickly. We can make a league or so by nightfall." Sart turned and whistled to the east for Crunch, the mule having wandered off into the woods while they spoke.

A minute later, he was rubbing his stomach, and Crunch was eyeing Thistle, who was now leaning on Jared's shoulder. Jared watched the animal warily and said, "Thistle, Sart has this rambunctious mule named Crunch. I would introduce you; alas, he has a bad habit of leveling his new acquaintances with his nose. You can ride him, hopefully, he will...."

That was when Crunch made his charge. He went straight for Jared's stomach. When the half-elf was on the ground, Crunch stood gently rubbing his nose into Thistle's side.

Thistle laughed. "I think he already greeted me, Jared, yet he does seem to have it in for you."

Fifteen minutes later, with Thistle tied loosely on Crunch's back, the small party headed west, paralleling the path they had followed earlier, but staying in the cover of the trees. By full night, they had covered at least a league. Soon thereafter, they settled into a small rock-enclosed clearing that promised some protection from the westerly wind.

Charging Forth

Ge-or woke before dawn, stiff from his labors the previous day, yet anxious to move on. He began gathering everything he could find that might be of use on a long journey.

As he had worked honoring the dead, he had picked up all the weapons and tools that were in good shape and laid them in a pile near the southeast corner of the square. Now, he went through all he had gathered carefully. Since he had not been able to find his own quiver, he selected another. He filled it with as many decently crafted arrows as he could find that would suit his draw length. His own sword was the best of the lot remaining, so he took it and his back scabbard. He added to his weaponry a stout staff for walking, several throwing knives, one in each boot and another in a thigh sheath, a long dagger, and his hunting knife in his belt sheath. He also added some basic tools to his backpack, anticipating he would have need of them eventually.

His sword was a cross between a short sword and a bastard sword that his father had insisted he make. He and Jared had sweated for five years assisting at the blacksmith shop, learning the trade so they could have the skill to make a decent blade, but more importantly learning to recognize quality workmanship so he could purchase well-made items for a fair price. It was somewhat crude and basic in form, yet was well-tempered and balanced to his hand. It would have to do until he could find or purchase something better.

Next, he gathered a change of clothing, foodstuffs, rope, and a variety of other assorted items that might prove valuable. The Qa-ryks had either taken or destroyed what they had readily seen. Many of the cabins, however, had deep-set cupboards as well as ground lockers for storage. He was able to glean a good bit from those that had not been destroyed by the pillaging beasts. Ge-or found enough that he had to make hard choices as to what he could fit in the pack and on his person. He wanted to make good time in the hills, though as yet he was undecided exactly which path he would take south.

By mid-day he was ready to go. He set out through the south-eastern exit of the stockade and thence up into the hills. Turning as he started up the slope, he nodded a goodbye to the village that had been his life. He set his mouth and went on. His tentative plan was to head south and eventually east until he reached a town called Aelfric. His father had often spoke of the place as a gathering point for adventurers and as a replenishing source for anything a person planning a quest might want. It sounded like just the place for Ge-or to gather what he needed to accoutre himself well enough to be able to go after the dragon. He also hoped that he would be able to glean some information about the great beasts. Sart had suggested there were still those alive who might be privy to such information.

He had decided to take the cleric's advice – better to prepare oneself for battle than to rush out and get killed by being rash. He had learned a good bit about the dragon by recalling the one attack he had seen. Later, he had learned even more by pacing off the damaged areas in the village while he had worked the day before. Though the heat of the dragon's blast had been intense, incinerating everything except the finest metals in its direct path, peripherally the damage had been minimal. In all three attacks – the two against the stockade and the last one that he had witnessed in the village square – the dragon's focused path of destruction had been twelve to fifteen feet wide. Those caught within a five-foot span on either side of that width had been severely burned. Outside that range the damage to anything caught near was much less severe.

The length of the fiery discharge was harder to calculate, as it had been partially stopped by the stockade walls or the makeshift barriers and people in its path. From what Ge-or could deduce, the maximum effective range was about fifty to sixty feet. To completely incinerate the stockade logs during its attack, the dragon looked to have swooped down within fifteen feet of the ground before releasing its inferno – maybe even as low as nine or ten feet off the ground during its final attack on the defenders of the inner barricade.

He had also noticed other things about the dragon's attack that might prove useful should he ever face the beast. It was obviously, in spite of its age and size, highly skilled at maneuvering. He had seen it turn on its tail in mid-air to swoop back down to retrieve the sword. The entire attack and retrieval had happened in less than a minute's time. Its long wingspan – Ge-or guessed the spread to be seventy feet across – meant it had to have quite a bit of room in order to truly use its flying ability to advantage.

While he couldn't identify any specific area of the dragon's body that might be vulnerable, he had burned into his memory a picture of the beast flaring its wings, belly toward him as it turned in mid-air. It appeared to be heavily scaled all over. However, if its coloration meant anything, the darkest and perhaps thickest and most impenetrable areas were the back, lower throat from the base of the neck down into and covering the chest area, and its head. The stomach was a lighter, yellowish-orange color; and the areas on the inside of each leg between the leg and the body were a light tan shade. The underneath of the throat, right below the chin, was also a light shade.

He figured there must be an old warrior or two still alive who could tell him more about the beasts. It would probably take some doing to track someone down, but it might be well worth the effort. Aelfric seemed like the place to start. He knew that knowledge about one's enemy was a key component to success and survival. The cold anger that now molded Ge-or's resolve could wait a few months to be assuaged.

Ge-or was loping easily upward, when he stopped abruptly, looking down at a large number of heavy prints on the rock-strewn path ahead. Qa-ryks had been there; and from the looks of the markings, one had been killed. Blood spattered the rocks in several places. Later, the beast had been carried away by his brethren. As Ge-or carefully inspected the immediate area, he saw other partial prints as well – a man had been here, too.

It took him a while to sort out the mess of superimposed prints. From what he could read, he guessed that a tall man had been chased from the village by a large Qa-ryk. This person had ambushed the beast in a hollow off the main path and managed to kill the monster. Whoever he was, he had headed further up the path. Large spatters of dried blood on the trail to the south suggested that the fellow had been badly wounded in the encounter. When the other Qa-ryks had trailed their comrade to this point, two of them had gone after the man up into the hills. With or without their prey, they looked to have returned sometime later to join their fellows in removing their dead comrade.

Ge-or worked the area carefully, following the blatant signs of the beasts'

72

heavy feet and the blood splattered here and there on the path from the man's wound. He had not gone even a half league further when he came across signs of another struggle. Footprints and scratches on the rocks spoke of two sets of human prints. These were badly marred by the clawed paws of the two Qa-ryks stomping about the area. Puzzling over the evidence, Ge-or determined that the taller of the men had attacked the smaller by coming at him from behind. The resulting scuffle had ended quickly. It appeared as if the two had ended up heading further up the path into the hills together. The Qa-ryks followed them for a while.

After another half league or so, the Qa-ryks stopped in the middle of the path and abruptly turned around giving up the chase. Though the spatters of blood were fewer here, there was still clear evidence that the two humans had continued upward. Ge-or did not know what had dissuaded the beasts in their pursuit, but there was no doubt they had given up on chasing after the refugees from the battle.

By early evening, Ge-or came to the stream where the two humans had rested. The blood spots ended at the stream. He guessed that the small fellow had finally bound the other's wounds. They had rested for a short while in this spot, and then, much more slowly and deliberately, had gone further to the south.

At dusk, Ge-or found a small cave. There he could easily read the evidence that the two wanderers had used it for at least a night or two. Since he was still tired from his monumental efforts of the day before, he decided to take the natural defensive posture of the cave's size and shape and stay there himself. He searched carefully, yet could find no evidence that would tell him any more about the pair who had stayed there before him. He ate a meal of dried fish, stale bread, and water, content to stay as unnoticed as possible. Placing his weapons close to hand, he lay with his boots facing the corner of the cave and fell quickly asleep.

The Power of the Earth

Sart stood at the edge of the clearing where they had stopped for the night. He had finished his evening meditation and was feeling as good as he had for many days. This eve had been what he had needed more than anything. The hours he had spent in his communion with Gaia had helped him rejuvenate much of his inner strength. He knew he would need it in the days ahead.

He didn't move, but stayed rooted in the spot he had chosen. His feet were bare and in contact with the dirt. He hoped the earth would offer him some insight into the puzzles he was trying to unravel, for he was troubled. Forces and devices were in play that he could not have guessed at. Aberon had given no hint that a powerful artifact, as the stone Jared had found, was a part of his plans. Now, with these two youngsters wound up in some way with the events that were unfolding, Sart's surety was being tested.

He was more concerned with their safety than his own. Yet, in searching his soul, he knew there must be a reason Jared and Thistle were part of what was happening. They were either caught in the web that Aberon was weaving, or else the greater forces of this world had drawn them in for some purpose he could not yet fathom. He believed the latter, for it was at the root of his trust in Gaia.

Jared was concern enough. He had obviously stumbled onto the stone fortuitously. Sart probably would never know whether providence had a hand in the young half-elf's killing of the Qa-ryk chieftain and his taking of the pendant, or whether it was simply a coincidence. The healing the half-elf had received from the talisman, and the protection from Aberon's fire blast after the stone had been taken, marked the artifact as being quite potent and, likely, extremely old. It could well be something from the first age of the world when magicked items of this kind were more commonplace. Such devices often seemed to choose the circumstances of their import into the affairs of the world.

Sart kept wondering as he continued his meditation. What chain of events had brought it to this place? Into the hands of, until this point, an inconsequential young lad from a small northern village? Everything he knew and felt told him that this powerful artifact had come to the boy for a reason. To abandon that, without making an all-out effort to get it back, might mean something far more disastrous to the kingdom than any of their lives might prove. Yet, he could not fathom what reason that could be. Until he saw and held the stone, he would not know any more. However, he also knew that artifacts of power were hard for even the gifted to fathom.

Thistle was another concern altogether. Did she have a power that she did not know about? How else could the Grand White Wizardess of Borea know of her and make this intense effort to protect her from that dread priest? There was something hidden here. On the morrow, when he was fully in his power again, perhaps he would be able to sense if she had some form of natural power.

Sart readjusted his feet, moving both legs back and forth so he could feel the good earth between his toes. In spite of his many concerns, he was deep within himself and much more relaxed than one would think. His mind was like a dozen gossamer threads in a gentle breeze – one thought floating upon the other as his slow deep breathing took him deeper still. He gave himself over to it again.

An ovietti? The creatures were almost mythical. Yet, in a small coastal village in the far northwest of the kingdom, the one she has named Yolk comes and chooses a wisp of a girl. Ovietti reputedly only chose those exceedingly gifted in the ways of magic, so why this child? It was another imponderable until he knew more.

If she indeed were a latent magic-user, how could she not sense the force of it within? He well knew the power that was needed to create the orb that had partially protected her. He had been friends with Meligance long enough to have a good sense of the power she wielded. Though he did not understand how potent sendings were done, nor how much of the force involved, if any, had come from the White Wizardess, he did know that the girl would have had to be involved in some way, else it could not have been controlled and would have destroyed her.

That was the thread that concerned him most of all, because if she had even a modicum of magic – and he figured she must have to have survived the sending – then she was in considerably more danger from herself than from outside. One truth that was certain in the realm of magic use was that if you had the gift, you had to learn to control it; else it would eat you up from within.

His dilemma thus came from several considerations: How much time did he have before Aberon struck again? His own deeper being answered... Not much. The priest was pressing forward, and the artifact obviously had been part of his plan all along. And how much time did this child have before she must be placed in the hands of a competent mentor? How much time did she have before her own power began to take its toll?

Sart sighed; he readjusted his feet yet again. His connection with the earth was a comfort few others could understand. His sect was small, for they kept to the old ways; but as all the older religions, they used the energy that they could connect with readily. He took another deep breath. Letting it out slowly, he sank deeper into his meditation. Perhaps Gaia would give him further insight this night.

Jared also spent an uneasy night. Yolk and Crunch were ostensibly standing guard; nonetheless, Jared paced the small camp at odd intervals trying to resolve the conflicts in his mind. He gave Sart a wide berth, instinctively knowing the good priest was doing what he needed to rejuvenate his powers. Throughout his young life he had been certain of both his direction and his grasp of reality. Suddenly, he had been thrown into this chaotic world where his knowledge, skill, and elven dexterity appeared of little consequence. Spells of devastating power, healing potions, talismans of protection, and magical-sendings were things that he had never had to deal with in his secure seacoast hold. Things such as these were only whispered about late at night with his brother, when the two imagined what the world was like far away in other towns and cities or deep in the wilderness. The physical world where he had been so positive of his place had changed, only to be replaced by a confusion of new powers that he could not control or understand. His mind reeled with the enormity of this new dimension to his life. He did not know in which direction to turn.

Thistle, whom he had begun to accept as a true companion, had also manifested, albeit indirectly, a power he could not understand. And Sart, who had talked of his own healing powers, had also referred to Aberon's evil magic with cautious respect. Magic? Good and evil? Dragon fire? These were forces beyond his ken that confused him all the more. When he and Ge-or had whispered of grand quests, their imaginings had turned to fierce battles with stupendous beasts, long treks after beautiful maidens or even elven princesses, and great feats of heroism and

strength in overcoming tremendous odds. They had always prevailed; returning victorious to great acclaim, and, of course, with the beautiful maidens on their arms. Magic, when they considered it, was always a positive force, one that somehow never failed to help them achieve their great quests.

There had never been any users of magic in Thiele, only the one old lady, whom everyone referred to as the Hag. In the coastal villages, this title was a type of odd deference. She, like others of similar ilk in nearby villages, take the title as a form of respect. Despite his father's reservations, she was an accepted member of their enclave, and she did provide services for many. Mostly she mixed herbs or distilled potions that were for minor ailments or injuries: a poultice for a cut, tea for the ague in the winter, ground herbs to relieve pain, and the like. Occasionally, a villager would go to her for a foretelling or to ask for a salve to remove warts; but for the most part, the villagers did not believe she had any true powers.

Jared felt uncomfortable, as well as vulnerable. He did understand, albeit in an oblique sort of way, that he was now actually in the midst of an adventure. He also knew that this had none of the feelings of power and greatness that were part of the adventures he and Ge-or had envisioned. The quests they had dreamt up always started with a firm determination to head out to right some ill or challenge some fell beast. This was altogether too real, and it felt like he had it thrust upon him when he was completely unprepared.

After pacing for a long time fro and to, he resolved to ask Sart for more information in the morning. Jared finally lay down and slept fitfully the few remaining hours until dawn.

When he awoke, the sun had already risen and Sart had breakfast cooking over a cheering fire. Thankfully, Thistle's eyesight was almost back to normal, though she was still quite weak. In spite of what had happened, she was bright and bubbly. She had taken it upon herself to care for Crunch, having already made a lasting friend of the large, ornery mule by carefully grooming his long-neglected coat. This she accomplished with a brush that Sart had grudgingly admitted to having "somewhere in my saddlebags."

Jared on the other hand was feeling the effects of having stayed up far too late. He ate his breakfast in silence, trying unsuccessfully to keep to himself. His feeling of ill-ease had deepened, and he answered Thistle's questions only with sullen grunts.

Exasperated by his moodiness, she snapped at him. "Well, the least you could do is grunt musically or something." Then she stalked off to tend to Crunch again.

Sart, aware that something was bothering Jared, interrupted his morning meditation and returned to the fire. "If you are concerned about whether I will take you with me on this quest, you need not be. I have searched my soul and prayed for guidance. Though I have misgivings, it does seem that our paths are destined to continue together for a while."

Jared shook his head, still unsure of himself and what he was to face. He was not even sure what questions to ask. "Nay, Father... ah, Sart, it is not that. I am confused about all that has happened... is happening. I have a hundred questions and know not where to start."

Sart raised an eyebrow, waiting for Jared to continue.

"As I understand it, you have the power to heal. You have the power to cast spells that cure various ailments and wounds. Aberon is also a priest of a sort?" Jared looked up at Sart questioningly. The cleric nodded.

"As you have spoken of him, it appears he uses his power with malevolent intent instead of for healing and blessing. He is in league with dark forces, and thus can cast destructive spells as well. Is...?" He stopped, trying to think of the right way to phrase his questions. Suddenly, everything came out all at once. "Is this power, this ability to cast spells, available to anyone? If I or Thistle learned these ancient formulas which you or Aberon speak, will we have this power for ourselves? Where does this force come from? How does a person like Aberon learn to grasp so much power? What...?"

"Hold, hold." Sart held up his hand to stop Jared's stream of questions. He whistled softly toward Thistle to catch her attention and gestured for her to join them. Sart looked down toward the earth, trying to think of how to answer. When Thistle was seated opposite Jared, he took a deep breath and looked back up. He caught both Jared and Thistle's eyes. "My son, you are confusing two types of power; or perhaps two different ways that power or force, if you will, are manifested and used."

Sart smiled. Gesturing to his sides, he said, "First, there is the power that is in all living things, let us call it life-force; and second, that power which makes up all things, which is, as I understand it, a form of energy. In the simplest terms: that which we feel as living beings, and that which we don't necessarily feel, but see as objects. Perhaps at the deepest levels of 'the making' they are the same, and they all come ultimately from the same source.

"We all have energy within, Jared. I believe what is most relevant to your many questions is that priests gather their power in a different way than magic-users or mages. The clerics, priests, and druids, whatever their religion or beliefs, tap the power of life, the energy of living things. They use this force to bolster their own inner strength and reserves. We connect with life, or perhaps more to the truth, to the pulse of things, for even defining life can be difficult.

"Those of different religions and persuasions use varying sources according to their natural leanings. When I heal, I am directly calling upon energy that is within me, energy that I have drawn to me in large part by my connection with Gaia, the earth herself, the source of life."

"A mage," Sart said, "a user of magic, as I understand it, for I do not truly ken how it is done, primarily uses energy from outside themselves to cast spells. I have been told that perspective is not wholly accurate either. Mages do have a reserve of inner energy, as all people do; however, they have much more than most. That is an important caveat, because they need to learn to control it, else it may do them damage. Best put, they need to learn to focus that energy and control it for the purpose of manipulating the energy they gather from outside themselves. The energy they use in their conjurations comes from wherever they can draw it. It can come from the ether about them, from a speck of matter, or from another plane of existence altogether.

"Have you heard of the Nine Planes of Hell?"

Thistle and Jared both nodded, wide-eyed at Sart's dissertation. Neither of them had ever heard any of this. Magic had been something whispered about in their villages and protected against by hand gestures or devices sold by their Hags. Magic meant Wizards, dragons and other creatures of amazing aspect, and more: all fantasy, because if they truly existed, it never was a part of their wilderness lives. The Nine Planes were simply warnings of horrid other worlds offered by passing clerics to gain advocates, or else they were parts of epic tales sung by Bards.

Satisfied that the two were focused on what he was saying, Sart went on. "I do not understand this as well as a powerful mage would, like the White Wizardess, Meligance. My understanding, both religiously and practically, is that there are infinite planes or dimensions. Those realms that mages can readily tap – our own and the so-named Nine Planes, and others – are 'closest' in a sense to this plane of existence, and hence easier to draw energy from."

Sart reached down and picked up a piece of dirt from the ground. "Meligance assures me that the energy, or perhaps I should say, the potential energy, contained in this miniscule amount of earth, or any other piece of matter, is almost incomprehensible. Understood and manipulated in the right way, a powerful mage could destroy a city or move a mountain with it. Or perhaps, if one knew truly how to tap it and control it, one could build wonders and heal legions.

"The problem that arises," he said, "has more to do with the ability to control the power that one is capable of drawing to oneself. The more control a magic-user develops, the more energy she can draw to herself and use. Those who dabble in magic, especially those who are incautious or not well-trained, can injure or destroy themselves by drawing more energy than they can control. It is a fine balance, that is certain. It is not simply the ability to draw energy to them that makes a Wizard or Wizardess; it is their ability to control that energy."

He flicked the piece of dirt off his finger. "As a priest, the power I garner to me, which I choose to use primarily for healing, is most easily gleaned from life. Through my meditations and my connection with the earth, I can strengthen myself, renew myself. It is hard to describe, because it is in some ways quite individual. Let me think…" He stroked his chin and stared at the ground.

"When I stand with my feet in contact with the earth, I can feel the power

78

flow through me as I focus. It is calming as well as reinforcing. If I am at peace while I do, I feel renewed. Nay, more than renewed. I feel alive, imbued and empowered with all that life is." Sart's eyes sparkled.

"Though I have not in any way tried to connect with the energy that magic-users draw upon, my sense is that there is a difference. The energy of life, of living things is... well... I guess I would have to say, 'in motion,' in a different sense than the fundamental energy of all things. Meligance assures me that all energy is in motion at the deepest levels, but life-energy seems to have a more directed flow. It perhaps can be thought of as having direction to it that is determined by the essence of the life or being that it is." Sart paused and looked at the two of them.

"To answer one of your questions more directly, Jared... Yes, in small ways you can learn to tap the type of power I use. We all have inner energy; it is the essence of life at its most fundamental. Some religions refer to this as the soul. I prefer to think of it as our life-force, for that is how it feels coursing through me. The task of a priest, whatever the religion, is to learn to concentrate and focus to a greater and greater extent, so that he or she can be open to the flow of this energy from its source. For me, that source is the earth. Other religions draw life-power from the sun, moon, or plants, all of which are alive with life-energy. Some of these – for examples, the Crosses and Mythras – use symbology to focus their power. Their fundamental source, however, is much the same as mine – life-force. All religions focus power found in life, for it is all around us: from the tiniest animals too small to see without a special glass, to Gaia herself, the sun, the other planets, and the stars in the sky. There is a special pulse to all these that gives them their form, their essence, their direction to be."

Sart paused, trying to think of a way to illustrate what he had said. "Have you heard of auras? A type of light or effect that surrounds all living things?"

"A type of glowing?" Thistle asked.

"Yes, exactly. For example, if I pay attention, if I look for it, I can see it most easily around people. But trees, plants, and animals also possess their own unique auras. Yours is easy to distinguish, Thistle. It is predominantly golden, with hints of vibrant white light on the outside. And yours, Jared, is blue – a light, peaceful healing blue with highlights of white light as well."

"And yours is brownish, earthy with..." Thistle said.

"Blue overtones..." Jared added.

At that, Sart cocked his head and looked at the lad opposite him. He had expected that Thistle would be able to see auras easily. If she indeed had magic about her, it was common for those with power to see them. Jared showed no signs of having such a force within. Perhaps the stone had influenced his inner sight as well. "You can see my aura, Jared?"

"Certainly. And Thistle's as well; both are very strong. Cannot everyone see these?"

"Nay, few can, actually. It usually signifies a sensitivity to the life-force of others, the 'flow' I spoke of earlier. You have seen these before around people?"

"Well, only when I pay attention. As you suggested, one has to focus to see them. I used to watch my father and mother when I was little. Theirs were different, but when they were together and close, they seemed to blend. I found it fascinating. But I also believed everyone could see them. I guess I never thought it was anything special, just interesting. Later, as I grew older, I guess I lost interest in watching them. I haven't really considered it much since I was quite young."

"And you, Thistle?"

"The same as Jared, I suppose. I have always been aware of them. If I looked for them, I could see them easily. My sisters' auras were all different. I felt that was interesting. It was one way I could tell the twins apart."

"Well, that makes this discussion a bit easier. Can either of you discern auras about plants and animals?"

Thistle nodded, "Yes." She glanced toward Jared.

"Never looked." He scanned the area about them. "I don't know, perhaps faintly. They are not nearly as strong as a person's."

"No, that is true," Sart said. "The strength of the emanation varies with each being, with each life form. What you both see when you observe a person's aura is the flow of life-force about them. It acts not only throughout our bodies but creates a sense of who we are as well. It is an emanation we give off. How we feel, who we are with, what we are doing, and so forth can all affect the color and vibrancy of our aura."

"Is that why Aberon's aura was so murky?" Thistle asked.

"Darkish gray, with hints of purple and dark brown?" Jared looked at Thistle. She nodded in agreement. "I guess I do still notice them; I haven't mused on it for so long that I am not even conscious of the auras I notice. I should start paying attention."

"Do so, they can tell you much," Sart said. "And yes, dark beings often have dark auras, though that is not an absolute. Mood also affects a person's aura, as well as what is in their heart."

"Our ill-ease in his presence was confirmed by his aura, then" Jared said. "Had we paid attention to them, we might have avoided spending any time with him."

"Perhaps," Sart said, "but he would have likely attacked without attempting to garner information from you. You are beginning to understand – auras reflect our personal power – who we are fundamentally.

"So," Sart continued "think of this force, this life-force represented by the aura surrounding things, as what we clerics tap into. When I root myself in the earth, I connect with all the life that is the earth; and I draw a miniscule amount of that totality to bolster my inner force. As another example, druids connect with flora and fauna as primary sources, as well as with the earth. We healers each choose, or better said, generally have a proclivity toward, a specific source for renewing our power. For me, it was a natural thing to connect with the earth.

"Religions, as far as I have been able to understand, all started from this connection with life-force in one way or another. In some religions, much of that direct communing with a source has been lost over the years in favor of symbols, rites, and rituals that attempt to draw energy/power through conventions. Well... each to his own, I guess."

Sart stood and motioned toward their camp. "We need to move on. I will talk more of this while on the road. It is something you will both need to ken if we are to face this dread priest and his minions together. Let us pack and set off. I will set a fast pace, for we have lost time already. Aberon is wily, and he is planning something else; I can feel it in my bones. It would be best if we can press him. Mayhap, it will dissuade him from his plans or at least delay him. Jared, will you help Thistle onto Crunch? It would be best for her to ride this day."

80

A Task Ahead

Ge-or was back on the southern trail by dawn. He kept a steady pace, skirting the higher elevations and staying low enough in the hills that he hoped he would avoid wandering parties of gzks. The forest-bred cousins to goblins tended to stay in the evergreen groves further up the hills and on the edges of the mountains far to the south. He knew, however, from patrols he had taken with his father, that they would sometimes come further down to attack trappers or mining camps. Luckily, the beasts had dwindled in number with the Qa-ryk advance eastward into their range. Still, it paid to remain alert.

He was in good shape. Years of mountain toil and hard training by a master of arms had hardened his body. Whatever the cleric had done in his healing, it had served him well. He had no residual effects from the clout on the head. In fact, he felt good except for the darkness deep inside that he refused to face.

Something nagged at him for most of the morning, but he kept avoiding thinking about anything except his mission. Every time his emotions pushed up from within, he forced them back down. What he held onto was his anger; and with the anger came the image of the dragon, ever the dragon.

There was a moment when he came to a sudden halt at the crest of a hill. He took a sharp breath, fell to one knee, and struggled unsuccessfully to rise. It was Jared. His brother was... He couldn't accept the truth, so he did the only thing he could, he pushed the thought and the horrible emotions back down. Sart had said he had seen no other half-elven amongst the slain. He had not recognized his brother's remains amongst all he had gathered for the funeral ship either. He was unwilling to think of what might have happened to him elsewise.

His brother was likely dead, and now it didn't matter how. The dragon would pay, and somehow, sometime in the future, he would make the Qa-ryks pay, too. When his anger took control again, pushing down ever further the feelings he would not face, he stood and went on.

By midday, Ge-or had to make his first major decision. Continuing to the southeast would lead him through hardwood forest and former farmsteads further toward the mountains and eventually high enough to be in goblin country. It would be a more direct route to Aelfric, but the cave-dwelling vermin were as thick as ever. Ge-or, alone as he was, would not stand much of a chance against more than a score of the wiry creatures.

The route to the east and back south would delay him several days, but he would be able to stay out of the worst of the gzk and goblin ranges. If he were lucky, he would find old mining or trapping trails that led generally in the direction he wanted to go.

His third choice was to head east for ten days or more. Finally he would cross the King's Wall, a barricade that had been built centuries earlier that was now mostly overgrown and derelict. Once on the other side, he could take roads leading south. He would make better time if he could somehow acquire a steed.

Any of these three choices meant he would soon be in territory he had never traversed. He was already at the limit of his excursions with his father. They had more often gone further west and south, near and occasionally into the Dark Forest. He was a good tracker, though not as skilled as his brother. He had few qualms about continuing into the unknown, but he knew he would have to be even more cautious and alert once he was wandering through unfamiliar territory.

Finally, he turned east and decided to choose whether to continue in that direction or head back south once he had made it over the larger hills. After a few days, he would see better what his options were.

On the Trail of Darkness

For most of the morning, they pressed ahead with only minimal talk between them. Jared had taken the point, both to scout for any danger, and to choose the easiest routes through the hilly terrain. Sart stayed close to Thistle. Weak and tired from her ordeal, she fell into a fitful doze upon Crunch's back.

They were able to make good time. Sart had suggested they cut away from the Qa-ryk route, as the beasts tended to take old wagon roads that suited their bulk. These wider paths followed the terrain and were thus less direct. The priest was fairly confident about where Aberon and his minions were going, so he hoped to gain on the beasts by heading more directly southwest. He also knew that the larger paths might be watched by young Qa-ryks, who were fond of setting ambushes for unsuspecting travelers. Once Jared knew which way the cleric wanted to head, he was able to pick out well-worn and easily-travelled animal trails that wove in and out amongst the groves of hardwoods, occasional conifers, and the overgrown vales they traversed.

Thistle was still suffering from the residual effects of the fire, so Sart took her aside during one of their short breaks and laid his hands on her brow. Now that he had rejuvenated his inner power, he was able to ease all her discomfort. Though he could not give her back her strength, she was much more vibrant after that. The two enjoyed chatting as they continued ahead.

During the healing, Sart also used his power to gently search the girl for any sense of hidden force within. He did not want to probe too deeply without her permission, as he did not want to frighten her. Yet, he felt it was important to her own well-being that she eventually be made aware that she had such inner reserves. He did sense something – oddly, it was buried much more deeply than he would have expected. He wondered at that. At her age, if she was indeed a witch, it should already be coming forth. The girl was proving a perplexing problem. They would need to talk at some point about his concerns.

Thistle enjoyed Sart's company immensely. He was jovial, had a wealth of knowledge about their world, and more to the point, was more than willing to answer a young girl's plethora of questions. Nevertheless, he did not return to their discussion of the morn, preferring to wait until Jared was back with them.

By mid-day, they guessed they had gained at least an hour back on the heavy-legged beasts. After a short break, Sart urged Jared to press ahead. They were still well over a day behind; and though the large creatures were slow afoot, they had incredible endurance. He knew they would not rest until well into the evening.

When they came around a bend in the path, the cleric was surprised to see Jared half crouched at an opening in the trees overlooking a wide expanse of grassland that dipped down into a verdant vale. The half-elf gestured behind him with his right hand, indicating he wanted the two of them to stop. At the same time, his focus seemed to be slightly to his left toward a small, grassy knoll. Even as he watched, Jared was slipping his bow carefully off of his left shoulder.

Sart laid a hand on Thistle's shoulder. He could tell that Jared did not appear to be alarmed, only alert, so he wanted her to be reassured.

Unfortunately, Jared's gesture meant nothing to Crunch. Impatient at having been brought to a sudden halt, he made a "whuffing" noise, which sounded much like a krummhorn being blown. The sound did not startle Jared, but it did jump his prey. Some twelve paces out, near the base of the knoll, four birds flushed and winged away.

Witnessing the fastest move he had ever seen an archer make, Sart's mouth actually dropped open when Jared reacted to the birds flushing. Grouse were fast; Jared was faster. He pulled an arrow from his quiver, nocked it, drew back, and was drawing aim on the birds in the time it might have taken the cleric to blink, except he would have missed the motion altogether if he had.

What was even more odd to both Sart and Thistle was that Jared then paused. At full draw, he followed the birds for a long breath with the tip of the arrow moving synchronously with their flight away. It wasn't until the grouse were at what Sart would have considered a long shot for any short hunting bow that Jared released.

The shaft flew true and speared the last bird in the formation neatly behind its left wing. Passing through the grouse easily, it hit the next bird forward and a little to the right, also full in the body. As both fell to the ground, Jared was already running toward them.

Grinning broadly on his way back with the two brush grouse in hand, Jared announced, "Dinner!"

Sart tried to say something, yet all that came out was, "I... Did...? How...?"

Thistle jumped in, asking the question the cleric was trying to get out. "Did you actually try to hit both of those birds at the same time?"

Jared looked puzzled for an instant. His answer flabbergasted the cleric even more. He said matter-of-factly, "I didn't want to lose the arrow. If I had hit only one bird, the shaft would have carried on and likely been lost in the tall grasses. These are hard to make." He held up the bloodied shaft. "Well, at least good ones," he added. "Plus, we need two birds for an adequate dinner."

"That was incredible," Thistle said. "I've never seen anyone shoot like that. I..." Her voice trailed off.

"Oh," Jared said, flushing slightly, "I guess I forget sometimes that Ge-or and I were trained incessantly on all facets of weaponry, warfare, and... I... Well, I guess archery always came naturally to me."

84

He grinned again, adding, "We used to practice shooting doves like that, as well as lots of other creatures. When we were small, we went on mouse hunts with our bows." He laughed brightly, and Thistle heard a bit of the light tenor voice she had enjoyed so much the one eve she had spent in Thiele. "It seems silly now; on the other hand it was good practice."

As he continued to speak, Jared handed the birds to Thistle to tie over Crunch's neck. As he cleaned the arrow shaft and point with a handful of grass, he asked, "Should we move on?" replacing the shaft in his quiver.

Sart nodded. He did manage, "I am more than impressed, young Jared. I think I have misjudged you both. There is more to each of you than meets the eye..." He left the rest of the statement dangling, gesturing past Jared. "This vale, if I remember, heads west and south for a long pace. Let us walk together and return to our discussion of the morn. There is more to be said about the forces at play in our world."

"I guess I am confused about what you mean by life-force," Jared said, as they began to move down into the vale. "What I mean is... we certainly attribute life to all creatures – humans, humanoids, animals, even small things like insects and worms – but how is the earth alive, or the moon or sun for that matter? These are objects, orbs, though we do not truly ken what they are any more than the stars."

"Ah!" Sart said. "Problems the wise have contemplated for many, many a year. To answer your question, I must divert part of it, for that discussion itself could go on for some time. That is "what are the sun, moon, and earth?" There are many opinions. Mayhap they are each an orb in a vast universe that in some incomprehensible way relate to each other. The same question must be asked of the stars, comets, and other astronomical observations. The answer is 'We don't know.' Some day over a few pints of ale, we could have that long discussion." Sart's eyes twinkled.

"Let me speak of life instead. The key question I think we must ask is 'How do we define life?' Then we might be able to say what has the attributes we have set forth." Sart paused again, thinking about how to start.

"This is where things get a bit fuzzy, for truly we do not know what life is, or whence energy flows or how it concentrates. An early question might be whether life is sentient? Does a worm or other minute creatures perceive, feel, think? There are, according to the alchemists, even smaller creatures than those which we can see with our eyes. They move; they reproduce. What are these?

"You asked me 'does the earth have life.' My answer is a definite 'yes.' It teems with life of course, though we believe there is something more to it than that. Gaia lives and breathes in a sense. There is a flow to her. Whether it is the combined sentience of all the creatures living upon or within her, or an intelligence at the most fundamental roots of who she is, I cannot say. Truly, I have felt an incredible power from her when I meditate. I oft wonder if much of what happens with Gaia on a more global scale is her life-force readjusting – making changes to balance herself back to some form of equanimity. Hence, she creates storms, fires, lightning and thunder, earthquakes, and so forth. I do not know the truth of it, Jared, but I feel her flux. Perhaps that is what life really is – a flow of energy at a certain level above the root of all things, a flow that has direction or purpose beyond just being. Which is different from, for want of a better word – base energy – the energy that makes up all things, alive or not."

85

Sart stopped and wiped his brow, since they had now been trudging uphill for a while. As they crested a rise, they saw the vale stretching before them. "Perhaps, as Meligance has assured me, all energy is at its roots the same. As I tried to suggest before, except perhaps I did not say it very well, life-energy seems to have... well, I would have to say, 'a more active form'. As the White Wizardess has said, even a rock, or any inanimate object is, at its most fundamental energy level, highly active. The truth is we do not fully understand what life really is.

"Magic taps energy at that most fundamental level. Meligance connects with... ah... the ether – whatever everything is built of. I connect with life, or life-force. What I draw to me energizes my personal life-force, and that is what I use in my healings. The way I understand Meligance's use of energy is that, for the most part, she uses her life-energy to control that which she gathers from the base energy of all things.

"Some have the ability to gather life-energy more naturally than others. I am an example. I knew at a young age that I wanted to help others. I always felt power in me. I have spent many years developing this natural bent. Still, I have much to learn. The more I use my power, the more I learn about the world and life itself, and most importantly, the more I connect with life through the earth.

"Understand this: the power I have now can be used to heal or to harm. That is the choice of the wielder of the power. I attempt to use it for good; Aberon and the Black religion he follows, alas, use it more for ill.

"Every day I try to become more sensitive to the life teeming about me. My order believes that this force is not simply a life-force; it is a force of existence, a force that in some way, through some miracle, has come together to create life."

Sart smiled. "Also, understand that I do not 'throw' or 'cast' spells. From what Meligance tells me, that is not even true of magic-users. I do not know any spells. The words I say when I call upon the power of existence are merely a formality, a way to focus."

Sart took a deep breath before continuing. "To heal a burn, I must draw upon my inner force to alter the reality that exists. I use not only my own power, but through my connection with the person I am healing, I use his or her own ability and energy to heal. In a sense, I encourage their own life-force. I awaken the body's natural capacity to heal, and I give it a boost. Power is energy; and as you are well aware, energy can change many things and take many forms – just as fire is energy released from a piece of wood, a thing that was once alive.

"It is my guess, Jared, that this is how the pendant helped heal your wounds. It has been imbued with life-power or energy that is focused toward healing in some way. That is its 'magic.'

"Some religions use symbols, rites, altars, and sacrifices to concentrate power. We, of the earth, go to the source, Gaia herself; yet the use of symbols has also crept into our order.

"This rood I carry is a symbol of our religion." Sart pulled out the darkened bronze cross from under his tunic. He pulled it over his head and passed it to Thistle. "The symbology is simple, though it has become more of an icon in our religion than what it once represented. The cross signifies man, with his feet, the longest arm of the cross, the downward branch, touching the source of our power rooted in the earth. The side branches are his arms outstretched to embrace the world, the whole of creation. The top part of the cross represents a connection to the heavens, where we become one with the force of existence, the universe herself. The twisted icon sunk in the center of the rood is an oak root, which reminds us of the force of life rooted in the earth, the soil. The root is inset in the cross to represent death – a return of the life-force to the force of existence.

"You may note that it is not unlike the symbology of the Crosses. This is not an accident. It has been handed down that we were once a unified church. One broke from the other a long time ago, and such records have long been lost. Many of the religions of this world have symbols and rites that are similar and seem to have grown from much that went before.

"Never underestimate the power of symbols, my children. They can become a source of a great concentration of energy. Even I cannot avoid the feeling of power that courses through me when I touch this small device or hold it before me as I meditate. Unfortunately, to some, symbols become more important than what they represent. People begin to worship the trappings of religion – the figures and symbols – and fail to remember the source, the Godhead, the energy, the all." Sart had a wry smile on his face. "Sorry, I get carried away when I talk of power and religion."

"Nay, it is interesting," Jared said. "I know little of this. In Thiele, some prayed to various gods for help and healing; otherwise, we had no healer than the hag. My father did not have any particular beliefs, yet he often swore to or at the gods." He grinned.

Thistle was glad to see Jared's mood had changed. "In Permis," she said, "we did have an acolyte from the Crosses visit one summer. He tried to teach prayers and rituals to those who would listen; for the most part it didn't take. Western folk simply take life as it comes. They offer thanks to this god or that, the old gods more often than not, or pray for rain, a mild winter, and the like. It is more of an accepted part of life than a fundamental belief."

She smiled at Sart; then she asked a question that she had long pondered growing up. "I have always wondered if prayer was of any use. I think we naturally ask for things when we wish them to be different, but are there truly gods who listen?"

"Ah, an excellent question, child. Which I think would be answered differently by virtually any cleric. I will give you my perspective, as briefly as possible; as in a short while our vale will end, and Jared will need to scout ahead once again.

"I believe," Sart said, his eyes alive with energy, "that in its purest form, praying is the concentration of power. However, I prefer the concept of meditation over prayer.

"Prayer in the form of kneeling, bowing, abasing oneself to a deity has no interest to me or most in my religion. Though we believe in a God or Godhead, or perhaps better put, a power greater than we are – something or some being who unifies all – we do not worship anything or anyone. The universe is here for us to appreciate, to use, not to fawn to. I speak, or you might say 'pray' to the Earth Mother, to Gaia; I draw power from the earth to add in my healings; but I do not abase myself to symbols of any religion.

"What you have asked, Thistle," Sart continued, "speaks to the question of, 'Does praying make a difference?' That is hard to say. To answer this, I must first tell you that we all do it, even I pray in a sense. It is a natural thing when we do not have answers to our problems. Do I believe in it? I would have to answer you truthfully – I don't know.

"I do know this: I have seen prayers answered. I have had my own prayers answered. Was this a God answering me, or was it something I created out of need and from my own focus in making the request? Did I place energy into this thought? This need? Or did power come to me from without because I asked for it? Or was it happenstance?

"Truly, it doesn't hurt anyone to make requests to a god or gods, to pray. Maybe it does help. Maybe it moves the ether in some way if we put enough energy into it, and perhaps that can make a difference. I pray all the time because it makes me feel better. It is a means for me to put my concerns and ideas into words. Do I pray to a deity? Nay, not really; nonetheless I do focus on our earth, on Gaia, for that is my source of rejuvenation. When I truly pray, when I meditate, I am bringing all my focus to bear on the life-force of the universe. I draw upon that for renewal."

Sart stopped and stared intently at Thistle and Jared. He no longer looked like a tired, middle-aged man. He was younger looking now, vibrant, and full of intense energy.

Thistle was captivated by the cleric's strong feelings, except now she wanted him to go in a new direction. "Could you tell us more about magical power? This is also beyond my ken."

Jared nodded in agreement, anxious to understand all he could before they would face the evil priest again.

"I will," Sart answered, "but let us wait until later or perhaps on the morrow. Come. We will continue well into the evening, and for now it is best that we concentrate on our travels. Aberon will not delay his purpose."

Some time later, after a meal of the brace of grouse, braised with juniper berries and herbs until the meat was falling from the bones, accompanied by scavenged root vegetables and apples from long abandoned orchards, they settled in a deep thicket for the night.

The Power of Magic

The next morn, Sart had them up before the sun rose. Rain was on the northerly breeze. He wanted to be off, deeper into the forest before it came.

After a cold breakfast of leftovers and partially stale trail bread, they were on their way.

Several hours later, they were settled onto an old cart path, making good time to the south and west. It wended its way deeper into the woods so that a canopy of trees, still with enough leaves on, provided them some relief from the continuous drizzle. It was then that the cleric drew Jared back from his forward scouting position to continue their discussion of magic.

Sart immediately directed the conversation toward his predominant concern: "Thistle, if you have magical ability, you must learn to use it. I am far from certain, yet I sense there is a concentrated power within you that you have somehow managed to suppress to this point. I cannot imagine that Meligance would have anything to do with you elsewise. This type of ability cannot be long ignored, especially if you are truly gifted. Else it can destroy you."

Both Thistle and Jared felt uncomfortable with how directly Sart started the morning's discussion; neither knew what to do except to hear him out. Something was definitely at work that neither of them understood.

"As I tried to explain before, other clerics and I use our personal power. We enhance that through meditation and concentration to heal. It is a limited form of power because it is only as strong as we are ourselves. However! and this is important -- it is controllable because it all comes from the user. THAT, my young friends, is the biggest difference between the power I use and the power of magic.

"Mages can also use their own personal power to create and do "magic," but the best magic-users use it primarily to manipulate their conjurations. The energy they wield is taken from the ether; thus, tremendous forces can be drawn upon. Unfortunately, there is far less control because of this. True magic, in this sense, is extremely dangerous. Only the most gifted and most practiced ever learn to control it well. The danger is that those less skilled draw more energy to them than they can control, and many a magic-user has died because they could not understand this."

Sart gestured expansively. "The further afield a magic-user garners power from without, the more suspect it is. What a mage does through various incantations, symbols, complex conjugations, and the like is to find ways of focusing and drawing power to them. I was surprised to learn from Meligance that tapping into other worlds for power is often easier than gathering power from our own plane of existence. I do not ken why this might be; still, she assures me it is so. These other worlds have their own forces of existence. When a person connects with another plane, she can readily draw from that plane's power. Once a mage learns the way to such power, the power that can be drawn is almost unfathomable.

"One reason for this is that something natural in another world can be a horror in this one. Hence 'the flames of hell,' which are the natural order of things on another plane of existence, become devastating when brought into this world. A demon from another plane of existence may simply be a common creature there, like as a rabbit or mule would be in this world. When it is brought into this plane, it can wreak havoc because it doesn't belong.

"The best magic-users, like Meligance, try to focus only the power of this world, as it doesn't disturb the balance on this or any other plane. Some magic-users take the easier route."

Sart wiped his brow, not comfortable talking about a force he did not ken completely. "Magical power that is drawn from other universes or dimensions can never be wholly good, whatever the intentions of the wielder. Thus used, such energy disturbs the balance of power within both worlds. Some of these other worlds or planes of existence have been named: Purgatory, Hell, perhaps even Heaven, the Nine Lower Planes, and so on.

"If you have this type of power within you, Thistle, the power and talent to manipulate the energy of the ether, you must learn about it as soon as may be. I think, should we complete this quest expeditiously, that you will need to come with me to Borea to meet with Meligance. There is some connection there. For your own sake, you should understand it."

Thistle nodded, though her thoughts were still on the uses and power of magic; and truthfully, she did not fully comprehend what Sart was suggesting. "Is all magic evil, then?" she asked.

"No, my child, it is neither evil, nor good. Evil comes from its use. And, if you want to get down to the roots of all things, it is often about how we perceive the use of it. What may be evil to one person may be the greatest good to another. If I wield a magic that destroys my most feared enemy, a horrid mage for example, that might be considered good to me and my followers, and perhaps even to a majority of those people this person enslaves. Yet, the mage and his close minions will not feel the same. Evil or great harm may come from a magic-user making contact with other forces before she has achieved proper control. This can happen when the force she has tapped escapes her. Remember 'evil' and 'good' are always relative to one's perceptions. Always keep that in mind, both of you." Sart glanced toward Jared.

"That being said, when a person or group seeks to hurt, overcome, or dominate another, that seems to be what we might call true evil. Such are these Black Druids and their minions, the Qa-ryks. The ultimate answer to the question of good versus evil is a matter of choice."

"Why would one choose to use magic at all, if it cannot be completely controlled?" Thistle asked.

"It is a matter of power, my child. I have been sensitive to the things of the earth from when I was a child. It was natural for me to want to tap this power and to focus it.

"Meligance, the powerful Wizardess of Borea, from whom you appear to have received a sending, has an innate ability to sense and touch great power not only within herself, but from other sources. She and I have little choice as to the power within; thus, we need to learn to control it. She has spent her life learning to use that power wisely and with great control. She is immensely powerful. What makes her stand out above so many others is that she understands the nature of the forces she taps. She wields only what she believes she can control."

Sart caught Thistle's eye, so she was sure to pay attention to what he said next. "You, my child, may also have this same innate ability. Else your ovietti would never have found you, and Meligance would not have been able to even attempt a potent sending. If you did not have such a potential within, how was it that you were able to create a powerful energy sphere? Or perhaps better put, use the energy concentrated by... well, Meligance and your Yolk? For it is not the words that make the spell, they only focus the mage. The power could only have come from you, and likely was enhanced by your little friend."

As Sart finished this thought, almost on cue, Yolk eased out from under the front of Thistle's cloak and folded into her hands. His large unblinking yellow eyes stared up at her. "He seems to know what we are talking about," she laughed, as she cradled him to her chest. "You suggested Yolk was magical. How does he use magic?"

Sart laughed, too. "I know not, child. There are many tales of magical creatures from the past, most long gone from our world: unicorns, pegasi, sprites, and yes, even dragons. If what I have heard is true, the ovietti can intensify the innate power of an adept. Meligance could wax more eloquently on the subject, but not I. The little fellow does appear to ken much though."

"He certainly understands my moods," Thistle said. "He will change position when I am sad or irritated. Almost as if he wants to comfort me. If I am really angry, he may slide off my stomach and go to a chair and stare at me." Thistle laughed again. "Eventually, I just can't stay upset. Those yellow eyes keep following me around, and I realize I'm being foolish."

"He can sense danger, and evil, too," Jared added. "Thistle is right. Those eyes can be both a comfort and a bit unnerving. Does he ever blink?"

Just as Jared said that, Yolk rolled his right eyelid shut and back open.

"Oh, ho!" said Sart. "He is a comedian as well. Perhaps we had best watch what we say. He does ken much more than even I would have believed. I, for one, am glad he found you, Thistle. For some reason, it makes me feel comforted to know he is watching over you."

"He has become my friend," Thistle said; and at that, Yolk rolled both his eyes closed and eased up from her hands to cradle her lower chest.

For a little while they rode on in silence, content to ponder what Sart had told them while staying bundled against the slow dripping of moisture from the trees.

Thistle's thoughts were flying in every direction. One floated in her consciousness more than the others – that she did not recognize any power within herself, magical or otherwise. She had never noticed anything of the sort. Yolk was a comfort to her; now she was even confused about him.

Jared noticed Thistle's frown of concentration. He wondered what there was about her that had changed, for in that moment he sensed there was something that was different – a confidence, a challenge in her gaze, a self-control that hadn't been apparent before, he wasn't sure. Or maybe he had changed from his contact with all the forces that had played about them the past days. Perhaps he was simply viewing her and their places in this world differently. He wanted to ask her how she felt, what she was thinking, but he resisted. Somehow, he also sensed that there were more powers at play here than the cleric's.

Thistle, breaking the mood, began to ask Sart another question. Sart raised his hand. "It is time we press ahead and focus on our current task. I doubt whether Aberon will suspect you are with me, as he expects you are both dead. He will surely anticipate my return to his trail and will make all haste to begin the next phase of his plan. That is what concerns me the most. Once he and the beasts return to their enclave, he will believe he can safely relax. We must try to reach him before he gets there, or the pendant will be lost.

Sart adjured them, "Think on what I have said, both of you, because you are now involved in something far beyond what you could have imagined a little while ago. You will have important choices to make in the coming days. Choose as wisely as you may, for all our lives may depend on it."

Thistle and Jared knew Sart was right. For most of the day, they whispered back and forth, trying to understand all that was at play in this strange adventure -- good and evil, power, energy, and magic, and their place in it. They did not come up with many answers; however, they felt better for having talked through their misgivings.

For his part, Sart was thoroughly enjoying the two youngsters. He had been on the road many long months with naught except Crunch to converse with much of that time. He watched their interactions, listened to their banter, and drank in their youthful levity. It was a tonic to him after so much duress.

Occasionally, he would rejoin their chatter. He did not want to frighten either of them further. He was afraid he might inadvertently wake what was hidden deep within Thistle's being and thus open the floodgates. If that happened, the girl would have a more serious concern.

For much of the day, the three of them shared some of life together – the mundane, the normal, the simple beauty of what was about them.

Heading along the edge of the wooded hills, they followed the broad trail of the Qa-ryks further to the south with occasional short jaunts west. The going was easy, though it soon got colder as they gained altitude and the wind picked up. Sart gave Thistle and Jared additional heavy wool cloaks from his large saddle bags to help ward off the chilling breeze. The two were grateful that the cleric was well provisioned and generous with all he had.

They traveled on into the early evening, pausing only occasionally for a quick bite of cold dried food from Sart's ample supply and the rest of the venison. They paused twice to let Thistle walk for a half hour by Crunch's side. Sart led the way now, studying the ground carefully every so often. After, he would hurry forward with his steady, strong gait. By nightfall they had covered an estimated four more leagues. After an uneventful but watchful night, they pressed ahead the until the next morn.

Priest of Darkness

Aberon, with the coveted stone finally in hand, quickly caught up with the Qa-ryk company and their new chieftain. The beasts were still in a boisterous mood from the celebrations following the battle, and also from having chosen a new leader, Ka-ragh, son of Rauggh.

As was their wont, they had enjoyed the previous few evenings toying with the three prisoners they had taken at Thiele. The beasts had tortured the two men and woman for two long nights of contests vying to see which clan could inflict the most painful wounds without having their victim fall unconscious or die. The woman had lasted the longest. Aberon was sorry he had missed the final night's festivities. The beasts were quite skilled at inflicting pain. He licked his lips as he considered what he had missed. Ah well, there would be many other times if things went as planned, and not too far in the future.

With a new day dawning and another assault to plan, Aberon had Ka-ragh wake them at the first sign of light. Qa-ryks didn't make good time on their heavy legs, but they had extraordinary endurance. Now that their fun was over, Aberon would drive them west day and night, until they met up with his fellow priest and the additional clans he was to have gathered together.

They had time; still, Aberon did not want to waste any. The sooner the stone was sealed away forever, the better for his brethren's plans of conquest, and the better for him and his ambitions. His only real worries were centered around convincing the massed clans to follow his chosen chieftain for the assault on the outpost – Ka-ragh was new and untested as a leader. They would be reluctant to release the honor of battle leadership to him. It was necessary for the attack to be focused and massive. If there were any infighting amongst the clans, it would fail. Now that he had his own "boy" in place, he would have to find a way to get them to accept his dominion, at least for a brief time. Unfortunately, their clannish nature and extreme reliance on prowess as the definitive measure of leadership were major obstacles in encouraging these beasts to cooperate. They were, unfortunately, the only tool at hand. The gzks and goblins, no matter how many there were, would never have the force to bring the kingdom to its knees. Kan had certainly known this. His creation of these brutes must have been undertaken because he felt threatened by the east.

Aberon's most immediate task was using his guile and magic to ensure that the beasts remained focused on the task at hand, so that they did not break into factions until the fighting was done. After that, they could do what they wished. His focus would be elsewhere. Perhaps he could play the clan leaders against each other and find ways to give each a position of honor in the attack.

Another minor concern had also crept back over the past two days. It seemed that pestering cleric was back on his trail. Maybe this was the time to deal with that petty annoyance once and for all. It had been entertaining for a while to have the fellow chasing him about the countryside. Once he had enlisted the red dragon's aid, it had been time to forget such amusements so he could press ahead with his plans.

He was surprised that the old Earth-bird had been able to get back so quickly from their western trek. He was nothing if not persistent; Aberon had to give him that. Well, if his luck held, maybe he could pluck two thorns from his side at the same time. Once they were close, Sart was bound to hole up at the outpost for a day or two. That would be when his army would strike.

***

The Qa-ryks made good time. By dusk a week later, the extended clans, those he had brought from battle and his fellow priest's new recruits, stood on opposite ends of the wide, rock-strewn vale that Aberon had chosen as a gathering place. He could see his counterpart standing to the fore of the massed army. From this distance, Aberon was not certain how much control Druid Vaspa had over the beasts. One thing was obvious, his compatriot had managed to bring a couple hundred or more to the meet, which, considering their natures, was no small feat.

Aberon's beasts roared at the sight of their brethren across the way, and they immediately began thumping their chests and dancing. That is, if you could call a heavy stomping of the earth a dance. It was what he had expected. They were bragging of their conquests in the recent battle. They would keep this up for an hour or more to make sure their comrades understood how brave and fierce they had been.

The Qa-ryks across the way joined in the stomping and thumping. Partially to acknowledge the others' victory and partially to work themselves up to a battle frenzy, showing their fellows that they were brave and ferocious, also. It was, of course, too soon to let them get really worked up; an hour of chest thumping and roaring would be good for morale, and it would also give the two extended clans one more reason to get along for a while.

Aberon sat on the back of his mule patiently waiting while the beasts got good and excited. When he calculated it had reached the right pitch, he gestured to Ka-ragh to continue with the plan.

The great brute charged out in front of his company as he had been instructed. He roared a challenge, stomping heavily with his feet and thumping his chest fiercely. His fellows roared at his back, thumping their chests now in rhythm with their chieftain. The beasts on the other side quieted at this new development. But when Ka-ragh roared again and lumbered into a charge toward the other side, they roared as one and pushed forward, too.

Soon there were two great masses of the beasts charging down the slopes on either side toward the center of the vale. They were roaring loudly and shaking their arms and weapons in the air as they came. They met with a tremendous crash, chest smashing into opposing chest. Another great roar shook the clearing. Then, as if on cue, the Qa-ryks broke into small groups and began to boast of their exploits to each other.

Aberon smiled, so far so good. Tomorrow he would see if there were any fires he needed to put out. For now, he would ride across and share the news with his cohort. There was much to tell and more plans to make.

A Chance Meeting

Finding clear paths over the hills, Ge-or made good time. For three days he kept moving, loping steadily eastward. He relied on nuts, wild fall fruits, and what he had brought with him for sustenance. Several hours before dusk on the third day, he topped a rise, looking over a small pine-crested vale below. As he stood watching for any signs of humanity, he saw a large doe, followed by two young deer wander across a hundred paces below. As he watched them move behind a copse of trees, he slowly reached over and slid his bow off of his shoulder. Easing one arrow from the quiver, he grabbed both in his left hand; then he took a diagonal line through the trees to cut the deer off.

He moved silently, slightly crouched, across the pine needle-carpeted forest floor. Gliding from tree to tree, he watched carefully for any movement ahead. When he figured he was within twenty paces or so of the path the deer had taken, he knelt and set the arrow to the string. He drew the wound gut partially back, testing the tensile weight of the string. Satisfied, he settled in to wait.

The deer had been ambling slowly. It was a couple of minutes before he saw the tip of the doe's snout as she came in from his left through the trees. He had picked a good spot. If she continued ahead, she would walk past him broadside about fifteen or sixteen paces from where he waited.

The two spring fawns, now almost adult size and grown out of their red-brown coats and white spots, followed their mother. Ge-or decided to take one of them instead of the larger doe. She was a good size, at least three or four years by her mass, and he would not be able to carry even half the meat from her carcass. He waited until she passed in front of him. The first of the deer was passing a small pine tree when he drew back. If it followed its dam, it would walk into his shooting lane in two or three more steps. Pulling back in one smooth motion, Ge-or raised the bow, brought the shaft to eye level, and took aim. The small deer paused briefly behind the tree sniffing the air; then it skipped after its mother.

Just as its front near leg went forward, Ge-or loosed the arrow. It hit solidly with a loud thwack behind the deer's shoulder and penetrated through both lungs. The young deer jumped straight up, twisting slightly back as it came down. It fell to the earth, rose, and turned further back. It took three more shaky steps before collapsing in a heap. The other two deer had fled at the sound of the arrow's impact.

Ge-or trotted quickly over to the downed deer. Removing his sturdy hunting blade from its sheath on his belt, he set his pack to the side. He scanned the area to be sure there was no person or creature that might surprise him while he worked. Satisfied that he was alone, he knelt and placed his hand on the deer's neck, offering a quick thank you to the deer and the gods. This, too, his father had taught him, though neither of his parents followed any particular religion. It was more of a general thank you to the animal for the providing.

After the brief gesture, Ge-or got down to dealing with what must be done. He slit the deer's throat to further bleed her out, quickly gutting her. He reserved the liver and heart, as he expertly removed the entrails. Next, he flipped the carcass over so the deer could drain even more. Finally, he cleaned his hands and knife with pine needles.

While he waited for the chest and gut cavity to drain further, he cut a small length of rope from the coil in his backpack, swung the bag back over his shoulders so he would be ready to move on, and resheathed his blade. He stooped over the deer once again, turning it back over. Wiping the insides with handfuls of fresh pine needles to clear the cavity as much as possible, he made short work of getting her ready to haul. He tied the deer's four legs together so that they overlapped slightly at the hooves. Placing the liver and heart in the body cavity, Ge-or lifted the deer up by the legs and spun it around his back and hooked them over his head, onto his lower neck. He could bear the dead weight for a while. He hoped the vale below would prove a good place to spend the night. Angling back toward the path as it wound further down the hill, Ge-or looked forward to fresh meat for his evening meal.

Once he had regained the path, Ge-or ambled down the gentle slope. Scanning the ground ahead, he was able to find several drooping herb plants that were already giving in to the cool dry conditions of the early fall. Ge-or picked handfuls of wild sage, chervil, and creeping thyme. Coupling those with the bag of sea salt he had managed to find in a broken cupboard in the destroyed village, he would have a good repast of roasted venison strips.

As he came around the last bend before a broader opening, Ge-or saw that the small valley would likely provide an excellent camping place. A pond, fed by a rivulet coming in from the southwest, looked inviting for both drinking water and a much-needed washing. There was enough of a clearing leading up to the northern edge of the pond, that Ge-or could camp alongside using the pond as one defensive wall. The shelter of a large boulder sticking partially into the water would serve as another. He could place his fire in front and feel relatively safe.

Dropping the deer, most of his weapons, and his backpack near the boulder, Ge-or grabbed his water bag and a large bar of coarse soap and headed fully dressed into the middle of the pond where he stood waist deep. First, he filled the water bag, tossing it on the bank when it was full. Then he washed – first his tunic, followed by his pants, underdrawers, and socks, tossing each onto the boulder as he was done with them. Completely bare except for a knife still strapped to his thigh, he began working the hard, sandy soap all over his body and through his hair. He rinsed by dunking himself every few minutes while rocking back and forth in the pool.

The last time he surfaced from his ablutions, he was astonished to see a moderately-sized, lanky creature kneeling next to his backpack. The fellow had Ge-or's sword in his hands, with the point nestled in the dirt between his legs. To Ge-or, who had only seen a few in his day, he looked every bit the better part of a gzk. Ge-or, had never heard of them traveling alone, and this one did not look aggressive at all. Well, not if you discounted the two-inch fangs that were part of its grey-green visage.

Walking slowly forward through the water toward the edge of the pond, Ge-or slipped the throwing knife into his right hand, passing the soap to his left. He immediately realized it probably hadn't been the wisest maneuver, as the wet soap made his grip slippery, but there was naught for it now. The man-creature on the bank hadn't moved; he just stared at Ge-or as he slowly came up out of the water.

Thinking better of his action, Ge-or decided to take the judicious approach. Just before stepping out above his waist level, he returned the knife to its sheath. He swished his hand in the water to try to clear it of soap residue. As he stepped up the embankment out of the water, he said, "Hail, and well met, friend."

The swarthy-looking fellow stood up, dropping the sword to the backpack. He raised his hand palm outward and grunted in response, "Hail." His voice was rough and guttural.

"Do you mind if I dress?" Ge-or gestured toward the pile of clothes. He figured modesty might be more appropriate; the clothes would dry soon enough by the fire.

The gzk, or whatever he was, gestured with his left hand, as if to say, "Please yourself." He did say, "I will start fire." Or at least that is what Ge-or thought he said.

As the other fellow was gathering wood from a grove of hardwoods further up the trail, Ge-or put on his change of clothes. When he was done, he began to work on the deer carcass. He punched a hole through its skin above the rear tendon of one of the legs and inserted a loop of the rope. After that, he towed the deer to a tree, where he tied it to a low hanging branch so he could work on it. First, he skinned the deer, starting by loosening the hide from its haunches, then scrapping and peeling it all the way down to its neck. Slicing it off there, he laid the pelt, hair-side down, on the pine needles. Next, he cut the untied haunch through the large thigh joint, removing it from the body. He tied that in a similar manner to another branch. Finally, he began dismembering the rest of the carcass.

Ge-or first addressed the best cuts from the deer. The back strap he loosened from the bone. Easing his blade under the gristle, he slid it carefully down removing it in one long strip so that he ended up with a long solid piece of the best meat. This he laid carefully on top of the skin. He did the same to the other backstrap. Instead of removing the two lower limbs, he cut long strips of meat from them until they were cleaned of any readily usable pieces. Carving whatever pieces he could glean from the rest of the carcass he left the second thigh hanging to be stripped later.

By the time he was done, the stranger had a nice fire roaring and he had also gathered enough reserve wood for the night. Ge-or rinsed his hands and knife in the stream. He stepped up to the fellow, extending his arm. "Well met. I'm Ge-or, recently from Thiele."

The odd-looking fellow grunted. He reached out and the two clasped arms. "Stradryk au Ruum, lately of parts south."

Ge-or gestured toward the pile of meat on the skin. "You are welcome to whatever you wish. Help yourself to the liver and heart if you like those. I prefer other cuts myself."

Stradryk raised his thick eyebrows, staring at Ge-or. Though Ge-or had spoken the truth, it was even so an honor to be offered what many would consider the finest parts of the deer. When he saw that Ge-or meant what he had offered, he went over and lifted the liver from the skin. He went to the opposite side of the fire where he had placed a small boulder to sit on. Half-sitting, half-kneeling, he began to chew the raw meat.

Shrugging to himself, Ge-or went over and retrieved one of the backstraps. Rather than cut it crosswise into steaks, he decided to slice it lengthwise into thin strips, using a flat section of the large boulder as a surface. Once he had a nice pile of the strips, he took some of the herbs, rolled them in his hands, and sprinkled them over the meat; adding at the end a small handful of salt. Thinking too late that he should have offered this precious commodity to the gzk, Ge-or held the bag out toward him. The fellow shook his head; he was already half through the liver. He continued to chew on the raw, bloody piece in his hand.

Ge-or looked about the clearing and found a nearby birch tree. He took off several small branches, quickly stripped them, and threaded the meat along their length. He went over to the fire and sat opposite the gzk holding the branches over the hot coals. The meat cooked rapidly; soon Ge-or had joined the other in stuffing his

97

mouth. After his first two skewers-full, partially satisfied, he pulled out his other meager edibles – some dried fruit, old bread, and walnuts he had gathered earlier in the day. He gestured for Stradryk to help himself, while he started cooking two more skewers of the backstrap strips.

The gzk stood when he was done with the liver and next retrieved the heart. This he sliced in half, before stabbing the two halves with a long, sharpened birch stake he cut from the same tree as Ge-or. He held them in the center of the fire to sizzle.

They didn't talk. Ge-or's father had taught him that conversation during dinner while on a trek was impolite, unless it had been agreed upon ahead of time that things needed to be discussed. He decided he would wait for the other fellow to set the stage.

After having downed the two heart halves and another long strip of leg meat, Stradryk burped loudly, pushed his legs out in front of him, and leaned back, looking across the fire at Ge-or. He nibbled on a dried apple half. "I am half-gzk. You have not seen one like me before?"

Ge-or shook his head.

"My mother was human, raped by gzks. I was left on a doorstep in the wilds." He pointed to the south and west. "Miraculously, a steader family took me in. I left when I grew older. I travel alone."

Ge-or said, "I am sorry; I didn't know. I have never met your kind. I am a half-breed, too – human and elven."

"A better mix, hah!" Stradryk smiled broadly, his yellow fangs looking even more pronounced as he laughed. "Where are you headed?"

"Aelfric. You?"

"West, far west, to trap for the winter."

"Well met, then. Can you tell me the best route to Aelfric from here?"

Stradryk nodded. "Why do you go there? Nasty place in the winter, wet and cold... and evil."

"I am on a quest, and I need to provision – arms, a horse, armor, whatever I can find." Ge-or hesitated about telling Stradryk more. Yet, the fellow seemed straightforward enough, and he needed all the advice he could get if the half-gzk was familiar with the border town. "I seek to avenge my village. It was destroyed a few days ago by a company of Qa-ryks."

"Qa-ryks? Bad beasts, best to stay away, especially in their country. That is why I head far to the north and west."

"I am not after the Qa-ryks. It... it was a dragon that led the attack."

"Red? Old beast?"

"Yes." Ge-or was more than surprised; he had feared no one would believe his tale. "You have seen him?"

"Aye, he sometimes feeds south of where I trap. Good country, lots of beavers, muskrat, and mink. He will fly off the western mountains down into the valley twice or three times each winter to ease his hunger. I stay still; he leaves me alone." Stradryk stopped, staring intently across the flames at Ge-or. "Dragons be dangerous, and he is an old, wise one."

"It is a matter of honor," Ge-or said grimly.

"I ken," Stradryk said.

In the morning, they cooked more of the deer for breakfast. Stradryk helped

Ge-or dry the rest over the fire as they got ready to move on. They didn't speak, just went about their morning business. When all was done and they had each wrapped and packaged half the remaining deer, they clasped arms again in farewell. Stradryk pointed to the east. "Go east for five more days and you will come to the top of the last big hill before the Great Greensward. If you turn south there, you will pick up a trail that moves along the ridge for many leagues. After five days, it will dip down into the lower hills and join an old wagon road. It is in poor shape, broken and disused, yet it is still the fastest way south. Follow that for two more weeks and you will come to the old road west from Aelfric. Take that east for a few days or so."

"Thank you, Stradryk. Good chance out there." Ge-or gestured to the west.

"Ge-or?"

"Yes?"

"Go to the Druid's Hut. It is on the western edge of town. It is inexpensive, but decent. Less chance of danger. You can meet people there, people who know much." He paused, adding as an after-thought, "If you need money, look to the wine merchants. They are always in the need of good swords for protection as they head south and back all winter."

"I thank you, friend." Ge-or bowed toward Stradryk.

"Back to Back."

"Aye, Back to Back," Ge-or returned. "Stay safe."

They both turned to leave and made their separate ways out of the glen. Just as Ge-or was climbing into the tree-line, Stradryk shouted back to him, "I will return to Aelfric in the spring. If you are at the Druid's Hut, I will find you. Maybe we can find some business together."

Ge-or waved as the half-gzk disappeared over the hill.

Capture

It was nearing high noon, four days after they had met up with Sart. Jared was helping Thistle up on Crunch's back following a short break when he sensed something was wrong. Beginning to draw his bow from his shoulder, he looked toward where the cleric was standing.

Suddenly, he was grabbed from behind. Struggling fiercely, Jared spun out of his assailant's grasp just as Thistle screamed. Jared looked up to see her hauled off the mule's back and thrown to the ground. Coarse, rough men were all around them. As he lunged forward to help Thistle, Jared was struck on his head from behind. He managed to yell, "Sart!" before he collapsed to the dirt of the trail.

The first thing Jared became aware of was a steady throbbing in his head and a nauseating roll in his stomach. Sometime later, with neither sensation having dissipated, he tried to move so he could ease the heaving in his stomach. He discovered that he couldn't even shift his position, and the effort increased the throbbing in his head. A particularly nasty jolt to his gut caused his eyelids to flutter open. He shut them against the sickening spinning of the world about him. He blacked out again.

Jared awoke much later to Thistle's insistent whisper, "Jared...? Jared...? Wake up! Are you all right?" His head still throbbed painfully. Thankfully, the rolling sensation had stopped; but he still couldn't move about.

Cautiously opening his eyes, he croaked out, "What?"

It took him several seconds to realize where he was, during which time Thistle kept talking. "Oh, Jared, I'm so glad you're all right. Are you all right? We've been captured by a band of cut-throats and thieves." Her voice took on a nasty tone at the mention of the latter. "I don't know where they are taking us. They tied us to the backs of mules, and we have ridden all day like this. I can't move. I can't move at all. My wrists are numb. I don't even know what they have done with Sart. I..."

"Thistle!" Jared hissed. He managed to twist his head up toward her from his awkward position on the more-than-ample nether end of a large mule. "Quit jabbering! My head... How long have I been out?"

Thistle glared at him. Like Jared, she was lying stomach-down on the back of Crunch. Their hands were tied tightly behind their backs, and their legs were also trussed. "Jared! Someday I'm going to teach you some manners. I don't..."

Jared tried to twist around for a better look, but the effort caused him to grimace in pain. Dropping his head back down near the mule's flank, he tried to force away the dizziness and pain. Frustrated, he snapped back at Thistle, "Damn it, Thistle, I'm not in the mood."

"Hey, you shut up, or I'll give you another." A burly, heavily muscled, and quite hairy arm carrying a large dark club appeared in Jared's limited line of sight.

Thistle challenged the man, releasing some of her frustration and anger at him instead of Jared. "Don't you dare. I'll... I... We'll get you for this. The least you dirty beasts could do is let us sit up. We're not going to bite tied up. I think..."

"Shut up!" The rough voice growled. The club swung up menacingly. Thistle quieted.

The man moved away from them. Several minutes passed when they heard the same voice shout, "Move out." A minute later their two mules moved, jarringly following the rest of the long train of men and animals.

Jared lost track of the time. After a while, he fell into a much-interrupted doze. When he did wake, Thistle lay sullen and silent on Crunch beside him.

It was after dark when he was finally pulled off the mule by two of the robbers and slung indifferently to the ground under a sweet-smelling fir. Shortly thereafter, Thistle was unceremoniously tossed beside him. They both struggled, levering against each other, into a sitting position. The man who had spoken to them before came up carrying something in one hand and a long knife in the other. He was immense, roughly clothed, and smelled of smoke, grease, and dirt. His movements and manner were coarse as he knelt down beside Jared. He set the mysterious bundle off to the side, still keeping the blade in hand. "Sit still," he said, "and I'll free your hands, but don't try nothin'. We ain't got time for foolishness."

Jared nodded. He was famished, desperately thirsty, and his hands were numb. Thistle snapped out, "I'm not going to promise you heathens anything. You filthy rogues should have better manners. We have done nothing… nothing to deserve this kind of treatment. I..."

Thistle!" Jared nearly shouted. "For God's sake! We have to eat and drink. Control your temper for once. If you want to do something stupid, do it later when this ogre isn't threatening us with a knife."

She quieted, but pulled forward, trying to avoid touching Jared. It was very awkward for them both.

Though the light from the moon and stars was limited, Jared was able to see enough to be amazed at the size of the man working on their bonds. He massed at least twice Jared's weight, and muscles rippled across his huge chest. Even without the other twenty or so of the robber band Jared had managed to count, he didn't think he wanted to try anything at the moment.

The man talked to them as he untied the ropes on their hands and feet. "Your cleric friend ain't feelin' too good neither. We hadda make sure he wouldn't use his power against us. He'll be all right, iffen he cooperates. We need 'im, and it ain't likely we'd let 'im die after all the trouble we done gone through to catch you folks."

Jared rubbed his wrists and hands when they were finally free, looking hungrily at the bundle the man had put down in front of them.

"What do you need him for?" Thistle questioned, curiosity overcoming her anger.

The man finished loosening her hands. When he finished those, he went back in front to work on her leg bonds. "Well, I guess that ain't no big secret. We got ten guys down with Beze fever. It's almost always fatal if it ain't cured, and it's very contagious. We got two others feelin' woozy today. We needs that cleric to heal 'em. Hope he's a good 'un."

When he had finished untying them both, the man adjusted Thistle and Jared's position up against the large fir, so they had their backs to the trunk. He tied them securely, but not painfully tight, around their waists to the tree.

"Why don't you let him cure the sick ones and let us go?" Thistle asked snappily.

"They ain't here. They're at Xur." The man picked up the bundle. "Here's somethin' to eat – dried meat, fruits, nuts, and some water. Can't start no fire; too close to the Qa-ryks. Eat this and sleep. We move out before dawn." He stood up and moved back a few paces. "Iffen you don' give us no trouble, I'll see you ride proper

101

tomorra."

Another man, much slighter in build, stepped from the shadows. The large man continued, "'The Knife' here is gonna keep an eye on you tonight. He's mean with a blade so don' try nothin'. Eat. Rest!" And with that warning, the man turned on his heel and strode toward the main encampment.

The smaller, leaner man sat down cross-legged in front of Jared and Thistle. He twirled a wickedly curved dagger in his left hand, looking as if he would like nothing better than to have an excuse to use the deadly blade. Thistle shivered, snuggling up close to Jared.

The two prisoners ate slowly and silently under the leering smile of their guard. When they had finished, The Knife let each of them up separately to tend to business, even allowing them some privacy behind a grove of trees. For his part, Jared was so stiff and sore that he didn't think he could make an attempt to escape. When they were both tied firmly back to the tree, the fellow set his back to another trunk facing them; then he closed his eyes.

Jared leaned toward Thistle and whispered, "Where's Yolk?" since they had been riding all day on their stomachs.

She whispered back, "Under my right arm. He isn't particularly frightened though, which is odd. He was about to come out until this fellow showed." She shrugged her shoulders.

"Good night, Thistle," Jared said, already feeling drowsy. She didn't respond, but laid her head on his shoulder, seemingly forgiving him for his earlier curtness. Their bonds gave them little freedom of movement, so they settled as comfortably as they could against the trunk. Soon they were both asleep.

Jared woke shortly before dawn, even more stiff and sore from the cramped position they had slept in. The Knife had been replaced by a tall, gangly, younger fellow of maybe twenty-five. He had long blond hair and a beardless face. Unlike most of the robbers in the band who were quite unkempt, this fellow looked like he had come from a hot bath. He was sitting opposite them, toying with something in his lap.

His whole demeanor was completely different from that of the malevolent-looking robber he had replaced. He was humming a popular drinking song to himself in a high tenor range, and he seemed to be in a remarkably amiable mood considering the circumstances. When he saw Jared was awake, he smiled broadly, his ruddy complexion highlighting at least half a dozen dimples in his cheeks and chin. "Hail and well met, elf-kin. I am Thaddeus of Borea, though my comrades here call me 'Lute.' Sorry we have had to keep you tied up like this; Ruxkin doesn't take chances. We have to be extra careful out here in the wilds."

Lute put down the flute he had been holding and moved behind the tree to untie them. "We have a long ride ahead, so you need to be up and tend to what ye may before we head out. Will you give me your word you won't try to escape?"

Jared willingly agreed. Thistle, who had woken at Lute's greeting, by this time was more than happy to have a brief respite from their bonds. She mumbled a "Yes," nodding groggily.

Lute continued to chatter as he worked at the ropes. "Don't worry about anything. Rux will not harm you as long as your cleric helps out. He's not as mean as he looks, just practical. Overall, this isn't a bad lot... well, except for 'The Knife.' You might want to avoid him… or at least don't annoy him. Hah!"

"I'd be happy to avoid all of you," Thistle murmured. Still,,she did find the soft-spoken man a pleasant change from others of the band they had seen. His voice carried a natural rhythm as he spoke, as if at any moment he might burst into song.

"Now, now, my dear," Lute said as he came back in front, "we're not really evil characters, you know. The roughness, that's for show. We need the services of your companion." Lute helped them up, leading them down toward a small stream.

Thistle, feeling perkier by the second, started in on the young man... Jared almost laughed out loud. "Who are you? All of you, I mean. What do you do besides abduct people? Can we ride the mules instead of being slung like baggage? Is Rux your leader? And who is the big dumb guy who clouted Jared? Why...?"

"Whoa, young lady, you better watch your tongue. Rux may look and sound dumb, but that's an act. He is one of the wisest and most naturally gifted leaders I have ever known. And, as you noted, he *is* big and powerful. No one, not even The Knife, goes against Rux."

Lute stopped at the edge of the stream, turning back to face them, a broad smile on his face. "What are we? I guess you would say we are a band of thieves, robbers, and ne'er-do-wells; however, there is more to this gang than meets the eye. You'll never find a better, tighter-knit fighting group then Rux's Demons. You'll learn a good bit more about us when we reach our stockade.

"For my part, I'm truly sorry for the inconvenience," he said. "The truth is we don't often abduct people. What we do try to do on a regular basis is kill Qa-ryks. And yes, unfortunately in a sense, we do take what we need to survive. Right now, we desperately need your cleric.

"As to myself? I am a Journeyman Bard. With a little bit of luck, I will be heading back to Borea in a few weeks or so. My tenure with the Demons is almost up, though I have wondered if Rux will let me go. I think they have adopted me, like a lost puppy." Lute paused, smiling. "Well… I expect they will let me go, however reluctantly. A new Journeyman Bard will likely be sent to take my place when our replacements arrive.

"Now, go wash up, and do whatever is necessary. I'll wait behind the tree here. Yell when you are ready." Lute handed Jared and Thistle each a small piece of soap and a coarse towel from his knapsack. He turned his back on the stream and stepped behind a nearby tree.

Glancing shyly at Jared, Thistle moved slightly up stream past some bushes. The wind was chilly out of the north; nonetheless, Jared stripped off his clothes and plunged into the mountain stream, splashing and whooping in the icy water before getting down to necessities. Thistle also bathed, more quietly, shivering and letting Yolk splash happily in the middle of the stream.

Fifteen minutes later, feeling much cleaner and a good deal more comfortable, Thistle and Jared walked hand in hand up from the riverbank toward Lute. The Bard stepped out from behind the tree grinning from ear to ear. "Good, good, I'm glad you didn't try anything. Always nice to know you can trust people. I must admit you both look better, though a hot bath and comb could add to the affect. Come, we need to get to the mules right away. Rux wants to move as quickly as possible; the fever is spreading. I think we can let you ride today after all." Lute grinned again, bowing low with a flourish. He took Thistle's hand and kissed it gently. "Sorry we treated you so rudely, milady; one must be careful in the wilds."

Thistle blushed nearly to her toes, and Jared could feel his own color rising. Awkwardly she said, "I... I can't believe that... that brute is your leader. I..."

"Brute, huh?" A familiar husky voice said from behind her. "Well, now, it appears that someone might want to be trussed up for a few more days. Think we got us another ornery female for the camp, huh, Lute?"

"Hi, Rux," Lute answered lightly, not at all surprised at his leader's presence. "I don't know. She's a bit feisty. Probably goes for the big brutes like you." The tall Bard's eyes twinkled in delight at Thistle's increasing discomfort.

Thistle felt her blush reach the tip of her toes and start back up. She opened her mouth to retort, but Jared gave her hand a tight squeeze. She choked off the remark, glaring at him angrily, then at Lute, and finally at Rux. She looked as if she wanted to belt each one of them in turn. She pulled her hand out of Jared's.

"All right," Rux said. "I ain't got time for a battle. It's already dawning. Take them to the mules and let 'em sit; tie their hands in front. We ain't got time for foolishness neither. Move it. We leave in five minutes."

Lute motioned for them to follow him, whistling brightly as he led the way. Thistle rooted herself in one spot and began to object, "What about...?" Before she could get out her complete thought, Jared grabbed her arm pulling her roughly forward. She finished under her breath with effective vehemence, "breakfast?"

A few minutes later Thistle and Jared were bouncing along at a fairly quick pace on the backs of two mules. Sart was now in front of them on Crunch's back. They managed to find out by whispering back and forth that he was all right, except for a knot on his forehead similar to Jared's. He had otherwise been well treated by the band of thieves.

The countryside was rough and soon they were separated from the cleric. From that point on, they traveled in single file for much of the day with several robbers in sight on mules to their front and several behind. Lute had gone up to the front of the long procession. Occasionally, through the long day, they could hear his high, clear voice singing some cheerful song, often harmonized remarkably well in the

104

choruses by the deep basses and baritones of several of the others. Lute's voice was a rich high tenor. Jared marveled at his wonderful timbre and the incredible control of he had of his voice.

At midday they stopped for a cold meal. Lute came back to eat with them, carrying a small portative harp, which he set next to him while they ate. Jared admired it between mouthfuls of dried venison, cheese, and trail bread. Thistle sat sullenly apart, still peeved from the morning's ribbing.

Lute was as loquacious as he had been before. He was soon telling Jared and Thistle about his life as a Journeyman Bard. "...I guess you could say that I am the local entertainment. If you really want to become a Bard – and by-the-way, I have your lyre safe on my mule – after your studies you have to apprentice out in a town or with some wayfaring band under the tutelage of a Journeyman or a full Bard. It allows you to learn the ropes, so to speak. Three, four, five years – it depends on where you go and what experience you may have already had. After that you go back to Bard Hall for a couple more years of study. Finally, back out in the field again as a Journeyman. I've been out here three years this time. I've learned a great deal, about life mostly. I'm ready now to go back and hopefully pass the final tests."

"You mean you have even more to go through after all that?" Jared wondered. "You sing so beautifully. I thought you were a full-fledged Bard."

"No. Not at all," Lute answered. "I have certainly studied: music, theory, history, lore, lute, harp, singing, solos, chorus; you name it. If it is musical, I have probably read about it or worked at it. That is only the first step to becoming a Bard. You also have to learn how to fight, all about weapons, warfare, armor, physical development, and so on – all those things and much more. There's also Bard lore, history of the kingdom, mathematics, economics, and so on. You do all of that before your apprenticeship. If you pass all of those tests and trials and remain alive in the process, you can begin the study of the true lore of the Bards. That's when you really learn. The rest of it is simply preparation for the real thing.

"Jared, my young half-elf," he continued, "there are many wandering musicians in the world, a great many who have picked up instruments and learned to play for the joy of music. Most of them serve a wonderful, useful purpose; only the best, the smartest, and the hardest workers become Bards.

"You have to be special – not only musically talented, also skilled and wise in many areas. You have to have a willingness to acquire a breadth of knowledge that few possess. I don't mean to sound conceited, really; but if you walked into Bard Hall and announced, 'I want to become a Bard,' they would probably throw you out. Unless, that is, someone was having an unusually benevolent day. In which case, they might put you through a series of rigorous auditions and tests. A real Bard has many talents. He learns the true power of music. It is not an easy road."

"How... how long did you study there?" Jared asked.

"A long time," he replied. "I'm older than I look. I was lucky enough to come from a wealthy family with some influence -- I was given a chance others might not have had. Even so, I had to work hard and pass each level. Being from a prominent family only helps get you in the door. There are no shortcuts to the learning process.

"Have you ever considered becoming a Bard, Jared?"

"Me?!" Jared stammered. "Well, not really, not beyond dreaming a little. I... I don't think I've ever met one. We often had minstrels and jongleurs come through our village. That's how I learned to sing and play. There was one I especially liked who came through several years in a row. He taught me a bit about playing the lyre, or portative harp, and some about the lute, rebec, and fiddle. His name was Josquin. Do you know him?"

"Yes, Josquin." Lute's voice dropped in pitch and his face saddened. "I knew of him. He was anointed some five years back; maybe he came through your village during his time as a Journeyman. Unfortunately, he was killed a few years ago in the south. He was exceptionally talented and well-liked. It was a sad day for Bard Hall. Though he was young, many believed he might take over the Grandmastership one day.

"So, he gave you some pointers? That is good; it says something to your musical abilities. He was a good teacher, one of the best." Lute smiled, "I would like to hear you play, Jared. Maybe you do have potential."

"Becoming a Bard?" Jared replied uncertainly. "I really don't know. I have lived a life as far from Bard Hall in Borea as you can get. Becoming a Bard always seemed like a childish dream, as remote and unreal as becoming a great warrior hero. My brother and I used to dream of such adventures when we were younger. In a western seacoast village, however, reality sets in early in life. You learn to enjoy what you have."

Jared glanced at Thistle. A wisp of a smile creased his lips. She smiled back, having relaxed enough during the meal and conversation to forget her anger. Lute had a natural ability to put you at ease; his mellifluous voice was like a soothing tonic to the soul.

"I always found music fun," Jared answered. "It was a part of my life in the village. When my mother saw I had a gift for remembering tunes and a decent enough voice, she asked my father to purchase a portative. Luckily we found one left at a local tavern that I fixed up. I used to make up tunes and songs all the time, as well as sing all the old favorites at village dances. Now, the farm, our house, everything is gone. I don't know where I will go or what I will do." Jared's voice trailed off. Thistle eased her hand into his and gave it a light squeeze.

He looked up at Lute. "I don't have any real musical knowledge; I just play – whatever comes into my head, I guess. I pick up the local songs by ear. No, I never really seriously considered becoming a Bard. Outside of Josquin's visits and other travelling musicians, I did learn quite a bit from one old fellow who visited some years ago. He stayed for the better part of two weeks and sang all the old ballads for us. He would sit with me for hours. We would sing duets, or we would make up musical repartees together. Lassus was his name. He never came back, but he did tell me I had a good ear."

"Lassus? *The* Lassus? Tall, thin fellow, with a reedy baritone and an impressive grey mustache?"

"Well… yes, I guess that does describe him," Jared said, puzzled at Lute's outburst.

"Well, my young half-elf, you have indeed met a Bard. He was one of the greatest of our age. Old, yes, he is quite old, and now retired and reclusive, I am afraid. He was wounded in a tavern brawl some years ago. His only fault, I'm afraid, was the drink. If he said you had a good ear, that is a high compliment indeed. He is renowned at the Hall. I was lucky enough to take Lore from him. It was probably the best class I ever took there. He is a bit of a legend for us younger students."

Lute seemed excited as he went on, "Well, this is all very interesting, Jared. When we reach Xur, you must play and sing for me. Maybe, if we get a chance, you can also show me what you can do with a sword and bow. I'll see if you have real potential. It would be interesting to me from a professional standpoint. One of the things we apprentices and journeymen are supposed to do is keep on the lookout for prospective students for the Hall. Unfortunately, I haven't had any call with this bunch to do that. They weren't brought together for their musical talents." He grinned ruefully.

"I can't make you any promises, Jared, or even give you any hope. The tests are rigorous, and the chances of failure are great." Lute stood and gave Jared a pat on the back. "We'll see."

Jared managed to nod when Lute mentioned him playing, but he felt his stomach tighten. So many of the people he performed for were now gone; he didn't want to think on it. "Thanks, Lute... well, I don't know if I really want to play anymore. It... I..." He, too, stood up, turning away toward his mule. A minute later, the call to mount up came from the front of the line. Jared welcomed the interruption to the anguish that had threatened to overwhelm him.

As they mounted and had their hands tied again, Thistle whispered to Lute. The musician nodded sadly, before returning to his own mule near the front of the long train.

They traveled for six more days, deeper and deeper into Qa-ryk lands, taking a winding route through the forests toward the mountains to the west and south. They rode from dawn to dusk. Some eves, if the sky was clear and the moon was up early and bright, they went on into the night.

Though Jared couldn't be certain, the trail they followed appeared to be in the same general direction the marauding Qa-ryks who had attacked their village had taken. Rux pushed them hard, hoping the herbalists at the outpost could keep the sick men alive long enough for Sart to reach them. The men were a hardy lot; and Beze fever, while deadly, took time to fully develop and to kill.

The trip continued with the band heading mostly south now. Each day was much as the first, except that Jared and Thistle were allowed to ride with their hands free, after promising, on Sart's urging, not to try to escape. Lute continued to visit with the "prisoners" during the halts. They all soon became fast friends. The Journeyman Bard often sang softly in camp at night. Jared did not offer to join him, usually preferring to keep to himself or to go on short walks with Thistle, always keeping within sight of the camp.

Eventually, they got to know Rux and several of the other thieves fairly well. "The Brute," as Thistle now fondly referred to him, had actually become a kind and gracious host now that he trusted them well enough. He went out of his way to make sure they were as comfortable as possible in the rough camps. They received the same amenities as any in the group and were allowed a certain amount of freedom as long as they stayed within shouting distance.

Thistle and Jared sat alone one evening and discussed whether attempting an escape would have any merits. They finally agreed that since they were headed west and in the company of men whose life's mission seemed to be to kill Qa-ryks, that for now they would bide their time to see what developed.

Sart was content to follow the troop, though he had not shared his reasoning with them. Both Jared and Thistle felt strongly that heading back to the east offered them few viable options, so they agreed to see what developed. Besides, Jared was now a long way from any territory he had ever traversed, and here Qa-ryks were numerous. According to Lute, they were adept at ambushing small groups of unwary or poorly armed travelers.

Near the end of their seventh day with the band, Rux rode back to them on his great goatsteed, a rare crossbreed of horse and goat found only in the southwestern mountains. It looked like a horned horse and was much larger than a goat. Capable of carrying heavy loads, it was also more agile than a horse. Because its hooves resembled a goat's, it was able to easily maneuver on questionable rocky terrain. The big man slid to the ground and motioned for Jared and Thistle to dismount as well. "I'm afraid we'll have to bind and blindfold you again for a short time. We'll be cuttin' off the main track and heading for our fortress.

"Dras here," he hooked his thumb at the animal, "knows the way. He ain't goin' ta throw you on the rough paths ahead. Once we get to Xur, I hope we can make up the uncomforts to ya." Rux helped Thistle and then Jared aboard the exotic animal, binding them loosely in place and tying dark cloths tightly around their eyes. Finally, he ordered all to move out, letting the goatsteed pick its way over the cluttered narrow maze of paths that led toward the stockade home of Rux's Demons.

All that Glitters is not Gold

Ge-or quickly picked up the trail that Stradryk had mentioned. After a few days, he intersected the old cart path, which this far to the north looked rarely used. It was overgrown with weeds, brush, and even little trees. Finding an old travelers' rocky niche about half a league along it to the south, he settled in for the night.

At dawn, he began his trek further to the south. For some distance the going was difficult, with so much undergrowth on the old pathway that the animal trails in the upper hills were beginning to look like a better choice. Eventually the trail was crossed by other similar tracks, and it began to look recently used. He kept moving almost due south along the rough path for two more days. Soon thereafter, he began to see indications of heavy-wheeled wagons drawn by both mules and oxen. By mid-day of the sixth day out from meeting Stradryk, he saw relatively fresh mule droppings.

Though he still had a few days left of the dried venison, he hoped he could catch up to the waggoneers and spend an evening or two with company sharing the trail. He increased his pace, trying to close the distance. By dusk, he could see a campfire flare up against the night sky ahead.

Moving up cautiously, Ge-or took a couple of minutes to study the scene. Three men, farmers or workmen by the looks of their clothing, had pulled their wagon to the east of the road and built a campfire in an indentation in the rocks on the other side. They were beginning to roast what looked to be a brace of chickens, spitted and stuffed, over the coals on the side of the fire. One of the men was kneading fresh dough in a rough wooden bowl; another looked to their four mules, giving them nosebags for the night. The third sat by the fire working a heavy pot of what smelled like kaffa, the scent wafting on the slight breeze toward Ge-or. The men were a bit rough-looking, with beards of at least a few days. Ge-or, feeling his face with his hand, probably looked much the worse for wear as well.

After watching for several minutes, he noted nothing untoward about the scene. They looked like a group of men setting down for an evening meal. Ge-or decided to venture forth and hail them. He raised his voice before stepping forward, "Greetings, fellow travelers…" he began.

The men, startled from what they were doing, reacted quickly. The one with the pot let it settle back into the coals, and immediately drew a long knife from his belt. The man by the mules spun around, drawing a heavy short sword from a belt scabbard in one fluid motion. And the one with the bowl of dough, stood, stepped back, and grabbed a heavy cudgel, while setting the bowl down carefully with his other hand.

Ge-or stepped into the light, his hands empty and his palms out. "No harm from me. I only wish to share your fire and camaraderie for a night or two. I am heading south to Aelfric, if you go that way."

The men seemed to relax only slightly. The one with the knife gestured for Ge-or to come further into the light.

"I am just a traveler, Ge-or, formerly of Thiele," Ge-or continued. "I have dried venison and fresh apples, picked today, if you would care to share. I do not want trouble."

The knife wielder gestured for Ge-or to sit by the fire on one of the many large rocks surrounding it. "I'm Grogan; that's Harky," he said, pointing to the man by the mules. "T' other's Slam. Have a seat, we gots some chicks and taters goin' and a bit of swee-bread. You thirsty?"

Ge-or nodded.

"Here." Grogan sheathed his knife, and handed Ge-or a tin mug, pouring out a stream of thick dark liquid from the kettle. "Good stuff, this. Rich and mean." He laughed, showing rotting teeth in his grizzled smile.

"What brings you on the road to Aelfric," Grogan inquired, after Ge-or had taken several sips of the strong liquid. Kaffa was a rarity in the northern villages. They typically only had the luxury of its pungent aroma and slightly bitter taste for a few weeks after the boats came on their runs during the spring and fall. Otherwise, they drank predominantly teas made with local dried herbs.

Ge-or slightly raised his mug. "Good. I haven't had this in a long while." He lowered his eyes and stared at the dark brown liquid for a while before speaking again. "My village was destroyed by Qa-ryks over a week ago. I have decided to seek my fortune elsewhere. There is nothing left for me there."

"Half-elf, be ye?"

"Aye."

Grogan nodded. "Ya probably can find work. Tough this time of year for most. Merchants ain't trustin' strangers, and unless you're keen on goin' down into holes and diggin' with the dwarves and gnomes, that's about all there is."

"I appreciate the advice. Where are you fellows heading?"

"South, maybe east. Hard to say. Wagon's only half filled and we needs more loot before…"

Ge-or sensed something was wrong a moment too late. He had only just begun to turn when he was hit hard from behind.

He woke in a haze with his head pounding. The regular bumping and jostling he felt throughout his body weren't helping any. It took him a long time to realize that he was trussed up like a hog, lying in the bottom of the wagon as it rolled down the rough road. Twice in a week, he groaned to himself. By-the-gods, my head hurts. I've got to learn to watch my own back.

Eventually he managed to roll mostly onto his back, from where he looked around as best he could. As near as he could tell, it was early the next day. There was a light drizzle of rain coming down, and he was already getting soaked through in the uncovered bed of the wagon. Though his stomach was empty, and he was quite thirsty, he knew he had far more dire concerns.

As Grogan had indicated, the wagon was filled with miscellaneous loot, which was likely taken from other unfortunate travelers or farmsteads they had raided. There were a variety of weapons, crocks, boxes, piles of clothing, and tools. From his perspective, it wasn't much of a haul. He also knew that whatever their plans for him, he was in serious trouble.

Ge-or was too low in the bed of the wagon to see the men. He gathered from the occasional shifting of weight and grunting that two of them were seated above him on the broad wooden seat of the wagon, with the other striding along in front helping to guide the mules.

Grogan broke the silence. "You think he might bring a price in the south?"

"Half-elven? I would think a good price. They last a long time in the mines in the deep south; better'n most men."

Ge-or guessed the second speaker might be Harky, though neither of the two others had spoken before he had been hit.

"What iffen he's somebody important?" the same voice said. "He might bring a whole lot more on the black market in Aelfric."

"Wha's someone important doin' in a village like Thiele?" Grogan asked. "That's way to the godforsaken north and west... at least I think it is."

"Mayhap he's related to some elf prince or somethin'."

"No way to find out, I reckon."

"Spyder might know someone who knows such." The last fellow, Slam, who was the one walking ahead, offered that piece of advice.

Grogan rejected that with a snort. "Yeah, and Spyder'd take most of the profits, too."

"Well, in any case, it's all profit, so somethin's better'n nothing,'" Harky added.

"Maybe we can get the idiot to talk," Slam said.

"Good luck with that," Grogan said. "He's a big-fella for a half-elf. Did ya take notice of that?"

Harkey agreed. "Yeah, kind of broad in the chest and arms."

"Maybe he ain't 'half.' Maybe he's a quarter or something."

Slam again, figured Ge-or.

"Shit, don't matter none, does it." *Grogan's voice.*

"Guess not... When we gonna stop?" *Harky's nasal whine.* "I need to use the latrine."

"Bout another hour or so. Hold it."

Grogan is the leader, for certain, Ge-or mused. He would need to take him out quickly if he got a chance.

As they continued on, Ge-or tried to formulate some kind of plan to escape. His head hurt; but they hadn't hit him as hard as the Qa-ryk, so he didn't think he had a concussion. If he could get free, even partially free, he calculated he might have a chance at escape. These louts didn't look to be well-trained; they mainly relied on brute strength and deception. Taking the opportunity of having another hour to prepare, Ge-or worked to loosen up his stiff arms and legs within the constraints of the ropes.

While he worked on his bonds, Ge-or searched about the bed of the wagon for a sharp-edged tool. He saw none and the weapons were piled far enough away that he could not reach them. It was difficult to move around much anyway, as everything was piled about where he lay. His bonds were tight, yet not incapacitating; so he was able to achieve a minimum range of motion by twisting about. He rubbed his hands to promote circulation, pushed against the bonds with his shoulders and thighs, and tensed and untensed his muscles over and over. He didn't expect to get free, but he was able to increase his range of motion slightly during the exercises.

When they finally did stop, Harky pulled down the rear gate of the wagon and roughly dragged Ge-or out. "Don't try anything, half-elf. We all got weapons, so behave and you'll live. I'm gonna loosen your legs and let ya hit the latrine. I'll stay right behind with my sword. Grogan's got a bow, so don't try to run. Do your business and that's it."

This was just the opportunity that Ge-or had hoped would present itself. If they intended to keep him alive for trade, they would have to let him partially loose on occasion. While he had been flexing his bound body, he had devised a simple plan. He hoped these oafs were as slow as he thought they might be, gauging from their bulk and lazy mannerisms.

Harky pulled him to his feet once they were untied. He grabbed Ge-or's tunic near the neck and shoved him toward the side of the road. "There, that'll have to do ya."

Ge-or partially squatted, saying, "I need you to pull my pants down. I can't reach the belt."

"Bloody hell, I always get the crap jobs. Stay still, my swords right at your back." Harky placed the point of his sword toward the center of Ge-or's back. Standing just behind Ge-or, Harky reached out to grab at the half-elf's belt buckle with his left hand.

From his half crouch, Ge-or suddenly straightened up and back, flinging his head as far back as he could. He caught Harky flush on his chin; the small man fell backward at impact. The sharp sword blade slid along Ge-or's back, penetrating into his side.

Twisting sideways and rolling down to the ground, Ge-or raised his legs in one motion. Pushed his tied hands over his butt, he drew them up and to the front. Just as he began to twist onto his knees, an arrow shot past the side of his face and splintered into the rock behind. Instinctively looking in the direction from which it had come, he saw Grogan drop the bow and go for his knife. Meanwhile, Ge-or was able to gain purchase with his knees and had come halfway up. He quickly assessed the situation as he continued to move.

Harky was out of the fight for now; he might even be dead. His sword was in his hand, lying across his stomach. Grogan was coming straight at Ge-or with a long knife in his right hand. He could see Slam, cudgel at the ready, rounding the end of the wagon. With his hands outstretched, Ge-or flung himself on top of Harky, hoping that the lout still had enough of a grip on the hilt that he could cut his bonds. Luckily, the blade was quite sharp. It only took a split second for him to cleave the cords, grab the hilt out of the thief's fingers, and twist sideways to scurry away from Grogan's attack.

As Ge-or moved, the blade of Grogan's knife caught the edge of his tunic; it ripped upward as he slid away, cutting cloth, and only scratching his chest lightly. Continuing to stay low to the ground, his legs stiff and not fully responsive, Ge-or pushed hard in a low dive for the wagon. He rolled under it, foiling a swing of Slam's cudgel.

Ge-or stayed put for a few seconds, trying to catch his breath. He was bleeding badly, but he didn't think anything vital had been cut. It had been a close call with his kidney. He could hear the two thieves cursing him as they maneuvered around the wagon to get at where he was. Ge-or rolled further under the wagon. Moving forward from there, he pressed himself between the mules. Placing his hands upon the first pair's backs, he heaved himself up and over to the right.

Though they hadn't anticipated his movements, Grogan was quick. He came around the wagon at a run, knife at the ready. Ge-or had already set himself to throw the sword. He sent the heavy blade spinning end over end toward the big thief's chest. It struck point first and buried deep, right in the center below the bottom ribs. Grogan gasped once, sinking to his knees before coughing up a flood of blood.

Slam now appeared behind Grogan as the thief collapsed into the dust of the path. Seeing that his opponent was now unarmed, he pressed forward, club raised high. Ge-or didn't hesitate; he ran forward and dove under the swing of the club. He hit the heavyset man right in the soft part of his stomach with his head. The two went down in a pile, the thief doubling over as Ge-or spun sideways out of the way. Ripping the sword from Grogan's chest, he swung around. He had it at Slam's throat in a flash.

Ge-or first tied Slam's hands to a wheel of the cart. Next, he checked Harky, who was indeed dead, his face smashed in. Satisfied that he was now completely in control, he began a search of the wagon.

Most of the stuff in the back was of limited value; the food stores he knew would be welcome as he made his way south. There were jars, bags, and barrels filled with different flours, honey, blackstrap molasses, grains, dried fruits and vegetables, a smoked ham, a small keg of mead, and another of a dusky wheat ale. There was also a small pile of corn that regrettably had begun to mold. The weapons that were lying in a pile on one side were of inferior quality and would bring only a few coppers each. The tools, and there was quite a selection, looked to be first rate. Ge-or guessed they had been stolen from a farm with a blacksmith stall. There were clothes as well, but these were also of limited value. What had been quality wear at one time were stained by rains and mishandling by the dirty ruffians.

He tried to separate everything in the wagon as much as possible, keeping the foodstuffs and clothing apart from the rest. Otherwise, the contraband would have to wait until he was in a better position to sort completely through what was there.

Ge-or next turned his attention to the two bodies. He carefully searched each, finding several other knives and small purses. The purses contained little enough – a few coppers and a couple of silver each. He went over to Slam and cut off his purse as well. It, too, had only a few coins in it.

Finding his hunting blade, Ge-or stuck the point up against Slam's neck artery. "Do you want to live?" The thief spoke hesitantly, trying to avoid moving and cutting himself.

"Please."

"Where is the stash?"

For a moment, Slam looked like he wasn't going to say anything; however, when Ge-or applied a bit more pressure on the blade, he said hoarsely, "Yeah." Ge-or eased the blade back about an inch away from his pulsing jugular and waited.

Slam blinked wildly, swallowing hard. "Under the wagon seat; it's a puzzle box. Slide the back board left, the middle right, and the front one right. It'll spring open. You... you gonna let me live now?" He twitched, stifling a sob.

Ge-or didn't answer. He was pretty angry at the way the thieves had fooled him. Still, he knew he had been stupid – both in trusting strangers, and in having failed to thoroughly assess the situation before jumping in. Had he even glanced in the wagon, he would have known something was amiss.

Climbing up on the running board, Ge-or flipped the seat up and forward. He followed Slam's instructions and the top sprang open. Within the seat cavity, he found a long tin box. Prying the lock apart with his knife, he opened it. There he found several hundred coppers, about forty silver, and three gold pieces by a quick count. He wasn't going to be rich, but the money would buy him some reasonably good chain mail and a few other things he had decided were necessities for the quest he had set for himself. He could trade the mules as well. They looked to be from sturdy stock and were in good condition. He might get enough for them to purchase an adequate steed. Of the rest of the loot: the tools would fetch a decent price, the clothing was too ill-used to be of any value, and the foodstuffs he could use on the road. He felt confident he would be able to trade what he didn't use for other necessities.

Ge-or closed the box, reset the boards, and replaced the seat. He stepped off the wagon and faced Slam again. "What's your real name?"

The robber was really nervous. He began to babble. "Herv of… Well, just Herv now, I guess. I'm a farmer, really. Things got tough. I didn't have any choices. My wife left with the kids, east and…" his voice trailed off.

"There are always choices, Herv. Always. Now, what else is there?"

"Nothing… Nothing I know of. I joined them a couple a weeks ago. We been raidin' places east of here, now headin' south. Please don't kill me. Please…" The big man was whimpering now, literally shaking against the wagon wheel. He was sweating profusely.

"Enough!" Ge-or barked at him. He spun around and eyed Grogan's body. He had appeared to be the leader. Taking more time now, Ge-or went over, bent down, and felt his way from the top of the thief's tunic down to his feet, checking seams, looking for hidden pockets, and feeling for any bulges. When he got to Grogan's feet, he took off the fellow's boots and checked them. Taking his knife to hand again, he pried off first the right heel, and then the left. Nestled in a hollow crudely dug out in the left heel were a small, quality ruby and a medium-large, perfectly formed pearl.

Herv grunted when he saw them. "That bastard! By-the-gods, I bet he took them off that gent the other day, and he goes and keeps 'em for 'emself."

"That's what you get for consorting with thieves," Ge-or said, as he placed the two valuables in his own purse. He stood, grimacing when he noticed the pain in his back from the wound he had received from Harky's sword. He reached his hand gingerly under his tunic and felt carefully for the cut. It was a clean slit that was still oozing blood. He probed gently. From the angle and depth, he was fairly sure it had missed his kidney; yet it had been close. He knew he had lost a fair amount of blood; he also knew enough about wounds to know that he needed it stitched, the sooner the better.

Taking the cleanest-looking cloth he could find from the wagon, Ge-or ripped it into a couple of long strips. The first he folded into a compact wad, which he placed on top of the cut; the second he used to wrap tightly about his waist several times. He hoped these makeshift bandages would hold enough to staunch the bleeding until he got some assistance.

After he was done, he took one blanket, a short hunting knife, a handful of venison strips, and a full waterskin, and moved back to where Herv sat. He placed the pile on the far side of the road in front of the thief, finally cutting the rope holding the fellow to the wagon wheel. "You ought to be able to get over there and cut your hands free within a half hour. Best do it before dark, anyway." Ge-or leaned over and glared at Slam. "You try to come after me and I'll kill you on sight. I'm heading south. Go north, if you want to live the night. Choose another profession. You won't survive this one for long." He turned quickly away, boarded the wagon, and heighed to the mules.

Ge-or was hoping to find a stead, or at least a road leading west or east before dark. He needed to get his wound tended if at all possible. He was already feeling weak and light-headed. He would try to gather his reserves as he drove the wagon. Thankfully, the mules, having had an unexpectedly long break, kept up a steady pace on the path.

114

Just as the sun began to wester toward the mountains, Ge-or pulled up the mules. He took his bearings – to the east was a broad road, deeply rutted, that led down into the lower hills. It appeared to head to the wide valley below, the Great Greensward before the King's Wall. He could see a long way down into the vale, but he saw no lights or signs of a nearby stead. To the west he could see that the road continued; it was narrower and less used. He pondered his choices. He doubted there was any kind of farm or tavern along this old road south. Stradryk had suggested it was not used enough to support any business venture. Ge-or could see that the immediate environs were too rocky for cattle or crops. Eastward, he knew, was a long, low plain – arable, only sparsely inhabited now because homesteaders could expect little protection from the kingdom's troops. The few farms that remained were large and widely spread, controlled by extended families and hired hands. According to his father, they were not typically amenable to wanderers on their lands. To the west, up and down the hill line from the far north to the desert, were rich vales. Unfortunately, many had been abandoned because of frequent gzk and Qa-ryk raids. Still, if there was a place within a reasonable distance, westward might be his best hope.

Slipping unsteadily off his perch on the wagon seat, Ge-or examined the trails leading both east and west. Someone riding in a small wagon looked to have been back and forth from west to east, and later back west, within the past several weeks. Other than that, neither way appeared to have been used except in the distant past. He hoped he was right. He climbed back aboard the wagon and urged the mules to turn right. He knew his life might depend on whether he was making the right decision. He was starting to feel weak and nauseous, and there were only a few hours of light left.

It was near full dark when Ge-or found himself drowsing on the wagon bench. The mules, tiring, had kept moving; they were now plodding slowly along, up yet another rise. Ge-or realized he was in bad shape. His forehead and face were burning, and the wound was stinging sharply. Gulping water to slake his thirst, he spurred the mules up to the crest.

When they got there, Ge-or stood unsteadily on the wagon's seat and scanned the horizon. For an instant, he thought he saw a flash of light, fiery against the deep darkness of the hills, off to his right and down low. He stared for a couple more minutes, but he did not see it again.

Seeing no other course except to investigate and hope his sight had been true, Ge-or unhitched one of the mules and anchored the wagon with rocks to the front and back of each wheel. He gave the other mules free rein to follow. Taking his sword, bow, and backpack, he scrambled up on the first animal's back, kneeing it ahead down into the darkened vale.

A half hour later, feverish and barely able to cling to the mule's back, Ge-or gave the animal free rein as well. He hoped that if there was a stead nearby the animal would sense it and head for shelter. He wrapped his arms about the beast's neck and held on as best he could. In any case, he didn't think he could last much longer.

After what seemed like a long time, Ge-or woke to find he was still slumped on the mule's back. The animal had come to a complete stop and was standing patiently. The other mules were gathered about, nibbling sweet grass. Ge-or looked up ahead and saw the reason they had stopped. They had come to a split rail fence and were facing a two-piece gate, closed for the night. On the other side of the gate stood another mule; it was nuzzling Ge-or's mount.

Sliding off the mule, Ge-or's knees buckled, and he nearly collapsed. Somehow he had managed to hold onto the mule's mane. Reaching out, he pulled himself along the top rail of the fence until he reached the gate latch. Loosening it, he pushed it open and fell through, barely catching himself. Allowing that the mules would follow, he half-crawled, half-stumbled up the path. Several minutes later, he rounded a small hillock. Looking up he saw a light gleaming from the window of a cabin that was set atop a hill just to his fore. Afraid he would not be able to make it up the slope, he cupped his hands and shouted as loud as he could. "Hail! Hail! I need some help… Help!" Then he fell to his knees.

He woke as strong hands around his arms pulled him up. The last thing he remembered was a female voice saying, "Latch that gate, Father; I'll get some water on to boil, this man's been stabbed." He blacked out again.

Preparations for Battle

Five days had passed. The Qa-ryks were well in hand, and lieutenants had been chosen to lead the various prongs of the assault. Aberon was now on his own. His brother priest had been called back by the Nine to attend to some other dire matter. No matter, he preferred to work by himself. This glory he would not have to share. Once the stone was sealed away, his ascendance into the brotherhood would be assured.

Aberon had been garnering his own power over the past four nights. He did not have a dragon this time to blast the gates, so he had designed the assault around his ability to break through the strong fortifications. Aberon had shared his plans with Ka-ragh and his lieutenants. Though they were notoriously slow-witted, he was fairly certain they understood the importance of waiting for the right time to attack. Unfortunately, Qa-ryks were best when they had really worked themselves into a battle frenzy. He was not sure whether they would hold back long enough for him to work his magic.

He hoped it wouldn't matter. His personal power was strong enough for the task. If they lost several dozens or even scores to the outpost's elaborate defenses… Well, the beasts bred like rabbits and flies. In that respect, they took their heritage from the gzks, cousins of the prolific goblins of the mountains. Their size and ferocity came from the mountain ogres to which Kan had bred them.

A Qa-ryk female often had six to eight pups in a litter, and they grew rapidly. In the early days, the pups had instinctively fought each other until one emerged as the only survivor of the litter. Kan had managed to breed that negative trait out for the most part, but the siblings were still overly aggressive and extremely competitive. By the time they were two years old, they were larger than a man and considered battle worthy. At three they were assigned to patrols and expected to become blooded. When they had thrown down their first victim and bit its throat, they were considered a potential member of the clan. At that point, each went through their clan's initiation, which was typically cruel and brutal; yet it was effective in weeding out any further weaklings.

The one thing Kan had never been able to breed out of his "children" had been their fierce clannishness. This failure had been the fundamental cause of his eventual defeat, or so the wise had speculated. He could never mass a large enough force of the beasts to make an effective weapon against entrenched troops. Eventually, they had turned on each other, and on Kan himself. It had been a nasty end by all accounts.

Aberon actually had doubts about this tale. It did not explain the utter dissolution of Kan's empire, nor the complete destruction of his massive fortress, There was not even enough left in the ruins to tell where the main entrance had been. He speculated that something else must have been at play. The Qa-ryks were not disciplined enough to have created an upheaval so powerful as to destroy a large fortress. One thing was certain, Kan's defeat had come from within. The Kingdom of Borea had not had anything to do with that dark mage's final annihilation.

The Black Druids had solved the problem of bringing the diverse clans of the beasts together through magical means and guile. So far, their efforts had produced effective short-term results. Their eventual defeat in the first Qa-ryk wars had at its roots the same concern. They had been able to hold the enmeshed clans together long enough to drive the gnomes and dwarves from the mountains. And most human settlements west of the King's Wall had been abandoned during the long conflict as well. The aftermath had been a bloody mess, because clans began fighting for territory and dominance. His brethren had lost what control they had established over the beasts. The extended Qa-ryk clans, so carefully developed, had been vastly diminished by the war and finally by infighting.

Now the brethren were using ever-more-powerful magic to control larger and larger amalgamations of extended tribes. The population of the beasts had begun to swell again, as they forsook their clan infighting for the honor of destroying gzks and humans. Unfortunately, their overall control of the beasts was still tenuous. Aberon was about to put some of their new spells and skills in manipulating the beasts to the test.

There was nothing like staying in touch with your army and using plain old bull to let them know who really is the boss. The real key was to keep the immediate goal at the forefront of their limited intellects. Therefore Aberon, as he had done the past four nights, was striding about the large camp interacting with the members of each diverse clan, reminding them of the battle-honor they would achieve when destroying the human stockade.

His tactics were simple: give them a slap on the back, the harder the better with these monsters; let them know that if they did well there would be many throats to bite and lots of loot (the creatures were enamored with little things – baubles, child's toys, and the like); praise their clan; and be sure to praise the individual in some way – his sharp claws, long fangs, sturdy arms, prowess in battle, clan status if he was blooded, and so on. As most intelligent and semi-intelligent creatures did, they responded first and best to what was most important to them.

Actually, Aberon found the whole process somewhat amusing. They were like little children much of the time. They even fought like children, flailing about in a frenzy for the most part; though the more battle-hardened, and hence longer-lived, had developed a certain amount of control and skill with their claws and with select weapons. These individual leaders were the ones that Aberon was counting on to maintain discipline at the critical junctures in the attack. He didn't care if he lost half his contingent of young pups, so long as his veterans got through the openings he provided and effectively crushed the resistance.

Late that afternoon, Aberon called a final meeting – more as a formality than as a true war council. The clans had already moved into position. He had them stay far enough away from the fort that the rangers' outriders would be unlikely to make contact. They were dealing with an epidemic of Beze fever anyway, if the reports he had received were correct. Those at Xur would be mostly focusing inward.

He needed to see that they all were aligned for the attack. Calling in the clan leaders would put everyone on alert that something was about to happen. It was useful to show all the other beasts that in some extra-special way Ka-ragh and the selected lieutenants were exceptional. It also gave him the opportunity, separated from the troops, for him to renew the spell that bound their obedience to him. It was a minor spell, took little power, and for that reason, it didn't always work. Yet, it was better than wasting his energy on more powerful incantations when he had work enough to do on the morrow.

The five arrayed themselves in a semi-circle in front of Aberon's tent. They tended to squat when being spoken to. Ka-ragh, to show his importance, was standing in the center. Aberon was always impressed with their size when he was close to them. He stood over six feet – these beasts, even the smallest, towered over him and easily massed thrice his own weight. At the same time, their close proximity helped him to feel powerful because he knew that with a wave of his hand he could easily dismiss them, or kill them, if that was his desire. Power was a nice feeling, after all.

"I wanted to have a last meeting before our attack tomorrow," Aberon began. Nods all around. They at least appeared to understand what he was saying. "What you do, how you lead, will make the difference between a crushing victory," he paused for effect, "... and a tail-between-your-legs defeat." They liked visual analogies. Since wild dogs and wolves were some of their favorite foods, they understood the meaning quite well.

"Remember, there are traps everywhere. The place is well defended. Keep your troops back as long as possible. I will create the openings in the stockade that you will need to get inside. Keep your best buoa throwers back at the beginning. They will find better targets once the wall is breached, while the men defending are otherwise occupied. When you do charge, make for the walls as quickly as possible. Many of their weapons are designed to fire long distances over the ramparts. When you are close, they won't be able to reach you. Understand?"

"Yes," a guttural growl from Ka-ragh, and throaty growls from the others. They made no other comment, and truthfully, rarely said much, which Aberon found quite refreshing. He hated conversation. These fellows were more likely to take your head off with a swipe of their claws if they disliked you, rather than make any effort to discuss why. Generally, if you faced a Qa-ryk, negotiation was not an option; just prepare yourself for a fight.

"The stockade entrance," Aberon took his staff and drew a large triangle in the dirt in front of them, "is to the south. Hra-rygk, you will have the honor of taking the road to the gates. Here." Aberon pointed to the center of the side of the triangle facing the five Qa-ryks. "It will be dangerous, but you will be first to the fight." The beast squatting next to Ka-ragh grunted, proudly raising his chin in the air as if to tell the others, "You see, I am chosen. I am the best."

Aberon knew this was a delicate moment in his presentation. He had briefed Ka-ragh only minutes before the others showed up, reminding him again that this perceived honor he bestowed on his rival was not without purpose. They both hated Hra-rygk. From Ka-ragh's perspective, he was the only challenger to his position as leader and chieftain of the horde. The fellow easily massed Ka-ragh's weight and was only an inch shorter. He was also from the newcomers, those who had not fought in the battle at Thiele. He had been the one most vocal about positions and honors. This was the reason Aberon had given him the most dangerous avenue of attack. The road to the fortress was heavily defended with many nasty traps. He would let the arrogant beast charge ahead as he knew he would. Hra-rygk would likely destroy half his clan, and hopefully himself, in the process. It would give Ka-ragh's reserves a safer path forward.

The other lieutenants were not happy with the battle arrangements either, but none of them had any real chance at disputing Ka-ragh's claim to leadership of the combined clans. Though they growled and shuffled when Hra-rygk postured, they didn't try to gainsay Aberon.

Qa-ryks had a hierarchy within each clan. They had leaders – captains and lieutenants for all practical purposes. The rest of the clan members were ranked based on prowess and strength. Since the youngsters grew rapidly, changes in leadership were frequent. Sometimes it was hard to keep up with who had the reins, especially if Aberon left them to their own devices for a few months. After, he would have to apply himself to cultivating, often with magic, the newest beast at the top of the pile.

Another thing that Aberon disliked immensely was trying to pronounce the guttural, deep-throated-derived names of the Qa-ryks. If one listened to them speak to each other in their own tongue, it sounded like an argument between two bassos growling in their deepest range, punctuated by noises closely akin to burps and farts. He had decided to make the effort to learn as many of their sounds and words as possible. To give them credit, the males had picked up a rudimentary understanding of the common tongue, albeit with many guttural inflections. The problem was it was virtually impossible to understand what they said. They had extreme difficulty with any type of "S" or "Z" sound, and their deep growling tones made it hard to decipher what they were trying to get across. Typically, they used many hand gestures and grunts when speaking to each other. The subtlest finger motion, punctuated by some rumble in their throats, seemed to be significant.

He made the effort – to not only understand them and their ways, but to speak an occasional word in their tongue or to call them by name. It gave them the illusion that he considered their culture important. He always ended up with a sore throat after these types of briefings. It was the price he paid for increased influence over them.

"Braggh, you will be here, in the forest on the left front, and Qrragdryk on the right front." Aberon pointed to both sides of the roads. "Remember, when you charge forward you will swing around both points and attack the corners as well as the walls." He pointed at the tips of the triangles to the east and west and to the walls on either side. "Ja-raggh you will come up through the woods in the back. You must stay back in the beginning!" Aberon caught the youngest and smallest of the lieutenants in his stern gaze. "Stay in the rocks until you hear fighting in the front. If you don't, your troops will be slaughtered."

Aberon set the end of his staff firmly on the ground in front of him, grasping it near the top with both hands. He let his eyes sweep back and forth across the group of clan leaders. Though they didn't realize it, he had just reinforced his incantation binding them together, as well as to his will. "We are agreed?"

More grunts and nods.

"Good. It is time to get ready."

This announcement was met by a roar, followed by all of them pushing to their full height and stomping thrice. Aberon knew that over the next twelve hours the beasts would work themselves into a barely-controlled frenzy that, if all went as planned, would erupt at the right time against the men and women defending the stockade.

It was time for him to prepare as well. He would need to be strong for the morrow and the days following. His quest was coming to an apex. Afterward, he would know true power.

Xur

When Jared and Thistle were finally released from their bonds and allowed to take off their blindfolds, they were astounded by what they saw. Before them stood a massive monolith of what appeared to be solid stone, surrounded in part by a large triangular stockade.

As the band of thieves entered a massive double gate at the southern side of a large triangular stockade, they could get a good perspective of the home of their captives. Each wall of the stockade looked to be over one hundred and fifty paces long, and the heavy pointed logs that formed the ramparts were twenty feet high; they were scraped white and glistening in the setting sun. A walkway ran along each wall some fifteen feet up, and these were connected at the point of each triangle, as well as some thirty feet from each point, by crosswalks between the sides. At regular intervals, the walls were cut for archery slots or for the other numerous war mechanisms that lined the walkways.

Inside the outer stockade, set back by approximately fifty feet, was a second barrier of smaller sharpened logs. These were lodged in the earthen floor of the enclosure at a forty-five-degree angle or so to the ground and were set only about Qaryk chest high.

The two youngsters hung back a bit from their recent trail companions. They watched as a group of men hauled on ropes attached to sets of pulleys, folding two large sections of the inner wall back and in. Jared noted that these two sections were on wheels so they could be easily rolled back or pushed into place. Once the gates were fully open into the inner stockade, Rux's men were met by a swarm of women and other men. They greeted husbands or friends from the band enthusiastically. This was an isolated post, deep in enemy territory. The return of any patrol was a cause for thanksgiving; this one even more so because they had brought hope for their sick in the form of a powerful healer.

Excitedly chattering, the crowd of milling people slowly made their way into the second enclosure. Jared and Thistle followed. They could now see many unusual wooden siege-type mechanisms dispersed throughout the inner triangle. These were facing toward the outer walls, ready to repel any attack that managed to get inside the ramparts. At the center of the triangle were several dozen small, roofed huts, which surrounded a huge block of solid granite that thrust straight up toward the sky and towered some fifty to eighty feet above their heads. As the whole party neared the southern face of this odd monument, a slab from seemingly solid stone parted from the wall in front of them. It slid out and to the side on some mechanism Jared couldn't see. This allowed access to a large cavity within, and ultimately to a set of steps carved into the granite that descended beneath the earth.

Lute managed to separate Thistle and Jared from the main swarm of people before they reached the entrance to the underground stronghold. "Things tend to get exciting around here when a raiding party returns. When things calm down a bit, I'll show you around the enclosure. Stay here and make yourselves comfortable." Lute gestured toward a small brazier in front of one of the huts on the eastern face of the rock mound. "Don't stray far. There are too many things here that could cause you harm. I have someone to meet. I'll be back...

"Oh! There's some ale and wine in the hut. Help yourselves."

Jared was sore, tired, and thirsty. The idea of something stronger than water to drink was very appealing. Smiling at Thistle, he motioned toward the hut and led the way. The small shelter had no door, so Jared poked his head through the opening and looked around. The one-room structure was filled with a wide variety of weapons – axes, arrows of various sizes, lengths, and shapes, spears, swords, heavy spiked iron balls, and other forms of weaponry. All were ordered in bins for easy access. Against the wall by the door stood several large kegs, and lined up overhead on the rafters were leather tankards. Hung on the walls on all sides of the room where there was any free space were down-stuffed mattresses.

Jared stepped into the hut with Thistle following close behind. He reached up and took two tankards from the ceiling rack. These he filled from the nearest keg. He knew that if Thistle came from a seacoast village like his, she would probably prefer ale to wine. Handing her the frothy flagon, he raised his to his lips and downed it in one long draught. Then he leaned over to refill the tankard with the dark hopsy brew. As he began to straighten up, Thistle came up to his side and handed him hers, which she had already emptied as well. Grinning broadly, he filled hers again. He laughed heartily for the first time since before the attack on Thiele. He said, "Come on, wilderness girl. Let's look around."

After they exited the hut, they turned left and were soon standing next to an odd machine built from wood, rope, and gears. Jared took some time to examine it carefully. He could not be sure what the machine did exactly, yet he was fairly certain it was a type of purposive weapon, capable of hurling projectiles of some sort over the stockade walls at an enemy.

Sipping the ale in his tankard, Jared was beginning to feel quite relaxed. He started to walk toward the next contraption, which stood some twenty-five feet to the north. After about three strides, he turned back to see if Thistle was coming. She had paused near the first machine to remove her shoe and was rubbing her foot. She smiled at him, took a long drink from her flagon. Pointing toward the fence, she started walking toward a small animal that was penned near the wall. "Look, Jared, it's a weas...."

"Thistle, watch out!" Jared yelled. He dove towards her, tossing his tankard to the side as he went.

Thistle stopped in mid-step, wobbling for a second as she tried to regain her balance. Just as she was about to fall forward, Jared managed to grab her outstretched arm with the tankard still clutched in her hand. Getting thoroughly doused with ale in the process, he fell backwards drawing Thistle down with him. She landed on top of him, her face only inches from his.

Not knowing what he was doing, Thistle stayed in his arms. Jared, feeling the effects of the hastily quaffed ale, took advantage of the situation by planting a kiss on her lips. Thistle immediately pushed herself up, furious at him for the ploy. "Jared... Jared, that is the most inconsiderate, ignorant, totally..." She turned away from him, stomping her right foot angrily in the dirt.

Jared rose slowly to his feet, blushing deeply, and trying to wipe the dirt and ale from his tunic. He only succeeded in making a smear of mud across his chest with his hand. "Thistle..." He reached out toward her with his hand, but she spun away. "Thistle, I'm sorry. I didn't mean to... to hurt you. I thought... Look! You were about to step into a pit." He raised his voice, starting to feel irritated himself. "I'm sorry I saved your life!" Hurt by her reaction to his kiss and embarrassed at having shown her his feelings, he turned away. Stalking toward his tankard, he picked it up; then he strode angrily back into the hut.

Thistle stomped her foot again, embarrassed herself, and confused by the strong emotions she was feeling. She yelled after him, "What pit?" Turning around, she looked down, and bent over to examine the ground near where Jared had tackled her.

Several minutes later, Thistle peeked around the opening in the hut. She called out sheepishly, "Jared?"

He was hunkered down in the northernmost corner of the room with a full flagon in his hand, his face turned away. He made no move to answer her.

Thistle came in and knelt beside him. She gently pried the tankard from his grasp and took a long draught from it. Leaning over, she kissed him lightly on the forehead, then went to her knee and kissed him on his lips. She whispered, "I'm sorry, Jared. I didn't see ... I..."

He responded by reaching up and drawing her closer. This time the kiss lasted several seconds.

They were interrupted in their embrace by a cheerful, "Hello, there! You two sober? I didn't mean you had to stay in the hut. It's not *that* dangerous around here." Lute's face appeared in the opening of the hut. "Come on, I'll show you around."

Thistle pulled out of Jared's arms at Lute's first words. She stood, blushing slightly when Lute waved at them. Jared got up, a bit unsteadily, and trailed Thistle out of the shed as she followed the Journeyman Bard. As they emerged, Lute smiled broadly and announced, "Now I want you to meet the most important person in my life." He drew a small girl around from where she was hiding behind him and presented her to Thistle and Jared.

"Rose, I want you to meet Thistle and Jared. They are companions of the cleric, Sart. He's the man who is going to help your friend Artos get better. Jared and Thistle, this is my daughter, Rose. She's my reason for living and singing, since her mother was killed in a raiding party a little over a year ago. She's a bit shy at first, but you'll get to know each other after a few days."

Thistle stooped down to greet the small blond-haired girl, who was obviously related to Lute. She had his facial features, hair, and even mimicked his stance. She appeared to be three or four years old. "Hello, little flower. My, you are a darling. How old are you?"

The cute little girl smiled up at Thistle. Lute laughed heartily. "You won't get much out of her for a day or so. She is three years old. We didn't know her mother was pregnant until we arrived here; by then it was too late to go back.

"Come on, it'll be dark soon. There will be a big party in the great hall after dark to celebrate the success of our mission. If you want to be free to move around, you had better find out about Xur's little anomalies."

"Thistle discovered one of them the hard way," Jared said. "A pit, over toward the northeast, there," he pointed to where he had tackled Thistle. "I must admit it wasn't an altogether wasted experience." He grinned impishly at Thistle.

Thistle chose to ignore him, instead, taking little Rose's hand and following Lute toward the pit Jared had indicated.

"You have good eyes, elf-kin. I have trouble spotting these, and I know where they are. You will soon see that the fortress of Xur is well protected. We are in the heart of the Qa-ryk sprawl. We can't be too careful here."

For the next hour, Lute led Jared and Thistle around the compound, pointing

123

out the numerous war machines, traps, and weapons that had been prepared for any exigency. They were amazed at the intricacies of the layout, as well as the complexities of the machines themselves. Each of the contraptions throughout the inner and outer sections of the stockade was a form of weaponry. Some were arrow or spear launchers, capable of hurling long shafts or wicked barbed darts over the barriers; others were catapults of many different designs. Some of these were used to throw large stones long distances over the main wall. Others were designed to hurl a variety of other objects shorter distances, at enemies that had breached the outer walls. These included small, spiked balls, a stinging, poisonous brew of local herbs, and barrels of razor-sharp flint chips.

The whole compound was also mazed with traps, each a slight variation from the others. Some were simple pit falls, others were craters that had spikes, sticky tar, or sharp rocks waiting at the bottom to greet the unlucky intruder, and more.

Lute took them up onto the stockade walls where he explained to them that there were many more deadly traps and pitfalls amongst the tall fir trees outside the compound. These included moss-covered tunnels that led down at steep angles into the hold's large oven where red-hot coals would char the unfortunates who slid all the way down the slick grease and sharp flint-lined pits; large snap snares that could impale a person or beast on a spiked wooden trellis; and a log gauntlet that lined the main path in the woods leading to the front gates. Other pits and snares were scattered throughout the woods, around the open, plowed perimeter of the stockade, and along the main cart path into Xur. They walked around the large triangle and saw the archery slots with box quivers next to each; large crossbows set at twenty pace intervals in the walls that could shoot broad-bladed steel arrows into massed troops; and piles of heavy stones that could be rained down on anyone trying to breach the walls – all of these chipped so that the many edges were sharp and would do the most damage.

As they walked about the ramparts, Lute told them that in the early years of Xur the Qa-ryks had indeed assaulted the stockade. After their war parties had been devastated by the defenses, the place had become an island in the midst of their territory. For the past several years, none of the beasts had come within three leagues of the stockade.

He explained that the compound held only about two hundred souls, mostly men, some women, and a few children – all except the youngest were expected to pitch in to support their daily survival. In the event of a major assault, everyone had an assignment. "It can be a rough and demanding life out here. Because of the many dangers, we are a close-knit community. We manage to survive, and we even manage to make a good life of it while we are here. Biannual caravans from Borea bring in what we don't grow, gather, hunt, or make ourselves. We are well-provisioned most of the time, so there is little to want. After a time, one wishes to see more of the world and the loved ones we left at home." He gestured toward the east. "The rest of my family is in Borea, and they have yet to meet little Rose."

Both Jared and Thistle were amazed at Xur's defenses. They were also amused and somewhat astonished at little Rose's knowledge of everything Lute showed them. She would scramble energetically over each of the ballista platforms when they came to them, relishing the challenge of climbing over things, rather than taking the long way around on the stockade walkways. And though she didn't speak, she pointed with her tiny index finger to each apparatus as Lute spoke about it.

After they had toured the compound, Lute took them down one of the two stairways on the southern stockade wall and thence to the stone entryway. He told them the stairs led below to vast interlocking natural caverns beneath the stockade. Little Rose, hopping ahead now, pointed down into the opening. She stood as tall as she might and spoke her first word to them. "Foods."

Lute laughed heartily. "My little Rose loves to eat. She knows there is a party about to happen. I think she eats twice her weight every day." He scooped her up into his arms and carried her across the threshold laughing. "You're bigger again, my little flower, and I have been gone only a couple of weeks." He tickled her. She squirmed out of his arms and led them into the open maw of the cave.

"These natural caverns," Lute explained as they descended, "are used for storage, for sleeping quarters in winter, and for cooking, eating, and cleaning. A warm underground spring bubbles up in one of the deeper caves. It provides clean water, a natural bathing pool, and warmth in winter for the sleeping quarters just above. During the milder seasons, many of us sleep outdoors within the inner compound. No matter how bad the weather, the ramparts are manned by at least ten men throughout the day and night."

Lute led them down to the hot spring; and after finding new clothes from a community laundry, he also brought them towels and soap. He left them to clean off the dirt and grime of their long journey. Even here things were organized, with a private area for women set aside from where the men bathed.

Jared and Thistle (and Yolk) enjoyed a long soak in the luxurious waters. Combined with the effects of the ale they had drunk and the soothing warmth of the water, much of the tension in their bodies eased away. When they came together again in the fore chamber to the baths, they shyly took each other's hand before ascending back up the granite stairway. Lute met them again on the way up.

As they made their way through some of the smaller caverns to the main gathering hall, Lute told them about the lifestyle of the people in the stockade. "There are only a few small children like Rose. Most of those who are born here remain with their parents, though a few are sent off to study or learn a trade when they are old enough. About half the men are married, and if their wives are here, they are expected to fight and work alongside their husbands. If they wish to remain, they learn the ropes of the place, as we all do. Some choose to stay; some don't.

"We must all learn to repair, maintain, and fire the weapons and traps in and around Xur. Everyone pitches in with the daily tasks as well. Thankfully, I do not have to do much in the way of cleaning and cooking, because I earn my keep by singing and playing. It is highly doubtful that they would want me in the kitchen, anyway. My talents definitely lie elsewhere." He chuckled, his blue eyes twinkling in the torchlight.

"How do you feed and clothe this many people?" Thistle asked, as they passed a large cave opening that was busy with men and women carrying platters of food and drink into the great hall across the way.

"Through raids on outposts, other robber bands, and unsuspecting travelers like you," Lute grinned.

At that remark, Jared stopped in his tracks and looked at Lute, trying to determine whether he was jesting. Even if their overall purpose was for the good of the kingdom, Jared did not like the idea that they took what they willed from anyone, without consideration.

Lute, grinning, noted Jared's discomfort. "Sorry, I am being a bit flippant. The truth is we rarely raid anybody except the Qa-ryks, and then just to keep them at bay. Only when the need is dire, such as our need for your cleric to curtail the Beze fever, do we stoop so low as to raid common folks. This is not the best farming country; however, we do manage to grow some usable grain plants for food, and others for feed, clothing, rope and so forth. The horses, cattle, sheep, pigs, and other animals we raise have ample forage ground about the stockade; and game, wild herbs, and nuts are in abundance. Within a ten-league radius there are some remnants of orchards from old farmsteads. We gather what we can in season. We also raise a large vegetable garden, which is carefully tended during the spring and summer. On occasion, we venture far enough afield to trade with the coastal villages to the north. We try to send out expeditions two or three times a year to trade furs and other goods we have accumulated, yet often that is not feasible because of Qa-ryk activity. As you will see, we are as self-sufficient as we can be. Most of what we harvest, we use.

"Truthfully, this raiding party was extra. We do not have a cleric or physician powerful enough to do the kind of healing needed for a dread disease like Beze fever. Our herbalists are knowledgeable about what to use and mix for common ailments, but this disease is beyond their abilities. Luckily, they were able to keep the men alive long enough for Sart to get here."

"You are all comfortable? The women as well?" Thistle asked.

"You will see anon. I would say, 'yes,' if one doesn't mind hard work. Daisia, my wife, loved it here. She was a bit of the rustic sort anyway. We met during my apprenticeship when I was travelling a good bit. I would have to say most of us genuinely enjoy it here. The few that don't usually don't request a second assignment to Xur when their first is up."

"You have some contact with the outside world? With Borea?" Thistle asked another question, and Jared laughed.

"She's an inquisitive sort, Lute. Be careful or we may never get to eat."

That comment earned him a hard poke in the ribs. Still, Lute was happy to answer.

"Only through the caravans, two or rarely, three times a year, and occasional messengers keep us in touch. The convoys often bring us extras – like mail and packages from loved ones. They also include many items that simply raise peoples' spirits: books, manufactured goods, soaps, perfumes, preserved treats and candies, even trinkets and the like. We also get replacements for those whose enlistments are up, or... well, have been killed, like my Daisia. Sometimes a cleric will come in the spring to deal with any illnesses that may have lingered through the winter. The spring arrival of the column is a time of celebration and renewal for all those here. We make do and enjoy what we have when we have it.

"A contingent is coming soon. Rux and many of his veterans are finishing their three-year commitments in the field. Some will leave the service upon their return to Borea. Others, including the commander, will take the winter to be with family and friends; then they will return here in the spring. It will be both a joyful and sad time for many of us. I will return to Bard Hall with the group departing and will leave many friends here. The new company is due within two weeks."

"It seems like an isolated and difficult life for children," Thistle remarked. "Does Rose like this kind of life?" She squeezed the little girl's hand, who had not relinquished her grip since they had started back from the underground spring.

"I don't know. It is the only life she has known. She has a few children to play with. Otherwise, it is not much different from your coastal villages – a community that mostly thrives on its own." Lute brightened as he continued, "Soon, if all goes as planned, she will be in a school with lots of children, and I will have the help of my parents in raising her. I plan to spend some years in Borea as I finish my studies and start my true work as a Bard.

"You should be aware that Rux's war council is to meet tomorrow, and your friend Sart has been invited. From what I have heard, he has given our leader important news. It may bring much that we have been striving toward here to a head. If so, our mission may change. We should know more tomorrow. I am not privy to the war council, but I do keep my ear to the ground!" Lute grinned again, impishly.

"I do long to see Borea again -- the guildhall, old friends and teachers, and my family. This has been an adventure, a good learning experience; still, it is not my life. I was born to a softer existence, I am afraid. For the most part, my traveling days may be over. Few Bards actually wander about the kingdom, unless they are mentors, or it is the life they crave. Our lot is to study, teach, and to learn. The wisdom and lore of Bard Hall is its true value to our society.

"Ah, here we are." Lute gestured toward an empty space at a table at the far end of the large cavern they had entered. Everyone was already digging into the sumptuous repast.

"As you can see, the party has already started. I will soon be asked to sing. Seat yourselves; eat, drink, and enjoy. You are welcome to all and we will not watch you. Try not to think of yourselves as prisoners. While we will not hold you, I would recommend that you stay within the confines of the complex. It is dangerous outside the stockade, especially at night." With that word of warning, Lute winked and grinned. "I'll try to get away later to talk. Come on, Rose, you can see Thistle later. It's time to eat, and they're going to want you to sing a little song or two with me."

Lute left Jared and Thistle to fend for themselves. They watched as the Journeyman Bard wound his way through the maze of seats and tables heaped with food and drink to the front of the hall. Rux and The Knife, with several other men, were seated there on a slightly raised platform. They did not see any sign of Sart, but Jared supposed he was caring for the sick.

Rux grinned at Lute as he approached. He waved at the Bard with a large bone in his right fist, gesturing for him to sit at the end of the long table. The Knife glanced up at that, and his lips curled into a sneer when he saw the Journeyman Bard. A sudden chill went up Jared's spine. The fellow looked dangerous. He was glad he was "on their side."

He turned back toward their table to help Thistle get settled on the long bench. The two newcomers made themselves as comfortable as possible. They were soon eating from the bounteous assortment of meats, vegetables, cheeses, and breads laid before them. Even Yolk, who was content to spend most of his time either on Thistle's chest or back, appeared to find the atmosphere of the hall relaxing. He slid from under Thistle's tunic and unrolled happily on top of the table next to a large roast. From that vantage, he looked about with his big yellow eyes. Jared glanced up only once in the direction of the main table. He saw Lute and Rose eating contentedly at the end of the platform.

Thistle smiled at him when he looked up. She reached out and brushed back a strand of his drying hair that had fallen across his face. For some reason, he found the gesture quite intimate. He wanted to take her hand in his and hold it, remembering how smooth it had been when he had touched her. Suddenly, he felt very shy, so he just smiled back. He turned his attention back to making up for all the food he hadn't eaten in the past week.

After a half hour, some of the men in the hall began clamoring for music. Jared looked up and saw Lute unsling his instrument and settle on a small podium in front of the main table to sing. His high tenor voice rang out in the great hall. Soon Jared found himself humming and tapping his foot to the popular drinking songs he knew so well. After a half hour of singing by himself, Lute drew Rose up on his knee. He accompanied the little girl's sweet soprano voice on his harp. He changed the tunes from the more boisterous to the carefree simple songs of young children. A hush settled over the hall as a sense for the reverence of years gone by affected all there. Finally, after several songs together, Lute set Rose down, where she was corralled by one of the women nearby. He returned to singing songs of men, love, nature, and beauty.

Jared had almost dozed off when he heard someone shout, "Let's hear the new fellow sing." Several others soon joined in, clamoring for "The lad with the harp," or "That tall fellow." Still dazed and half asleep, he was pushed toward the front of the hall. Once there, a man shoved Jared's portative harp into his hands. Lute leaned over and whispered in his ear, as he stood there feeling lost and very foolish, "I tuned it for you. Do you know Harper's Row?" Jared nodded dumbly. "Key of D." Lute started into the song. "Harper had a pretty little lass...." Jared stood looking confused. Lute stopped and looked up at him, "What's the matter, Jared?"

"I... I don't know what you mean by Key of D." He blushed deeply.

"Oh, sorry. I guess I assumed... well, 'D' is the tonal center of the scale." Jared nodded. He did know his notes by ear, though he did not read music. "Here, follow this chord pattern." Lute plucked a series of chords on his own harp.

Jared picked up the progression easily. The second time through, he felt more comfortable. He joined in when they reached the verse. Jared sang softly at first, unsure of himself and apprehensive about what he might feel; but the song and music soon caught him up. He began the reprise with a full-throated, clean medium tenor, which he harmonized easily with Lute's melody, "Harper had a pretty little lass. Her eyes were clear and bright..."

They continued for what seemed like hours, alternating roles singing and accompanying until Jared's throat and fingers were sore. Finally, as many of the men and women had fallen asleep or left, they stopped. While Lute finished the festivities with a haunting melody of longing, Jared went over to where he had left Thistle and Yolk. The two were sound asleep; Yolk was curled up next to a large roast bone, his eyes poking up on top of the roll of his body.

When Lute was done, he suggested that Jared pick Thistle up. Letting her head rest against his shoulder, Jared eased her off the bench. She woke just enough to stretch out both her arms around his neck. She said sleepily, "That was beautiful, Jared." She nodded off again. Yolk moved slowly up Jared's body until he rested neatly rolled up between Thistle's arm and his neck. He carried them up to the open air. It was a glorious, cool fall evening with bright stars covering the sky.

Once outside, Lute took some mattresses and warm blankets from one of the huts. Laying Thistle, Yolk, and Rose, who was also asleep, on one, Jared and Lute shared another of the large, soft bed rolls. Before they settled back, Lute took Jared's hand and shook it firmly. "You sing and play well even though you have no formal training. I'm sorry about earlier. I assumed you knew some basic musical theory when you said Lassus had taught you. Can you read and write?"

Jared nodded. "Both common tongue and high elven, but not musical notes. My mother taught my brother Ge-or and I to read scrolls and books. Our father insisted we keep it up. He would buy books each year from the traders for us to read, mostly chivalrous romances, histories, and the like."

Lute clapped him lightly on the shoulder. "You have passed the first initiate tests, Jared. You have true musical talent; I can bear witness to that. You have an excellent ear and sing perfectly in tune. You also have a knack for harmonizing and improvisation, which is a bonus. It is a natural gift you have. You will certainly need a good bit of musical training and study to catch up with others your age. Goodnight, my friend, for I count you as such. Tomorrow maybe we can continue your tests and trials."

Jared wasn't quite sure what he meant by "tests and trials." Still, he didn't think he could be any more nervous than he had been earlier. He reached over to Thistle, who was fast asleep on the other mattress. As if to return the favor from before, he brushed his hands across her forehead, pushing her hair back from her eyes. She is incredibly beautiful, he thought. He settled back with a smile on his face.

***

Dawn was beginning to streak the sky when an alarm rang out. "Qa-ryks! Qa-ryks! Man the ramparts!" Jared sat up, startled awake by the cry. He looked over toward Thistle; she was already getting to her feet. Lute was up and running toward the hut behind them. "Come on, we'll need your help!" he cried. He disappeared into the opening. Rose was already running toward the steps that led down to the caverns. Jared grabbed the mattresses and followed Thistle at a run.

Accused

Ge-or woke to feel a cool compress against his hot forehead. He opened his eyes but couldn't seem to focus. He could barely make out general shapes in the flickering candlelight. Voices were carrying on a conversation; he couldn't focus on that, either. Finally, he gave up and slid back into oblivion.

When he next awoke, it was to a pressure behind his neck. It took him a moment to realize that a feminine voice was urging him to drink something. "Please drink. It's a tea for the fever – feverfew and other herbs."

Ge-or opened his mouth slightly. He felt a hot, bitter brew flow into his mouth. At first, he couldn't swallow; he coughed and sputtered, spewing the stuff across his chest. His eyes flew open at the struggle; still, he couldn't make out anything except for light and dark shapes shifting in his field of vision.

The woman spoke again. "Drink. You have to keep trying; it is all we have for your temperature." Ge-or opened his mouth when he felt the press of the cup on his lips. This time he managed to get some down his swollen throat, then a bit more. He drifted in and out of consciousness as the woman persisted in making him drink as much of the tea as he could. Eventually, he dropped back into a heavy slumber.

When he woke again, there was daylight in the room where he lay. His eyes were heavy with sleep, and he kept dozing and waking for what seemed like a long time. He was jarred awake sometime later by the sound of a man and woman arguing.

"It's full of contraband, I tell you. 'e's a brigand... a thief, Daughter. Best to cut his throat and have done with it."

"Father!" The female voice was just as vehement in protesting what the man had said. "Give the man a chance to speak. He may die anyway; he's not out of the woods yet. He lost a lot of blood, and the infection is barely contained. Why have his life on your hands?"

"How many did he kill for all that stuff out there? Tell me that?"

Ge-or tried to raise himself up; the red haze of his fever beat him down. He gave up and croaked out, "Not thief..." He began coughing. The woman rushed in through the open door to him, placing her hand on his chest.

"You see..."

"Pah..."

Between racking coughs Ge-or tried to continue. "Captured... I escaped... wounded..." but the coughing fit continued. He ended up gasping for air, unable to say anything else. Just before he fell back into unconsciousness, he thought he tasted blood.

Attack!

Shaking his head to clear out the cobwebs, Jared ran after Lute into the hut, dragging the two mattresses with him to get them out from underfoot of the defenders. Thistle had gotten there first. As she ducked into the doorway, she was helping Yolk get underneath her tunic. Lute gestured toward a neat row of bows and quivers of arrows near the entrance. "Can you shoot, Jared? Thistle?"

"I prefer the shortbow, but can shoot either," Jared answered. He hadn't considered asking for his own bow back the previous eve, so he reached out to receive the mountain shortbow and a quiver of arrows Lute handed him. It would have to do. Thistle, standing at his side, shook her head, "No."

Lute, grabbing a longbow himself, moved over to the next stack of weapons. He pulled out a short sword and said, "Take one of these, anything else will be difficult to use on the ramparts." Jared reached out and took a sword from the stack, didn't like the feel, dropped it and tried another. Lute looked at Thistle questioningly.

She shook her head again. "I'm only good with knives, throwing, if you have them."

"Over in the corner," Lute said, pointing toward a small bin. "Jared, come with me to the south ramparts. We'll need the extra men there. That's where the brunt of the attack will likely be." Lute was already moving toward the door of the hut. "Thistle," he yelled over his shoulder, "it would probably be best for you to stay here in the inner wall and help with the machines. The dart thrower to the northeast is minus a man from the fever. Please make sure Rose went down into the cavern as I told her. Stay safe!"

Thistle waved in assent. She turned to go, then paused and reached out to Jared. "Be careful, half-elf," she said softly.

Jared, smiled. He reached out and touched her fingertips lightly. A second later, he followed Lute.

The whole compound was alive with running figures. Many men and women were climbing the ladders and stairways to the ramparts; others were hastily getting the various war machines in the stockade loaded and ready to fire. Lute led Jared up a ladder near the eastern corner of the south wall. As they clambered up on the walkway, Jared could see a large company of Qa-ryks milling around off in the distance. A few small groups had made tentative penetrations into the forest areas on either side of the main road; however, none of the creatures had ventured into the one hundred and fifty paces of cleared terrain surrounding the stockade. Most of them appeared to be waiting for something. Jared half-expected a great red dragon to come circling out of the gray morning sky toward the gates.

Lute motioned Jared toward a part of the wall where they found several free archery slots. Just as they were getting positioned, a roar went up from the Qa-ryks. The roar continued as a tall black clad figure swept through their ranks. "Aberon!" Jared exclaimed. Lute glanced at Jared in surprise.

The dark figure of the druid, floating above the ground, came at an incredible speed toward the main gate as if he were being pushed by some unseen force. When he was within fifty feet of the gate, he abruptly stopped, raised his long ebon staff, and shouted to the sky. A flash of light burst from the staff, which immediately formed into a fiery ball. It sped toward the gate and burst on impact.

The men and women on the wall began to react as soon as they saw the dark priest rushing toward them; but the attack was so fast that most only had time to duck down. A few were wise enough to dive backwards for the ground at the sight of the fire speeding toward them; they were the only ones to evade the full force of the explosion.

The whole southern wall of the stockade shook from the force of the blast. The gates burst asunder, with the men and women who were on the ramparts at that point dying instantly from the explosion. Others nearby began to scream as their clothing burst into flame.

On either side of the burnt section, archers with longbows drew back and loosed their arrows at the now slowly retreating dark priest. Though the bowmen were good marksmen, none of the arrows found a mark. Many seemed to be deflected by some force encircling the evil druid. The others simply disappeared when they got within two feet of his body. As soon as Aberon was out of bow range, a tremendous roar shook the trees to the south. This was taken up by the beasts all around the stockade. As it roiled back around to the front, the Qa-ryks launched their assault down the road and through the woods.

Jared realized that there were many more Qa-ryks than he had first believed. This was the equivalent of a full regiment of the powerful warriors – many more than had attacked Thiele. The whole forest to either side of the road was full of the large humanoids charging toward the walls. As he glanced to his left, he could see others pouring out of the woods to attack the eastern wall of the triangle. Setting an arrow and raising his bow to get set up to shoot, Jared was stopped by the touch of a hand on his shoulder. "Wait, Jared. You'll see a few surprises, before you will have a chance to shoot. This attack will fail in spite of that dark priest's fire. The Qa-ryks are afraid of this place for good reason."

As Lute spoke, Jared saw the Qa-ryks coming down the center of the road suddenly engulfed by huge swinging logs suspended from the tall trees on either side of the narrow wagon trail. Catching the foremost ranks of beasts from each side, the heavy logs swung out in long pendulum arcs, crushing them like flies. One large beast to the fore of the others was struck simultaneously by two of the logs and literally torn in two. The impact of the logs flung the pieces of his body into the forest on either side of the road.

As the log pendulums swung back off the road, more Qa-ryks were pushed forward into the gauntlet by the press of their comrades behind. These also met their deaths as the huge logs once again swung in. Soon the whole mass on the road was fighting backward to get out of range of the swinging deathtrap.

Cries of fear and pain echoed from the woods on all sides as well. Jared saw one Qa-ryk hauled high in the air by a snare. As the tree snapped back, the beast was impaled on a well-placed set of spikes. Others disappeared into ground traps. Before the attack had gained a hundred paces, the Qa-ryks began to pull back.

Jared shuddered, realizing he had been standing with his bow half drawn in his tense grip. He tried to relax as the Qa-ryks retreated. Lute grinned at him, "They will need more than magic to defeat Rux's Demons." As he spoke, a wave of flame rose behind the beasts on the road. More magic from Aberon, Jared thought. The fire drove the Qa-ryks forward again to the assault.

This time the Qa-ryks moved cautiously along the side of the road. They also began to creep more slowly through the trees. As he swung around to try to catch sight of Thistle below, Jared saw Sart. The priest was near the main gate, working with some of those burnt in Aberon's flaming attack. He almost jumped from the walkway when he heard Thistle's voice behind him. "You don't look as if you've done much shooting yet," she said.

He spun around the other way and saw that she was busy placing arrows in a small box next to his archery slot. "We're ready to go at the dart thrower, so I volunteered to take some arrows around." She looked at him worriedly. "It's Aberon, isn't it?"

Jared nodded, taking her free hand in his. Lute asked, "Who is this Aberon?"

Before either of them could answer, there was a loud roar as the main mass of Qa-ryks reached the edge of the woods.

Thistle gave Jared a quick kiss on the cheek; then she was off in a crouching run, placing arrows at every position from the large quiver she held in her arm. Lute and Jared eased up to their respective archery slots.

With the fire threatening to engulf them from behind, many of the beasts were beginning to charge out across the open plain. The men with longbows began to launch their arrows as more Qa-ryks lumbered into effective range. Lute drew back and fired while Jared watched with fascination the slow unfolding of the battle. He would not be able to shoot with any accuracy until the Qa-ryks had come within at least sixty paces of the wall, preferably forty or fifty. Now that the initial excitement had passed, he clutched his bow loosely at his side. He had chosen the more flexible shortbow, because once the enemy was within range, he would be able to shoot more quickly than with a longbow; and he would have the ability to shoot from anywhere on the rampart, not being restricted, as the longbowmen were, to archery stations.

While he watched, he saw Qa-ryks run forward, pause to launch a buoa, and then continue ahead. At this range, the buoas were still deadly, but unless you were preoccupied, they could easily be dodged. Jared watched several fly toward the ramparts with only one finding a mark. The man hit by the buoa was caught full in the chest. He had been firing his longbow at another Qa-ryk when the spiral hit him. The force of the blow sent him backwards off the rampart. Jared watched numbly as the man grasped awkwardly at his chest in mid-air. He landed with a sickening thud, sprawled grotesquely on the earth below, unmoving. Turning back to the battle, Jared saw more Qa-ryks mutilated by traps they stumbled into, and others pierced by arrows from longbows. Yet the beasts were so numerous, that as a group they were inexorably moving closer to the fort. A large group of the creatures had returned to the road after passing the section where the trees had crushed their comrades. These joined the rush to the fort.

Now that the beasts were within his range, Jared drew back his bow and took careful aim at one of the leading Qa-ryks. As he released the arrow, the Qa-ryk suddenly disappeared. The arrow struck the thigh of the Qa-ryk behind and to the side of the one he had aimed at. The whole area in front of the rushing Qa-ryks opened up, and a dozen or more pitched into a deep, spike-lined pit. Terrible screams and hoarse shouts erupted from the area. Jared set another arrow to his string and took aim at another beast.

The air was suddenly filled with showers of missiles from the fort. Spiked metal balls capable of cruelly gashing the skin, sharp stones, larger boulders, arrows, and spears rained down, sending the Qa-ryks into a milling mass. For several minutes, the attack was stalled. The men and women archers of the fort continued to pick out targets from the ramparts, as the beasts pushed forward and back in their frenzy to avoid the death coming from above.

Jared nocked one arrow after another, drew back in one smooth motion, brought the bow to his eye, and released as he came onto a target. His aim was true; he placed his arrows in the chests or sides of six of the beasts as the mass closed in on the fort. Once they came within twenty-five paces of the walls, he began aiming for the thick necks of the beasts, skewering three Qa-ryks in quick order. At that close a range, he could have hit the center of their eyes; but you could not always account on what direction they might twist or turn once your shaft was released. His father had taught him and Ge-or to aim at the surest killing spot with the greatest diameter. Using a shortbow against these massive beasts at close range, that was the neck.

It was at this juncture of the battle that Aberon attacked again, this time on the eastern wall of the triangle. Another ball of fire exploded into the stockade creating a second gaping hole. Qa-ryks on that side charged for the opening, while men inside tried desperately to fill the gap.

To the south, the beasts now coming up had skirted the spike pits and were massing before the destroyed front gates. Many others had closed to the stockade walls to escape the deadly hail of missiles from above. At the blasted gates, Rux, who was directing the defenses below, led a charge of strong fighters to block the entrance. Men and beasts were soon locked together at close quarters with swords, pikes, clubs, and wicked claws flashing in the morning sun.

Jared and Lute continued to shoot quickly and accurately from their positions on the rampart as the main body of Qa-ryks attacked the walls. Many were massed at the fiery openings, trying to fight their way into the stockade. Others jumped at the walls of the fort trying to claw their way up like cats. The hard, smooth, greased logs, however, afforded little purchase even for their powerful claws. Only a few were able to climb up high enough to reach over the top and haul themselves over.

The defenders were now aiming directly down with their weapons; and

134

though their arrows knocked the scrabbling beasts off the walls, often they would rise again and continue their frenzied clawing to get up and over. Even well-placed arrows rarely killed the beasts quickly. They had thick skins, incredible stamina, and a frenzied energy that kept them going until they simply collapsed in death.

The fight at the gate became increasingly desperate as the powerful Qa-ryks forced their way into the enclosure. Slinging his bow, Lute drew his sword and rushed across the rampart, yelling for Jared to follow. "Come on, we can't do much more here. We need to fight on our way to the inside perimeter. Remember to watch for traps."

Yelling hoarsely and realizing he must have been shouting for a while, Jared followed close behind. He drew his sword and struck out at a Qa-ryk that had managed to climb to the top of the ramparts. His powerful blow hacked off the beast's claw and the creature fell backwards from the wall. Soon Jared and Lute were fighting several of the beasts that had clawed their way onto the crosswalk near the burnt gates. Lute picked up a shield that was lying against an arrow bin as he moved up, but Jared relied on his agility to counter the blows of the two creatures to his fore. He successfully ducked under a swipe of a claw and stabbed one beast deep in its stomach. Jared then swept his blade up to counter a savage swipe from the other. Following through, he brought the sword across in a slicing arc, cutting through the throat of the beast he had wounded. Parrying again quickly, he heard Lute shout, "Jump down. We don't stand a chance here. They've broken through the wall below." He disappeared with a leap over the edge of the walkway.

Just in time, Jared dove sideways off the rampart as a Qa-ryk came up behind him and swung wildly at his back with an axe. He spun as he landed, managing to hit another Qa-ryk in the back with a slicing blow as he somersaulted to his feet. He rolled quickly up away from the wall and scrambled toward the inner fence. The beast he had cut spun around, swinging at him with its bloody mace. The blow glanced against Jared's right side, tearing through his tunic, crushing and ripping the flesh. Forced to his left, he fell to one knee.

Pulling his knife from his belt, he parried the next swing of the mace with his sword. Plunging upward with his left hand, he sank the long blade up through the beast's soft belly and into the Qa-ryk's lower chest. The creature roared, reeling back in pain. Jared stepped forward, and with a wicked stroke brought his sword down onto its neck in a powerful blow, almost decapitating the Qa-ryk. Not pausing to see his opponent fall, Jared ran to his right where the fighting was fiercest.

The Qa-ryks meanwhile had gained considerable ground inside the compound. Only a few pockets of men were managing to hold off the full assault from gaining momentum toward the open inner gates of the stockade. Rux was fighting alone near the center, a sword in one hand and a huge battle axe in the other. As Jared pushed forward, he sliced at the hairy backs and shoulders of several beasts as he passed. As he got near Rux, he saw three more Qa-ryks break through the opening and attack the huge man.

As if from nowhere, The Knife came up and neatly slipped his long, wicked blade into the back of the neck of one of the beasts attacking Rux. As the Qa-ryk slid to the ground, his spinal cord severed, the lean wiry man spun on his heel and struck again and again with deadly accuracy. Two more Qa-ryks fell; then he and the robber leader were swarmed over by a fresh attack.

Several moments later, Jared managed to again cut his way through to Rux. Fighting desperately, he and two other men drove the beasts back long enough for the big man to retreat. For The Knife, unfortunately, they were too late. The little man had been raked by sharp claws during the worst of the melee. He lay in a pool of blood between Jared and Rux. Weeping openly, Rux dropped his huge battle axe and picked up his friend with his one arm, carrying him back through the inner gates.

Jared did not have time to watch where they ended up. He dodged another Qa-ryk's attack as he turned to face the assault once again. He hoped he and the other men could give Rux enough time to get safely within the inner perimeter. He drove forward, not so much inflicting mortal damage with the whirl of his blades, as trying to get some breathing room. Yet with the beasts pressing the attack anew, he had to retreat slowly, fighting his way back toward the inner compound with the others.

All around Jared was mass confusion. Everyone who could get free were streaming toward the spiked fence. With the men breaking from their defensive line, the Qa-ryks paused momentarily in their assault.

Taking advantage of the lull, Jared spun about and sprinted for the entrance. Just outside the gateway, he turned around to help form a defensive semi-circle, as other men fought toward the protected opening. The Qa-ryks roared and charged forward en masse. The fight whirled all around where Jared stood as he thrust and parried. With friends to either side, it was difficult in the confined space to inflict deadly wounds to the beasts. Jared's blades danced in his hands, biting sharply into his opponents' sides, arms, and legs.

Slowly, the diminishing group of defenders fell backward toward the enclosure. At the last minute, before turning to rush inside himself, Jared saw Lute trying to cut his way through to his left. The Journeyman Bard was separated from the gates by two Qa-ryks; and though he fought bravely, he was being pushed further to the side by the beasts, unable to fight through. Instead of breaking back, Jared pushed out ahead of the thinly held line to engage one of the beasts attacking his friend. Faking a stab with his sword, he used the knife in his left hand to slice deeply into the Qa-ryk's upper thigh. As it stumbled before him, Jared flipped the knife in his left hand and threw the blade at the other Qa-ryk. Caught between the shoulder blades by the sharp weapon, the beast reared back, giving Lute the chance to bury his sword in its lower chest. Jared finished off the first Qa-ryk with a chopping blow from his sword, almost taking the beast's head off with the fierceness of the downward sweep of the blade. He joined Lute in a dash for the enclosure.

They barely made it to the inner defensive line when a signal from within the compound warned the small rearguard to break off their defense and make a run for the opening.

Almost immediately, the Qa-ryks charged forward following the retreating men. The gates never got completely closed, but the assault was stymied there for several minutes as the beasts tried to deal with the sharpened spikes. Jared and Lute stumbled into the inner compound.

Lute suddenly gasped as he ran, sprawling heavily to the ground. Jared, turning back around, saw his friend clutching his side. He could see a steady stream of blood leaking through his friend's fingers. "Lute!" Jared exclaimed, reaching out to help the musician to his feet. "Come on, let me help you bind that."

Lute pushed his hand aside. "Don't. Use your bow. I'll manage. Fight, Jared, fight! We can't afford to lose. You don't understand the importance of this fort." Lute coughed. Jared saw blood on his lips as the musician drew his hands back from his mouth. He smiled weakly up at Jared. "You have passed all the trials, elf-kin. You are quick and brave in a fight, a true friend and fighter. Don't worry about me. I'll manage.

136

Go, fight. I'll get below."

Lute wobbled out of Jared's grasp and unsteadily made his way back toward the stairway leading up to the granite block. Seriously worried about his friend, Jared nevertheless turned back to the battle. Unslinging his bow and choosing his aim carefully to avoid hitting any of the rangers, he began to fire into the mass of Qa-ryks engaged with the defenders near the gate.

All about him, the inner missile machines were discharging their loads over the spiked fence. Only at the gate to the inner compound were the Qa-ryks making progress. There the defenders' swords, axes, and knives rose and fell, and the claws of their opponents flashed as men and beasts fought to the death.

After shooting the last few arrows in his quiver, Jared picked up his sword again and rushed toward the gate to help with the defense. Before he could reach the barrier, the Qa-ryk attack suddenly drew back, opening a pathway through to the destroyed main gates. As the Qa-ryks gave way, a tall black-clad figure strode self-assuredly through the partially open inner gate. It was Aberon. He held his staff high in the air and began to speak in a dark, strident voice.

Sart came forward from amongst the defensive line forming near the entrance to the caverns. With his staff in his left hand and his rood out in front, the good cleric stepped toward Aberon, shouting, "Begone foul creature, vile priest. By the power of the Earth, I say begone!"

Aberon did not seem surprised at Sart's presence; and though he took one step back as Sart approached, he brought his staff level with his chest, holding it forward in his two hands. Continuing to shout in a language Jared did not know, the evil priest thrust the head of his dark staff toward Sart's chest. Facing each other several paces apart, the two priests struggled for dominance.

After several minutes, Sart began to waver, drawing slowly backward before the silent onslaught. Aberon, laughing wickedly, stepped ahead. He raised his staff above his head as if to strike the now-faltering cleric. Instead, he stopped with it raised on high, with the gnarled end pointing directly at Sart's chest. His eyes rolled back, and foamy spittle came from his mouth as he screamed a series of syllables. Faltering to one knee, the good cleric tried to gather reserves of energy to combat the wicked incantation; but he knew he was spent. He had used much of his inner force working to heal those injured by fire and claw.

Jared shook himself, coming out of a trance-like state. Looking desperately for a weapon he could hurl, he suddenly remembered the buoa he had taken from the dead Qa-ryk Captain. Reaching for the pouch tied to his belt, he tore the top open and withdrew the deadly spiral. Relying on instinct and luck, as much as an understanding of the weapon Jared had received from his father, he launched the spiral blade at the evil druid the very second Aberon swung his staff down toward Sart's head.

The blade flew true enough. Though missing the mark he had aimed for, it sliced at an angle across the dark priest's right side, below the armpit. Shrieking in pain and rage, Aberon, his focus disrupted, fell backward. Seeing Sart getting to his feet, he panicked. With a flash like a lightning strike, followed by a thunderous clap, he disappeared from the compound.

All motion in the enclosure appeared to hang for a moment. Then, with the dread priest gone, the people in the stockade exploded into motion. Men and women who had gathered at the opening to the caverns rushed forward to the attack. Those in the front lines pushed ahead to engage the beasts anew. The Qa-ryks, instead of continuing their fierce assault, were milling about, confused by the loss of the power that had kept them focused and driven. Loaded machines were fired, unloaded machines were left empty as the crews joined the attack with swords and spears. Within two minutes, the whole atmosphere of the battle had changed. Qa-ryks were now struggling for their lives, trying to fight themselves free from the stockade and the battle fury of their assailants.

Jared, stunned, stood watching the last of the battle. By the time he had recovered enough to rearm himself and join the fray, the Qa-ryks were streaming out of the stockade. Wearily dragging his sword as he reentered the inner compound, he was met by an exuberant Thistle wielding a bloody knife.

"Jared, you're safe," she cried with relief, hugging him closely. "I was terrified that you hadn't made it back in when the perimeter fell. I've been over to the northwest. It's been hand-to-hand. What happened here?"

"Aberon," he answered. Then he saw a familiar figure lying near the entrance to the caverns.

Aftermath

Aberon was more than angry. "Where had that half-elf come from? And why was he still alive?" His fire should have consumed the whole grove. Yet, unless he was mistaken, the bastard had hit him with a buoa. It stung, too.

He had teleported back several hundred paces from the stockade to where his horse was tethered. One thing he had learned long ago was to be prepared for a hasty exit. Things didn't always go your way no matter how carefully they were planned. He had no thought of going back and reorganizing the battle. Let the Qa-ryks fend for themselves. Now, before that cursed cleric could get organized enough to trail him, he would take this opportunity to get to Kan's Altar. There he could at least salvage something from this bloody mess.

Perhaps he had been too greedy for a decisive victory; perhaps he should have taken care of the stone first. Destroying Xur would have negated the Borean attempt to find the altar. That would now have to wait for another day. Neutralizing the stone was of the utmost priority. He could yet snatch victory from this field of battle. Hopefully, that meddling cleric would be overwhelmed with taking care of the wounded at the fort. Aberon would make all haste west.

Many of the Qa-ryks would survive. They would disperse back to their clannish existence, until the next time he and his brethren decided to draw some of them together. It would be more work, but not so much as one would suppose. By that time, the whole leadership would have changed within the clans. Their chieftains did not live long. There were always young pups growing up quickly, and loyalty had no place in their culture. The hierarchy was entirely based on the biggest, strongest, and most willing and able to kill.

Opening his saddle bag, Aberon took out his kit and smeared a salve on the wound under his arm. Then he took a special cloth, magically designed, and slapped it in place. The wound would heal in a few days. His clerical powers did not include healing. Such was too antithetical to his brethren's dark ways. They did know a great deal about using dark magic to facilitate healing with herbs and poultices. He himself had forwarded an approach to his brethren that included many new types of bandages and other devices for tending wounds, and for use in surgery as well. The patch he had applied not only helped keep the herbal salve in place, it also kept the wound clean and bound. Its magic helped knit the edges of the wound together more quickly; and later, after a couple of days, it would fall off. He would be sore for a week or more. That would serve as a reminder to him that he had been careless. He couldn't remember the last time someone had gotten through his defenses. Someday that boy would pay and so would that pestering cleric.

Aberon grabbed the reins off his horse's neck and hoisted himself into the saddle, grunting at the pain in his side. He could take some herbs for the discomfort; however, occasionally pain was good. It kept one alert. It was something that he had never quite understood about himself – for some reason pain always made him feel more alive. He knew that at least for a little while he would use it to his advantage, and in an odd way, his pleasure. When he tired of it, he would take something. Pain had its uses, yet after a while he grew weary of its nagging at him.

He turned the horse's head to the west. He would rest later, when he was well away from this debacle. There was one thing he did feel good about from this day's labor – the Qa-ryks had, except for isolated incidences, followed their orders. Their spells had worked. That was some important news he could bring back to the Nine.

***

Rushing over to his friend, Jared yelled, "Sart! Sart, come quickly, Lute's hurt." Jared knelt and picked up the Journeyman Bard by the shoulders. The ground around Lute's body was soaked with blood. Jared saw another wound in Lute's lower thigh where a buoa had struck him.

Lute opened his eyes when Jared lifted him. He smiled weakly, "I never made it up the stairs. Too weak... Wouldn't you know they'd get me when…" He coughed, "when I was ready to leave." As he spoke, a trickle of blood came out of his mouth. He continued to talk, haltingly, as if something important needed to be said. "I want to... to tell you... before I die. I want to write..."

Sart came up and knelt by Lute's side, bending down to examine him. Lute had closed his eyes for a minute; he opened them at the touch of the cleric. "Bless you, Father, I am afraid you can't help me." Anxiously Jared looked at Sart as he examined Lute's wounds. The cleric looked up sadly a second later and shook his head. Even if he hadn't been exhausted from his battle with Aberon, he wasn't sure he could have saved the musician. His wounds were grievous. Having been left unattended during the heat of the battle, he had bled far too much.

Jared bowed his head, tears welling up in his eyes. He had only known the cheerful musician for a little over a week, yet Lute had reminded him of something that he believed he had lost forever – the power and beauty of music. He had also given him hope of a new life, something to replace the familiar life he had lost when his village had been destroyed. Most importantly, he had offered him and Thistle friendship, when that was above all what they needed.

"Don't mourn for me, Jared," Lute said weakly. "We did what was necessary." He closed his eyes. When he opened them a minute later, he continued, "See that Rose is taken to the east. My parents... in Borea... they will care for her." He coughed again, spewing more blood on the front of his tunic. Closing his eyes, it was a long time before he spoke again.

When he opened them, it took him a little while to focus on those around him. "Ah, Rux." The rebel leader had come up and knelt opposite Sart. The Demons' leader was wounded himself in many places. He picked up Lute's hand and held it gently. "My good friend and leader, there is one thing... please do for me." Lute managed a weak smile. "A note to my guild... introduce this young half-elf here. He passed the trials. He will make... a good Bard. Promise me... this."

"It is done." The deep voice of Rux was heavy with sorrow.

"Where is my Rose?" Lute cried suddenly, slumping in Jared's hands.

"Father!" A small voice cried. Lute's daughter rushed forward out of the grasp of a woman who had brought her up from below. She flung her little arms about her father's neck and cried.

Jared eased Lute's shoulders to the ground, tears streaming down his face. Thistle gathered the distraught little girl in her arms as they all mourned the Journeyman Bard's loss.

After Thistle had insisted on carefully binding Jared's bloody and badly bruised side, they both helped Sart with his work: bandaging, applying herbs and salves, and helping with surgeries. As they worked, the sun rose to its height, warming the war-torn arena with welcome heat. When the most life-threatening wounds had

140

been taken care of, Sart, exhausted from the healings and his fight with Aberon, sat down heavily on the edge of a mattress drawn from one of the huts. Jared, his side aching badly, slumped next to him. A few minutes later, Thistle came over with welcome bowls of hot stew prepared by those in the caverns below.

They ate in the middle of the ruins of the battle, exhausted almost beyond measure. The whole compound seemed to reflect the deep sadness they were all feeling. The few people who were moving about were doing so reverently, as if they were attending a service. Even the moans of the wounded had subsided.

When they had finished eating, the three of them lay back on the mattress, their heads almost touching. Jared, for his part, felt like the nightmare of Thiele had come to visit him again. As he tried to rest, he couldn't help feeling that somehow this was all a bad dream. If he could wake up, all would be as it had been before the dragon. "Yet," he speculated, "then I would not have met Thistle." On impulse, he reached up over his head, twisting slightly so he could see her. He touched her face lightly with his fingers. She smiled, and responded by leaning into his touch and murmuring, "Oh, Jared." He could feel tears begin to slide down her cheek.

He was about to turn fully around to comfort her, when Sart suddenly sat straight up, his eyes opening wide as if he had been startled. Both Jared and Thistle popped up as well, wondering if he was all right. The cleric, who they had thought to be in silent meditation for the past ten minutes, began to speak, as if they were not there. "That's what it must be. It all centers on the pendant."

Sart turned toward them, twisting his rump on the mattress. "Jared, Thistle, I think I understand something of how this all fits together – the importance of the stone you found, and Aberon's intentions." Speaking rapidly, he continued, as if time were suddenly terribly important. "At first I could not understand why he would dare to attack here; now I think I know. He wanted me dead and he wanted this fort overcome. He does not want me or Rux's men to interfere with what he plans to accomplish next. Part of his purpose all along has been to lure me on so he could eventually kill me. By following him, I was led directly into his trap. He knew that as long as I was after him, he could not hope to destroy the pendant freely without opposition. When he realized I was still on his trail, he gathered more forces for a strike on this compound. It was a daring move, and he almost won. If it hadn't been for your..." his voice trailed away. He looked over Jared's head, as if pondering another concern.

"Yet, perhaps...? Yes! I guess that would make more sense," Sart mused. "He must have planned the assault on this fort a while ago. Our being abducted and being taken here, were simply bonuses to his over-arching strategy. He felt he would be able to take care of me in the bargain.

"His power is far greater than I first believed. He has been toying with me. All the time I followed him, he was playing his game, a game with a larger purpose. With that buoa throw, you saved my life, many lives here, Jared. I thank you.

"Providence does move in strange ways sometimes. Perhaps you were destined to find the stone, to meet up with Thistle, and perhaps I was also destined to come across your path at the right time." Sart shook his head, looking again at Jared and Thistle, who were now sitting holding hands and watching him closely.

"I hope he doesn't realize that you two are alive. It is possible he may have recognized Jared, at the last; maybe not as he was focused on destroying me. That fact may be of importance for what we have to do next, if you are willing?"

"If it means paying him back for this," Jared gestured at the devastation

141

around them, "and for Thiele, count me in."

"And me," Thistle challenged the cleric. "I won't be left behind."

Sart didn't answer her implied challenge; he was completely focused on what he was about to say. "I believe he is heading for the Altar of Kan. The wise of the kingdom have been seeking it for many long years. Finding it has been one of the key reasons Xur was built. It is the real reason Rux's Rangers are here. Once he trusted me, Rux and I talked about their mission on our ride here. Finding that dread altar has also been a fringe element of my own quest in seeking more knowledge about the Black Druids." Sart paused; his eyelids narrowed intently.

"I believe that now Aberon's plans to destroy Xur and to kill me have failed, he will make all haste to get to Kan's Altar. It is where he is most powerful; hence, it is the place where he will try to destroy the stone. For whatever reason, whatever powers it holds, he understands that this artifact is best moved out of the kingdom's reach. He will press with all speed to get there before we can recover from this assault...

"Do you see? It is the stone that has been his focus all along. Thiele, your father's sword, me, even Xur, were secondary aims. Important, yes, but only meant to help him toward his goal. They were never the most critical elements.

"There, at Kan's Altar, he will work dire magic – magic to destroy, or at least seal away, this stone you found. He cannot afford to have us find the altar, not until his mission is complete." Sart glanced up. Jared and Thistle followed his gaze with their eyes. They saw that Rux had come up behind them. He was nodding at what Sart was saying.

Sart continued, "Rux entrusted me with all that they have been doing here. Aberon certainly understands their mission. He also knows that it is only a matter of time before the altar is discovered. He does not want us to recover the pendant, and he is wise enough to know that I may figure all of this out eventually.

"Jared, there is far too much we do not know of this device you found. There is no doubt that it is a powerful artifact for the Good. Else he would not have gone to such lengths and deception to acquire it. I wonder more how the Qa-ryk came upon it?

"You said the beast you slew was a leader or chieftain," Sart mused to himself.

Jared nodded "Yes," anyway.

"And the stone was about its neck?" This time the cleric did look up at Jared. He nodded again. "That is very strange. Are you positive that he was of import in his clan?"

Jared shrugged. "I don't know much of these beasts, except what my father taught me. He was certainly of higher rank. He wore heavy chain mail, and I remember he also had an ornate sword. I took him for a lieutenant or captain. He was a big brute; bigger than others I saw that day."

"Perhaps a clan leader then, which may be why Aberon was reluctant to take the stone from him. He may have hoped the brute would die in the attack on Thiele. When the beast followed you and you killed it, he changed his plan. For him, that was only a small inconvenience. He knew he could take the pendant at his leisure. He was under no compulsion to hold back once it was out of the Qa-ryk's possession.

"Now, we must assume he will try to take it to Kan's Altar to destroy it. It is the only evil place near here with enough power to counteract an artifact of its nature and power.

"Jared, Thistle, I am afraid that you two have fallen into a web of many threads that started far, far back in time. Few realize it, but the kingdom is being threatened from within and without. Though we are far from the center of power of the Borean world, the strands that play out here may be key to its survival. Today, many years after his death, the power of Kan, still serves evil.

"It has long been thought that the Black Druids found his altar years ago. They have used its dark power to build their influence. For these many years, we have not been able to locate it; and until this outpost's recent work, we did not even know where his fortress had been, only its general location."

Sart paused a moment, looking up at Rux. The big man nodded, as if giving the cleric permission to continue. "I don't know how much you two have learned in your brief time here; this fort, this 'band of thieves,' is really an outpost of the Borean army. Rux is a captain in the service of Borea, a company commander who volunteered for this duty. Their primary purpose has been to find the Altar of Kan, as well as to forestall the growth of the Qa-ryk ranks. They believe they have narrowed the altar's location to a slope of ruins where Kan's old palace once stood. So far, they have not been able to find an entrance that would lead down to it.

Sart fixed Jared with his eyes. "Because you are somehow wrapped up in this, Jared, I am afraid that this lot falls in part to you, and to the few men who are whole enough to come with us. You must trail after Aberon. He must be pressed. He is wounded, not badly, yet weakened and drained by the power he expended here. Our best chance to overcome him is now, when he is not fully in his power. I…"

The battered fort commander raised his hand to interrupt. "I will come, too, Sart. The lad can lead the way, but he will need all the force we can give him. I know those ruins as well as any."

At first, Sart looked to dissuade Rux. The captain had received many wounds in the recent battle. However, he also knew Rux would be a stalwart leader and fighter even in his wounded condition. Sart also knew how powerful Aberon would be once he got close to that seat of evil. Sart shrugged his shoulders, accepting his decision. "Understand this, both of you," he looked up at Rux and finally at Jared, "he is extremely dangerous, even wounded. He will be more dangerous the closer to that dread altar he gets. You must take all care.

"Now, to the present -- his powers of teleportation are limited. He would not have been able to go more than a hundred paces or so to some planned escape route. Perhaps he had a horse waiting. You should be able to pick up his trail to the south and west. You are a good tracker, Jared, as you proved in the woods with me. So are many of Rux's men. Press him, force him to keep moving. Our best ally is speed.

"I am sorry, Jared; I must ask you to accept this burden because the stone came to you. Powerful artifacts oft make such choices. It may be you are the only one who truly has a chance to recover it." Sart wiped his face, looked into Jared's eyes, and saw only resolve there. He smiled grimly at Rux. They both knew that this tall thin lad had solid mettle. He had proved it well enough in the recent fight.

"He will likely be alone, Jared. The Qa-ryks have scattered and will return to their stockades. The power holding them together has been removed for now. With any luck, they will fight amongst themselves and not prove any threat here for many months, perhaps even for years to come. If you leave now and keep hounding him, Aberon will not have time to gather any other forces to him.

"If you are willing, you should all leave within the hour. Sleep on the mules, but keep going. I will follow when I have done all I can here to help those who are in need of my skills. First, I will need to rest this eve to recover my vital powers. If he does not have the chance to recover fully, I believe I can best him when I am fully rested. With any luck, the stone's aura will have worn on him a bit, too…

"Do not engage him! Our best hope is to find and attack him as a unit. I will try to catch you on Rux's goatsteed before Aberon reaches the ruins. Watch for me in three or four days. I...."

"I am going!" Thistle interjected, emphatically.

"Yes, I guess you are, my stubborn young lady." Sart smiled at her. "I don't approve, nor will Rux, I imagine. Yet, you seem to be as much wrapped up in this affair as any of us. Perhaps you may help where we do not ken. Meligance's blessing is with you; so who am I to go against what she has blessed with her power, much less gainsay a strong-willed woman. I must admit that I have already seen much in the last few days that suggests the divine kens far more than I in these matters. If the gods will it, let it be so."

Sart stood and faced the three. "I must get back to easing the pain and suffering of the many wounded, both in body and spirit. Get everything ready as quickly as you can." Sart reached out; placing his hand on each of their heads in turn, he blessed them. "Earth Mother, bless and keep them safe from evil. So be it.

"Hurry now. May the power of Gaia herself be with you."

Less than an hour later, Rux, with bandages plastered over his body from head to toe, was on Crunch's broad back. Thistle, Jared, and five other men rode with him on sturdy mountain mules through the blasted gates, then south and west. They picked their way carefully around the carnage of the battle, pausing only once to look back at the battered ramparts before turning west on another path.

Riding West

The small company kept a steady pace toward the mountains. Exhausted, with his wound stinging painfully under a tight bandage, Jared dozed fitfully in his saddle, lulled by the rolling motion of the mule. By evening, they had covered several leagues in the rough terrain. Just before dusk, one of Rux's men came riding back from the trail ahead. He announced that they had found tracks of a lone horseman traveling to the south and west.

Except for a brief stop for food and a chance for Thistle to re-bandage Jared's and Rux's wounds, the quest continued throughout the long night. Progress was tediously slow as the men tracked the lone steed by torchlight. By the early light, they had determined that they were only a few hours behind the fleeing priest.

***

Aberon rode throughout the day and long into the night. His horse was mountain-bred and could pick his way through the rough terrain. He let the animal have his lead while he got some needed rest. Finally, a few hours before dawn, he stopped and settled down in a small grove for a few hours sleep. Taking some medicinal herbs for the pain in his side, he set a magical perimeter, three hundred feet in diameter, that would allow him ample warning should anyone approach.

He woke with a start before dawn, pondered trying to sleep again, but decided it would be better to press on. He wanted to stay well ahead if any were following him. He still had days until he reached the ruins.

He wanted to cast a scrying spell to see if anyone might be on his trail. However, the bout with the cleric had weakened him, and he had used much of his residual energy teleporting back to his horse. Soon enough, he would be closing in on Kan's former fortress. There was great dark power there. Once he was within a day's ride, he would begin to rejuvenate his own energy from that evil aura. By the time he reached the Altar of Kan, he would be at full strength. The presence of that evil edifice would also weaken his enemies, while it would give him a boost of vigor and confidence.

These thoughts brightened his mood. He urged his mount ahead. Power beckoned.

Home is where You Rest Your Head

Light was streaming in through the window when Ge-or woke fully. He was lying on a comfortable down bed with his head, neck, and back supported by several pillows. His fever seemed to be gone and with it the red haze that had obscured his vision.

The room he was in was spacious. It appeared to be the main bedroom in a large old log cabin. The one window, which looked out over a hillside pasture, was paned with glass, a luxury rarely found in these parts. Unfortunately, several of the panels had been cracked and had not been replaced. Heavy woolen curtains were partially drawn. The logs of the walls were fitted, as they often were in the north country coastal villages -- partially hollowed out so that the curved surface of one heavy beam fit snugly into the concave part of the other. It meant a slower build, but less caulking with mud and straw, thus providing better protection against drafts.

Ge-or managed to push himself further up so he was resting against the headboard of the bed. He was a bit surprised that he felt much weaker than he expected. His wound was sore as he moved. When he reached behind and felt his lower back, he could tell that it had been carefully stitched under the light bandage.

The room was typical for a sleeping chamber in a wilderness cabin. Furs or blankets lined each of the walls. These helped to insulate the space further during the harsh winters. A large chest of drawers built from local pine wood stood in one corner, and there were two similarly constructed necessity chests at the foot of the bed. One straight-backed chair, with woven reed seat, stood next to the head of the bed. Ge-or wondered whether his hosts had a family. He could remember only hearing two voices during his fever – a father and daughter.

While he considered trying to shift his body and perhaps swing his legs to the floor, he heard a door open in the next room. Someone came in from outside. The person walked across the plank floor and opened the door to what sounded like a cast iron stove. Ge-or guessed by the clunking sounds that they were adding some wood. A moment later, the door to the bedroom opened; and a woman walked through, smiling when she saw him awake.

She was slight of stature, perhaps only a little over five feet tall. Ge-or figured she likely weighed in at less than eight stone. She was comely in a rustic, hill-bred way. Her hair was the color of hay in the sunshine, with a few sprinkles of gray throughout. Her cheeks were ruddy with the cold of the morning. He guessed she was in her mid-thirties, but it was her smile that drew him. She had the kindest, most accepting visage he had ever seen.

"You look good. I am glad. You have been really sick. Whatever blade struck you, it was fouled. You spiked a nasty fever, and quickly by the looks of that fresh wound. I am Leona, and you have been in my care these past three days.

"No, don't try to get up."

Ge-or tried to shift his body. Leona put her hand to his chest, keeping him down without much effort. She reached behind him and adjusted his pillows so he would be more comfortable. "I have some soup ready, a hearty chicken stock with strength-building herbs. I want you to eat and rest for a bit; then we will talk.

"Aldred, my father, is tending the goats. He will be in for lunch midday. Later we will see how you are doing." With that, she spun around lightly and exited back to the kitchen/entry room. Ge-or closed his eyes and listened to her puttering about.

Leona chatted lightly about this and that as he ate – telling him about their stead, the hidden vale, the goats they raised, and many other things about life in the area. Though it was obvious she was trying to keep Ge-or from asking questions, he didn't mind. From what little he could remember about getting here, her father's reaction to finding the wagon, and his fever, he figured most of this would come to a head when the man returned. Perhaps, by then, he would have more energy to face up to an explanation. For now, he was content to listen to her, enjoy her company, and bask in her radiant smile. It was the last thing he remembered as he dozed off.

Ge-or awoke with a start when the outside door slammed. "Is he awake yet?" A heavy, gruff voice, none too friendly, followed the bang.

"Father! He's not a thief. You heard him, he…"

"He needs to explain a wagonload of stolen goods he has out there. That's what he needs to do. 'Til then, I ain't gonna have any truck with him. Now get outta my way."

"No! Let him rest. Move…"

"I'm awake." Ge-or shouted as loudly as he could – he still felt drained of energy.

The door to the bedroom swung open. Leona, entering first, looked behind her sternly as if to keep her father at bay, or at least to delay his interrogation until she had seen to her patient.

Ge-or waved for her to let him in. He didn't relish defending himself. However, he knew he had nothing to hide, except his shame at being incautious enough to get captured in the first place.

Leona's father, also short in stature, was surprisingly broad and solid in contrast to the petite frame of his daughter. Ge-or was taken aback that the man was so much older than he had expected. He looked to be in his mid-sixties, already old for an edge-of-the-wilderness lifestyle. He was balding and gray and slightly stooped, though he looked like he could lift his weight in hay to his shoulders. He was missing a good many teeth; and when he pointed his right hand out the window, Ge-or saw the third, fourth and fifth fingers had been cut short by some accident.

"What's all that stuff out there and where'd you get it?" He gestured at what must have been the wagon Ge-or had gotten from the thieves. It was below the sill of the window, so Ge-or couldn't actually see it. Ge-or suspected he had drawn the wagon in from where he had left it. "Speak up; I won't abide a thief in my house."

"Father!"

Ge-or waved again at Leona. "It's all right. He has reason to be suspicious."

Ge-or stared steadily into the man's brown eyes, returning the challenge. "I am Ge-or, lately of Thiele. My village is… was on the north coast, out to the west." Ge-or motioned toward the far wall. "It was destroyed by Qa-ryks nigh unto a week ago… Nay, closer to two now, I guess. I have lost track of time. I was bashed in the head by one of the beasts and managed to live. I was lucky; they left me for dead. Since then, I have been on the road south and east. My plans were to head to Aelfric to get better equipped, so that I could set about avenging my family's and friends' deaths.

"Being wilderness born and bred, I was too trusting of strangers; and while sitting at the campfire of three men, fellow travelers who had invited me to stay the

147

eve with them, I was hit from behind. I woke the next morn in the bottom of that wagon out there..."

Ge-or spent the next half hour, interrupted once by Leona when she brought him some hot herbal tea, describing in detail his capture, escape, wounding, and attempt to find help. Aldred's demeanor stayed hard, up until Ge-or related the story of his escape and wounding. He saw the man perceptibly relax and grudgingly accept what he was saying.

"I didn't know what to do with the goods they had taken, and I knew I needed help. The wagon and mules were my only chance of finding someplace in time. You are welcome to anything there that would be of use to you. I imagine those ruffians stole much of it from other farmsteads like yours."

"You shouldn't of let that other bastard live," Aldred said. "You're a kinder man than I woulda been."

"I left him little. Unless he is resourceful, he is unlikely to survive anyway. I... I found even in my anger and embarrassment that I couldn't kill someone who was at my mercy."

"Which says much about you," Leona added, glaring at her father.

"Alright, I can admit my mistakes, Daughter. I apologize to you, young Ge-or. I mistook you. In these evil times, one needs to be careful."

"I have found that out the hard way." Ge-or managed a smile. "No need to apologize. You both saved my life. I owe you a debt. If I can do something for you when I am back to health, I would be pleased to help where I may."

Following Darkness

When they found themselves on a wide cart path through the foothills, they were able to quicken their pace for a few hours. Jared, who had dozed through the night, was stiff and sore but more alert. The herbal poultice that Sart had made for him was easing his discomfort considerably. Unfortunately, the curative effects of the pendant had obviously worn off. He would have to let his own body deal with this wound. He and Thistle rode next to Rux, who had also taken the opportunity to rest during the night.

Thistle and Jared were both surprised by how much the rebel leader had changed. Though weakened by his wounds, Rux held himself proudly as befit the captain of a Borean command. He no longer played the part of a rebel leader. His tavern drawl and coarse manners had changed to those expected from a highborn officer. Now that he had no reason for dissimulation, the leader of thieves had become a champion of Borea.

Thistle seemed captivated by his manner. With her overwhelming curiosity, she asked him numerous questions about his assignment to the Qa-ryk lands, finally leading up to the one question she really wanted answered, "Who was Kan?"

"Kan?" Rux mused, rubbing his hand across the dark stubble of his beard. "That would be best answered by your friend, the cleric. He is well versed in the lore and history of the kingdom. Sart has focused his search in recent years for knowledge, at least indirectly, related to Kan's sources of power. I will tell you what I know.

"Kan was an elf, by all accounts, born in Moulanes – one of the pure-bred. They say he was developing into a credible mage by elven standards, considering his relative youth. Be that as it may, he was supposedly turned by some dark force many years ago and went into seclusion in the west.

"Wherever he came from, he slowly grew in power, gathering minions to him from the bowels of the earth: goblins and their ilk, the gzks and chats, ogres, trolls – any creatures he could twist to his cause. For years, he was believed to be dead, because neither the elves, nor any in Borea, heard anything from him. His true might was not felt until he built his fortress in the west.

"The site we ride to now is where he bred the beasts we now fight. It appears he sought to develop a creature that had the best characteristics of two evil races: from the goblins or gzks – no one knows for sure which creatures he used for stock – their fearsome fangs and claws, their agility, and their ability to procreate quickly; and from mountain ogres – their strength, resilience, ferocity, and size. The Qa-ryks were all that he desired and more. However, he had not bargained for their fierce competitiveness and clannish tendencies. Ultimately, he could not control them."

Rux tried to adjust his seat, grimacing at the discomfort the small shift caused him. "The Borean world first felt Kan's power when his minions began to take over the Dark Forest. They spread slowly, fighting themselves as much as destroying the villages and trapping communities that had built up in the west during the Borean expansion. Inexorably, they expanded ever eastward, destroying farms and ranches as they multiplied.

"Eventually, Borea had to take notice and make an effort to protect its people and borders. A century or more ago – you would have to ask Sart of the actual timing – the king's army made several excursions westward to fight Kan's forces. When they came within twenty leagues of where his fortress was suspected to be, they were attacked fiercely by goblins, gzks, and Qa-ryks, any creatures Kan could draw together to throw at them. They were forced to withdraw.

"The odd thing was that, even though he was certainly extremely powerful and did wield some control of his minions, Kan never actually mounted an attack eastward against the kingdom. The minions he drew to him, and these monstrous beasts he bred, were solely for his protection. It seems he was inclined to keep to himself; he wasn't a conqueror.

"One last expedition was launched a decade later out of Borea; and except for isolated skirmishes with outlying Qa-ryk clans, they encountered no resistance on their march westward along the north side of the Beze mountains. When they reached the mountainside where Kan's fortress had supposedly rested, they found nothing. It had been completely destroyed, leveled to the ground, with nary one stone left upon another."

Rux scratched again at three days' growth of beard. "Kan's Altar and the fortress built above it is a mystery even to the wise. Some speculate he built it above the labyrinthine dungeon of an old citadel. Others say that he took over a great fortress that had been built in the first age by the dwarves for men, yet had since been abandoned. Others believe Kan used magic to create his dark citadel. Whatever the truth, refugees from the west spoke of stronghold set against the mountains that none dared approach. Deep beneath this fortress is where Kan practiced his most powerful and dire magic. By all accounts, great evil emanated from there.

"How he was destroyed is a mystery to even the wise. Many say with the breeding of these great beasts he overreached his power and was destroyed from within. There are fantastic yarns of the Qa-ryks turning on him and torturing him for weeks in retribution for his enslavement of them. No one really knows the truth. That he was destroyed from within, there is no doubt of that; and it could have been the Qa-ryks. He wanted an army of powerful, evil beings that he could wield as one wields a sword. Yet, he never gained the control he would have needed to form them into a viable fighting force."

"The Black Druids, brothers to Aberon, have used this place since?" Thistle asked.

"The Black Druids took advantage of Kan's demise and whatever power source he left in place beneath his fortress," Rux answered. "We believe it is this altar that was spoken of. They use this source to gain power, and thus to help them control these beasts, the Qa-ryks. They, too, have had problems keeping them directed to their will. The first Qa-ryk wars, the battles your father fought in, Jared, started nigh unto fifty years ago. They were not ended by the beasts' defeat, but by their eventual breaking of the spell-bonds that the Black Priests held them under. Their army dissolved at the height of its conquest. Now, these dark druids have begun another fight, using these same beasts, except with more powerful magic to hold them together. We are facing more war, though few understand that. The attack on your village and, this one on Xur, are early forays in that new fight."

Rux fell silent. Thistle, however, was not satisfied with all the ranger leader had told them. "What is this altar or shrine of evil we are trying to find, and why is it so important for it to be destroyed if Kan no longer exists?"

Rux laughed. "You are an inquisitive sort, milady. Yet it does help pass our time a-saddle." Jared nodded his head vigorously at the "inquisitive" part of Rux's statement. Thistle reached out to slap his shoulder. They all had a short laugh before Rux began again.

"Evil breeds unto itself," Rux said. He paused again as if to give them time for his words to sink in. "These Black Druids – evil clerics and mages who came together after Kan's demise – may have originally been followers or minions of his. We don't know. Or perhaps they were dark priests who came seeking his power source. In either case, they appear to have searched for the ruins of Kan's stronghold for many years, hoping to gain wisdom and strength from the evil that had so long dominated the place. When their power grew rapidly, approximately seventy years ago, the wise knew these dark priests must have found something.

"What they found and where it was located were other problems that had to be solved by the kingdom. Unlike Kan, these dark priests are determined to gather forces so they can destroy the east. We believe that the first of the Qa-ryk Wars was a result of the powers they gained when they found the dark one's shrine. Gaining enough control of the Qa-ryks to breed a formidable army, the Black Druids drove the beasts eastward, threatening the kingdom. In the process, they displaced the dwarves and gnomes from their homes and digs in the Beze mountains.

"These dark priests overstepped themselves, and the invasion collapsed back upon itself when the clans of Qa-ryks began to fight amongst themselves. Though the dark priests survived the collapse of their army, they were forced to draw back and regroup.

"Since then, partly through divination by our mages, and partly through our efforts here in the wilds, we have learned a great deal. We now know where Kan's fortress used to be, as we have discovered the ruins. Unfortunately, we have not yet located the altar itself. That is where we ride now," Rux pointed ahead with his chin.

"Over these intervening years since the first Qa-ryk War, the Black Druids have not been idle, either. No one really knows much about them, not even where their center of power is located.

"Sart believes it is far to the west. He is resolved to know more about them – their work, their plans, and whence their strength derives. Their power does grow anew, and they seem to have discovered new ways to control the Qa-ryks. The beasts have been proliferating again over the past decade. The massed attack on Xur is an indication of how powerful they have become. The kingdom is again at risk."

"What is this altar and its import?" Rux mused, returning to another segment of Thistle's query. "The one bit of information we have to go on was that beneath this edifice, deep within the earth, Kan had built a shrine where he worked his most powerful magic. There he communed with the Nine Planes of Hell and... well, some believe with realms even darker and more aberrant than those.

"Meligance, the great White Wizardess of Borea, saw this much one night in her crystal; yet she could not scry where it was located. The task of finding the ruins was laid upon the shoulders of the army. Over the last five years, my men and I have narrowed our search to a mountainside of ruins five days ride or more from Xur, depending on how much we push our mounts. These, we are convinced, are the remains of Kan's once great fortress. Unfortunately, we have not succeeded in finding the entrance to this evil place of power. Perhaps that is because we are not meant to find it. These dread priests have taken great pains to keep its whereabouts hidden.

"Why it is so important to Aberon? Sart appears to think that this stone that Jared found is of some import, and that Aberon may be able to destroy it, or lock it away forever, with the help of the evil that permeates the altar. I do not know. Truthfully, I do not wish to know; but Sart came willing to help my men, so I will help him. Besides, my primary mission has always been to find the altar. In a few days, if we are lucky, we may accomplish that. My men and I do not have the power to destroy such an evil place. If it is saturated with dark magic, as has been suggested, then it will take some other power – power that priests like Sart wield – to harm it; or perhaps a force even greater than he wields."

"Meligance?" Thistle asked.

"Aye, her and others. We do not know what power it might take to undo so much evil."

"Why did you capture us if Sart knew all of this?"

"Because we did not know Sart. We had to be sure he would help with the illness at the fort. And once we did, the assault on Xur by Aberon and his army affirmed the suspicions he talked about to me.

"I must apologize again for the way we treated you initially and for the subterfuge thereafter. I would have released you sooner, if I had known you better. When you have lived with evil surrounding you for many years, you do not take chances." Rux grinned at Thistle and Jared. "I do ask again for your forgiveness at the mishandling, but our needs made us cautious."

"Well, except for sore muscles and Jared's head hurting – not that he couldn't use a bash now and again – I suppose everything worked out all right." Thistle smiled back. Jared reached across and poked her in the ribs this time. Thistle was inclined to reciprocate; on the other hand, she didn't want to aggravate Jared's wound.

The rest of the day was spent in the same slow, steady pursuit. By all the signs, Aberon was able to maintain his distance. The demands of the trail were wearing on all of them. Jared's wound flared painfully at intervals; and Rux was also suffering – his face was wan, and he grimaced at every jolt upon Crunch's back. All the others were beyond weary from the battle and the long time in the saddle.

As the sun was setting in the west, Rux knew that despite the risk of losing ground on the dark priest, they all needed to rest. Selecting as comfortable a spot for camp as they could amongst the rocks, he ordered a halt at full dark. As they settled in for the night, Jared, Rux, and Thistle were troubled that they had not seen anything of Sart.

***

Aberon was feeling better by the minute. His mountain horse was making good time in spite of the terrain. He could now sense the dark aura ahead; and though it was many hours away, its pulse energized him. The altar's evil power was beginning to permeate his body.

He took a brief rest in the predawn. After refreshing himself with some dried meat and his strong herbal brew, he decided to see if he was being pursued. Bolstered by the emanations from the ruins some leagues ahead, he felt strong enough to cast a scrying spell. What he discovered was troubling for several reasons; however, it was nothing he couldn't deal with.

They were closer than he had expected, less than a half day back; but they had also stopped to rest. Their party was small, seven in total, and unless he was mistaken, the cleric was not with them. He knew Sart's power signature well. There was no sign of it in or near their camp. If that were true, and he did not doubt his ability to sense the cleric's energy since he had been doing so for months, this motley crew of men would be of little concern once he reached full power.

He had felt something else – another type of power, hidden deep within one of their group. It felt familiar – yet it took Aberon a while to remember where he had

152

sensed it before – it was the girl!

Now that he recognized the signature of her energy, he found this information most troubling. How had she survived the fiery blast he had called forth upon that grove? Both of them? He had seen the column of fire, felt its heat, witnessed the fierce blaze and charred trees as he rode off. How had they both survived?

Was she a potent magic-user, able to keep her power almost completely hidden? No, that did not seem feasible; she was too young. In addition, she had not had any ken of the nature of the ovietti. Aberon knew enough about the creatures to know that they did not cast spells; they only enhanced magic that was already present. They could help add energy to a spell, not create one. She obviously had some power and some potential to use it. Unless he was mistaken, it was latent, buried deep within, unused. He had sensed that from the time he had caught up to the two. That is why he used such a powerful fire spell to destroy them. Yet, for some reason, it hadn't worked.

Perhaps it had been the stone, its residual effects. The thing was powerful enough, that was certain. Aberon could feel its radiating coolness by his side in spite of the energy he had used to encase it in evil. With all he had done, its inherent goodness was still not completely contained. This is why he had made it a priority to seal it away in the most evil place accessible – the Altar of Kan.

The ebon altar stood deep within the old mage's palace. It had been the centerpiece for his most dire magic, sacrifices, and torture. Aberon had been there many times, as had his brethren. It served as a place where they could release themselves to its aura and drink in its powers. This would be his first time back in several years. Rux's Demons' closing in on the location had limited the brethren's willingness to expose the entrance. With Sart chasing after him, he had figured discretion would be better than taking the chance at revealing where it was. Thus, he had led the cleric on long circuitous routes about Qa-ryk country, while preparing for his plans to come to a head.

Now, he would return to encase this dreaded stone in the altar's massive ebon block. There it could remain for eternity, impotent to spread its wellness throughout the world. He knew he could not destroy it. From what he had learned, there was only one true way to neutralize it completely; and that method, unfortunately, would also destroy much of the evil power ensconced in the west. For now, even that choice was out of the Black Druid's reach. It was not likely a choice they would make anyway, for it would undo all that they were. This way they could keep its goodness and influence out of the empire's reach, and keep it from affecting, or infecting, the world at large.

When he succeeded with this task, all else would be forgotten. He would undoubtedly be asked to join the Nine. He might even be considered as the next successor to one of the Three. After that? Well, time would tell; he had his ambitions. Those did not include bowing to anyone for much longer.

Whatever the reason, the two of them had survived his fiery blast. They were both in the group trailing him. Aberon was positive of that. He could think of no more fitting an end to his quest than to pluck those two up and take them prisoner. Perhaps he would visit the Qa-ryk camp after all. These two morsels would help placate Ka-ragh and his clan following their defeat. They would spend many nights playing with their victims, causing them ever more pain. By the end, the beasts would think better of Aberon, and they would have forgotten their losses. He would enjoy seeing that girl and lad squirm in agony for several days, as much or more than the Qa-ryks.

Smiling, Aberon gathered his few belongings and leapt on his horse. He was on a clear path, so he spurred the animal ahead. He might as well finish the task at hand.

***

They all woke feeling considerably better, yet knew they had lost ground to Aberon. Rux gave them little time to refresh. Breaking their fast while riding further into the west, they chewed on old biscuits and dried meat. Soon they were pushing hard along the edge of the mountains.

More confident of where their quarry was headed, they kept a faster pace. By dusk, they had gained back some of the ground they had lost, though they were still four or five hours behind the dark priest. Rux ordered them on through the night.

The morning of the fifth day out from Xur found them all dragging again; nevertheless, by all the signs, they were once again within an hour or so of the priest. Rux knew they were close to the ruins. He ordered a short half-hour break for everyone to eat a hurried meal and gather their strength.

They were all worried now that something had befallen Sart on his way out to join them. The goatsteed should have been able to easily catch them. It could travel twice the speed of their mules. Rux felt their only choice was to push ahead after the dark priest.

After the brief respite, he brought them all together. "We must continue on. Gods willing, our priest is hard behind us. This bastard druid must be pressed. Now is the deciding time. There is no doubt where Aberon is headed; the ruins are to our fore and only hours away. Maybe we can still surprise the rabbit before he goes down his hole. Come!"

***

Aberon drew the horse up behind him on the narrow twisting path. It was steep and difficult, but the animal had been here before. Aberon wanted him close to hand once he was finished at the altar. He did not know if he would be tired after he sealed the stone away, or exhilarated and energized. He didn't want to take any chances. He would depart as quickly as possible to be safe.

As he approached the entrance to the old palace's dungeons, Aberon was radiating with dark energy. He was also gasping for breath from the steep climb up. This energy fed his magic, not his body. He had to stop and rest for a half hour to gain his composure.

They were close behind; he didn't care. He would deal with them whenever they arrived. He would kill the four soldiers. He had other plans for Rux, Thistle, and the half-elf, especially the half-elf. Aberon had decided that he would enjoy their company for several days himself, before turning them over to the Qa-ryks. Some of his torture methods did not leave marks. If he was careful, he would quite enjoy putting these three through some agony for a pace. It would enliven his spirits a good bit to see them squirming and screaming. After his own fun, he might stay a day or two with Ka-ragh's clan and watch them torture the three as well. One could always learn new tricks.

Finally, feeling rested and full with power, Aberon turned and walked through what appeared to be a solid wall of rock. Once inside, he descended the stairway beyond the illusion down into the depths.

154

An Unusual Request

Though he was improving, Ge-or spent another two full days in bed, only rising to attend to necessities. He didn't know where Leona and her father were sleeping, and he felt guilty for depriving one of them of their comfortable room. They both insisted he would heal better where he was.

Leona plied him with poultices for his wound, mugs of tea with odd concoctions of herbs, and her rich broths. Even as a child, sick with the ague, Ge-or had never felt so pampered.

For the most part, Aldred left him alone and tended to farm chores. He did poke his head in on two occasions when Ge-or was awake to ask him how he was feeling. Elsewise, he appeared to be embarrassed about everything that had gone before. Leona was more than happy to have Ge-or to herself.

She gave him wonderful fragrant broths, oat and barley cereal sweetened with honey or molasses in the morning, and on the third day after he awoke fully, a delicious thick stew with chunks of goat meat and late fall leaf vegetables. In between his meals, she would bring in a variety of herbal teas: some that were "good for him," (they did not taste particularly good, even with honey added); others he recognized – peppermint, chamomile, and the like. They reminded him of what his mother had given him when he was ill as a child. Leona and her father obviously had a well-tended garden to be able to produce such a variety of herbs and plants. Ge-or was thankful he had fallen into a capable household.

When he awoke the next morning, Ge-or felt considerably better. Still, he had slept late. Swinging his legs to the side of the bed, he tentatively tried standing on his own. He still felt weak and drained, but he was no longer dizzy. He stood up, took a moment to make sure he would be all right, and walked to the door. After pausing there for a several seconds, he swung the heavy oaken panel inward and stepped out into the kitchen.

Leona was seated at a small wooden table near the stove, working on some knitting when he rounded the corner. She looked up in surprise and smiled. "Up, I see. I'm glad. Come, sit. I will fix you some eggs and a rasher. You need some solid farm food today."

"Thank you, Leona. I feel much better. Thank you for all you have done. I wouldn't have made it without your care."

She blushed and waved, as if to say it was nothing. Then she went directly over to the cabin's cold cupboard. It was built, as many were, so that the doors were flush with the wall with the storage area extending to the outside. As Ge-or well knew, these served for storing perishables in the fall, winter, and early spring. Aldred and Leona probably had an underground storage area near the house as well. Blocks of ice, cut from a nearby pond in the winter, would help to keep things cool in the summer.

As Leona drew some packages wrapped in oiled cloth from the locker, Ge-or asked, "Where is your father? I would like to thank him as well."

"He went to the south pasture to check on the breeding stock. He should be back by noon. You can talk with him when he comes back to eat. I think he is feeling a bit odd, you know, discomfited, about accusing you of being a thief. Don't worry about it; he is an honest old soul. You two will get along well, I warrant."

155

"After you eat, if you feel up to walking a bit, I'll show you our place. You can see most of it from the porch. Father wanted Mother to be able to see him when he was working, so we are perched on the side of a hill looking into the valley."

Leona went to the large cast iron stove that served for both cooking and as the cabin's main heat source. She began frying thick slabs of bacon she had taken from one of the packages. Next, she chopped onions and potatoes which she had fetched from a large woven basket hanging from the rafters nearby. As Ge-or looked about, the home reminded him of the well-designed, efficient living and eating spaces typical of wilderness cabins.

Feeling somewhat awkward, Ge-or made an effort to keep the conversation going. "Leona, you have a beautiful smile. Seeing you so has helped pull me through the rough spots the last few days. I can't thank you enough."

This time, Leona did blush hotly. She turned to the side quickly so Ge-or couldn't see her reddened cheeks. When she had recovered her composure, she turned back toward him and smiled. "I see you do feel better; you have gracious manners, sir."

Ge-or flushed a bit himself at the formality of her words. He wondered why she had replied in that a way.

While she was cooking, Leona chatted some more about this and that to do with the stead, weather, and their animals. Ge-or enjoyed listening to her. He took the opportunity to take in more of his surroundings. The log cabin appeared sturdily built, well-caulked with clay mud where needed, which looked to be recently reinforced for the winter. The room he was sitting in served as an entryway from the outside, a dining room, kitchen, and as a general gathering area. It was large, roughly fifteen or sixteen feet wide and twenty-five feet long. At the far wall, opposite the entry door and past the stove, was another door set in the wall. Ge-or guessed it led to another, perhaps smaller, bedroom.

The place was homey in a rustic way – utensils and pots hung over and around the stove; in a corner stood brooms, a mop, several buckets, and other cleaning items. The room held what one would expect for a cabin built in the wilds: accoutrements for the outdoors, including boots, coats, and various tools that were all set near the door; a large woodbox was placed on the opposite wall from the stove; a tall, pine cupboard filled with blue china stood in the corner between the stove and the front door; hooks hanging from the rafters above held drying herbs and plants that gave the room a slight, pungently sweet scent; and a variety of baskets filled with an autumn bounty of root vegetables, fruit, and nuts were set about or also hanging from rafters above. A ladder to the side and back of the room led to what he guessed was a loft for storage and perhaps, for now, as another sleeping area.

Ge-or settled back in the chair and took a deep breath. He felt at ease, safe, and almost at home.

Fifteen minutes later, Ge-or was digging into the heartiest breakfast he had ever had. Leona had fried five large brown eggs, courtesy of chickens he had heard cackling in the yard. Thick slices of bacon with potatoes and onions shared his plate. Leona had served it all with a hearty oat and honey peasant bread that was slathered with newly churned butter. She had given him warm, honey-sweetened goats' milk to drink. He hadn't realized how famished he was. He ate with gusto, enjoying all of it. When he finally finished, he pushed the heavy stoneware plate away and sat back, groaning slightly. He was quite full and felt considerably better. Leona's broths and teas had worked wonders; however, they did not fill one's stomach.

While he ate, she told him about the different kinds of goats and sheep they raised. Her father was particularly proud of a hardy hybrid of angoras he had bred, which seemed to thrive in the vale's rich pastures. Though most of their income and meat came from the variety of animals they produced, right now the herds were depleted because several weeks ago they had sold more than half the herd at the fall market.

When Ge-or was done, Leona led him out to the expansive porch which ran the entire length of the front of the house and around the western corner. She explained to Ge-or how much her father and mother used to like to sit there on summer and fall evenings looking over the vale. "They had a good life." Leona tried to smile, but a tear rolled down her cheek. "She died ten years ago from Beze fever. By the time we got her to town, it was too late. It was a bad year for illness, and it took a big toll on the steads around here.

"Already people were leaving, because of the raids that had escalated the years before. Gzks coming down from the mountains were pushed further east and north by the Qa-ryks. And bandits, like the ones you met, were becoming more and more brazen. Mother had grown despondent over the loss of so many good people. I don't think she had any fight left in her. She was always small and a bit frail anyway."

Ge-or, saddened at the picture she described, placed his hand on Leona's right shoulder. "I'm sorry, Leona. It must have been hard for both of you. Your father

157

decided to stay?"

"Father's stubborn; and, well, as you can see, we are isolated here, which has helped to keep us safe." She pointed to the high walls of rock surrounding their small valley. "My parents, Aldred and Cilia, came here forty years ago, a young couple seeking their fortune in the west. At the time, the kingdom was offering land grants to those who were willing to stay for ten years."

"The expansion after the first of the Qa-ryk wars," Ge-or said. "Borea wanted to repopulate the west. That is also when my father went west and north."

"Yes, it was a fine dream, and life was good for them for a long while. Father found this hidden vale – more remote than other plots further north and east, it had a natural protection from the surrounding foothills. You probably didn't notice in your fever, but there are only two constricted access points. The one you came through with your mules is a narrow path that leads through a small gorge. It is only wide enough for a mule. It is amazing you found it."

"I think it was my mule that led me through it. I was not in particularly good shape by then, as you saw. He must have smelled or sensed your animals. I'm not sure I was even cognizant of where I was at that point."

"You may be right. The breeze must have been southwesterly. I remember that our mules were agitated and brayed a few times that evening. Not enough to cause an alarm. They will run in circles and make a racket if wolves, coyotes, or other dangerous creatures are near.

"The other access trail is further to the west in the hills. It is steep and treacherous, but wide enough for a cart. Aldred has let it overgrow with weeds and small bushes, so others won't find it easily. We only use it for our spring and fall trips to the nearest town for provisions, or for treks out to cut wood in the hardwood groves for the winter. That is how he brought your wagon down.

"The bacon you had for breakfast, we just smoked from a pig we brought back. If our wool crop is good and we get a fair price for our goats, we try to bring a fat one back to butcher. We smoke a good part of the meat to keep for the winter. It gives us a nice change from goat, fowl, and wild game."

"How far do you have to go for provisions?" Ge-or asked.

"There is a small trading post within a day's mule ride; it is mostly aimed at travelers. If we need something urgently, Father might take a mule and go there. Typically, we take our goats and wool to the market. It is a trading post about two days travel east by cart. We plan a week when we go. It takes three full days driving a herd, and we typically stay two nights at the tavern inn there while Father bargains. We could probably get better prices south in Aelfric or further east. That would take much longer, several weeks or more with a herd."

"How big is the whole vale? Do you farm all of it?"

"It is not much bigger than what you can see. To the south there," Leona pointed in the distance where a large rocky outcropping jutted into the grassy valley, "it takes a turn to the west, but only for another quarter of a league or so. The valley floor from here to there is about a league in length, less than half that at its widest point. And yes, it is all ours. Father was so proud the day he came back from the magistrate with the deed papers. That is when he bought the glass and put the windows in for Mother." She turned, nestling closer under Ge-or's arm, finally daring to look up at him.

At that moment, Ge-or had a strong urge to kiss her. Just as suddenly, he felt very awkward. He dropped his hand off her shoulder and took a half step back. Leona

158

flushed and turned away from him toward the vale.

"I... The goats do well here," she said hesitatingly, trying to fill the awkward space between them with words. "They are sure-footed creatures and will climb even to the highest points to find the richest grasses, lichens, and mosses among the rocks. Luckily, they know their place; we have rarely lost any. Wolves have been more plentiful of late, though, and occasionally they manage to find their way into our vale. Father is not much good with a bow anymore; you've seen his hand?"

Ge-or nodded.

"Sometimes he will put out a fresh goat haunch and poison them. You do what you must to survive here."

"I know," he said. "Life can be hard. It was the same in the coastal villages where I grew up. It makes you tough in the process. You and your father have accomplished a tremendous thing surviving alone out here and making all of this." He gestured toward the large barn, outbuildings, and fields before him.

"It is beautiful, Leona. And you..." Ge-or wanted to say something about her, but again, he felt uncomfortable. He spoke of the farm instead. "You both have accomplished a great deal from what I can see."

"Come, Ge-or." Leona reached out with her hand to take his. "If you feel like walking, I will show you around a bit more. Father and Mother worked hard." She helped him down the three wooden steps to the dirt path in front of the house.

Leona kept hold of Ge-or's arm as she led him around the path toward the large barn. There were several outbuildings, including a good-sized shed and two separate outhouses. She pointed out her father's workshop-smithy, which was set to the west of the main cabin. "The barn has enough room to house all of our breeding animals, plus our mules and two cows. As you can tell, we don't do much actual farming. Snow is typically light here most years because of the mountains and hills, so the animals can forage all year. We do plant small plots of grain, corn, and hay or alfalfa, as well as a nice-sized garden. Father never liked the plowing and tending of crops. He's more of a rancher at heart. He loves tending the animals, even in the worst weather."

"Remember, Leona," Ge-or said, "I was born into a community that farmed and raised animals, as well as worked the sea. You both have really done an amazing job. The place is well-cared for, repairs kept up from what I can see, and you keep everything clean and organized. I'm impressed. There is care in it all and a women's touch."

"It is our life," she said. Ge-or tried to detect any regret in her tone of voice, but when he looked at her face, she was smiling at him.

"It is a good life, Leona, hard, at times, I would think. You... you should..." Ge-or started to say, "You should share it with someone," then quickly realized she might misinterpret the remark. She was a handsome woman, dedicated to her father and the farm. He had a quest; his fate lay elsewhere.

"I should what?"

"Enjoy it... for what it is." Ge-or hoped that she didn't hear the hesitation in his voice. "I... I think I better go in. I am getting tired."

When Aldred returned, Ge-or was resting again, so Leona and her father went to the barn to begin preparing it for the winter. As in all farms, there was always work to do and never enough hands or time.

159

Ge-or felt considerably stronger when he woke late in the afternoon. The food and extra rest were the perfect medicine. Satisfied that he was better, he tested his strength by walking about the porch. He decided to investigate the work at the barn. As he walked down the pathway toward the sturdy structure, he could see Leona working vigorously. She was using a pitchfork to fill a sturdy cart with old hay and muck that she and her father had raked out the open double doors.

As he approached, she waved to him. "You look much better."

"Your cooking hit the spot, and the extra rest also helped. I feel much better. Can I help?"

"Better not today; on the other hand, depending on how long you stay, winter is coming and there is much to do to get ready. We can use the help." She almost finished her sentence as a question. Ge-or could hear the slight rise in pitch at the end. Jared had taught him to listen for that.

He wasn't sure whether she was indirectly asking him how long he intended to recuperate with them; he chose not to answer. He was already considering how soon he should try to get back on the road. He was having mixed feelings about the farmstead. It reminded him of Thiele and the life he had been forced to leave behind. Something, however, told him that he would never be completely satisfied with that life again. He had tasted the freedom of the road for the first time; and though he had made some mistakes and had a bad experience, he liked the sense of being on his own and responsible for what came next in his life.

He had never shared this with his father, or even with Jared; but the last few years in Thiele he had begun to get really antsy, especially during the long, cold winters. When he had gone afield alone for hunting or trapping trips, he would often stretch them out a few extra hours, so he could explore over the next hill or into the next vale. There was something that always drew him on. He often imagined that an adventure lay over the next rise.

Finally, he said, "I expect I should stay at least a few days yet to regain more of my strength. I don't think I can fend off robbers just yet." He grabbed the handle of the wood rake set against the barn door. "Here, at least I can help get that into a tighter pile for you. I don't think that will strain me, and I need to do something. I've been too long abed; my muscles need some stretching."

They worked silently together for the next fifteen minutes. Ge-or took it slowly; yet surprisingly, far too quickly, he could feel the effort was sapping his strength. He was sweating by the time the last of the goat leavings were in the cart.

"It's hard to believe that I could get so sick from so small a wound," he said, leaning against the rake and smiling at Leona. She was the perfect model of a wilderness-raised lady, he thought, as a wisp of hair fluttered across her face. He smiled, seeing that dirt from her effort was smeared on the front of her heavy work skirt. There was strength in her – a sturdiness that spoke of hard work and long days outside. At the same time, there was also something womanly about Leona. Ge-or found her quite comely in her frock.

Leona did not seem to notice him looking at her so intently. "Fevers can come on quickly. Without a healer in these parts, we have to rely on what is at hand. I learned herbal craft from my mother. Even so, some fevers do not respond to home cures. You were strong and able to fight it off."

"And lucky to have found your stead."

"Come. Let's go back to the house. I should start dinner. If you are comfortable talking about it, I would like to know of your village and family. We have few visitors anymore, and I love hearing about the outside world."

"I should tell you about my brother, Jared. We were very close, and we could get into the most interesting situations together. I guess we were like any two boys growing up in the wilds. We could always find something to get into; more often than not, it had mischief at its roots."

"Through no fault of your own, I suppose."

"I am an exemplar of innocence." Ge-or grinned, feeling a bit lighthearted for the first time since he had left Thiele. He was actually looking forward to an evening with Leona and her father.

It wasn't until later that he realized he had spoken of his brother without feeling he had to push down a flood of anger and other confusing emotions. Perhaps it would not trouble him again. He decided that such things were best not dwelt on.

The next morning, Ge-or woke feeling yet more like himself. The pungent smell of goat sausage and herbs was filling the cabin. Before he went into the kitchen to join Leona for breakfast, he took his sword from where it was leaning against the wall. Stepping back and slightly to the side so he had a bit more room, he swung the blade in a long-practiced drill. For several minutes, he spun the weapon in the air, enjoying the heft and balance and the feeling of his strength having returned closer to normal.

Setting the sword back, Ge-or washed his face and hands in a basin that Leona had refilled earlier that morning. It was a chilly fall morning, but he felt good. In a few days, he could be back on the road.

Aldred was back from early morning chores. The three sat at the heavy table enjoying a breakfast of fried goat sausage with onions, sweet griddle corn cakes with maple syrup, and an herbal tea sweetened with a touch of honey. Leona was unusually quiet. Ge-or sensed that she and her father had been discussing some difficult matter before he had come out. They had both suddenly quit talking when he opened the door from the bedroom to the kitchen.

After eating his last bite of sausage, Aldred broke the silence. "You have color back in your cheeks, young man. I am glad you are feeling better."

"Much better, my strength is returning. I hefted my blade before coming out. I feel good. I would be happy to help about the stead today. If you have the time, I think we should also go through that wagon. You both should take anything you need or want. I will not have much use for most of what is there, since I will be on the road."

"Some of the tools would be most welcome, certainly," Aldred said. "After forty years, many of mine are wearing down. I only replace them when I need one for some task."

"Take them all, please. I have the few I need in my pack. I would see these put to good use. Take the foodstuffs as well. I will pack a few things when I leave – there are crocks of molasses, grains, and many other items, also a small bag of some quality kaffa. Perhaps we can have some of that on the morrow, and a mug of the mead or ale this evening would be a pleasure to share."

"We thank you, elf-kin. These will be welcome additions to our winter stores," Leona said.

There was an edge of nervousness to her voice; and what she said and how she said it seemed a bit stilted, almost formal. Ge-or wondered if she and Aldred had been fighting over something. When he had been in the bedroom, their voices had been low enough that he could not make out what they were discussing. There didn't seem to be any indication that they were in dispute with each other, either.

When Leona stood, she kept her eyes looking down, avoiding his. "Would you mind if I went through the clothes. There might be something I could clean up and use. Even rags, when cleaned, are welcome for making quilts and bedding."

"Please, it would give me pleasure to see you make use of any or all of it." Ge-or smiled at her across the table.

Leona finally did look at him; she blushed when their eyes met. Turning quickly away toward the stove, she said, "Maybe I will go down now and sort through what is there while you men finish your tea. It will feel like Yule season early with so many things to choose from." Leona laughed nervously when she came back to clear their plates. Ge-or thought he saw her hands shaking. He wondered anew at what was going on between her and her father.

After Leona had gone, Ge-or waited politely for Aldred to speak. Her father also was unwilling to meet his eyes. He was looking into his mug of tea. He cleared his throat thrice, as if he were going to say something, but didn't. Finally, he decided to break with whatever it was he wanted to say. Clearing his throat once again, he looked up at Ge-or, blushed red under his dark tan, and dove in. "Ge-or, may I ask a boon?"

"Anything, Aldred. As I said before, you saved my life. I owe you a great debt."

Aldred waved his hand in front of his body. "That does not matter. This is past a debt owed that I would ask of you. Please do not answer me based on what we have done for you. I only ask this as of a friend, and as someone who understands the hardships of this life."

Ge-or was dumbfounded. He could not imagine what could have transpired this morning that would have caused Aldred to speak so formally, and for there to be so much consternation in his hosts. "If it is within my power and will, I would be happy to do a friend a deed," he answered, also a bit more formally than he might have fifteen minutes before.

"Well, I will have out with it, though this is mayhap one of the hardest things I have ever spoke to another man in my many years.

"Ge-or..." Aldred cleared his throat once more. He kept his eyes riveted on Ge-or's. "Leona is getting older by mountain standards; she has only a few years left, well, ah... left to bear children."

Ge-or straightened and began to open his mouth. Aldred rushed ahead, not wanting to stop before he had it all out. "She... she is in her window, if you understand what I mean, and she would be with child. Ah... if you are willing that is. There, I've said it. I hope I do not offend or presume too much." He stared at Ge-or, almost as if challenging him to take a swing at him. His face was flushed a deep red now.

Opening his mouth and shutting it several times, Ge-or's mind was awhirl. What he understood of Aldred's request was that presumably, with Leona's knowledge and permission, her father had asked Ge-or if he would bed his daughter and try to get her with child. Besides being flabbergasted by the request, Ge-or suddenly had dozens of questions circling in his head, not to mention a flood of emotions. Aldred sat staring at him, obviously expecting a response.

"I... I'm honored," Ge-or managed to stammer out. "I... It's just that..."

"I know, son, I know. I wisht there was an easier way to broach such a

162

subject. Again, please don't feel obligated. If you can't, or won't, I'll... We'll both understand. It was hard for both of us to even talk of this. She... she likes you, and there are no suitors about this area anymore. I can't get her to leave me to seek one, either. She would love to have a babe, and I... I would leave this stead to a grandchild, if the gods are willing." Aldred stood to leave. Ge-or grabbed his wrist, pushing down hard to get him to sit again.

"Truly, Aldred, I am honored. Please understand that there are so many things, ah... factors to your request, that I cannot consider this lightly. Leona is a beautiful and kind woman. I do not want to hurt her in any way; she has been an angel to me. You both need to understand something at the outset – I *will* be leaving, and I think that would hurt her. I..."

"This she understands, Ge-or. We have talked about it at some length. She wanted to ask you herself; but I felt it was best if you and I talked first. We both think we understand a bit of what drives you. She... I... We are not asking that you should marry her, or even be responsible for..."

"I will be responsible!" Ge-or set his mouth, making sure Aldred met his gaze. "If there is a child, I will not abandon it. That is not who I am." Ge-or stood, placing his hands on the table. Leaning forward, he gave Aldred an even more piercing look. He was now speaking with passion. "And right now, without thinking further on it, I don't see that there is a solution to that."

"Perhaps we can find one together."

"Aldred..." Ge-or backed up slightly, trying to ease some of the tension. "Though I was thrust onto this path unwillingly; now I cannot imagine going back to the life I led a short while ago. I think I am destined to this life of exploring and roaming. What you have here is beautiful, peaceful, almost idyllic; however, if I pledged to stay, I do not think I could keep that promise. As much as Leona, this vale, and what you have built draw me, I feel my destiny lies elsewhere."

"If there is a child, Ge-or, come back when you can or will. We do not want you to feel obligated in any way."

"Yet, I will feel that way. It is who I am. It is how I was raised."

Aldred nodded. "I understand. Leona will understand as well. It speaks to your upbringing and your honor. We can accept this decision."

"Hold a minute, Aldred, I have not decided yet. Give me more time to work this through. I do understand, or I am beginning to understand, the depth of your request. It is a courageous thing to ask, more-so for her than for you. I ken the hardships she faces, the loneliness and emptiness. She is a brave soul to have stayed this long. She must care for you and this life very much."

Aldred nodded, tears now leaking from his eyes and shining on his cheeks. "After her mother died, I thought to leave. I even begged her to leave all of this and head east with me, because I knew it would be hard for her in many ways if we stayed. She refused, and I could not change her mind. In that respect, she has always been like her mother, stubborn to the core."

"Can you both give me a day? I need time to think about this in every possible way. Please tell her that I am deeply honored; I... I need to work through my own issues. I need to understand what this means to me as well as to her. Please help her to understand that if I decide 'Yay,' that eventually I will leave. It is who I am now, and I do not want her to think elsewise."

Aldred opened his mouth to speak; Ge-or silenced him with his hand, held palm outward.

"There is one other thing you need to understand, Aldred, both of you. I am half-elven. It is my understanding that there is something about our heritage, as the elves are, that makes it difficult to father a child. Even if we are willing and try, it may not happen."

"She understands this. You are her chance, perhaps her only chance, to have this... this miracle in her life. There is also, equally important to her and to me, the fact that... well, I'll out with this, too, though she begged me not. She really likes you, Ge-or. Perhaps she even believes she loves you. I know that makes it better in one sense; more difficult in another. It may also affect your decision, I ken that. It is better that it is out in the open."

"Tell her that I care for her as well. She has come to mean much to me these few days. It is not just her kindness that makes me feel so. It is important she know that, whatever I decide."

"Thank you for understanding. This has been difficult for us both. If you wish to be alone, there is work today in the far pasture."

"Good... that would be good."

The Altar of Kan

Within two hours, their small party had reached the edge of the ruins -- a whole mountainside composed of a mass of broken stone with only stubby, dark, twisted shrubs scattered amongst the piles of dark rubble. Jared, shielding his eyes from the sun's bright glare, scanned the slope, as the others did, hoping to see something that would give them a clue to Aberon's or the altar's whereabouts.

They had lost Aberon's trail as soon as it entered the rocks. They could only plod forward slowly in hopes of seeing something, however insignificant, that might lead them in the right direction, or point to where he and his horse had gone. Rux's men had been here numerous times. They had never found an opening in the rubble. What force had destroyed the fortress so thoroughly was unknown. It did look as if no stone remained standing with another, as Rux had said.

"Up there!" Jared yelled, only minutes after they had begun picking their way upward. "Something moved."

With his keen elven eyesight, Jared had detected a slight movement of some tiny black object that had gone against the breeze from the north. He jumped off his mule and scrambled over the rocks. Ten minutes later, with the rest of the party trailing a hundred paces behind, he whispered back to Thistle who was closest. "It's a horse. I can see his ear. He appears to be tied behind a boulder, about a hundred feet up." Jared pointed up the mountain. Following his gesture, Thistle saw a tiny black point sticking above a large rock; as she watched, she saw it dip and straighten again.

Rux motioned for Jared to wait for the others to catch up. A few minutes later, they were all gathered around the Borean captain. "We must wait for Sart. We can do no further good until he arrives. Aberon is too powerful for us. We..."

"No!" Jared whispered vehemently. "We must press Aberon. Above all else, that is what Sart told me. If we give him time, any time, he will gain power, especially here. Then even Sart will not be strong enough to stop him. If none will come with me, I will go myself. He must be pressed."

"I'll go," Thistle said determinedly, stepping next to Jared.

Rux looked troubled, but finally agreed. "Lead on, elf-kin; and may the power of the gods, and all forces for good, go with us. We will have to leave the animals below. The path up is too dangerous for them to go further. Perhaps they will serve as a marker for Sart, so he knows which way we have gone... if he yet comes."

Minutes later, Jared led them stealthily up to the place where the horse was tethered. He flitted from rock to rock, trying to keep something between himself and where he had seen the animal.

When he reached the horse, Jared saw it was glossy with sweat. Soothing him with whispered words, he slid in next to his flank and patted him while the rest of the party eased past the animal, continuing up a narrow path. Looking down the slope, they could see that a narrow, winding path had been chipped into the mountainside to this point. They could see it went up another hundred paces or more.

The path was steep and difficult. They had to hold onto the rocks about them and haul themselves up. Fifteen minutes later, breathing heavily, they were all staring at the solid wall of a cliff directly in front of them. They saw no other direction they could go, more hard rock stretching upward. Elsewise, all about them were large broken rocks.

Jared's first thought was that Aberon must have used his magic to penetrate the wall. He did not know if that was possible. What Sart had said about magic did not help much. The granite looked impenetrable; and though he had climbed many a cliff as he was growing up – answering challenges that often came from his brother – this wall was sheer. It looked like it had been carved from the stone of the mountain to be perfectly smooth, with nothing to grasp a hold of for many feet above their heads.

They all looked carefully around the relatively flat crescent of rock in front of the cliff. It was small, barely twenty paces from end to end and maybe twelve deep at its widest. Finally, Jared walked right up to the cliff face to examine it more closely. All at once, he felt disoriented and a bit dizzy. He thrust out his right hand toward the wall to steady himself. He fell forward and, to everyone's surprise, his hand disappeared, followed by most of the rest of him. He hit the ground with a loud "Oomph." All the others could see only his boots.

An illusion! Jared had heard of such things, but he had never witnessed anything more elaborate than the sleight-of-hand tricks displayed by travelling entertainment groups. As Jared pushed himself up, he found that he had passed back out into the light.

It took them a few minutes to test the illusion further. It appeared to be simply that – a realistic rendition of a solid wall that had no substance. No harm came to them when they stepped through, yet they each felt a bit strange the first few times they approached and stepped into the illusion.

Once back inside, Jared could see steps that led under a worn arch down into the bowels of the mountain. At one time, the stairway must have been fully thirty feet wide; now it was partially clogged by rubble. The archway itself had been ornately carved with hideous heads lining the upper section. Time had taken its toll on these symbols of evil. They were pitted shadows of their former horror.

After examining the entire entryway carefully, the small band was ready to descend into the depths. Thistle, Rux, and the other men brought up the rear. Stepping once more through the ethereal wall, Jared led the way. Behind Jared, two of Rux's men lit torches before following him into the blackness. Thistle, Rux, and the other men brought up the rear. As he went down, a shiver ran through Jared's spine.

At first, Jared felt his fear was just apprehension at entering this unwholesome place. However, as he descended, a cold, clammy, filthy aura began to permeate everything. He began to avoid the threatening walls by staying to the center of the stairway. The others followed his lead.

The place felt close, as if the walls were pulsing with a power that threatened to overwhelm. He drew his bow forward and nocked an arrow, though there was nothing to fight, only a feeling of fragility.

He had gone down a hundred steps when the malevolence began to feel more and more like a real force, trying to drive him back and up. It was all he could do to force himself down the last few steps.

At the bottom of the stairway, Jared came to a sloping pathway leading further down. It took a formidable act of will for him to take the next step ahead.

Once he had gone about ten more paces, Jared found himself on a small platform which was lit by a reddish glow emanating from the walls. Twenty paces further, he came to more stairs.

With Rux close behind, Jared went on. Thistle, walking behind the big man, also felt a deepening sensation of pressure coming from all sides. The deeper they went, the more an oily filth seemed to penetrate their beings.

The red-evil glow of the walls gave their descent an eerie, hellish quality.

The crimson light reflected ghoulishly off the polished steel of their drawn weapons. As they continued, Jared soon noticed something unsettling – if he strayed far from the center of the stairway, he would start to feel terribly afraid. In the narrow corridor in the middle, oddly, it felt almost pleasant, wholesome, as if something holy had recently blessed the area. Wary of even this small blessing in this evil place, Jared moved ahead more cautiously.

The red glare continued to light their way as the small group pushed ahead for a long time, ever further down. Occasional landings interrupted their descent, but they never saw any other corridors or doors to either side. After what Jared thought must have been the better part of an hour of slow, steady descent, he saw a brighter glare ahead. He hesitated while the others came up behind. As soon as they were all gathered together, a sinister voice boomed out. "Come down, come down. You have arrived too late, my friends." A strident laugh followed, sending shivers up their spines.

Stepping hesitantly forward, his bow at the ready, Jared moved into a bright circle of reddish-orange light. Set on massive boulders before him stood a rectangular black altar with a glowing red flame burning fiercely in the middle of its thick top slab. Aberon, priest of darkness, stood behind the altar. His hands raised over the flame. He did not look up as they came in, keeping his gaze on the intense blaze. The flare of red, yellow, and orange lit his thin bony hands and sharp face to horrid aspect.

He laughed again as the others entered behind Jared. "Behold your stone, elf-kin. Soon it will sink into the altar and be beyond the grasp of anyone. Kan's power lives, and it is mine!" At those words, Aberon did raise his head. He turned and grinned wickedly at them, bringing his arms up to chest level.

The dark priest's movement shook Jared from his trance. Drawing his bow in one smooth motion, he brought it to his eye and loosed the arrow at Aberon. In a split second, he had set another shaft. As he moved, the others behind him also reacted. Rux and his men rushed forward, splitting into two groups toward the sides of the altar, circling the oval chamber with their swords held high.

Aberon laughed horribly again, mocking them. He brushed aside the arrow as if it was a fly. Continuing to laugh, he gestured indifferently to his right. Rux and the two men with him froze in mid-stride. Turning back toward the other side, he reached out with his left hand and touched the nearest soldier's sword as the man came around the corner of the black slab. An intense white spark flew along the blade, up the man's arm, and through his body. The man went rigid, his entire body blackening as he collapsed to the side of the altar. His charred remains crackled as they broke to pieces on the floor. The soldier behind stopped, backed slightly, and suddenly fell in a heap next to the altar.

It was then that a deep earthy voice broke into Aberon's mirth. "Do not rejoice so soon, evil one," Sart said, striding from behind Thistle.

Whether out of fright or judiciousness, or to be close to Jared, she had stayed back near the entrance to the cavern. As still as if molded from the stone at her feet, Thistle stared straight at the dark priest, her haunted green eyes reflecting the fiery kaleidoscope of multi-colored flames to her fore. Even at Sart's words and movement, she did not stir.

Passing Thistle, Sart stepped forward, his rood held out toward Aberon. "Now is our time," he said, "and this time you are matched." He approached the altar. Bringing his staff high, he pointed it at the evil priest's chest.

Aberon seemed little disturbed by the good priest's presence. He bent slightly, picking up his own dark staff from the altar.

"Foolish cleric," Aberon sneered, "the power of Kan is with me here. It is you who are overmatched." Raising his black staff, he pointed it at Sart and began to chant dark syllables none except the two priests had ever heard. The language appeared to match in form and substance the horror of the evil force the dark druid commanded.

Sart was suddenly stopped as if struck by a solid wall of energy. Having no more power to resist the malevolence of the Black Priest, he slowly crumbled to his knees, his rood falling from his hands and his staff dipping to the floor.

"See, my foolish enemy. My power here is unmatched." Aberon's smile broadened. Exerting more force, he pushed Sart lower.

Sart strove with all his might against the grip of the evil that drove him ever downward. He gasped, fighting the crushing power. He knew he was too weak to counter the energy Aberon commanded, so he tried desperately to focus on his connection with Gaia. Yet this place held no good at its roots. It had been too long the womb of evil.

Frozen for a second by the horrid tableau unfolding before him, Jared finally was able to look away; he raised his bow to eye level again. It was as his aim came to bear on the priest's neck that he heard Thistle's voice. Spinning around, he saw that she had stepped sideways, following the shadows of the cavern wall to her right. Walking like she was a puppet being manipulated by another, she moved toward the fallen cleric. Alarmed that she was under the Black Priest's control, Jared swung back around and fired his shaft. As before, Aberon simply flicked the arrow away with a slight movement of his finger.

Thistle continued to move steadily toward Sart. Jared could see her eyes were glazed, and that her right hand clutched at something underneath her tunic. He drew another shaft from his quiver, though he had little hope it would find a mark. Drawing back the bow string one more time, he hesitated as it stretched back to his cheek.

Thistle began to intone a long stream of syllables in the old language, bright and glorious words that Jared was certain had never been uttered in this abominable place before. The intonation and rhythm of old Elvish his mother had taught him many years before defied the negativity emanating from the priest and altar. Thistle continued to move until she was close enough to rest her hand on Sart's bowed head.

Aberon, bent on the destruction of his enemy, and keeping his peripheral vision on the nuisance half-elf with the bow, did not see what she was about until it was too late. Just as she touched Sart's brow, Thistle spoke the last word of the incantation. In a bright flash, a globe of blue light began to form around the cleric. It took several seconds to fully encase Sart, which was enough time for Aberon to readjust his focus and point his staff toward Thistle.

Sart reacted at the same time. Released from what held him, and now protected by the power of Thistle's conjuration, the cleric regained his feet. He wavered there a moment, then took two quick strides toward the altar. As he did so, Thistle collapsed to the floor. It was not, however, Aberon's power that felled the girl, for at the last second, he had to deflect another shaft from Jared.

Screaming in anger, Aberon raised his staff to refocus his energy back on Sart. By this time, Sart had raised his staff above his head. Standing across the altar from Aberon, he grasped it in both hands and brought it down in a savage swing. Knowing now that he did not have the power to overmatch Aberon in this dark place, Sart focused his energy and the full power imbued in his staff at destroying the source the dread cleric drew from. The knotted head struck at the center of the fire on the altar. A split second before the staff hit, Aberon screamed and vanished.

Sart's staff found its mark as it shattered in dozens of pieces on the altar block. As the staff hit, the pendant was flung through the air, landing near Jared's feet. A great crack slowly opened across the top of the ebon slab. It spread across the thick, wide expanse quickly, the altar breaking in half and crashing to the floor.

As if in slow motion, the tableau around the altar began to change. Jared dropped his bow and quiver and ran to Thistle. Kneeling down, he reached out and drew her to his chest. She was not moving; he did not know if she even lived. Rux and his three remaining men, released from Aberon's power, began to move as well. They stared about blankly, and only slowly were able to orient to what was happening in the altar chamber. Sart, trying to overcome the draining effects of the enormous power he had spent in the destruction of the altar, began to turn around.

Seeing Jared with Thistle, the cleric reacted as quickly as he could manage, even though he was barely able to remain standing. He gestured toward the floor. "Jared, the pendant, you must take it. We must leave!... Where is Aberon? Did he…?" Sart gasped for air. "She swoons. We must away in case he returns. The power here is not broken. Come."

Jared, weeping bitterly and feeling he was in the midst of a long nightmare, reluctantly left Thistle and went to retrieve the pendant and his bow. Pocketing the gemstone, he turned back toward Thistle.

Rux, seeing Sart was still struggling to catch his breath, went to lend the cleric his support; he half-carried him to the entrance to the room, whilst the other men and Jared picked Thistle up. Aberon was nowhere in the room, yet no one had seen him leave.

Driven by the malevolence of the place to hie ever upward without pause, still it took them a long time to ascend. The weight of the place dragged at them as well as the length of the stairway. Drained as they were by the oppressive atmosphere during the descent, the ascent was a struggle through hell.

When they finally reached the place where Jared had found Aberon's horse, they discovered that the evil priest's steed was gone. Shortly thereafter, they also discovered that Aberon had driven their own animals away from the base of the ruins.

Sart urged them on. Hurrying as quickly as possible, they made their way along the winding path and out of the ruins. When they were well back into the trees and out of sight of the destruction of Kan's fortress, they all sank gratefully to the soft mat of pine needles of the forest floor.

Jared held Thistle while Sart bent to examine her. She was deathly white, cold, and unresponsive to his touch. The cleric eased Yolk out from under her tunic and discovered that the little creature was also limp and unconscious.

"What... what happened?" Jared cried. "What did she do?"

Sart answered, "She must have spoken the words that Meligance sent her in her dream; words to help her focus her energy. A conjuration like that is only controllable by a powerful magic-user. It is a miracle that it worked, that she was able to connect with her power. She did have the ovietti; she had Yolk. His power would help. He appears to have paid dearly. Though she saved my life, perhaps all our lives, it was a dangerous thing to do. I don't know if I can do anything to help her, Jared. I am drained and she has gone deep within. Mayhap... if you let me freely use the stone."

Jared looked puzzled. "Certainly, you can use it. Why didn't you take it?"

"Magic works in odd ways, my friend," Sart replied. "Especially objects long imbued with power. They oft have a way of their own in this world. Sometimes artifacts work only for the person who has rightfully acquired it. This stone could work in many ways. I may not be able to use it; with your permission, I will try."

Fumbling in his pocket, Jared brought out the pendant. As he handed it to Sart, he looked at it for the first time in the light. It was an unusually large and irregularly shaped milky white stone, with hints of blue in its depths. Turned a certain way, it almost looked as clear as a crystal. It was in a simple setting of silver wire with a loop at one end, through which the leather thong had been passed. It was cool in his hand and somehow it felt comforting. Momentarily, he felt reluctant to hand it to the priest.

Sart lay Yolk back in Thistle's hands. He took the pendant when Jared proffered it, pressing it onto the center of the girl's chest. Placing his right hand on her forehead, Sart stayed in that position for several minutes while Jared looked anxiously down at Thistle. Just as Jared thought nothing would happen, he saw a spark jump in the depths of the gemstone. A moment later, Thistle's eyes fluttered open. Yolk rolled open his large yellow eyes at the same time.

Smiling up at Jared and Sart, Thistle asked, "How did we do?"

Jared laughed and cried at the same time. He reached down to gather her close in his arms.

Sometime later, satisfied that Aberon was indeed gone and not likely to return, they managed to retrieve two of the stockade's mules, Rux's goatsteed, and Crunch. Facing back to the east and north, they began the long trek back to Xur, trying to get as far as possible from the evil mountainside as they could before full dark.

Darkness

Aberon was dazed when he emerged from the depths next to his horse. He clambered aboard the animal and gave it a sharp rap with his heels. He remembered heading down the mountain, rushing to escape; after that, no more for a long time. When he came out of his trance, he was leagues to the west, his horse lathered from a hard ride. He was furious at the turn of events.

When the horse stopped to drink, he slid to the ground and knelt by the rippling stream. Wiping his face with the cool water, Aberon tried to reconstruct what had happened. All had gone as planned, and yet, he had not prevailed; he had not succeeded in his task. The wisp of a girl had cast – it seemed inconceivable to him – she *had* spoken the incantation to a powerful spell of protection, which formed about the priest. He had known instantly that he would not be able to penetrate it, not while it lasted. How had she wielded so much power? Her own magical signature was weak at best. How, indeed, had she known the words used to focus the energy? That much power should have destroyed her. This was a conjuration known only to the most powerful of mages. It took an immense concentration of energy. Yet, she had spoken the words and created the sphere right in front of him. How had she tapped into so much power?

What had happened next?

It took him some time to remember. Sart had... had taken his staff and struck? He obviously had not struck him... the altar? That would make sense, he guessed. What of the stone? He had left too soon to see what had happened. Maybe he had succeeded after all. For now, he knew he had to get away. He felt drained, completely devoid of any power in a way he had never felt before. As he mentally examined himself, he realized that something had changed within him. There had been a flash, just as his teleportation spell had taken effect. It had emanated from the core of the block as he dissolved into the ether.

And now? Something was different; something from that flash of energy had penetrated to his core. He felt it burning brightly, deep within his gut. It was a fiery, red hot force; and it frightened and exhilarated him at the same time. There was power in it, a different type of power, not accessible right now, but there nonetheless. Soon, after he was rested, he would explore what it was.

There was something else, too – a darkness had penetrated his inner vision. He felt it as if it was at the periphery of his mind, encircling him. He sat heavily on the ground next to the stream and gave himself to it. For a long time, he knew nothing else.

A Decision for Life

Ge-or spent the day in the south-west field gathering sheaves of hay that Aldred had cut and stacked several weeks before. He had hooked two of the mules to the large wagon that was now empty of its contraband. With it, he was able to haul ten to twelve of the large bundles in each load. Though he felt much better physically, the work was tiring. He had to pause frequently to rest. He was far from full strength, but it felt good to be exerting himself. He knew he was past any danger in his recovery.

The long slow labor gave him plenty of time to think. One thing that Aldred and Leona didn't know was how inexperienced he was with women. He was young, as half-elven, physically only a few years able to call himself a man.

There had been one young lass in their village that Ge-or had spent some time with. They had avoided consummating their relationship. If they had, marriage would have been expected, and Ge-or had definitely not been ready for that. They had enjoyed exploring each other's bodies and their budding sexuality on more than a few occasions. When he had taken the time to honor his fellow villagers after the Qa-ryk assault, her body had been the hardest for Ge-or to deal with. She had been clawed horribly and bitten on the neck repeatedly by the Qa-ryks. There was a great deal of anger burning deep in his gut about that. That revenge would wait until he had dealt with the dragon.

Because of his upbringing in the coastal village, the notion of bedding a woman without offering marriage also gave Ge-or pause. He had been brought up in a time and place where such meant a proposal was in the offing. His father had been tolerant of the boys' flirtations, and had also warned both of them many-a-time about the consequences of taking things too far.

So much depended on the family unit and the extended family in these close-knit wilderness societies, that one did not take liaisons lightly. The traditions continued from generation to generation; certain things were expected, though not written in any code. Ge-or's father and mother had been first generation in their village, yet they had respected and abided all that held the community together.

Ge-or had also been brought up to respect others, as well as to respect life – to consider his actions in relationship to how they would impact not just himself, but anyone they might affect. This decision was not about providing his host with an heir, nor in giving Leona her heart's desire, to have a child. He knew that if they were lucky and managed to conceive, he would always feel a responsibility to her and to the child. He would not be able to ignore that. Somehow, he would want to help ensure they were safe and provided for. That responsibility he would own and not relinquish.

He also knew, deep down, that life in this vale, as idyllic as it might seem and even be on occasion, was not what he wanted. It was not who he was. He had often talked with Jared about what they would do once they were of age. As youngsters they had dreamt of grand adventures together: going out and rescuing maidens, fighting dragons and fell ogres, finding lost treasures, and the like. Each tale was more wondrous than the next. Yet, now that he was in a sense living such a tale, now that he had been thrust on the adventurer's path, he knew that their imaginings had been simply boyish dreams.

Still, there was an underlying excitement, energy, and drive within him every time he thought of his quest and his promise to take his revenge on the dread winged beast. Though the two lads had never honestly believed they would ever fight real dragons, Ge-or had now set for himself exactly that task. He knew that, despite all that had happened in the past weeks, it was the right thing for him to do. He knew instinctively that it is what his father would have done and probably would have expected him to do. It was, he felt very strongly, a matter of honor for him and especially for those who had been killed. It was not just a task of revenge.

If Leona could accept that about him, that he *was* going to leave, that he needed to fulfill another destiny, perhaps... perhaps...

He was considering all the ramifications of his decision as he rode the last wagon full of hay toward the barn at sunset.

Ge-or found Leona in the kitchen preparing a lamb stew for dinner. The pot was simmering at the back of the stove, and she had taken several loaves of bread from the side oven. Aldred was sitting at the table sipping a mug of what Ge-or expected was "fortified" tea. They both turned as he came in the door. Aldred nodded at him, his face set in an impassive mask. Leona blushed, managed a partial upturn of her lips, and quickly turned back to the stove.

Though he needed to clean up after the sweaty work in the field, Ge-or felt strongly that they should resolve this as soon as feasible. "Leona, I would talk with you alone," he said, striding across the floor toward the stove.

Aldred stood to leave; Ge-or waved him back down. Leona half turned as Ge-or reached her. He put his hand on the side of her shoulder. "Come. Let us go outside. It is a beautiful eve. The stew will keep a while." He slid his hand down her arm and took her hand and drew her toward the door. Aldred nodded again as he went past.

Ge-or led Leona silently around the back of the house to the stream that came out from the northwest corner of the vale and ran down west of the barn. There was a small hillock in front of a natural pond that Aldred had spoken of as his "fishing hole." Turning toward Leona, he pulled her close and kissed her lightly on her brow. He gestured for her to sit. As she settled, her long skirt spreading around her, Ge-or cleared his throat and started to talk, choosing to stand in his nervousness.

"Leona, I want you to understand that I am overwhelmed by what you and Aldred have asked of me. It is... I don't think I know the right words... for me, it is an honor; yet more than that as well. You have become special to me, both as my savior and caregiver when I was near death, and also as a companion these past days. I owe you and your father a great debt. What you ask, as your father said, is something beyond a debt owed. It is something I have had to think seriously about, because I cannot dispel the responsibility I feel attends such a decision.

"You are a beautiful, handsome, and... and desirable woman." Ge-or was more than a little happy that he had chosen this shadowed location. He hoped Leona would not be able to see how red in the face he was; he figured she must know his discomfort from the hesitation in his voice. "Please understand this – I do find you attractive. I think any man with good taste would find you very attractive." Ge-or felt himself flush even more; because the truth was, once he had begun to heal from his wounds, he had found it difficult not to think of her in that way the past few days. She had a fine figure for so petite a woman, and his wilderness background helped him appreciate the strength and fortitude she exhibited in everything she did.

He held his hand up to signal a pause. Suddenly, feeling hot even in the cool breeze, he turned toward the stream, knelt, and quickly washed his face, neck, and arms. He also needed to gather his thoughts for what came next.

Leona was nervously wringing her hands, trying to accept that what Ge-or was saying might seal her fate – as a lonely maid, or not. She had considered little about any of this until a few days ago, because she had never found a man she considered worthy. His stumbling into their vale that night had awakened dreams and feelings she had put aside long ago. She had believed herself content to live as she had for many years: working, producing, and enjoying the fruits of her and her father's hard labors. She also knew, instinctively, that her time for being able to bear children safely was almost up. With Ge-or's presence, the desire to have a child had blossomed overnight. Other feelings, strong ones, had begun to surface as well. A child would make all the difference in the meaning of both her and her father's lifetime endeavors. She sat waiting as Ge-or washed, because that was all she could do.

Turning back, Ge-or swallowed hard. "Leona, before I answer you, I need to know that you understand who I am, and what I can and can't do. I know... I know that you do not wish me to feel obligated, yet I will. That is my choice and my honor. I also understand that you are not truly asking of me anything except some nights together, so that you may conceive a child. I hope and feel that it is more than that exercise. I believe you care for me, and that is a good thing; it is a hard thing, too, because I care for you as well.

"I... I was brought up in many ways like you were – to the hills, farming, trapping. It is a life of hardship – simple, yet beautiful in a way many would not understand. I believe we have a deep kinship there. When that life was destroyed for me a few weeks ago, I found myself free from all that I was and had been. I realized that freedom was something I have craved for a long time. I do not think I could settle into that life, this life," he gestured with both hands to the vale and structures about them, "again. I would grow restless, quickly. The open road has called to me, and I know I am already given to that new life.

"You need to understand that whatever we choose, because once you know my feelings you will have to decide again whether this is what you truly want as well, that I will not stay. Whether I stay a week or until the snows, I will leave here. And it is not just the quest I have pledged myself to, it is the man I have become. I need to be free. Do you understand what I am saying?"

Leona nodded. Tears were running down her cheeks, but Ge-or could not see them. The moon was yet to rise, and darkness had now settled into the vale.

"The other important part of this for me is that I cannot, in due conscience, forget my responsibility to you and to the child, if one comes. Though we may not marry, you and I will have shared something, something special and unique. If we do this, and if you do conceive, the child will be of my flesh as well as of yours. I will not ignore that. Somehow, I would want to ensure that you are both safe and provided for."

Ge-or took a small step toward Leona. He wanted to reach out to her, but he hesitated. "I know that what you have here is more than adequate for raising a child, a family. I understand that your father will do all in his power to care for both of you. I would want, however, to make sure as well. I am not positive what that may mean: whether I would be able to come by on occasion to see how things are going and to bring something that you may need, to send money when I may, or to simply be in some way a part of you and our child's life. That would remain to develop as it would.

"This is perhaps the most difficult part, because I do not know what my future holds. I may be killed in my quest; it is perhaps even likely. If three scruffy ruffians can fool me, I may not be much good against a wise old dragon." Ge-or smiled grimly. Right now, he could barely see the outline of Leona's face as he stood before her. He did notice that the moon was beginning to peek above the hills to the east. "If you conceive, mayhap I can return in the summer when the baby is due, or if not then, soon thereafter. Perhaps I can visit once each year. Leona, I do not know what my future holds; and I don't know what I can promise, except that you and a child, should it come, will matter to me, and I will not forget you. It is not who I am at heart. I cannot leave that which I am responsible for."

Ge-or took another step forward and reached out for her hands. He drew her up until she was less than a foot from him. "Leona, I want to grant you this boon. Not because I owe you, because I care for you. Can you accept who I am, what I have said here? Do you truly understand all that this portends for you, your father, and for me?"

She lifted her face. Ge-or could now see her tears and her smile. He bent and kissed her on the lips, lightly at first, but there was a hunger in both of them that called from their depths. They kissed for a long time before they sank to the earth, bathed in the light from the moon.

It was much later when they opened the door to the cabin and tiptoed in. The house was quiet. Aldred had set the pot of stew toward the side of the stove above the oven to stay warm and wrapped the fresh breads in oiled parchment. Leona pulled Ge-or toward the stove. "I'm starving... would you like to eat?"

In response, he pulled her back into his arms and kissed her deeply.

They ate later.

Powerful Magic

Sart insisted that Thistle ride on Crunch. Though she said she felt fine, he wanted to be certain that she had no ill effects from what had happened. He didn't tell Jared that she had come close to dying. There had been very little pulse when he had checked her. Using the stone, he had to pull her back from deep within.

Tired as he was, the stone had been the catalyst for him to help awaken her spark of life again. As he had knelt with her, there was a moment when a flash of energy had jolted into his left hand from the pendant, and thence, in an instant, through his whole body and back out through both his hands into Thistle's core. He had never experienced anything so powerfully intense and focused. He had simply been the means to an end. The stone had provided the energy for the healing.

He felt awakened by that flash of energy in a way he had never been before. The power of it had been amazing, almost instantaneous in its effect. Something deep within him was more alive. As he rode, he felt it occasionally flare up within. It was as if the stone had allowed him access to a depth of his being that had been closed off. Tonight, he would meditate on it. Although he was not sure how or why, he was certain he had been blessed in some way.

Sart felt re-energized, yet the others were in varying ways beaten, tired, and worn down by the evil they had faced in the depths. Rux was on the goatsteed; Jared rode one of the other mules. They both were both drained and flagging. Sart rebandaged their wounds with new poultices. Unfortunately, he had used all his healing potions in the aftermath of the attack on Xur, which explained why he had been so late in meeting up with the group at the ruins. Following the battle, a new wave of Beze fever had hit the compound. For two days, he had called upon all his energy and skill to quell it. Afterward, he had ridden with all haste, day and night, to catch them. He had almost been too late.

The soldiers, though unwounded, were lethargic and exhausted from their struggles against the spell they had endured. The dread of that dark place had also taken a toll, as well as the horrible death of their comrade before the altar. Still, two led the way, scouting some hundred paces ahead of the small procession. The other held back a pace to ensure there was no pursuit. They wanted to get as far away from that evil mountainside as possible before they stopped for the eve. They pressed ahead.

The only one not showing any ill effects from their travails was Yolk. The little fellow had remained in Thistle's hands once they had both been restored by the pendant. During the ride he had spent the time looking about. At one point, Thistle had laughed. "I think he is keeping watch for us." At that, Yolk had folded his way in between Crunch's ears and sat there for quite some time with his eyes wide open. As the eve approached, he went back to Thistle, folded up into his favorite position on her upper stomach, and closed his eyes.

Thistle wasn't sure what to think of the little fellow and what he had just done, yet she felt like he was telling her that they were now out of danger.

For his part, Jared relaxed when he heard Thistle laugh. She was herself and did not appear to have any ill effects from her casting of the spell or her healing by the stone.

Rux called a halt shortly thereafter as the sun was almost to the horizon. All of them were now past being exhausted. They picked a spot within a hardwood grove that had a half-circle of boulders in the center which would provide them with some protection. A small rill crossed in front of the campsite, affording them not only a source of fresh water, but an early warning, should anyone approach from below. It was as good a spot as they could have hoped to find.

It had been a long ride, yet Jared was already beginning to feel better. This time he knew his improvement could be traced to the effects of the pendant he was wearing. Whatever its powers, it definitely seemed to have healing properties when worn. He had wanted Thistle to wear it; she had insisted she was fine. Sart, though concerned about her, had told Jared to keep it safe.

When they stopped, Jared, the only one with any energy, decided to circle back along the trail they had traversed. He had seen signs the past few hours of both deer and wild boar, and he was determined that they should all enjoy a hot meal of fresh meat. Leaving Thistle in Sart's care, he scouted back to the north and west of their route of travel, picking up fresh signs almost immediately. Boar had been somewhat of a rarity as far north as Thiele; still, occasionally he and Ge-or managed to bring one down on their longer treks. Here they were more prevalent. Jared decided that stalking one would be a nice change of pace, both for the challenge of the hunt and for dinner, should he shoot one. They were warier than deer, and far more dangerous, so he expected a bit of a test to his skills as a woodsman. The prospect of the challenge helped him forget his residual tiredness and the soreness of the mace wound.

Typically, wild pigs come out to forage in the evenings, first showing themselves near dusk. Jared could tell from the signs that several had recently moved from their bedding area, a dense thicket he had come upon. They seemed to have gone toward a stream further down the slope. The copse was upwind from where he knelt, so he was confident they had not scented him. He decided to set himself between two trees that formed a natural blind because they had grown at an angle to each other. They crossed above Jared's waist.

Setting an arrow to his string, he stood at the vee formed by the two trunks and waited. He was guessing that if he were patient, some of the sows and younglings would still be in the thicket and would come out soon enough.

When he heard a slight rustling ahead, he drew back and waited. A few seconds later, a snout appeared protruding from the edge of the thicket. Boars cannot see well at all, and hence Jared had not felt the need to build a better covering blind using the two trees as an anchor. The pig sniffed about, relying on its two keenest senses, smell and hearing, to wary of any danger.

With the wind as it was, Jared was not worried about his scent. Unless it shifted or some creature came at him from behind, the pig should not bolt. Had he waited until the pig had stuck its nose out, it likely would have heard the slight sound of his drawing back of the arrow.

He waited at full draw for the pig to be satisfied that all was safe. Though he preferred to shoot in one smooth motion, aiming as he brought the bow to eye level and then releasing as soon as he was aligned with his target, he had practiced this stationary technique frequently as well. One never knew what type of shot would present itself in the field. He could hold at full draw for several minutes if he needed to. His father had insisted that he and Ge-or practice that very technique until their arms shook. Eventually, they had developed a steady sure hold on target for periods of up to three or four minutes – a feat that took a steady hand and a good bit of strength.

Finally, the boar moved out into the clear. It was a large sow with several good-sized piglets following behind. She looked healthy and fat. Jared decided the young ones were now large enough to fend for themselves, so he set his aim behind the sow's shoulder and released.

There was a loud thwack as the point hit; the arrow plunged deep into her side, penetrating to the feathers and slicing through both lungs. The pig squealed; diving forward, her snout plowed into the ground. She rose up again, twisted sideways, and ran straight toward where Jared stood. Knowing how dangerous the beasts could be, Jared had set his bow down as soon as he had shot and drawn his long knife. He braced his foot against a root and watched, as the pig charged right at the opening beneath the trunks.

His shot, however, had been true. She once again plowed into the ground only a couple of paces to his fore. The other pigs had scattered at the impact of the shot.

Jared waited several minutes before rounding the tree, just to be sure she would not raise up again and charge. As he approached, he reached out and poked her in the belly with his sharp knife. She was dead.

Working quickly, he gutted her, saving aside the heart and liver. After making sure he had cleaned her thoroughly, he tied her legs tight for dragging. She was a nice size; and even if he had been in top form, Jared didn't think he could have lifted the dead weight. Ge-or probably would have tried, and maybe would have succeeded. He smiled, wondering where his brother was and what he was doing at this moment. They had both shared many a time like this hunting in the hills south of their village. He shook his head sadly at the memories, hoping that his brother was doing well in spite of all that had happened. He started up the slope, drawing the sow behind on the end of his improvised drag-sling.

By the time the fat sow was sizzling on a large spit in front of the fire, they were all in a more boisterous mood. Sart had brought loaded saddlebags, prepared by those at Xur. For the past hour, they had been passing around a bottle of what Rux and his men referred to as "the brew." It was a potent concoction of distilled liquor created from, as was often the case in remote villages and camps, whatever was at hand – in this case, corn, grain, and "other items of an organic nature."

Thistle was the only one who hadn't imbibed. Sart had warned her to be careful for a few days. The cleric did not know the nature of the power from the stone that had helped heal her; and he wanted to make sure she was in good health, and remained so, while they travelled. The road would be demanding enough as they worked their way back to Xur.

Jared, on the other hand, was feeling quite pleasant. Already his aches and pains were better since he had left for the hunt, or else the whiskey made it appear so.

They all enjoyed the fresh meat and close camaraderie until fatigue and the effects of the strong brew began to take their toll. Sart volunteered for the first watch; he wanted to meditate to rejuvenate his powers. He stood facing the opening in the grove with his bare feet firmly planted in the earth. Though he would meditate almost to a trancelike state, his mind and body were tuned to respond to anything out of the ordinary. He would know if something approached them.

Jared and Thistle took their bedrolls and settled down on the eastern edge of the circular space. He was feeling quite tired, but also a bit frisky. When he tickled Thistle for the third time, she pushed his hands away."

"Sh-h-h, you're drunk."

"I know, and after all that has happened to us, it feels good." He sobered a little, and asked, "Are you sure you are all right?"

"I don't know. I feel fine. Sart sure seems concerned. He wants me to tell him what happened on the morrow. I am not sure I remember much. I felt like I was in a dream. It was ethereal – like I was looking at the whole scene from a different place."

"You had me... all of us, dreadfully frightened, Thistle. I... I care about you," he said awkwardly. He also blushed, though she could not see it in the dwindling orange glow from the campfire.

She reached out and touched Jared's face. Drawing closer, she kissed him lightly on the lips. "I care about you, also, elf-kin." When he leaned closer to her, she put her hand on his chest and drew back. "We have been through much together in the past two weeks, haven't we?"

He didn't respond. In spite of her retraction, he reached out and drew her close once more, letting his lips barely brush across hers. "Good night, Thistle."

"Good night, Jared."

They both settled back, and Jared fell quickly asleep. Thistle stared up at the stars for a long time, wondering.

The next morning, as breakfast was being prepared, Sart drew Thistle and Jared aside. "It is important that you tell me all you remember, Thistle. Your life may depend on what I can deduce. Twice now you have created a protection sphere that only a powerful mage could invoke. As I told you, words do not make spells, energy does. That you could create a powerful focus of energy, speaks more to a force or forces at play within you, than the words you spoke.

"Somehow, from within yourself and perhaps bolstered from without, though I do not know how it would be possible, you were able to manipulate a great deal of energy. The first time this happened, from all that you were able to relate to me, it had to be a sending from Meligance, the White Wizardess of Borea. How she knew to whom and when to make this sending, I can only guess. I warrant that it has something to do with your little friend, Yolk. When did you say he came to you?"

"A couple of years ago, not much more. He was just there one day when I woke, staring at me with those big eyes. I don't know why, but I remember I wasn't afraid at the time. Since then, he has always been with me, except for when I came to Thiele. He... he didn't appear to like the man I was to wed. He came back to me after I met up with Jared."

"Ovietti are powerful magical creatures. My understanding is that they enhance a person's innate magic, or perhaps, better said -- support the user's ability to use energy. Again, that is something to ask of Meligance. I am beginning to think that it is imperative that we get to her as soon as possible."

"We?" Thistle and Jared said together.

"Yes, well, actually only Thistle needs to see her. I will explain momentarily. Jared, you are welcome to come with us; that is if you truly want to become a Bard. Lute thought you would make a good one. The capital is where the Hall of the Bards is located. That is also where we will find the White Wizardess. I, myself, must head back with all haste to Meligance to report all that has transpired here. She will also wish to know about the stone you found. I hope to spend some time researching it in the kingdom's archives. Unless you have else to do, I would have you both come with me."

Jared looked at Thistle. She shrugged her shoulders. He wasn't sure what she was suggesting with the gesture; he assumed that she was willing to go if he was. It felt good to know she was with him whatever they decided.

"Thistle, tell me now of what you remember by the altar; after, I will share with you my concerns for your safety."

"It was much as before in the glade," she said, "though this time I was awake from the start... or at least I felt awake, only different... like I was looking at everything from above and slightly to the side of where I stood. Something inside me compelled me to help.

"For some reason it was easy to remember the words of the 'sending.' I had no vision this time of the woman in white and blue; nor do I remember what caused me to step forward and place my hand on your head, because in some ways I was removed from what the physical me was doing. I don't know how, but I knew what to say and what to do to create the effect.

"I felt extraordinarily energized. I do remember that. It also seemed natural that to protect you, I had to touch you." As she finished, she reached out as if she were reliving the last part of her actions. When she noticed what she was doing, she flushed and withdrew her hand to her lap.

"Had you any sense of power within, or of an energy that flowed through you or to you from without?"

"No, I would not describe it that way. As I said, I felt energized, and Yolk was somehow connected to that energy. I did not notice that it came from anywhere in particular. It just was. If I could describe it best, it might be to say I was imbued with a sparkling, almost white energy throughout my whole body."

"Do you feel any such energy or power within you now?"

Thistle thought for a moment, examining herself with her mind. "No, not really. I feel good. Perhaps my stomach is a bit upset from eating so much boar last night. That is normal for me. I have always had a sensitive gut, or so my mother has said. Otherwise, I feel fine; no ill effects at all."

"Strange, very strange, indeed," Sart said, musing on her description of being energized by the words of the conjuration. "Yet you obviously possess innate power, and in no small amount. We must get you to Meligance, and soon!"

"You have said that thrice now. What is the concern?" Jared said, feeling afraid for Thistle.

Sart hesitated, as if what he would say next was of the utmost importance. "If Thistle is magical – that is, if she possesses an innate talent for magic – it can be dangerous for her and for those around her.

"It is not a small matter; you both need to understand that. Magic does not 'just happen' to someone, not normally, not to my understanding. Typically, there is a long history of the practice in one's family. Yet, Thistle, you told me that you know of no relative who had or has any talent in any of the magical arts. Perhaps it is a talent that has skipped a number of generations. It matters not a whit. If you have it – and I would dare say that considering what you have told me and what I have witnessed recently, you do have power, and in no small measure – then it can be dangerous. You almost killed yourself back there. That should be warning enough."

"But I know no spells or incantations. I can do no tricks or sleights of hand. Except for this sending, I have no sense of the power you speak of. I am a farm girl. I do not understand." Thistle felt overwhelmed by what Sart was saying; she was close to tears.

Sart reached out, touching her shoulder lightly. "I know this is difficult to comprehend, my child; however, if I am right, it would be best to be sure. You need to come with me to see Meligance. Mayhap, she can enlighten us as to how all of this transpired. Are you willing to find out?"

"I don't know. I... Jared?" She turned and looked at him, reaching out to clasp his hand.

"I agree with Sart," he answered, "though this all confounds me, too. If there is a chance of what he speaks, you should be sure. To be safe, it is best to know. Our quest for the sword was ended almost before it started, and the Qa-ryks we went after have been defeated. The gods seem to have designed other things for both of us.

"It is truly a dream for me to think of becoming a Bard, Thistle... I am willing to try. I would feel much more at home if you were in the city with me, near to me. Else, I think I would be overwhelmed by it all. Our only other choice would be to return to the life we once led, or to try to."

"I should go home," Thistle said. "Not to stay; I want to see my parents, my sisters, and friends. I should let them know I am safe. Could we find a way to stop at Permis before we go to Borea? It would help me feel better about continuing on in a new direction."

"That might be feasible," Sart said. "I will talk with Rux. He has told me that he plans to march with most of his company back to the capital. They are due a long break. A refitting contingent has already been sent and should be on its way to the fort. Xur will be rebuilt and reinforced. The Qa-ryk threat is here in the west; and though we have destroyed or damaged the Altar of Kan, it would be wise to keep an eye on it, as well as on these destructive beasts.

"Aberon, unfortunately, is merely frustrated, and he is only one of these dark priests. From what I know of them, there are many more; and there are those that wield even greater malevolent force than he.

"Perhaps," Sart added, "we can go with the company for some days, then cut off to the north, and rejoin them later after we visit your village. They will be a large group, so they will move more slowly than we can. For the first part of the journey, it will be best to have their protection through the wilds. We will be able to stay only a day or two. Would that suffice?

Thistle nodded. She looked questioningly at Jared.

He shrugged.

"Are we agreed? We will make for Borea together?"

This time Jared looked to Thistle. He felt it was more her decision than his. She pressed his hand. Looking up at Sart, her face set, she answered. "Yes, I am willing to make this journey for myself and for Jared."

Later that day, when they stopped for the night, Sart took Jared aside while they washed off the dust of the road. "A word, Jared? We must discuss something regarding Thistle. It could be important for you both."

"Yes?"

"You are fond of her?"

"Yes," Jared blushed. "We have become close; so many things have happened. I..."

"No, my son," Sart said kindly, "there is nothing wrong with this. Love and caring are good things. Would there were more in the world, and that it was more universally shared. Never feel bad about caring, genuinely caring for another. No, what I wish to discuss is specific to magic. There are... ah, dangers."

"To?"

"Potentially to you both."

"I don't understand."

"I'm sorry, Jared. This is difficult for me. I feel I am intruding where I shouldn't. Know this, I am seriously concerned for her... for you both. If... if Thistle is truly magical, she must learn to control it before... Well, what you must understand is that emotions and passions can cause magic, energy, to flare from within, potentially causing damage to her, and even to others."

"Huh? What?"

"I'm sorry, Jared, I have to tell you this, though it will be difficult for you to hear and accept. You cannot be with her, have a sexual relationship with her, not until we know for sure. You, Jared, must take responsibility for this until she can meet with Meligance. If I had thought you two had already... well, if you had, there might not be a concern. I... Jared?"

Jared was staring at Sart as if the cleric had hit him with his staff. "What? How? I... By-the-gods, Sart, we haven't. I'm not..." He was blushing a deep red, and his embarrassment was quickly turning to anger.

"Please, Jared. I am sorry to have to say this, but it is important! She could kill you; she could kill herself if I am right about her powers. Please understand how hard this is for me. I care deeply for you both. In some ways, I wish I was wrong; yet, I don't believe I am. If she is as magically talented and as powerful as I think she is, she could hurt you both. It is why... why I feel I must warn you now."

"By-the-gods, Sart." Jared's ire started to dissipate; still, he felt really uncomfortable with the direction the conversation had taken and confused as well. He sat down on a large stone sticking up from the water.

"I know, Jared. There was no good way to bring this up. Please think about what I have said, if you truly care for her."

Jared stood up again, stepping out of the stream. He sat heavily on the ground, cradling his knees. "I'm sorry, Sart. This is so difficult, and I don't know... so unexpected. I felt maybe you wanted me to keep my eye on her. This? This is really hard for me, because I do care for her. I have never felt this way before."

Sart reached over and put his hand on Jared's shoulder. "I know you don't think I understand. I do, better than you might imagine. I was young once, myself. I understand how difficult this will be for you. Even if you had no such thoughts, what I have said sets a wedge where there was none before. For now, I think it is best that this be kept between you and me. Thistle should hear this from someone who understands it better than I do, and... and well, she should hear it from a woman. It was hard enough for me to tell you, and I can't say I did much of a job."

Jared managed a smile. "I understand and I don't blame you, Sart. More than anything, I want Thistle to be safe, too. You are right about that. Give me a few seconds. I will be all right."

It took them another four and a half days to return to Xur. Though they were anxious to get back, Rux figured it best that they keep to a reasonable pace so they could all recover from their ordeal. They rode through the reconstructed main gates shortly before dusk and were met by a crowd of their friends and comrades in arms.

Life on the Farm

Leona and Ge-or were enjoying themselves immensely. Neither of them had any real experience in lovemaking; but they had been told the essentials – Leona by her mother when she became of age, and Ge-or by his father when he was old enough to begin to comprehend that men and women were different and that there were reasons for it. For the rest, they had a good bit of fun learning; and they were both very enthusiastic.

Even so, there was work to be done about the farmstead. The winter snows in the foothills would be on them soon enough, likely only a few weeks away. Ge-or had been going up out of the vale in the mornings with Aldred to harvest hardwood for next year's wood supply. In the afternoons, while Leona and her father tended to the herds, Ge-or split the older logs into manageable pieces for the winter.

He loved the physical nature of the work. It felt good to be stretching and exercising his muscles. In Thiele, he and Jared had done many different chores; these were in addition to the many hours each day their father had made them spend learning weaponry, tactics, and all forms of combat. He did miss sparring with his brother, yet this was good honest work that would help him return to form. It also felt good to see the piles of wood, against the house and in the open shed, grow higher and higher through his efforts.

For Leona, each day was a dream come true. She had often imagined what having a man would be like, to enjoy his closeness – not only the sensuality of it. Just having him somewhere near during the day was a pleasure; she enjoyed the simple pleasure of taking his lunch out to him. Sometimes, she would watch Ge-or for several minutes while he chopped wood, watching his broad shoulders and muscles shining with sweat as he worked without a tunic in spite of the chill air.

In her view, he was an ideal lover. He was a bit shy, as she was – awkward at first, but gaining more confidence with each tryst; and he sincerely cared about making sure she was enjoying herself. He was gentle when she needed him to be; eager, willing, and energetic when she was on fire, desperate for him to be a man.

Every minute she was in his arms was heaven, with a tinge of hell thrown in because she knew the minutes were finite. She understood, even when lost in passion, that she only had a few days. With each moment of ecstasy that she experienced, she was that much closer to losing him. She tried to hold as many of those memories as possible in her heart and in her whole being.

The hardest part for her was that she did genuinely love him. Leona had waited for a long time to find a man that she felt deeply attracted to. When he had fallen into her life, it was the most natural thing in the world to let those emotions flow; yet, she refused to let him see her inner pain. She didn't want him to experience anything negative during their time together. Though she often cried when she was by herself, she also smiled. She had something that she knew would last her through this life, something that she could remember when he was gone.

After their first night together, she had told Ge-or that she had been engaged for a brief time. It was when she was a young lady of nineteen – in mountain terms a very marriageable age. Back then, there were enough homesteaders in the region that there would be meets, barn-raisings, and dances a few times each year. She had met, talked with, and danced with many a young lad and man from when she was twelve on; but beyond girlish flirtations, she had never been truly attracted to any. Eventually, her mother and father had begun to push her to make a decision. She had acquiesced to a betrothal to a man, six years her senior, who had lost his young wife to the fever the winter before. He was a good man – sturdy, hard-working, and he was willing to accept Aldred's offer to come and work their stead and to become his heir.

They had met three or four times and kissed once before the announcement of their engagement to the community. Leona had not loved him, not truly; but she had liked him well enough. He would have made a good husband; he was kind and even a bit shy. She felt a duty to her father as his only child to ensure the survival of his line and what he had worked so hard to build. She had been determined to make it work. They were to be wed in the spring.

He had been killed three days after they became formally engaged, during a foray to chase a clan of Qa-ryks from the hills to the west. After an appropriate mourning period, she had refused to consider any more suggestions or offers for her hand. It was not long after that their community had slowly dissolved because of the many troubles from the Qa-ryk expansion. As a result, many families had left the area.

In some ways, Ge-or was like a teenage boy having his first physical experiences with a girl. It was new and exciting. Yet, he really wanted to please Leona; he wanted to make her happy. He often asked her what she liked, and they had fun trying new things to add to their lovemaking.

In spite of his inexperience, awkwardness, and his youthful exuberance, he really cared for her. He cared about how she felt, about trying to fulfill her need for both a man and a child, and about being as much a lover as he could be with the time they had together. Deep down, he did understand that he was causing her pain, and that it would be very difficult for her when he left. His parents had instilled in him a respect for others, for life.

He knew he didn't love her, not in the classic sense of falling in love with a pretty lass and wanting to spend his life with her. A part of him could not respond to this beautiful woman in that way. It was as if a piece of his soul had shut down. Whether it was the circumstances of knowing he would be moving on, or the recent tragedy he had faced, or something else that held him back, he didn't know.

The hardest part for Ge-or was knowing how idyllic it was here, yet also knowing that something had awakened in him that would never be quieted. This vale, the life that Aldred had carved into these foothills and made his own, was something many men would spend their whole lives dreaming about, and if they had the fortitude, working toward. Ge-or recognized its value, yet this life had never been a dream of his.

He had never understood why his father had given up the life he had as an adventurer and as a renowned warrior. Even with the loss of his arm, his father was more than a capable fighter, as he had proved many times in bouts with his two sons. It had only been in the last few years that Ge-or and Jared had bested their old man.

There was also the added bonus of having a kind and loving woman who would be devoted to him for as long as she lived. He rejoiced in her firm, strong body, soft in just the right places. He loved everything about her womanliness, and he tried to show her how he felt. He loved being close to her. He found it difficult not to touch her, even when they were with Aldred.

If he had been truly in love, his heart would have been soaring; as it was, he was having the time of his life. What mattered, and he would potentially carry it as a

184

burden most of his life, was that as half-elven, he could live three human lifespans or more. He guessed that for whatever love his father and elven mother had shared, her choice many years ago had weighed that consideration. Their love had won, and ironically, it had been his father who had outlived his fair wife by many years.

The other consideration that weighed occasionally on Ge-or was his desire to remain responsible and connected should he and Leona's union result in a child. Whatever he had gleaned from his heritage, one thing that was paramount to him was the importance of family. In remote villages, extended families were commonplace. They formed the core of their society. Family was first, the village a close second, and neighboring villages third. All others were considered a distant fourth – welcomed, treated well as long as they respected traditions, but not part of these key units. He was determined, even if they did not conceive a child, to stay in touch with Leona and Aldred when he could. If they did conceive, he would not only visit, he would make sure the child was provided for. He wanted the child to at least know that his father cared.

It was the sixth day since Ge-or had made his decision to accept Leona's proposal. He and Aldred were at the kitchen table eating another of Leona's hearty breakfasts. She joined them a few minutes later, having brought over a steaming plate of fresh biscuits from the oven. Nothing had been said of Ge-or's time with them. Yet they were all aware, more and more each day that passed, that the amount of time he had agreed upon staying would be soon up.

Taking a biscuit from the warm platter, Ge-or split it carefully with his knife, slathered it with fresh butter, and smeared a dollop of honeycomb on top. Afterward, he sat and stared at it as if he hadn't quite got it right. He cleared his throat and looked up at Leona and then at Aldred.

Leona's eyes dropped and she swallowed. She fought hard to keep the tears from starting, dreading what he was about to say. So soon, so soon. Please a few more days, she thought.

Ge-or cleared his throat again and tried to catch her eyes. She refused to look up, because she knew she would burst into tears if she did, "How many days," he asked, "until you would know if you are with child?"

Leona was completely taken off guard by the question. She was only able to stammer out, "What? What did you say?" Finally she did look up.

He was looking at her like he always did in the morning, with affection and caring, though she sensed there was tension beneath his slight smile. Ge-or repeated the question. "How long before you would know if you are with child?"

Leona, still unsure what he wanted and why, said, "Two weeks, maybe longer, it would depend; it can vary."

Ge-or nodded; his smile broadened. "I will stay until we know." He ate his biscuit.

That evening Leona made sure Ge-or had a particularly enjoyable time.

Return to Permis

They remained in Xur three days while they prepared for the changing of the guard and the long journey east and north to Borea. The relief caravan had arrived while they were traveling back from the ruins of Kan's fortress.

Everyone pitched in to repair the parts of the stronghold that were most vulnerable, though the task of completely refurbishing after the battle would take many months. Rux spent much of the time in conference with the new captain, planning repairs to the old defensive systems, and designing new and better war machines for the future. They had learned much from the assault, and they hoped to make the fortress even more impregnable. Among other improvements, they would double the thickness of the outer stockade and reinforce it further with earthen and stone works inside, supporting the heavy logs.

The last night, a subdued but lavish banquet was set to welcome the newcomers and bid farewell to the many who were leaving. A new Journeyman Bard was introduced, and he played appropriate tunes for the occasion, singing throughout the evening of comradeship, valor, and especially poignant ballads for those who had fallen. Jared stayed in the background, happy to let the new fellow begin his tenure on his own merits.

Though Sart was anxious to get to Borea as quickly as possible, he felt leaving with the company would be safer and ultimately faster. He, Jared, and Thistle were all put to work. They, like all the others, fell onto their mattresses beneath the stars each night, exhausted from the long days of physical labor.

Early one frosty fall morning, Rux led the long procession of almost a hundred souls out of the gates. Thistle and Jared, with Lute's daughter, Rose, were some of the last to wave goodbye as they left the stockade. Fulfilling one of Lute's last wishes, they were taking the little girl to her grandparents in the capital.

Rux chose to take a more northerly route, not only to accommodate Sart's plans to visit Permis. He was also determined to gather intelligence as to the growing concerns in the west. It had been some time since his men had ranged so far to the north. He and Sart knew that the attack on Thiele may have had specific motives, yet it spoke to increased Qa-ryk activity toward the coast. There were other communities potentially at risk along the shoreline, should the Black Druids decide to push their charges increasingly in that direction. The journey would be a bit longer overall; he hoped it would be worth the effort.

They were nine days out from Xur when Sart, with Crunch, Jared, and Thistle with Rose in her lap, turned from the main group to head northeast. Rux's company would continue to the east.

They made good time, keeping to animal trails and the occasional cart path carved out by trappers. By the eve of the third day, they could feel the fresh salt air coming out of the north off the ocean. By nightfall, they were riding toward the lights of Permis, having intercepted the road from Thiele a half league west.

When they were hailed at the barred gates, a new precaution that Thistle assumed was the result of the destruction of Thiele, she answered for them. "I am Thistle, daughter of Roald of Permis. I survived the battle at Thiele and come home with friends."

Minutes later, she was being swarmed over by her mother and father, sisters,

186

aunts, uncles, her grandmother, and many other friends and acquaintances. Jared, Sart, and Rose stood aside, watching the joyous reunion. After introductions were made, they were roundly welcomed as well. By this time, most of the village was out of their homes and at the west gate.

Jared was also pounded on the back by older men and women from Thiele who had managed to flee during the battle and its aftermath. He was surrounded and hugged at the knees and waist by the many children from his village who had survived. They all knew him as the musician who oft played them tunes of an eve. He was happy to see so many had made it to Permis, though there were few of the young women from Thiele and only two young men who had survived, those who had been caring for their pregnant wives. After the furor of his surviving had eased a bit, Jared also was able to tell them that Ge-or had been healed by an itinerant cleric, and had chosen to seek the dragon that had taken their father's sword.

There was a loud cheer when Sart was introduced. Healers were always welcome in remote villages. Sart knew he would be busy on the morrow; such was his personality that he would welcome all. He promised he would spend the next day tending to concerns.

After the initial furor of the miracle that others had survived the devastation at Thiele had run its course, Jared and Sart were taken in by two families. Almost every family in the village offered to take in Rose. Thistle, however, felt she should remain with her. The little girl would have her four sisters, one almost exactly her age, to play with.

After they were all settled, Thistle's father came by and insisted that they all come over for a late meal. He had discovered that they had not stopped to eat in their haste to get to Permis before it got too late. Thistle's family and the adventurers sat at the long table in the cabin's crowded main room. The three were asked a myriad of questions while they ate from a spread of smoked meats and sausages, rich country cheeses, and hearty bread washed down with mugs of dark ale.

Finally, Thistle gave up trying to eat and sipped her ale as she told the story of her escape, her meeting up with Jared, his killing of the Qa-ryk chieftain, and much of the rest of their adventures. She left out the finding of the stone on a nudge from Sart at that point in the story, and she purposefully did not say anything of the magic she had been involved in casting.

Her sisters and parents sat spellbound as she told of their capture by "bandits," the assault at Xur, and Sart's fight with the evil priest at the Altar of Kan. Once she was done, they all looked toward Jared and Sart, who both nodded in agreement. Jared, his mouth stuffed with bread and a creamy goat cheese, managed to mush out, "Your sister was very brave."

They immediately began to ask questions again. Sart raised both his hands, palm outward, and said, "Enough for tonight. Your mayor has proclaimed a feast for tomorrow eve; there will be more telling of tales and perhaps some music?" He raised his eyebrows and looked at Jared.

Thistle's sisters, who were more than a little bit entranced by the handsome young half-elf, and quite jealous of their sister's escapades and adventures with him, clapped, giggled, and begged him, "Please, please, play and sing for us."

Though he did not feel up to performing, Jared could not refuse these people who were more than neighbors now, having taken in so many refugees from Thiele. He agreed to play his portative harp and sing popular local tunes at the feast.

In the morning, Sart set up shop in his host's house and began seeing patients. His jovial nature and accepting manner brought out the villagers in droves. He happily helped all he could; many came just to make sure they were hale and whole. He discovered that the local healer was quite adept at the many forms of care she provided. Much of the afternoon, he spent sharing healing remedies with her and recommending this salve or herb combination for some sore, injury, or the ague. He also saw the occasional reluctant farmer, whose wife dragged the poor fellow in to have his corns removed, or a neglected wound tended.

Thistle spent the morning with her family, retelling her story and catching up with all the local gossip. Though her parents were considered poor by village standards, having all girls and no heirs, they had willingly taken in a four-year-old boy and his two-year-old sister from Thiele when their parents had been killed in the battle. Rose had a grand time playing with the four youngest children while the adults chatted. Many of Permis' families had taken in one or more refugees. It was the code of the wilderness.

The younger girls and the boy soon were playing games with Yolk. Their favorite being a silly variation of hide and find, where Yolk would close his eyes, wait for a few seconds while all the children would rearrange themselves around where he sat, and then open them suddenly. A great deal of giggling would ensue when those big yellow eyes popped open, staring at the next "victim," who would be out of the game for a while. The little fellow seemed to have the uncanny ability to shift his position without anyone knowing, so no one could predict who he would be looking at when he opened his eyes.

Jared worked all morning helping the men gathering, chopping, and stacking more wood for the winter. He thoroughly enjoyed the heavy work. By mid-morning, the down-home attitude and country humor had lifted his spirits tremendously.

At noon, Thistle sought out Jared and Sart. She had them come to her family's home for a short meeting. She wanted them to be there when she told her parents, sisters, and extended family what her plans were. To this point everyone had assumed that she and Jared would be staying in Permis. Almost twenty people were crowded shoulder to shoulder in the cabin's main room by the time Sart and Jared arrived.

Sart offered to break the news, but Thistle insisted that she had to be the one. Standing at the end of the dining table near the stove, she raised her hands for quiet. "While it has brought me great joy to see all of you again, I wanted you to understand as soon as possible that my plans, our plans," she gestured toward Jared and Sart who stood to either side, "are to leave early on the morrow." There were gasps and immediate murmurings; Thistle raised her hands again. It quieted quickly.

"I wish we could stay longer, but there is much that we have left unsaid about our experiences. Sart," she nodded to the cleric, "believes, with what he feels is powerful evidence, that I have innate magical abilities that could…" This time the gasps and vocalizations drowned out Thistle's soft voice. She had to raise her hands once more.

When things finally grew quiet again, she had her audience's complete attention. "It is imperative that I go with Sart to Borea to be tested further, else I could hurt myself and those I care about. I know you will have many questions to ask of me; the truth is I cannot answer them, because I am not aware of this inclination. Sart has noted that things have happened that are not easily explained away by any other understanding.

"As for Jared, he has agreed that I can share with you the news that he has been recommended to the Hall of Bards for study. Since many of you have heard him sing and perform, I know you will congratulate him for this great honor." There were nods all around. Jared dipped his head to acknowledge them. "I would like Sart to say a few words. Also, I would appreciate it if you would not ask me further of this, for I have no answers for you.

"Sart."

The cleric smiled at her. "What Thistle has told you is true. We must make haste to Borea for many reasons, one being that she needs to be examined by Meligance, the White Wizardess of Borea, who has summoned her. I hope you will respect our wishes and not query us further about this delicate subject. In time, hopefully, Thistle will be able to return here to let you know what has transpired. It is also important for Jared to go to Bard Hall as soon as possible as their term has already begun. I, myself, have other urgent business at the capital. We will leave at dawn tomorrow. I am sorry we cannot stay longer with all of you. You have been most generous and hospitable to us. I will continue to see those who need my services at Bartlett's up until the festivities start this evening."

As soon as the cleric had finished, they all started talking at once. Thankfully, none of them broached any questions to the three at the head of the table. Sart started for the door, motioning for Thistle and Jared to follow. When they were outside, he drew them off a few paces from the house. "I mentioned Meligance, as that should help dissuade most inquiries. Her name alone inspires awe. If anyone does ask you, say what you are comfortable with; reveal nothing else.

"I have spoken to the mayor. The festivities will not last past midnight. We need to rest and be off early if we are to catch back up to Rux's company. Since the village is still preparing for winter, it would not be wise for them to lose the better part of a day recovering from too much of a good time either." He winked at Jared.

"Jared, it is likely you will be asked, nay, expected, to relate our adventures to the gathering. It is the lot of the Bards; and though you have not even entered Bard Hall for study, people will now expect you to hold the reins. Speak as Thistle spoke last night. Elaborate as much as you wish, that is also expected; but stick to what has already been related."

"Sart," Jared protested, "I… I have never done anything like this – told tales as you suggest. Except… well, I guess I have seen it done many times. Aren't adventures often set to verse and even sung? I fear I will bungle this badly."

"Yes, it is true that grand adventures are sometimes set to verse; however, few men have such a talent. Usually, only Bards with specialized training have the skill to create rhyme schemes as they tell a tale. Likely, many of the tales and epic songs you have heard were carefully crafted by Bard composers sitting in rooms for many a month. Once completed, they were memorized by the wandering minstrels and troubadours. These are the musicians who probably came to your village.

"Just tell the saga of our adventures as if you were telling a group of children a bedtime story. Everyone loves a good tale, so use your imagination to help embellish what you say. I would downplay the Qa-ryk assault and defense of Xur a bit. The memories of what happened to your village are too close to home for this

189

audience. Otherwise, I'm sure it will be great fun for everyone."

"I will try," Jared said, smiling wryly. "It looks like I am branded before I start."

"Witness my day," Sart said, slapping him on the back. "Indeed, we are almost always classified by others by what we do; and unfortunately, too often by our titles, deserved or not. You will do fine. When I heard you play and sing with Lute, I could feel music was in your blood. Don't lose that, Jared. It is a rare gift; something beautiful you can share with others. Music has the power to heal minds, feelings, and souls. It can also relieve much of the stress of life. Play on!"

Thistle took Jared's hand and squeezed it. He smiled and pressed hers back. Finally, he bowed at the waist to Sart. "For my friends and for the people of the villages."

Thistle spent the afternoon with Jared visiting friends and relatives, leaving Rose to play with her sisters. She felt the need of his support as she spoke with those she would soon leave again. He was amenable enough because he wanted to spend time with her. Often, they would find the person or family they sought hard at work at some task; they would both pitch in to help where they could. In some ways, it was the tonic both of them needed. It gave them a full taste of the life they had once lived, and yet, were soon to abandon, perhaps forever.

By late afternoon, they had made the rounds. Thistle, grinning impishly, pulled Jared out of a door in the stockade to the south. After being sure no one was about, she drew him close to her under the shadow of the tall logs. She kissed him lightly, seeking with her lips to let him know she missed him. Then, surprising herself, she felt an urgency to be even closer. She kissed him more deeply, pulling his body next to hers.

Jared moaned, wanting more than anything to give in to her need and his passion. Heeding Sart's warning, he pulled away. "Not now, not here, Thistle. I…" He touched her flushed face, brushing her light brown hair back from her forehead. By-the-gods, she is so beautiful and innocent, he mused. She reddened as he held her at arm's length.

"I'm sorry, Thistle. It's that I… I care so much about you, for you, that I get scared about going too far, not being ready. I…"

Thistle placed her right hand on his chest, her fingers lightly touching above his open tunic. Her hand was soft and alive with warmth. Jared groaned again. "You are right, Jared. Just hold me." She leaned into him and pressed her head against his chest where her hand had been. Her silken hair rested below his chin. "I've missed being close to you like this. Traveling with all the others, it has seemed inappropriate and…" Her voice trailed off as she pressed herself even closer.

"Soon, maybe we can be together," she said.

Jared knew that it might be otherwise, but that he could not, would not, tell her. The truth was neither of them had any idea of what was to happen. What they would learn when they arrived in Borea. And whether either of them would be accepted there.

Jared held her. Feeling her aliveness pressed against him, he wondered how soon it might be. Sart's words of warning had been more than ominous in many ways. He couldn't help wishing in some way that she would prove not to be naturally magical.

In spite of the sad news that Thistle, Jared, and Sart were leaving in the morning, the village party was loud and boisterous. Bounties from the fall harvest, fresh meats from the woods and range, and open kegs of ale and rum helped them all forget the hardships of their lives for the evening.

After eating his fill, but limiting his intake of the libations, Jared began to play. At first, he simply let his fingers fly over the strings of the portative harp, using popular tunes to create a long medley with many embellishments. As people began to finish eating and were well into their cups, he began to play drinking and dance songs. Soon the village square was filled with people whirling in and out or singing along to a rousing tune. Some villagers, who had a bit of expertise and talent on drums or recorder, joined him for the well-known tunes. When it grew late and they had mellowed a good bit, with most of the youngsters asleep at the edges of the open area on blankets, someone did ask for Jared to tell the tale of their adventure. The cry was quickly taken up by anyone sober enough to care.

Taking a long draught of rum to bolster his confidence, Jared began slowly. He felt awkward at first, yet after a couple of minutes he remembered Sart's advice to talk as if he was telling a bedtime story. He fell into an easy rhythm after that. It turned out that he was as naturally creative with words as he was with tunes. He had great fun embellishing their adventures with hyperbole and florid verbiage. He found that the older children were particularly entranced with his performance. They gathered in a semi-circle at his feet and clapped and cheered wildly at all his expressive nuances. They particularly enjoyed his dramatic beastly roars and the little musical phrases he played on his lyre that he used to punctuate certain events.

He timed things fairly well. Just after midnight, he played one last nostalgic song that had all who were awake singing. It was a perfect ending to a joyous time for the villagers. Jared needed little coaxing from Thistle to return to his lodging. Barding, if what he'd done that night were anything like it, was tiring; and they had had a long day before. She kissed him lightly goodnight. "Thank you, Jared. It meant so much to everyone. And to me."

Just as dawn began to streak the horizon, the three adventurers and little Rose exited the east gate of Permis. Thistle's parents and sisters and a few others were there to say goodbye. Tears were shed and promises made to not be too long apart, though none of them truly knew what lay ahead.

It took them four days riding well into the night for them to reconnect with Rux's entourage. Five more days and they passed the western Borean escarpment at the King's Wall, and a day after that they were on one of the main roads east to the capital. Sart told them at the current pace their extended caravan was going, that they should see the capitol city within two to three weeks.

Winter Cometh

Aldred and Ge-or had been working hard the past week gathering the last of the hay and fall crops. Each morning it was just a little bit brisker and the frost a bit heavier when they left the house. On this particular morning, Aldred stopped on the first step and sniffed the air. "Snow in the mountains today." He gestured southwestwardly. "Let's go up out of the vale to cut some more dead wood. Cold's coming in fast. You game?"

Ge-or smiled. He enjoyed heading up out of the vale to the hardwood rich slopes. Before they had returned to the fields on their last foray, they had discovered a new, accessible deadfall area that promised well-dried wood for this year. It would mean some heavy double-saw work for several days, then a couple weeks' worth of chopping once they had moved the stove-length logs to the vale. "You expect much snow soon?"

"Well, now, that's a good question," Aldred answered. "Don't get much normally, as we're alee of the high hills, a few inches here and there, enough to keep the grasses wet. We're high enough here that some clouds do come across from the northwest and dump on us; a good nor-wester may hit us hard once every three or four years. Truth is, we don't get much overall unless we get a southern or south-eastern flow. That's when we get hit. Build up right over our heads for whatever reason. Had a blizzard three, no, I guess maybe four years ago that kept us busy for a fortnight. We had to dig through drifts twice my height to get to the barn and sheds. It was a month before we could get out of the vale; and once out, you couldn't get anywhere, anyhow. Late February, that one came in. C'mon, I'll show you something."

Aldred led Ge-or toward the barn. As they approached the northeast corner, he pointed way up above his head. "See the markings there, and there?"

Ge-or could see what looked like notches, one in the edge post about fourteen feet above the ground, and the other over twenty feet up near the roof. He nodded.

"That's where the snow topped out. Had to dig a big tunnel to the barn doors. Once the powder set hard, Leona made me climb over in the middle there and fix the leak in the roof I had been putting off for two years. I couldn't use the excuse that the ladder was broken any more. I walked up the snow drift right onto the roof."

Ge-or grinned, picturing Leona getting her crusty old father out the door some cold winter morning to reroof part of the barn.

Three-quarters of an hour later, they had hitched up four mules to the large wagon and were headed up out of the vale. They rode west through the opening toward the hardwood grove. Keeping to the rutted path he had used for years, Aldred drove the mules forward as Ge-or walked alongside. Suddenly, a sharp high-pitched howl pierced the cold air, and the mules shied back and to the left, almost overturning the wagon and forcing Ge-or to jump forward to avoid being pushed down the steep ravine to his left.

Aldred hauled back on the reins, calling to the mules, as another howl and another pierced the early morning air. Ge-or moved up next to the closest mule. He grabbed the beast's bit and placed his hand on its nose to calm it. "Wolves," Aldred spat on the ground, "been a nuisance the last few years. Don't know whether the Qa-ryks have pushed them eastward, or whether they're proliferating; but I've had to set traps at the most likely places where they come into the vale. We have to watch the animals whenever they're in the pasture during the winter."

Ge-or asked, "What kind are they? Most wolves I know are shy of humans."

"Used to be so, not anymore. They're timber wolves, and they're big. Last year I must have trapped five, six of them and poisoned a couple that got through the traps. They smell the goats; think they can get a free meal. I sold the pelts in the spring. They bring good prices. You would think someone would come out and trap 'em for a profit. I don't really have the time; always something to do on the spread. They're a nuisance to deal with and that's a fact." He spit again over the nose of the mule on the right front. "And me with my bum hand, I can't shoot the beasts anymore. Used to be a decent shot when I was younger. From the looks of that bow you got with you, you probably have a practiced eye."

"I've shot a few, though the Qa-ryks have taken care of most of them from where I come from. They eat them, you know."

"Well, they could eat a few more, far as I'm concerned. This close, this soon, means we're in for a cold winter and likely a long one. Cold's coming in early, and they're already foraging down the mountain. We may need that extra wood."

Many hours later, the wagon laden with logs, the two drove back into the barnyard. While Ge-or stacked the wood for cutting, Aldred worked to bring the stock inside the barn for the night. He said he didn't want to take any chances; the wolves had been too close for comfort.

Later that evening, Ge-or sat at the table in the kitchen enjoying the warmth of the stove and simply watching Leona do her work. Aldred had already excused himself and gone to bed. Leona was sewing a new skirt and top from some of the nicer fabrics she had gleaned from the wagon. After carefully cleaning all that was worth preserving, she had found many uses for the bounty. Ge-or thought that the red and blue colored fabric she was working with would look quite handsome on her.

Ge-or was working with some straight birch shafts he had cut before they had left the grove. After hearing the wolves howling throughout the day, and heeding Aldred's warning, he had figured it would be useful to add a few more arrows to his quiver. He had a dozen extra points he had garnered from the detritus of the battle at Thiele. This was as good a time as any to put them to good use.

Leona was humming while she worked. Ge-or enjoyed looking up at her from his truing of the shafts. Right now, he would not have traded this life for any other. He could think of nothing more perfect than his current situation. If he could have forgotten everything else that fed who he was, he would have decided to stay with her for as long as she lived. He knew it wasn't love he felt for her; it was a deep fondness for what was beautiful and whole, perfection for this moment in time.

He wanted to keep this image of Leona sitting before the warm stove, needle in her delicate hands, humming a simple child's tune. It would keep him comforted on the road until he could see her again. He already understood that while the freedom of adventuring was rooted in who he was, there was a loneliness to the wanderer's life, too.

It must have been the fifth or six time that he looked up from his work and stared at her, that Leona looked up as well and met his gaze. She mistook his look. Setting down her work, she stood and reached out for him. It broke the mood, yet he didn't mind. They retired to their bedroom.

The next morning, Ge-or and Aldred were finishing their breakfast tea when Leona suddenly bolted for the door, ran down the steps and around the corner. Ge-or stood up to follow; he heard her retching by the side of the house. Aldred grabbed his arm as he started out the door. "Wait, big fella, this is a time for her to be alone."

"She's sick?"

"Aye," Aldred grinned, shoving Ge-or out on the porch with a push to his back. "She's with child, you nit-wit. Her mother got sick every morning for two months when she was with Leona. Leave her be, she'll be good in an hour or so. C'mon, we got wood to cut. Congratulations, Dad." He slapped Ge-or on his back hard enough that it propelled him toward the steps.

Ge-or spent the day in a daze, a myriad of emotions running through him. Aldred had to bring him back to reality a couple of times when he was lost in his feelings and had stopped in the middle of a saw stroke.

The understanding that she was surely pregnant hit Leona two-fold: she was overjoyed that she and Ge-or were to have a child, but she also knew all too well what that would mean. Her lover, friend, companion, her love, would be leaving soon – a day, maybe two or three if she were lucky, just so they would know for sure. Winter was coming and he would soon have to leave; else he would be stuck in the vale when the ice and snow came.

She sat for a long time in the middle of the day cradling her stomach in her hands, wondering one minute, crying the next. She had hoped that she would be able to hold onto the memory of Ge-or, of their lovemaking, of their intimate closeness. Now she knew that, though she would cherish those memories her whole life, they would not, could not, replace him. There didn't appear to be a way to hold onto happiness. Time, and what one did and who one was, moved forward in spite of what you wanted to keep within your grasp. It would ever be so; she wished she could hold onto to it a bit longer. Their time together had been far too short.

A few weeks before, her prayers had been partially answered. Now, they truly had been answered; yet, she felt a deep anguish at the notion of losing what she had finally found. She didn't want to hold Ge-or against his will. She couldn't do that to him. He had been completely open and honest with her; she would not do anything to hurt him. When he left, she would have to gather her inner strength and be braver than she had ever been in her life. She could hold onto his pledge to return. Then, maybe, she would have a few more days with him from time to time.

Surprisingly, Ge-or was dealing with much the same feelings. He found his fondness for Leona was coupled with strong feelings of responsibility and protection; yet, even with this news, he could not say that he loved her – not in the deeper sense that he had always thought of as the union of souls between two people. He knew that in spite of her beauty, her kindness, and all that he did love about her, there was something holding him back from fully loving her. The destruction of his town and of so many he had cared about, as well as the grim task he had set himself to honor their deaths, had slammed an inner door shut so firmly that he didn't know if he would ever find a way to open it again. In a very real sense, he felt that true love was lost to him forever.

Now that he knew she was with child, his child, he questioned the wisdom of his choices and the additional choices he would have to make soon enough. As Aldred had said, winter was just around the corner. If he didn't leave soon, perhaps within a

194

week or two, it would be increasingly difficult to travel out of these hills and far more dangerous.

He also knew that he could make other choices. He knew that if he did, that those choices would raise other questions, other dilemmas to be faced. They would in turn create ever more new choices to be made. He did not want to leave Leona. He cared for her. He loved being with her, close to her, and making love with her. Though he knew she and her father were both resilient and capable, having a child changed the stakes. As he had felt he would, he did feel responsible for her safety and well-being, and for the growing child's safety and well-being. He wanted to be sure that she was cared for in this remote part of the world. Facing a hard winter, he began to have his doubts.

Except for occasionally bringing him back to task, Aldred wisely let him think. He understood, as only a father can, how difficult the situation was for both Leona and Ge-or. He wished he could help them; he was even tempted to encourage them to marry. Nevertheless, he had made a bargain with the young half-elf, and he was an honorable man. He would let things take their course. He did, however, thank the old gods many a time that day for the blessing that fate had brought to his door.

When they entered the house that evening, Aldred went up to his daughter and kissed her on the forehead. She reached up and touched his haggard, sun-darkened cheek and rested her head briefly on his chest. It was the first intimate moment Ge-or had seen between the two. When she drew away, she turned and smiled at Ge-or. He could see tears shining in her eyes.

Ge-or walked toward her, and she stepped into his arms. He drew her into a close embrace, raising her up in his strong arms and swinging her in a circle. "I am so glad for you, Leona. For you as well, Aldred. I hope you both are as pleased as I."

"It is a miracle and a blessing," Aldred said as Ge-or set Leona down. "As you know, it is no small gift for both of us. Leona will have the child she always wanted, and I will have someone to continue with what I have built here. You have blessed me and my house."

"It is my honor to have served," Ge-or laughed. "It was no trouble at all."

"Ge-or!" Leona looked shocked, but she was smiling when she playfully swatted at his head.

Leona and Ge-or spent the evening lying on the bed in each other's arms. They touched each other, nuzzled, and kissed, nothing more. It was a time when they wanted to be close and enjoy knowing that they were still together.

After Leona fell asleep, Ge-or lay awake for many hours, finally drifting off into a deep sleep before dawn.

He awoke when a loud snort from Aldred pierced his consciousness. "Hah, he sires a child and thinks the work is done." His voice was loud and tinged with humor.

"Father, let him sleep. You have both been working hard. Perhaps it is a good day to rest."

"I'm up," Ge-or shouted through the door. "Ask your father who lifted all those heavy logs yesterday."

"Bah, it couldn't have been more than a few hundred-weight. Perhaps you've had too much of a soft life these past nights."

"Father!" Though Ge-or couldn't see her, he guessed rightly that Leona had blushed at that poke.

He opened the bedroom door to see Leona standing over her father with a raised skillet in her hands.

"Put that down, Daughter, and bring an old man his breakfast. Maybe you two don't have better things to do, but I do."

"Hold!" Ge-or broke in. "Enough, old man. You see, Leona, you put him in a good mood and this is what happens. Maybe we should shove him out the door hungry, and see when he comes crying back to the stoop."

"Hey, this is my house after all, young half-elf."

"Well, I guess I was mistaken. I was hoping you wouldn't mind sharing it for the winter."

"Oh, Ge-or," Leona gasped. She stared at him, wondering if she had heard right; then she rushed over and threw her arms around him. She started kissing his face, tears running down her cheeks.

Aldred harrumphed, "I'll be out back for a few minutes. Take your time with breakfast. I've starved before."

Later that day, the three of them sat at the table and laid out plans for the cold months. After thinking about it carefully and logically, Ge-or had reasoned that there would be little he could accomplish by heading to Aelfric for the winter. The knowledge that timber wolves were threatening the vale had both worried him and given rise to an idea that he hoped would prove fruitful. He felt that if he shot and trapped enough of the animals, the furs might bring good money at the market in a town and trading center the size of Aelfric. He would be able to equip himself with better quality weapons and armor for his quest as a result.

Leona was of course thrilled that he would be staying, though he emphasized to her when they talked alone, that at first thaw he planned to continue his journey. Still, it was far longer than she could have wished. She would have her knight for a bit longer, and that raised her spirits considerably.

They decided that Aldred should take the small cart and head to the nearest trading post for supplies. Ge-or knew he could provide wild game for them with his bow; still, there were other necessities that they would use up with three mouths to feed. Aldred's shopping list included many food items, another pig for slaughter and smoking, some kaffa, if available, and various requests from Leona that mostly centered around, "if they have this…"

Ge-or had told Aldred about the money tin in the cart some time before, but the old man had refused to take "stealins." He reminded Aldred of it now and told him to take all that he needed. Though he said that he and Leona had enough saved up, Ge-or insisted. So, he stuffed several small bags with coppers. Aldred told Ge-or and Leona that with the money he would also get some "extras" for them and for the baby to come.

While Aldred was away, Ge-or planned to continue with the wood-gathering. They had left several cartloads of cut logs up in the grove, so he and Leona would start with bringing them into the vale. She would drive the wagon, and Ge-or would do the heavy work. Leona, however, insisted that she could do any kind of work for months. Ge-or would hear none of it. He had quickly fallen into the role of protective lover and father-to-be.

Aldred left early the next morning, and for the first time in a long time,

Leona was without her father in the vale. It felt strange to watch him go; they had always gone to market together after her mother had died. Something seemed to nag at her when she saw the wagon disappear around the bend; however, Ge-or was waiting for her, so she didn't pay attention to it. It only came to her much later that her father had looked far older than she had ever noticed before. The wilderness life was a fulfilling one, but it was hard on a person as well. She could see that in his gray hair, the way he held himself, and in his eyes.

Wolves

Later that week, Leona and Ge-or took the wagon and mules up to the hardwood grove to load the cut logs. It was a brilliant, cold fall morning, and sitting next to each other on the broad bench as they rode up the bumpy path was like a little piece of heaven for that brief moment in time.

"Are you happy, Leona?"

She turned and smiled at him. She leaned over and gave him a hearty peck on the cheek. "I am joyous, Ge-or. I have longed so much for a child. You have given me this one thing and much more." She stopped, thinking whether she should say what she felt, in the end, she knew it was the right thing.

"You know that I love you?"

He nodded.

"You don't love me?"

Ge-or hesitated. He knew this was important to her, and he had to be honest. "I love you as much as I can love anyone right now, Leona. It is difficult for me to describe what that means. Since the destruction of my village, with so many friends and relations dead, I feel as if part of me has shut down. When I collected all the bodies for the sea burial, I honestly believed my heart was going to stop. The awfulness of it was almost unbearable. Over the period of time while I continued my labors, it hardened and set deep inside of me to a resolve and a… I don't know… a hardness to feeling."

Leona laid her hand on his arm as he continued. "You are special to me," he said, reaching over and rubbing her belly lightly, "as is this child. That will never change. I wish I could offer you more from my heart, but right now, I can't."

"It is enough that you care for me." Leona blinked back some tears. "I am full with what you have already given me. It…" She hesitated, not sure that she should continue; finally, she decided it was for the best to speak her true feelings and not hide anything from him. "It will be hard for me when you go. I have accepted that. I do not wish to make you uncomfortable about what you have to do. If you feel it is best to leave now, I will understand."

"Nay, this is the wisest choice. I have considered long and hard on it. We will have a good winter together. It will bring me joy to see you grow with our child. I…"

"Enough, now…" Leona interrupted him, instinctively knowing that they had said all that needed to be said. She had a sadness deep within, for now she was filled with other emotions that she wanted to relish.

"You are feeling well?"

"Yes, Ge-or. The morning sickness is normal. It will pass after a few weeks, perhaps longer. I will be fine. It is my body adjusting to all that is new. It is funny, though, because I mind it not at all. It reminds me that I am with your child, and that is a good thing."

"You look radiant, my mountain girl, sturdy and shining in the sun."

"Now don't go getting any ideas, we have work to do."

"The work will be there a while, yet." Ge-or drew back on the reins.

Once they reached the large log pile, Ge-or began heaving the cut lengths into the back of the wagon, arranging them to make the most of the space, while

Leona hobbled the mules. He worked steadily, relishing the heft of the wood as he took it from the pile to the wagon bed. As he turned his back to lift another log into the wagon, he heard a loud thunk from behind. Spinning around with the heavy trunk section in his hands, he saw Leona standing with a smaller chunk in her arms, ready to heave it into the bed.

"Leona, no! You'll hurt yourself."

"Ge-or! I am a sturdy mountain-woman. I can handle these logs." She seemed cross, though Ge-or had not seen her so before, except to her father. Standing there, he thought maybe they were going to have their first fight.

"Leona, I must insist that…"

"Ge-or! Listen to me. Think back. You come from a wilderness village; didn't the women there work even when they were fat and heavy with child?"

She was right. Ge-or had seen many women work right up to the time of birthing. One young girl had given birth in the corn rows during the fall harvest. A midwife had come over to assist her, and that had been all that was necessary. He had to agree with what Leona was saying.

"There! I am as strong as any. I'll not be treated like an invalid. Women know how much they can do. It is instinctive. I can lift logs twice this…"

"Leona, get in the wagon, now!" Ge-or interrupted her, his face suddenly stern and set.

"Ge-or!" Now she really did feel her ire rising. She was ready to dig her heels in for a fight; she could be as stubborn as any. Tossing her log into the wagon bed, she brushed her hair back from her reddening face and was preparing a stinging retort. She turned and saw what Ge-or was looking at.

"In the wagon, now," he said again.

Dropping the log in his arms, he sidled up the length of the wagon and reached for his sword. His scabbard was wedged in-between the seat and the sideboard.

He slid the blade out, pulling a throwing knife from his boot at the same time. "Get my bow," he said, while he slid up even further, until he was behind and to the side of the first mule.

Four gray shapes had eased out silently from the woods as he directed Leona. The wolves were now facing the mules in a semi-circle. The big timbers looked hungry. Three of them were larger than any Ge-or had ever seen. They easily weighed seven or eight stone and the largest could have been close to nine.

Ge-or couldn't tell whether they considered him a threat or not; however, they clearly saw the mules as meals standing ready for slaughter. He stepped cautiously forward, hoping the timber wolves would wait until he was clear of the mules before they struck.

He well knew how they attacked. In two steps, they could bound forward ten to fifteen paces. The force of their weight and speed could drive a big man to the ground. He wanted to get into a position where he could plant his feet and have enough room to freely swing his sword. Though he did not dare to look back, he imagined that Leona had the bow up and an arrow nocked ready to shoot. The bow would have too long a draw-length for her; but if she had any skill at all, she would be able to get at least an arrow into one of the beasts before they could be on them.

As he slowly took another step toward the head of the mule, the timbers turned their heads one at a time in his direction. Ge-or, his side brushing the shoulder of the animal, could feel it quaking as it stood frozen in place. A second later, he saw the largest of the wolves crouch. An instant after that, it launched itself straight toward him. Twisting sideways to clear a space from the side of the mule, Ge-or swung his blade in an arc toward where he expected the wolf's throat to be in another second.

His aim was true. The blade bit deep, severing both of the animal's neck arteries. The timber's forward momentum hit Ge-or full in his right side. He was tossed to the left, ending up on his knees as the other wolves attacked. He was getting to his feet when the next biggest wolf took three bounds and drove itself off its hind legs straight toward Leona, who was standing on the wagon in front of the seat. She had Ge-or's bow in her fists waiting to club the beast with it when it got close. She yelled, "Ge-or!" as he whipped his left hand behind his ear, then forward, sending the knife end over end toward the wolf. The blade buried deep into the wolf's eye as it crashed into the wagon, narrowly missing Leona.

One of the other wolves missed its mark and landed between the two front mules; the two terrified animals were stamping and trying to turn away from its attack. Hobbled as they were, they could do little more than jostle back and forth. The smallest of the wolves was coming, a bit more cautiously than its brethren, right for Ge-or.

Ignoring the screaming mules, Ge-or charged ahead, hoping to disable the lesser wolf so he would be able to deal with the frenzy behind him. Though he moved quickly, the wolf was faster; his stroke went wide as the animal sidestepped. Ge-or kept moving ahead swinging, trying to wound the wolf. It kept avoiding his blows. Cursing the time he was wasting, Ge-or reached across his body and drew his other throwing knife. He sent it spinning toward the wily animal. It struck the wolf mid-section as it twisted away. It yelped, spun around, and disappeared back into the woods.

Turning quickly around, Ge-or saw the strangest sight he had ever seen. The wolf that had gone for the mules had somehow gotten tangled in their hobbling ropes and harnesses, with its rump high up near the front mules' shoulders and its head hanging close to the ground. The mules were kicking, one after the other, in an odd sort of rhythm at the head of the obviously dead animal. Leona was sitting on the left hind mule's haunch, beating repeatedly on the back of the wolf with Ge-or's unstrung bow.

Shaking his head, he loped back, caught the bow on its next downward swing, and took it out of Leona's hands. He grabbed the dead wolf by its two hind legs and heaved it over the harness and onto the ground. Leona leaned forward, falling into Ge-or's arms. She let Ge-or ease her off the mule's back.

Leona held tightly to Ge-or's arm, following him as he looked over the immediate area to make sure they were safe. A few minutes later, he was satisfied that the three largest wolves were dead and the fourth gravely wounded and not likely to return. He figured he would trail it when they were finished loading the wood. By then, it should have died of its wound.

He drew Leona close and held her to his chest. She was still shaking.

"I'm sorry, Ge-or. I don't know how to shoot a bow. I didn't know what to do. I thought you wanted me to get it for you, so you could shoot."

"It's all right, we're safe. Two of the mules are injured – bites to their flanks and sides, but they will live. We can see to them when we get back. I'll smear some mud on their wounds; it will help stop the bleeding. We can clean and salve them in the barn.

"Come on." He took her hand and led her to the pile of wood, knowing that

200

the work and focus on something else would help. "Let's finish filling the wagon. After that, I'll skin the wolves. These will be nice-sized pelts." He turned her toward him. "We need to remedy one thing. I'm going to teach you to shoot. We have the whole winter; enough time for me to make you an adequate bow. Agreed?"

She nodded; then following his example, she grabbed a log and heaved it into the wagon bed forcefully. Ge-or smiled, "Some woman!"

***

Six days later, as they sat enjoying a mug of a mulled red wine that Aldred had been able to purchase at the market, snow began to sift down outside the window. Ge-or put his arm around Leona's shoulders and drew her closer on the bench. They watched the flakes as they began to stick to the porch and ground. Winter was upon them. Life was good for the moment, very good, for three people on the edge of darkness.

Epilogue

On a bright sunny day, four people stood apart from a company of soldiers that marched into the lower city of Borea. They waved one last time at the figure of Rux riding somewhat stiffly in his dress uniform, as befit his rank, at the head of the column. Then they turned to enter the city themselves.

Until this adventure, Jared and Thistle had never been in any town larger than their seacoast villages; and as they had passed through several big villages during their journey from the King's Wall to the capitol, the scale of this city almost overwhelmed them. The buildings were enormous by cabin standards. Many, both wooden and stone, had two or more floors; and some looked to be four stories or more. They didn't even have churches in the west that were more than two stories; rarely, the occasional inn would have an upper sleeping floor. From where they stood, they could make out the Borean Palace atop the hill to the east. It stood outlined against a blue sky with the sea beyond. Its limestone walls, mostly cut from the rock it sat upon, were bright in the sunlight. They stopped to wonder at its magnificence. The many towers seemed to touch the sky itself. To Thistle, who was soon to enter there, it was beyond her to fathom what there was about her that could have brought her here.

For a while they stayed on the main road, melding with the congested traffic that headed up toward the palace. After twenty minutes, Sart led them down a side street. He knew the city well, having spent much of his youth growing up in the western suburbs; and his training and acolyte service had been at a monastery near the palace. Thistle, Jared, and Rose marveled at everything they saw, though they all felt uncomfortable in the close limits created by the streets and buildings. Their whole lives had been spent in the wilds and in wide open spaces. This was a strange and wondrous experience, yet it would take some getting used to. Thistle let Rose climb into her arms soon after they left the main road. The little girl was frightened by the noise and commotion of so many people, animals, and carts.

Sart led the way through various streets and alleyways, until they finally came to a small, carefully groomed garden in front of a mansion near the northern inner wall of the city. Just beyond, another street over, they could see the high masts of ships anchored in the harbor. This was where they were to give Rose over to her grandparents. With tears in their eyes, Thistle and Jared said goodbye to the small child, whom they had grown to love and cherish on their trek out of the wilderness. It also felt as if they were finally saying "so long" to Lute for the last time when they waved goodbye. They promised to come and visit when they could; however, they knew the young girl would soon be a part of another world altogether.

Returning once again to the main avenue in the center of the city by another circuitous route, Sart soon had them climbing steadily toward the great palace on the hill. At last, with the final long rise to the Borean Palace gates looming ahead of them, Sart led the two young people to the north, down another long avenue to a magnificent gate of gilded metal set back from the street. Beyond the gate sat an impressive stone building and complex. They could hear a rich cacophony of sounds coming from the open windows nearest them.

For a minute, Jared stood rooted in place trying to take in the enormity of what was happening to him. Thistle stood at his side. She knew enough to wait for him to gain his composure. It was hard to believe the adventure they had been on together was suddenly coming to an abrupt, though expected, conclusion. And to replace this experience, they had mostly a blank slate – an unknown continuation that branched off at sharp angles from what they had just been through, what they had managed to survive together.

A young man, who appeared to be the outer gatekeeper, was standing near the ornate panels of the gilded entryway. He looked inquiringly at the three of them as they stood only five paces away, simply taking in the scene before them. Finally, the lad sang a musical phrase, "What bid you here?" Jared stepped forward at the musical challenge. He sang back a cadencing phrase with the words, "To study to become a Bard." Jared passed a scroll of parchment through the ironwork, followed by an ornate portative harp. The young man took the scroll and the harp. He briefly looked at the letter. He sang, "Wait."

Less than a minute later, an old man, who had been standing out of sight by the inner gate, returned with the scroll. Peering intently at Jared through the bars, he said, "Jared of Thiele." It sounded like a challenge. "Do you wish to enter?"

Jared nodded nervously.

The man read the parchment aloud in a booming bass voice, "I, Rux of Athalia, Captain of Borea, greet thee of the Hall of Bards. Lute of Borea, stout Journeyman of your guild, requested as he lay dying for me to convey to you the bearer of this letter, Jared of Thiele, as a novice trainee. He has proven himself to be brave and stalwart in battle, he has a natural gift in the musical arts, and he is true to his word and friends. As a Captain in the Borean service, I also commend this young half-elf for trial in your guild. He is of the best character and has proved of service to the kingdom.

"Furthermore, as he faithfully and without reservation fulfilled his commitment of service to my company as a Journeyman Bard, I request that you elevate Lute of Borea to the status of Bard, and grant his surviving kin, a daughter, Rose, all benefits pertinent to that title. Ruxkin of Athalia, Company Commander and Captain in the Service of the Borean Kingdom."

"Half-elf," the old man looked up, "once you enter these gates, you will be at the service of the Borean Guild of Bards until you are either dismissed or until you die. Your life will be difficult and your responsibilities many. Do not accept this trust unless you are ready to dedicate yourself to music, life, and Borea."

"I accept," Jared said, his heart leaping inside him; and though greatly nervous, he was already looking forward to the work ahead, the music, the learning, a new life. He felt Thistle's hand give him a squeeze of reassurance.

"You may enter." The old man opened the gate.

Turning to his friends, Jared extended his arm to Sart. The cleric smiled broadly while he gripped Jared's forearm in farewell, drawing him into a great bear hug at the last. "Take care, Jared. Learn. You can do nothing better in life. Remember to keep the stone safe. I will consult Meligance and the lore books to see what I can find. Magic works in strange ways. We don't know what other powers it may have. I will try to see you at odd intervals. Look for me. May the force of Gaia remain with you." Sart released his grip and turned to walk a few steps down the street.

Jared drew Thistle into his arms. He held her tightly for a minute. Though he did not want to let her go, he finally stepped back. Reaching up, he brushed a small tress of her light-brown hair back from her forehead. "Will you wait for me, Thistle?"

She nodded, tears welling up in her eyes. "Take care, elf-kin." Thistle stood on her tiptoes and kissed him lightly. Then she turned and ran quickly down the street to Sart.

Jared, fighting with his swirling emotions, turned to the gate and followed the old man into the courtyard. Swinging around, he waved at the disappearing figures as they made their way up toward the palace where Meligance, the great White Wizardess of Borea, waited to receive the priest and a young girl from the far west. Finally, he turned toward his new life.

The End

Next: **Book II: The Making of a Bard -- Gigue**

End Note

On Writing *The Chronicles of Borea*

In 1979-1980, I wrote the first book of *The Chronicles of Borea,* entitled *IXUS* (now the fifth book). At that time I sent this work out to a variety of publishers because it was still possible to do so. The book made it to several senior editors, from whom I received personal suggestions and comments re: revisions. Many of these were instrumental in the rewrites and the direction the series would go. Eventually, with my professional life taking up more and more of my time, I put this manuscript aside, and only sporadically returned to fiction over the next several decades.

The idea of a Prequel to *IXUS* crept into the picture fairly early. I finally wrote a short novel entitled *The Making of a Bard*, for my young son. Many years later, I envisioned expanding and finishing the *Chronicles.* From approximately 2007 to the present, I completely revised and expanded *IXUS* several times; and *The Making of a Bard* was extended into a series of four complete works: *Preludio; Gigue; Siciliana; and Ciaccona.* The initial drafts of the final two books of this series which follow *IXUS*: *Corrente; Civil War Threatens: Tempo di Borea; and The Great War: Grande Finale,* were completed in 2011. A short story, entitled, *The Hunter's Mark,* was completed in 2022 and serves as an introduction to the series. As a musician and an avid Sword and Sorcery fan, this series was a natural for me. I think my love of this genre really solidified when I read T.H. White's *The Once and Future King*, Tolkien, Lloyd Alexander, and others, and also when I was introduced to *Dungeons and Dragons* ©. (I still have the original three book set from 1974 – Thank you, Gary Gygax and Dave Arneson, MYRIP). I owe a great deal to all of these "mentors" and many other figures in this arena.

Music, Magic, and the Warrior mentality play major roles in these works. Each is wrapped around the other, and they are threads that tie the entire series together. I have tried to detail the development and unfolding of the three primary characters, who forward these roles throughout. Also, I have placed many references within for fun. I am not sure when all of this started, probably when I picked names for the first characters in *IXUS*; but it seems I like to play games with words, titles, names, sayings, and so forth, as well as, in an indirect way, give homage to authors and others that have influenced me through the years. Some of these are fairly obvious if your background includes the information to decipher them, e.g. Lassus is a Bard named in *The Making of the Bard, Book I* -- Orlando di Lasso, or di Lassus is a Renaissance musician (16th century). Others are much more subtle and personal, e.g. Aelfric (a town in my kingdom), was a dwarf character of a librarian (thanks, Carol) in one of my early *Dungeons and Dragons* groups (as well as a real abbot and writer). I hope you will have some fun finding the hundreds of subtle underpinnings and references within these books. I write and insert them as I go.

As a musician, I also like the sound of words, so I tend to play around with that a good bit in my manuscripts.

I have been influenced by many writers and works. I hope I have offered a nod to all in my own way, for I cannot fathom the depths to which my imagination takes me. I write and it all comes out, typically flowing as fast as my two index fingers can fly over the keyboard.

A brief perspective: Tolkien's orcs have become a mainstay of gaming for a creature with certain characteristics. However, as it was pointed out to me by a senior editor of a famous publishing house, they are uniquely Tolkien. Therefore, as a way of offering homage to the Dean of this genre, I have twisted this type of creature to my own usage with "goblin" (used fairly synonymously with "orc" by Tolkien) as the beginning reference point. My goblins, gzks, and chatts are creatures who are from the same heritage, but were mutated due to their environs -- therefore, I have chatts of the desert, goblins of the caves, and gzks of the evergreen forests.

My sincerest wish is that my writing is first and foremost enjoyable to read. I love a good tale, and I hope these books satisfy that criterion.

    Joe Koob

About the Author

Dr. Koob is a former college music educator, having taught: – Music Appreciation; Music History Course Sequence; Private and class Stringed Instruments –Violin, Viola, Cello, Bass; Music Education and Student Teacher Supervisor; Student Success classes; Interdisciplinary advanced seminars; and Music Theory. He also Conducted University-Civic Symphonies for many years and has performed in symphony orchestras in the United States and Europe.

Dr. Koob served in the United States Air Force during Vietnam as a C-141 Starlifter Navigator.

Education: Bachelor of Music – DePauw Univ; Masters Degree in Violin – Montclair State Univ; Masters in Counseling, Northern State Univ; and Doctorate in Education – Univ. of Illinois.

Writing Awards: *A Perfect Day – Guide for a Better Life:* **Winner – Best Book Non-fiction,** Oklahoma Writers Federation, and **Certificate of Merit,** *Writer's Digest* Self-Published Book Awards. Winner Various Local and Regional Writing Competitions

His background includes work as an Executive Coach and Motivational Speaker; Author of Music Educational Software, Music Texts, Manuals, and Adjudicated Articles; as well as many books and articles on "Understanding and Working with Difficult People." He has many additional interests, including bicycling, woodworking, painting, reading, archery hunting, fishing, and more. Joe is happily married and has two grown children. He divides his time between FL and MI.

Website: **chroniclesofborea.com**

Blog: chroniclesofboreabooks.wordpress.com

Made in the USA
Middletown, DE
29 January 2023

23018668R00116